KING
OF
Hearts

By

L.H. Cosway

Marie you're the wild blue sky
And men do foolish things
You turn kings into beggars
And beggars into kings

"All the World is Green" by Tom Waits.

Part One
Before

One

Johnson-Pearse Bank, Canary Wharf, London, 2009.

I was nervous.

I was also procrastinating as I sat on a bench and watched men and women scurry by, an endless parade of people with "stuff to do." I had ten more minutes before heading inside for my interview, and I was draining every last one of those bad boys the same way I was draining every last dreg of my coffee.

Despite having lived in London my entire life, I'd never actually been to Canary Wharf. There'd never really been a reason – until now. It was a strange place, so professional, the smell of money in the air, and yet, just a couple of feet away from me, the guy running the newsstand was very obviously dealing. Growing up where I grew up, it was the kind of thing I noticed. A suit would walk up to him, buy a paper, and he'd slip a little something extra inside. Then the suit would mosey on into his office building to start his day, casual as you please.

It was sort of depressing to know that even in a place like this, drugs were still prevalent. The only difference was that the people here could actually afford them.

Okay, time to face the music. Getting up from the bench, I smoothed my hands down my dress, inhaled a deep breath, and put on my game face. I was determined to bravado my way through the interview, and faking confidence was one of my true talents. Today I was competing for a job as an executive assistant at one of the top investment banks in the country, with only a diploma in administration and too many years' experience as a barmaid.

I was still a little flabbergasted as to how I'd even managed to score the interview. Address profiling was alive and kicking, and I had a feeling that Johnson-Pearse Bank employed a grand total of zero peeps from my neck of the woods.

I arrived at the reception area and smiled at the lady manning the desk. "Hi, I'm here to interview for the executive assistant position with Mr King."

She raised a speculative eyebrow, her gaze giving me a quick sweep up and down. It didn't take a genius to figure out what she was thinking. She heard my East End accent and immediately wondered what the hell I was doing there. She wasn't the only one, because despite my calm exterior, I was suffering from a distinct case of impostor syndrome.

Pursing her lips, she finally nodded and directed me to a large office down the hall, telling me to sit and wait outside until I was called. Several other people sat waiting quietly. Some of them looked just as nervous as I felt, while others seemed cool, calm, and collected. Maybe they were faking it, too.

Minutes ticked by. A couple of the other candidates were called into the office, some leaving with smug smiles, and others looking like they wanted to go home and have a cry. I could see myself in the same boat in the not too distant future.

The door opened, and an older man emerged.

"Alexis Clark?" he called, scanning those of us left waiting.

I stood immediately, again wiping my sweaty hands on my dress and stepping forward. I felt like everything outside my body was in slow motion, while inside my heart hammered a mile a minute. Having recently split with my boyfriend, Stu, and subsequently quitting my job at the pub he frequented on a daily basis, I needed employment.

Stepping inside the room, I found I was being interviewed not only by the elderly gent who'd called me in, but by a panel including two others, one male, one female. My eyes briefly scanned the woman, who appeared to be in her sixties and who was appraising me shrewdly. My attention then wandered to the blond guy sitting at the end of the desk nearest the window. He held his phone to his ear and wore a lazy smile as he stared out at the view beyond. He was fit with a capital "F," too handsome for a banker, if I was being honest. He didn't have the sleaze-ball look of the young City Boys, nor did he have the cold, money-hungry eyes of the older bankers. No, he had the carefree beauty of a male model, or a Hollywood heartthrob.

His eyes came to me for a brief second, looked away, then came back again in what seemed to be a double take. As he made a slow perusal of my body, a mix of amusement and intrigue passed over his features before his attention returned to his phone call. Okay, so that didn't make me a tad weak at the knees, no siree, Bob.

"Yeah, okay, Greg, I'll believe your trash and cash bullshit as soon as I start taking up belly dancing classes and piercing both my ears." He chuckled cynically, and I got a few goose bumps at the sound of his deep laughter. "I distinctly remember you pulling a stunt like this in '06. All of a sudden everybody's steering clear of The Phillips Group, and a week later you're swanning around in a brand-new BMW."

The other two sat and waited quietly as he wrapped up his phone call, which led me to believe that despite being younger, Blondie was the one in charge. Huh. After just a minute he ended his call, sliding his mobile onto the desk and clasping his hands together. Then he shot the older guy a glance that said he could begin the interview.

"It's a pleasure to meet you, Alexis. My name is Daniel James, senior managing director here at Johnson-Pearse," he began, and I shook his hand. "This is Eleanor Price, Mr King's current assistant, who'll be retiring soon and whose position we're looking to fill."

I shook Eleanor's hand next. She seemed strict but nice, in a head-mistress sort of way. I could now surmise that Blondie was Mr King, and I guessed he needed someone like Eleanor to keep him in check. If I got this job, I imagined keeping up with Mr Sexy Smile would have me well on my toes.

When Mr James was finally introducing me to Oliver King, head managing director, I felt my trusty bravado kicking in. I wasn't going to wilt and blush at his attention. No, I was going to hold my head high and be like Eleanor, tough as nails, no nonsense.

"Mr King," I said as his warm fingers slid against mine and we quickly shook hands. Yep, tingles galore, but I refused to acknowledge them.

"Alexis," he replied, eyeing me closely before sitting back down. "Thanks for coming."

I took a seat in front of the three of them and rested my hands in my lap.

"So, to begin, please tell us a little about yourself," said Mr James.

Okay, good. They were starting off with the standard stuff. I could do this. Clearing my throat, I began my spiel. I told them about my high A Level results, especially in computing and maths, then moved on to my bartending experience, during which I decided to return to education

9

and get my diploma. I told them my main reason for not going to university straight out of school was due to a lack of funds, and how I was eager to gain experience now that I had my qualification.

"You understand that most entry-level staff here hold university degrees, even in our admin departments," said Mr James. "What do you think you can bring to the role, given that you haven't had the same level of education?"

"I think I can bring people skills," I answered promptly. "Working in a bar might seem like it doesn't take much, but believe me, you get good experience dealing with all kinds of conflicts. I think that education is important, yeah, but I also feel that I can bring a lot more to the role in comparison to someone who's coming in with a degree but zero experience."

"And what if you come up against a problem that requires technical rather than interpersonal skills, something that a university graduate would be better equipped to deal with?" James went on. I glanced quickly at Mr King to find him studying me closely, and all of a sudden felt a little warmer under my dress.

"Then I'll ask for guidance. If there's a problem I can't deal with on my own, I always ask someone to teach me. I'm all about expanding my learning, and I hold the belief we should be continually gaining new skills."

King leaned forward on the desk to shoot James a grin. It said "I like her," and I felt a triumphant little rush in my belly. James was far more difficult to read, and Eleanor seemed to only be sitting in on the interview as a silent observer. I imagined she'd be giving her two cents after I left, informing the other two whether or not she thought I was fit to replace her.

"Okay, very good." said Mr James. "So, why is it that you'd like to work here at Johnson-Pearse?"

Relief flooded me and I was glad he'd asked this question. I'd spent hours researching the bank, so I knew my stuff. By the time I was done regurgitating all the reasons why I thought it was the ideal place for me to work, all three interviewers seemed impressed.

Then Mr King clasped his hands together, finally deciding to speak. "You seem to know a great deal about this bank, Miss Clark, but tell me, if you were to implement one change to improve how we run things, what would it be?"

His question took me by surprise, and I drew a complete and total blank. My mind scurried for an answer, any answer, and before I could take a second to properly think things through, I blurted, "Well, for a start, I'd call the cops on the dealer working the newsstand outside. I'm guessing high employees don't make for very productive ones."

James' eyebrows shot right up into his forehead. Eleanor pursed her lips, appraising me more closely, and King didn't show any outward signs of a reaction other than the slightest curve to the edge of his lips. He glanced out the window, where there was a direct view of the newsstand, scribbled something down, then shot James a look to continue with the interview. I saw him glancing at me again, differently now, like he was seeing something interesting he hadn't noticed before. The fact that none of them had commented on my answer made me feel sweaty and embarrassed, and my need to flee the room was palpable. Me and my big dumb mouth.

James threw a few more questions at me, asking how I'd cope with a number of scenarios. Unfortunately, though, after my comment about the dealer, his distaste for me started to shine through, and he quickly wrapped things up.

"Thank you so much, Miss Clark. As I said, these jobs do normally go to university graduates, but well done for coming along. Do you have any questions for us?"

I eyed him, feeling like what he'd said was a little patronising. I'd spent days preparing for this interview, and the fact that he was so quick to write me off got my blood up. This was why, despite having a whole host of questions prepared to ask, I said sharply, "If I'm not the usual candidate, then why did you call me for an interview?"

James' face flashed in surprise at my question, and I inwardly groaned. Technically though, I'd already screwed things up, so I might as well speak my mind.

He glanced at Oliver King. "Each of us put forward a number of resumes. I believe it was Mr King who thought yours had…potential."

Eleanor frowned, and King shot him a look that said he was in for it later, before turning to face me. I was under the impression that James was my biggest enemy in this situation, but then King spoke and flipped everything on its ear.

Levelling his eyes on me, he said simply, "You included a picture, Miss Clark, and I liked the look of you."

I swear, my jaw practically dropped to the floor. I'd sat through many interviews in my time, but this one was by far the strangest. Was he even allowed to say something like that? Since it appeared he was the one who ruled the roost around here, I guessed he was. Bristling, I rose from my seat. I knew I should have waited until I was dismissed, but I was so pissed off that I just had to get out of there.

Still, I didn't let my temper get the better of me. I settled my gaze on his and calmly gave him my best parting line.

"Well, then, Mr King, if I do get chosen for the position, I'll have to prove to you that my looks pale in comparison to what my brain can achieve."

King smiled.

I turned and left the office.

The very next day I received a call from Eleanor telling me that I'd gotten the job.

***

Gulping back the last of my coffee, I slipped my headphones over my ears, hit "play" on my favourite M.I.A. album, and set off for the tube. I lived on the tenth floor of a big grey tower block in Bethnal Green with my BFF, Karla. The stairs were a hassle, but I had to admit that hauling my arse up and down them every day did wonders for my glutes. Too bad my penchant for cake undid all the good work.

It was my first day working at Johnson-Pearse Bank. After the bizarre nature of my interview, and the even more bizarre fact that they'd actually chosen me for the role, I was putting my best foot forward. M.I.A.'s tracks always made me feel ready to take on a challenge; it was like my fight music.

I wore my most office-friendly pencil dress under my duffel coat. I also wore gloves and a scarf, which I buried my nose under in order to stave off the chill. It was January in London, which meant it was cold enough to freeze your nipples off.

Once I reached the tube, I savoured the heat of the carriage and head-bobbed my way through the journey, standing because it was rush hour, and I wasn't going to get a seat to save my life. Finally arriving in Canary Wharf, I made my way out of the gigantic tube station and completed the walk to the glass and steel tower where Johnson-Pearse was located.

This area was referred to as The City, a single square mile that housed the most powerful financial institutions in the U.K. Some of the buildings had funny nicknames. For instance, you had the Gherkin, which I personally thought looked like a giant Fabergé egg.

You could divide the district into three sections. Canary Wharf was modern, towering, soulless, and where you could find the all-powerful investment banks. The Old City was historical, quirky, and mostly home to the insurers and brokers. And lastly, you had the stylish and cosmopolitan Mayfair, where you could find the hedge funds and private equity companies. I'd only become so well-informed about all this since I started my job hunt. Before that it was just another part of London to me. But now that I'd discovered this city within the city, I'd become fascinated. With just one glance, you knew that this was a place where there was only one God, and its name was Money.

I disappeared among the throngs of professional types as I entered the building. I had to sign in at the security desk, since I hadn't yet been given my staff I.D. Once I was done, I stepped inside the elevator. I was still rocking out to my music, standing in the corner of the crowded lift, when I felt somebody's eyes on me.

Quickly glancing up, I spotted Oliver King a few feet away, wearing a suit and a smile, a newspaper tucked under his arm. Pulling my headphones off and letting them rest around my neck, I gave him a polite nod. My first instinct was to be embarrassed that he'd caught me bobbing my head, away in my own little world, but I tamped that bitch down. If I'd learned anything from growing up in a tiny council house with three overbearing brothers and limited resources, it was that you had to hold your head high in this life. Take what was your due and never let anyone make you feel uncomfortable or inferior.

When the lift stopped at our floor, both Oliver and I stepped off, leaving the crowded carriage behind us.

"Good morning, Alexis," he said in that refined accent of his that screamed of Cambridge and Eton, and all those other fancy places where the upper classes received their educations. He placed his hand on my lower back for a second as though leading me out.

"Mr King," I replied, making sure to step away and put an end to the touching. I wasn't sure if that was business as usual or what. I began removing my gloves and unwrapping my scarf from around my neck.

"Cold out there today," he went on, eyes scanning me, and I nodded. We soon reached his office, which had a large atrium area with two desks, one for Eleanor and one for the other assistant, Gillian. Eleanor had told me about her on the phone, but we hadn't met yet. The older assistant was already at her desk, tapping away at her computer, as was Gillian, who had short blonde hair and a slim build. She looked to be about my age. When she spotted King, she immediately jumped up from her seat, gathered a bunch of folders, and walked alongside him. She barely gave me a second glance.

"These are the briefs for this morning's meetings, your coffee is inside, and Kenneth Green called to schedule a lunch meeting on Wednesday." Her voice trailed off as they went into King's office, and I looked to Eleanor, who gave me a warm smile.

"Morning, love, come sit. You'll be shadowing me for the week, then next week we'll see how you do going it alone. I'll be here on and off for another month to make sure the transition runs smoothly."

There was something about Eleanor that put me at ease, and I began to wonder if she was the reason I got this job. When we'd spoken over the phone, she'd been really apologetic for what Mr King had said to me in the interview, and stated outright it was the kind of carry-on that set the feminist movement back fifty years. Needless to say, I liked her already.

After I'd made myself comfortable, she ran through Mr King's morning routine with me. I'd be responsible for ordering his breakfast and giving him a rundown of the headlines in each of the countries' main newspapers, while Gillian took care of the morning and afternoon meeting schedule. Apparently, Mr King had a knack for absorbing the news and making predictions on which way the markets would turn. I was sceptical of that, but we'd see.

The hours trickled by, and my new boss was in and out of his office several times. On instinct, I found myself observing how he interacted with people. He must have only been in his early thirties, yet he had this confidence that made people eager to do his bidding, to impress him. It was a little addicting to watch.

It was almost lunch when Gillian appeared at my desk and told me that Mr King wanted to have a quick word. I swallowed and stood, hesitantly making my way into the office. It was pretty impressive. Two sides of the room were all windows, looking out onto the hustle and bustle of Canary Wharf. King's attention was fixed on the screen of one of his computers (there were several set up around his desk) as his fingers typed rapidly. I wasn't sure if he even realised I was there until he started to speak.

"How's your first day going, Alexis?"

It was a little disconcerting that he wasn't looking at me, but I answered anyway. "Very well. Eleanor's giving me a good schooling."

A smile graced his lips. "She's something, isn't she? I'll be sad to see her go, but she and her husband are retiring to the south of France, and no amount of money I've offered will convince her to stay."

"Well, if given the choice between soaking up the sun in St. Tropez or staying cooped up in an office all day, I know what most people would choose."

As soon as the statement was out, I regretted it. He paused typing and finally looked at me. A long moment elapsed, and I wondered if I'd been too free with my mouth again. This wasn't a pub. This was an office. This man was my boss, and I really needed to learn that certain banter wasn't appropriate.

"Have you ever been?" he finally asked.

"Huh?"

"To St. Tropez."

"Oh, no, I haven't," I said, eyes glancing out the window and then back to him.

"Then how can you know it's the better option? We need evidence to prove a point, Miss Clark. Guesstimations are a waste of time."

"It wasn't a *guesstimation*," I replied, using his word, which definitely wasn't in the dictionary. "I was simply using my *imagination*." Plus, wasn't his whole career based around guesswork and taking risks?

Pondering me a moment, he asked, "Has anyone ever told you that you're very direct?" He smiled and tapped a finger on his chin as he studied me. "I like it. I'm direct, too. That being said, sometimes my directness can come across the wrong way. Which brings me to the reason why I called you in here. I've been told it would be wise to apologise to you for my behaviour at your interview. I sometimes have a problem with tact, and it seems what I said to you could be considered offensive."

Wow, he was apologising? I didn't want to show any weakness, so I simply stared at him head on and replied calmly, "You'll have to get up a lot earlier in the morning to offend me, Mr King."

His lips pressed together. "Really? How early are we talking?"

I suppressed a laugh and smiled. "The crack of dawn, pretty much."

He let out a playful sigh. "It's a pity I treasure my beauty sleep."

I didn't respond, only raised an eyebrow. In my opinion, his beauty didn't need any enhancing.

"Anyway, it's a good thing you don't offend easily, because teary-eyed assistants are a bother." He paused, eyeing me closely, his voice turning serious. "I value honesty, Miss Clark. Too many people in this world hide behind lies and duplicity. Needless to say, the way you so outspokenly responded to me in your interview left me truly impressed."

His compliment surprised me. I was at a loss for words, and when I couldn't think of anything to say, I normally made a joke. And that's exactly what I did.

"In that case, maybe I should have told you that I have a bod for business and a brain for sin," I quipped, humorously fluffing the line from the movie *Working Girl*.

After all, it was an appropriate theme. "Or is that the other way around?"

King's attention, which had momentarily wandered to his computer screen, snapped back to me, and for a second he looked halfway between amused and perplexed. Not the laughter I'd been aiming for, but not the worst possible reaction, either.

I cleared my throat, suddenly needing to get out of there. "Well, if there's nothing else?"

"That's all, Alexis. You can return to Eleanor," he replied.

It was only when I was halfway to the door that he muttered under his breath teasingly, "A bod for business sounds interesting."

I turned around, and he glanced up at me, flashing me a quick, heart-fluttering smile. I smiled back, and his attention returned to his computer screen. All at once, my uncertainty and embarrassment vanished. My chest felt fuller, and as I continued my way out of the room, I swore I felt his eyes return to me once more.

Two

I picked up some groceries for dinner on the way home, my thoughts centring on my new job, but, more importantly, my new boss. Yeah, he was appealing to look at, but there was something else about him. Something beneath the surface that got me curious. I had a feeling that there was far more to Oliver King than met the eye.

Counting the flights of stairs as I climbed my way up to our flat, I tried to remember whether Karla was working days or nights this week. Being a constable with the Metropolitan Police meant she didn't always work a simple nine-to-five.

When I heard the shower running, I knew she'd been on the day shift. As I turned the TV on and made a start on dinner, I heard the shower turn off. A few minutes later, she came out wrapped in a towel and gave me a tired smile. Wet tendrils of her bright red hair fell across her forehead, and her clear blue eyes seemed weary.

"Hey," she said, voice soft. "How'd your first day go?"

"It was good," I replied. "Good but weird. I swear, it's a whole other world over there."

She sighed and sat down on a stool by the counter, watching me chop carrots. "Tell me about it. Some days I just feel like chucking it all in and finding a rich man to marry. It'd make life a whole lot easier."

I snorted. "Yeah."

Despite her profession, Karla could actually be a very sensitive person. Some would even go so far as to say shy. She was hard-working, and tough as nails in her own way, but she was also quiet and kind. She fell into police work due to her dad being on the force, but I always wondered if that was what she really wanted to be doing.

"Did something happen today?" I asked as I studied her. She seemed more tired than usual.

Rubbing at the crease between her eyebrows, she answered, "I had to break up a really vicious fight between two kids today. One of them was hurt pretty badly and had to be hospitalised. He was only fourteen. I'm still kinda reeling."

"Oh, my God," I exclaimed, putting down the knife and going to her. I threw my arm around her shoulders. "Are you okay?"

"I'm fine," she said, accepting my hug. "It's just so hard sometimes. You try your best to help people and keep them safe, but kids are still out there, killing each other, stealing, doing all sorts. You end up feeling like there's no way the system can ever work."

I didn't say anything, just squeezed her tighter. Finally she let out a long breath and pulled away. "Don't mind me. I'm just being morose. A good night's sleep and I'll feel better."

I gave her an understanding look and returned to the carrots. Trying to take her mind off it, I said, "I think we should go out this weekend. I know money is tight, but we need to let off some steam."

Her eyes lit up at my words. One thing that the both of us loved was dancing, and every couple of weeks we'd go out to a club.

"The Silver Bullet is putting on a ska night on Friday," she said. "I saw the poster on my way home from work."

I grinned at her. "A ska night it is then. We'll paint the town beige, since red is reserved strictly for those age twenty-five and under."

21

That solicited a giggle from her, and I felt good that I'd made her laugh. She picked up a carrot and took a bite. "Well, of course."

***

The next morning I arrived at work bright and early. This time I didn't see King in the elevator, which I found curiously disappointing. Okay, all right, shut up. So my peepers found it disappointing, because he was one hot slice of A. Plus, remembering that smile we'd shared yesterday made my belly feel all a-flutter.

I was sitting at the computer, completing some data entry that Eleanor had tasked me with while she scanned the morning's papers. Gillian's lightning fingers danced over her keyboard like a percussionist portrayal of *busy, busy, work to do.* Her desk was on the other side of our atrium that led to King's large office. When he arrived at around eight-thirty, he gave each of us a nod hello as Gillian hopped up from her seat, the same as yesterday.

"Morning, Eleanor, morning, Gillian, morning, Alexis," King chirped. He gave Eleanor a sparkly-eyed look. "Have you heard the news?"

She glanced up at him, licking a finger before casually turning another page. "I don't partake in salacious gossip, Mr King. You know that."

I nearly snorted at her dismissive response but managed to hold it in. Eleanor was quickly becoming my lady hero, because I knew for a fact she was the only person who got away with talking to King like that. I also had a hunch that she was the one who'd suggested he apologise for saying what he said to me in my interview. I was seriously looking forward to being her age and gaining that "Miss Trunchbull, I don't suffer fools gladly" vibe.

King let out an amused huff and turned to Gillian. "Have you?"

Gillian seemed oblivious as she nervously cleared her throat and clenched the folders she was holding. "Oh, um, no, sorry, I haven't." She seemed disappointed in herself, like she considered letting down *the* Oliver King in any way was a failure on her part. I felt like telling her to buck up and be a woman, not a simpering girl desperate to please her boss.

Finally, he looked at me. "Well, you obviously haven't, either, newbie. God, is it so much to ask to have some ladies who like to gossip around here? I'm practically bursting at the seams."

Eleanor shook her head, but I saw her lips twitch with a hint of a smile. Mr King was obviously in an unseasonably personable mood this morning. While chatting with her yesterday, she'd told me that his moods could be somewhat unpredictable, so it was always best to err on the side of caution.

"Well, tell us what you know, and I'll be happy to oblige," I said. "Gossiping is my forte."

"Oh, thank God." King exhaled with false dramatics as he approached the desk and eyed me mischievously. "George Bacon, one of the top guys over at Citibank, died last night."

I let out a breath. "That's terrible."

"A-ha! But you haven't heard the worst of it. Poor Georgie boy popped his clogs during a rather intensive session with a lady of the night. His old ticker wasn't up to the challenge." He shook his head, but he clearly felt no sympathy for the man. Well, since we'd just been hit with a motherbutcher of a recession, very few people felt sorry for those working in the financial services industry these days.

However, being a banker himself, I thought Mr King might be able to empathise.

I stared at him, finding his choice of conversation topic surreal. Oliver King really didn't have any tact, but oddly, I didn't mind. In fact, I kind of liked it. When I'd taken this job, I thought I'd be stuck working with a bunch of stiffs.

I wasn't sure why I said what I did next. It was a mixture of being a smart-arse and having no filter. I grinned at King and deadpanned, "So, what you're saying is, he came and went?"

There was a beat of silence before King let out a loud guffaw of a laugh. Smiling widely, he leant in and rested his hands on the desk as he responded with a wink, "I prefer to say he arrived before departing."

I chuckled. "Well okay, then, if you want get all fancy about it."

We were still grinning at one another when Eleanor cut in, "Mr King, I do believe you have a meeting in twenty minutes that you need to prepare for."

King didn't look away from me for a moment as his grin began to fade. Having his eyes on me made me feel a little goose-pimplish. Finally, he nodded and turned, striding inside his office with Gillian following behind. I returned to my data entry, and a minute or two of quiet passed before Eleanor said, "I think you two might be a little too alike." She paused, and there was a smile in her voice. "After I'm gone, maybe let Gillian accompany Mr King on trips. I shudder to think what the two of you would be like unleashed on prospective clients."

I shot her a questioning look. "Trips?"

"Sometimes he requires us to accompany him on business trips. It's only really once or twice a year."

"Oh, right," I said, frowning a little. I must have blanked over that part of the job description, too full of glee when I saw the size of my yearly salary. Oh, yes. This year was going to see *quite* a lot of cake buying once the money started to roll in.

The morning passed quickly. When lunch time came, I declined accompanying Eleanor and Gillian to a sushi restaurant in favour of grabbing a sub from a nearby deli. I needed the carbs, and I never felt full after sushi. And okay, maybe I should have been eating more sushi than subs, because I was carrying a little extra weight, but I just couldn't seem to summon up the urge to care. My body was what it was. I'd inherited it from my curvaceous Greek mother, and life was too short to go around eating packets of zero-calorie jelly from Japan.

I brought my food back to the office and found the place relatively quiet, since most people were either dining out, or were in the cafeteria having lunch. I had planned on eating at my desk, then making a start on the remainder of the workload I had to complete, when my attention wandered to King's office door.

My nosiness was urging me to go inside and take a look around, and I knew from his schedule that he wasn't due back from his afternoon meeting until three. Bringing my lunch with me, I stepped inside his office and marvelled at the view. His desk was big and imposing, and there were a number of picture frames on the wall. Two of them showed his university certificates. He had a first-class honours degree in finance and accounting from the London School of Economics, and a masters in finance from Cambridge. I whistled as I took them in. An education like that must have cost a pretty penny. But then I realised that

King's family probably wasn't hurting for cash when I took in the next frame.

It showed an old concert poster for Elaine King, a world-renowned concert pianist who had her heyday in the late eighties/early nineties. She was now a renowned shut-in, think Agnetha from ABBA but classier. It didn't take much for me to put two and two together and figure out that she was related to King somehow, and taking in her blonde hair and familiarly refined features, I'd put my money on her being his mother. Wow.

I saw a door leading to an in-office bathroom and took a step inside, letting out a few choice swearwords when I saw the size of the place. It was probably bigger than my and Karla's entire flat. It boasted a large walk-in shower, a closet, and floor-to-ceiling windows with that special glass that went either clear or frosted at the touch of a button. The pièce de resistance, however, was the fancy designer sofa that went along one side of the room. I mean, a sofa like that in a bathroom like this just screamed extravagance, and since I only had a crappy threadbare one at home that had definitely seen better days, I couldn't help but to plop down on it and dig into my sub.

Yes, I was eating lunch in my boss's *en suite* bathroom while enjoying the view of the city beyond. Probably not the cleverest of moves. And yes, it was weird, but I couldn't resist taking advantage of the luxury. Who knew when I'd next have the chance?

Pulling out my phone, I browsed Facebook as I chowed down, intermittently chuckling at funny statuses or shaking my head cynically at the usual whack jobs. I came across a collection of photos from a distant cousin of mine, taken at her wedding vows renewal.

Hmm, bitch never invited me. I swear to God, it was the height of excess to have 350 pics of the same event, but like the weirdo that I (and, let's face it, all of us were) I couldn't help but to keep on clicking, like I needed to see ten variations of the same scene more than a crackhead needed her next fix.

I was lost deep in the Facebook vortex when the distinct clearing of a male throat caused me to jump and drop my phone in fright. Glancing up, I found King standing in the doorway, arms crossed and a curious look on his face. He was back early. *Of course* he'd come back early.

"Enjoying your lunch?" he said, raising an eyebrow.

What was that sound, I hear you ask? Why, it was my heart plopping right out onto the floor and crawling away in mortification.

"I, eh, uh…." I tried to think of an excuse, but drew a complete and total blank. Finally I went with, "You have a couch in your bathroom." Yep, that gem was all mine.

"I do. And you're in here, why?"

I let out an embarrassed laugh and hung my head in shame. There really was no excuse for this. It was like, when you see a giraffe walking by, you're more than likely at the zoo. This was me taking liberties plain as day. Wincing, I decided to go with honesty and face the consequences. "I'm really sorry. I was looking around your office and saw that you had a couch in your bathroom and that your bathroom is swankier than any bathroom I've ever been in, and I just couldn't help myself."

Oh, God, somebody gag my verbal diarrhoea, *please*.

I stared at King. King stared at me. His expression was indecipherable until he shook his head and let out a gentle laugh. Then he surprised the shit out of me when he closed

27

the door, stepped inside, and dropped down beside me. He threw his arms up and rested his head in his hands, kicking his legs out.

"It is quite swanky in here," he allowed.

A beat of silence elapsed before I had to ask, "Am I fired?"

King's eyes slid to mine as he let out a long sigh. I thought he might be enjoying making me sweat before he finally answered, "Luckily for you, I'm in a decidedly good mood today, so no, you're not fired. I'd appreciate it, though, if you let me know the next time you feel like eating lunch in my bathroom. I could have been in here taking a shower." He grinned at me before putting on a face of mock horror. "Or, God forbid, having a number two."

He whispered the words "number two," and I burst out laughing. I swear, it was the last thing I'd expected him to say. He was pretty funny when he wanted to be.

I swiped my fingers over my heart. "Okay, cross my heart, I'll give you notice the next time. Number twos are not something I want to witness."

He waggled his brow and leaned in a fraction closer, bumping my shoulder with his. "Ah, but you wouldn't be adverse to a shower?"

His question took me by surprise, and I was doubly surprised by the faintly heated look he gave me. My surprise, combined with my frazzlement, caused me to blurt out a whopper of a lie. "Oh, well, being a lesbian and all, seeing you in the buff wouldn't really bother me."

Why, why, why, Alexis? Why did you say that?

King eyed me shrewdly, his expression incredulous. "You're gay...seriously?"

I pursed my lips together and swallowed. Now that the lie was out, there was no taking it back. Then I'd have to come up with a reason for lying, and that would mean telling him the way he looked at me made me have some very unprofessional thoughts about him. And yeah, no way was I doing that. *No way.*

"Yep. Gay as a...spring day on the first of May."

Jesus. I had no idea where that weirdness had just spewed from. He studied my features, and I didn't know what he was going to say next. Then he gave me a playful grin before asking brazenly, "Always or mostly?"

The cheeky little...I stared at him head on and continued lying. "Always."

I wasn't sure, but I thought I saw a flicker of disappointment in his eyes. "Oh, well, at least this means we're ticking a box in the old equal opportunities survey." I could tell by his tone that he was joking. But still, I needed to change the subject. Perhaps he'd forget about the lie. After all, he was a busy man and surely took in a lot of new information on a daily basis. Perhaps the "Alexis being a lesbian" info would get lost amid the masses.

"You have a picture of Elaine King in your office," I said. "Any relation?"

His expression grew clouded, his demeanour more serious now as he answered soberly, "Yes, she's my mother."

"Wow. That's some talented gene pool you come from. Do you play piano, too?"

He leaned forward, resting his elbows on his knees. "Yes, actually. Mum began teaching me as a boy. Of course, I play purely for recreation. Mum is the star."

"She's very beautiful," I added.

"Yes," King agreed, frowning. "She is. It's a pity the world doesn't get to see it anymore."

I wanted to ask him why that was, but I didn't want to pry. Besides, I'd succeeded in changing the subject, and that was good enough for me. I wrapped up the last of my sandwich, got up from the couch, and gave him a friendly smile. "Well, Cambridge, I'd better get back to work. No rest for the wicked."

He narrowed his gaze playfully, and I was relieved to see the humour return to his features. I didn't like him sad and serious. "Let's leave Cambridge out of it. It's Mr King to you, Oliver at a push."

"How do you feel about Cambo?"

One eyebrow shot up as he joked, "Cambo as in Cambodia?"

"Nah, Cambo as in, I came all over your boobs."

What I'd said was probably pushing the limits of boss/employee appropriate chitchat, but he'd been overstepping the boundaries just as much as I had during our short time in the bathroom. Therefore, I wasn't as worried about his reaction as I might have been.

I'll give him credit — King didn't miss a beat as he laughed loudly and shook his head. "Oh, my God, you really are a lesbian."

Three

The rest of my first week went by, and I didn't see much of King. The man was one busy banker. However, on Wednesday, the day after our bathroom chat, I arrived back from my morning break to find a Post-It note stuck to my keyboard. It was from my boss. He had really messy handwriting, but I managed to make it out nonetheless. It read:

Alexis,

I have lunch meetings all this week, so my swanky bathroom is free and at your disposal should you wish to avail of it. Just clean up the crumbs when you're done.

Mr King

I was positively gleeful that he was giving me permission to use his bathroom as my own personal dining area and took full advantage of the offer. Besides, it was nice to have a little sanctuary away from my co-workers. I was fond of Eleanor, and Gillian was nice enough, despite her habit of flirting with any and every man who came into the office. But still, I cherished my hour in King's bathroom. It was my thinking time to eat and relax without the constant need to be conversational.

I had a swing in my step as I walked home from the tube station Friday evening. Karla and I were going to our ska night, and I couldn't wait to get dolled up and hit the town. After a week stuck in the office, I was more than ready to let my hair down. Maybe I'd even meet a man. Since my breakup with Stu was only a couple of months in my rearview mirror, I hadn't really given much thought to dipping my toes back in the dating pool. But now that I had this new job, I also had a newfound boost of confidence. Yeah, I could definitely pull tonight if I put my mind to it.

I ate a quick dinner that Karla threw together for us, then hopped in the shower. Fresh and clean and wrapped in a towel, I stood by my closet and took inventory of my clothes, trying to decide what to wear. My wardrobe was a bit of a mishmash of styles; I liked to wear eye-catching patterns. In the end, I chose a pair of slinky leopard-print leggings, a black halter top that cupped my tits nicely, a chunky gold necklace, big hoop earrings, and a pair of stripy green and black wedge heels.

Shut up, I looked fabulous.

Standing by my full-length mirror, I began straightening my wavy hair and took in my appearance. The mismatched patterns were purposeful. Besides, you had to dress funky for a ska night. It was expected.

"Great outfit," said Karla as she came into my room. "And those pants make your arse look fantastic."

"Why, thanks," I said, grinning and switching off the hair straightener. "You're not so bad yourself."

Karla wore a tight red pencil skirt and a stripy black and white top. She had the pale skin, red hair, and blue eyes of someone with a definite hint of Irish in their lineage. I, on the other hand, inherited my looks from my already mentioned crazy Greek mother (crazy in the best way) and had dark brown hair, almost black eyes, and an olive complexion. I also had an ample chest and a definite arse going on.

After I applied a bit of makeup, we shared a quick glass of wine before heading out. The Silver Bullet was totes hipster and always putting on random themed nights. At twenty-seven, and Karla being twenty-eight, we were probably a little old to be coming here. But whatever. The day I stopped going dancing would be the day they put me in my grave.

The ska night was in full swing when we walked in to the upbeat saxophone stylings of "One Step Beyond" by Madness. I didn't even bother going to the bar first to get a drink. Instead, I grabbed Karla's hand and led her to the dance floor, where we proceeded to bop and jump up and down like a pair of overenthusiastic toddlers.

I was lost in ska heaven when I felt a pair of arms go around my waist. Turning, I found my friend Bradley grinning down at me, wearing a wife-beater vest and a pair of canary-yellow jeans. Bradley was my brother from another mother who loved the cock. And yeah, *camp* as a row of tents. He'd gone to school with both Karla and me, and now worked as a pretty successful fashion photographer.

"Lexie! I haven't seen you in ages," he shouted in my ear. "What have you been up to?"

Fluttering my eyelashes, I replied jokingly, "Oh, you know, the usual. Leo Di Caprio offered to whisk me away for a dirty weekend and wouldn't take no for an answer."

He let out a yip of laughter and took my hand in his, leading me towards the bar. Karla followed, and Bradley turned to give her a quick hug and a kiss hello. He called to the barman, ordering a round of shots before turning back to me.

"I'm glad I bumped into you," he said. "I've actually been meaning to give you a call, because I have a proposition."

I grinned and knocked back the shot; it burned good as it went down. I liked Bradley's propositions. They were almost always guaranteed to have "fun" stamped all over them.

"Oh, yeah?"

"Yesss," he said. I could tell from the sparkle in his eyes that he was more than a little tipsy. "I've just started working for Baha. You ever heard of them?"

"Can't say that I have," I replied as Karla's elbow knocked against mine while she drank her shot.

"Wellll, they're a really popular fashion label, and I'm going to be working with them on an upcoming shoot for their plus-size range. They're looking for some new faces, and I immediately thought of you."

I sputtered a laugh. "Me? What, like, you want me to model?"

Bradley whacked me playfully on the arm. "No, I want you to make the tea. Of course, I want you to model. You'll be perfect."

I pretended to play it cool and joked, "Oh, well, I'd say yes and all, but if I showed up, they'd probably tell me to take my Kate Moss–lookin' self back from whence I came."

"Ha! Good one," Bradley deadpanned. "Are you up for it or what?"

"Eh, *yes*, I'm up for it. When, where, and can I keep the clothes after? But, more importantly, how much will I be getting paid?"

He gave me a little scowl. "You'll be very handsomely compensated, we'll see about the clothes, and I'll call you when I know more details."

"Coolio," I said, and turned to try and catch the barman's attention. I needed a drink to celebrate. It really was turning out to be my lucky week. I had new job offers coming out the wazoo. Before I knew it, I'd downed a rum and Coke, and Bradley was dragging me and Karla back to the dance floor. At one point, a brunette wearing a skintight shirt sidled up to Bradley and began what can only be described as booty popping at him. He continued dancing and arched a brow as she turned to face him, shimmying her boobs.

"Oh, you are *so* barking up the wrong tree, love," he sighed, and grinned.

I didn't think she heard, because she was now rutting against him. I snickered my laughter and grabbed a hold of Karla's hands, swaying her to the music. I was a happy, sweaty, dancing mess when I felt my phone begin to vibrate inside my bag. Stepping outside for a moment, because the music was too loud for a phone call, I glanced down at the screen and recognised King's number. Eleanor had me programme all the required numbers into my phone on Monday, and similarly, she'd passed my number on to King if he ever needed me.

I was curious, and yes, too tipsy to be answering a call from my boss, when I hit "accept." "Yo."

King's voice came down the line. "Alexis? Is that you?"

I grinned and leaned against the wall of the building. "The one and only. What can I do for you, boss?"

He cleared his throat, and there was a beat of silence, as though he was considering whether to continue the conversation. Finally, he went on, "I apologise for disturbing you outside of office hours, but I need someone to go collect some folders from Monty, and both Eleanor and Gillian are busy."

"Monty as in Burns?" Yep, definitely tipsy.

I heard the smile in his voice when he responded. "No, Monty as in Montgomery Charles. He works for me at the bank. He's drawn up some certificates, and I need the originals. Are you free to collect them for me?"

I sighed internally, knowing my night of fun was at its end. "Not exactly, but since you've allowed me to requisition your office bathroom this week, I suppose I do owe you one."

"Great," said King before rattling off where I had to go, alongside his home address, and told me he'd leave a key with the doorman. He also told me to keep my travel receipts for reimbursement. I went back inside, told Karla there was a work thing, and swiftly flagged down a taxi. Monty turned out to be a twenty-something guy with a big smile and a distinct eagerness to impress. He was adamant that I deliver the papers directly to Mr King, no detours. It was probably the way I was dressed that had him concerned, like I was some crazy leopard print–adorned lady pretending to be Oliver King's assistant.

The taxi was idling by the side of the road, waiting for me, when I returned and we continued on to King's place. It turned out his apartment was located close to the Thames, in a building that screamed *money*.

The doorman was expecting me and handed me a key card as I looked around the stylish modern interior. There were about ten floors, and King's apartment was at the top. Choosing to take the lift, since I had enough stairs to contend with in my own building, I hit the button for his floor.

I was fully sober as I walked down the long corridor to his apartment and let myself in. At first the place seemed quiet, but then I heard the music. Someone was playing a piano.

As I stepped around a tall column and entered the spacious lounge, I saw him. His back was to me as he sat in front of a black baby grand, his fingers skimming the keys as he played something classical. The tune was soft and hard at the same time, so intricate and beautiful. I knew I'd heard it before, maybe in a film, but I couldn't pinpoint where.

It made my pores grow tight and my lungs feel a little bereft of air.

There was something that was just so unexpected about seeing him like this, and it hit me square in the feelers. In the office I'd seen him professional, efficient, confident, and in control. But right then he was vulnerable, artistic, and totally absorbed in the music. And he was good, crazy good, so good I didn't understand why he was a banker when he could be playing music like this for a living.

The song became passionate, and his fingers pounded the keys right before my phone went off with a text. I had no clue who it was from, but I stood still as King immediately stopped playing and twisted around to face me. He seemed taken off guard, surprised to see me there even though he knew I was coming over. It was clear that he'd been completely lost in the music.

A moment of heavy, unexplainable tension fell between us.

Then he did a slow perusal of my body, and I swear he was holding back a grin. All in an instant, the tension was gone, and he wore a humorous expression.

"Oh, go on, say it. You know you want to," I sighed.

King let out a breath like he'd been holding it, and his voice was full of amusement. "What on earth are you wearing?"

"Hey, what I wear outside the office is my own prerogative." I scowled at him playfully. "But if you must know, I was out clubbing with some friends when I got your call, hence my fan-bloody-tastic attire."

He pursed his lips in an effort to stay his grin. "Well, in that case, I apologise for interrupting your night. Please, come and sit down. Do you have the receipt for your taxi and the certificates from Monty?"

"Yes and yes," I replied, walking to his couch, setting the folders on the coffee table, and taking a seat. "By the way, you play beautifully. Your mum taught you well." My words were restrained. What I really wanted to do was gush about how amazing he was, how the music had given me feelings I'd never had before, how it had made me see him in a completely different light. And I really liked that light.

King seemed to grow self-conscious as he ran a hand through his hair. "Yes, well, it's just a hobby." He paused and eyed my bag. "The receipt?"

"Oh, yeah, sorry," I said, and began rummaging for it while he waited.

As I handed it to him, I did a quick scan of his place. The Steinway sat by the window looking out onto the river, and I noticed piles and piles of paperwork stacked neatly all over the living room floor. He must have been working tonight. A bottle of red wine sat open on the coffee table, a half-finished glass beside it. There was an expensive-looking chessboard on the table, and I wondered if he played or if it was only there for show.

I remained seated as King disappeared into another room before returning with his wallet. Retrieving a few notes, he handed them to me. I took them and shoved them in my bag.

"Again, thank you for doing this on such short notice. I do try not to disturb my employees outside of the office."

"It's not a problem," I replied, and our eyes met. We both stared at each other for a moment, and my skin began to feel warm. King took in a deep breath. He didn't seem to want me to leave yet, so I nodded towards the coffee table. "Nice chessboard. Do you play?"

He glanced at the board before he brought his eyes back to mine. They were handsome eyes, intense, and so glacial blue they could almost startle you at times. I wondered if my sweatiness was from my earlier dancing or from King's unnerving attention.

"I do. Do you?"

"Yep. My dad taught me. We'd spend hours playing when I was growing up."

"Hmm, my grandfather was the one to teach me." He paused, studying me for a moment, before he said, "If you're not in a hurry to get back to your friends, would you like to stay and have a game?"

I shrugged, trying to play it nonchalant when really I was delighted with the offer. My new boss was an interesting (and sexy) one, and I wasn't going to turn down an opportunity to get to know him better.

"Nah, I'm not in a hurry," I said, shrugging off my jacket and laying it over the back of the couch. King's gaze wandered to my chest for a moment as he took in my halter top, before shaking his head and muttering under his breath, "Such a pity."

"Huh?"

"Would you like a glass of wine? I've already opened a bottle."

"Sure," I answered, still wondering about his comment. Was he referring to me being a "lesbian"? Couldn't be. Well, it could, but I was choosing to believe it wasn't for the sake of my employment. I didn't need to be having unprofessional thoughts about my intriguingly talented and handsome boss any more than I already was.

King went to the kitchen to grab another glass. When he returned, he handed it to me before picking up an expensive looking bottle of red. I considered asking how much it cost, but I stopped myself. Expensive indulgences always made me feel wasteful, and I just wanted to enjoy myself.

After pouring the wine, King began setting up the chessboard as I took several sips, and man, it was delicious. The rest of the bottle was in serious danger of being depleted by me if I kept this up. King's attention was on the board when he started to speak, holding a pawn between his fingers, "You know" —a pause— "you're not the usual sort of person who comes to work for me."

I wasn't sure how to respond to that. Finally I went with, "Is that a good thing or a bad thing?"

"Neither. It's just a fact. Eleanor is strict. She steers me in the right direction when I might be about to make a bad decision. Gillian is a wonderful organiser, and she never fails to compliment me in some way when she greets me in the morning. It's a nice little confidence boost."

I grinned at him, leant in, and mock-whispered, "Mr King, do you have a crush on Gillian?"

He chuckled, and it was an attractive, masculine sort of sound. "Don't be ridiculous. I simply enjoy her compliments."

I couldn't help teasing him. "Well, I wouldn't go getting a big head about it. That woman would marry a cup if it showed her enough attention."

"Alexis." Now it was King's turn to mock-whisper. "What a horrible thing to say."

Laughing, I replied, "It's not horrible. It's just the truth, and I'm not judging, but that Gillian is a flirt. You forget

I'm the one who has to listen to her giggle to men over the phone all day long."

King winced. "Giggle? Really?"

I nodded. "Uh-huh. You're not the only one who gets the compliments. Jealous?"

King shook his head and made his first move on the board. "No. And stop interrupting my train of thought. I was saying something, now, where was I? Oh, yes, Eleanor is my compass, and Gillian is my confidence-booster. Now that Eleanor's poised to leave, do you think you can fill her shoes?"

I bent forward to take in the board, then made a move. "Be your compass? I'll try my best," I answered, considering my strategy for the game.

"Your best is all I would ever ask," said King, a thread of seriousness coming into his voice. I glanced up at him for a moment, my eyes catching on a picture frame behind his head. It sat on a shelf beside a number of other pictures, and showed King with his arm around a good-looking woman with light brown hair. Since he thought I was gay, I felt relatively comfortable asking about her.

I nodded to the picture. "Your girlfriend?"

King turned to see what I was referring to. "My ex, actually. Mila and I broke up about three months ago." He shrugged like it was no big deal.

"I'm sorry to hear that. Breakups are tough."

"They can be, but not this one. Our parting was amicable. She wanted to get married and start a family, and right now I'm married to my job. There are things I want to achieve, and I'm quite single-minded about them. Mila is a career woman, too, so she wasn't hurt by my decision."

"I can understand that," I said. I could understand it, but I didn't believe for one second that this Mila woman hadn't been hurt. She'd probably just hidden it really well. I felt a bit sorry for King that he couldn't see that, or maybe he just refused to see it.

Eyeing his side of the chess board, I could already tell he was going to be a tough opponent and I was probably going to lose the game. We played for a couple of minutes in thoughtful silence before King spoke up.

"What about you? Any special lady in your life right now?"

His question and curious tone took me off guard, and I was answering before I had time to think it through. "Yes."

King rose an eyebrow. "Really? How long have you two been together?"

"Not long. It's pretty new."

"Do you think she's a keeper?"

Jesus, what was with all the questions? I felt like I was under interrogation. Needing to lighten the mood, I answered, "Who knows. For now I'm keeping my options open. I mean, just 'cause I'm tied to the fence, doesn't mean I can't bark at the cars."

He chuckled softly. "I've never had a lesbian for a friend before. I quite like it. It's pleasant talking to a woman who's essentially a man."

"Hey!" I protested.

He raised his hands. "I didn't mean it in a bad way."

I scowled at him. "Whatever. Besides, I'm not exactly your friend. I'm your employee."

King feigned a sad expression, like I'd just hurt his feelings. "You can be both."

I shot him a grin. "Well, all right, then. Let's try that. And since we're being friends, you won't mind me openly kicking your arse at chess."

42

His answering grin was wicked, and combined with his handsome face and tousled blond hair, gave me some distinctly un-lesbian feelings down below. What, oh what, was I getting myself into?

"Bring it on," said King.

Four

My mind was on my boss again as Karla and I walked to the nearby supermarket to do our weekly shopping. I'd stayed at King's place for another hour the night before, drinking wine and finishing our game of chess. I really enjoyed talking to him. I mean, he was so unlike the usual sort of men I'd grown up with. King was sophisticated and urbane, and he represented a world I knew virtually nothing about. And, as expected, *he* was the one to kick *my* arse at chess. I had to hand it to him — he was an excellent player.

In order to preserve my job, I left before I got too drunk, and told him I'd see him on Monday. It was only Saturday, and already Monday felt too far off. There was something about being in his presence and talking to him that I craved.

"Oi oi," I heard someone call as Karla and I were passing by a betting shop.

Talk about the sort of men I was used to. I turned my head to see Lee Cross, my ex Stu's younger brother, standing in the doorway, wearing a cocky smile. Lee was a handsome little shit, and he knew it. He was about twenty-five, and was one of four brothers that made up the notorious Cross family. Despite being younger than Stu, Lee was the brains of the operation, and I was fairly sure the garage he ran was also a chop shop. He held a toothpick to his mouth, still grinning, as he took in me and Karla.

"Haven't seen you around in a while, Clarky," he said, stepping outside and walking toward us. "What happened?"

"Stu and I broke up," I said, and remembrance lit in his eyes.

"Oh, yeah, I think I heard something about that," he said, glancing over his shoulder and back inside the bookies. That glance told me all I needed to know. Stu was inside, and I had the sudden urge to flee. I definitely didn't want a run-in with my ex right now, especially since the last time I'd seen him, he was being arrested for stealing cars. So yeah, their garage was most definitely of the dodgy variety. Lee's attention wandered to Karla, his gaze skimming lazily over her body and then back up to her face. By the glint in his eyes, I thought he definitely liked what he saw.

"All right, Gingersnap," he said, giving her a flirtatious wink.

Karla frowned and tried to hide a blush before looking at me. Although she'd met Stu a few times before, she'd never met Lee. And as I said, Lee was attractive in a bad boy sort of way. He had light brown hair, blue eyes, a muscled physique, and a perennially cheeky grin that promised pure naughtiness.

The supermarket was right next door to the bookies, and Karla sounded a little perplexed as she said, "I'm, uh, going to go inside and make a start. I'll see you in a minute."

And then she left, leaving me alone with the sexier, grown-up version of the Artful Dodger. Lee didn't even try to hide the fact he was checking out her arse as she went. He also didn't look away until she'd completely disappeared inside the supermarket, and that was when his attention returned to me.

"She single?"

I couldn't help it; I sputtered a laugh. Lee's eyebrows drew together as he chewed on the toothpick. "What's so funny?"

"My friend's name is Karla. My friend is also a cop."

45

Now Lee's eyebrows practically shot right up into his forehead. "For real? She's Old Bill?"

"Uh-huh."

He let out a low whistle. "Well, fuck me."

"Yep. She's also too old for you."

He flashed me a dangerous smile. "All the better. I like a woman with experience." Well, that statement was definitely wrong, because if what I'd heard on the grapevine was true, Lee had far more experience than Karla, even if she was three years his senior. He looked back inside the supermarket, and I could tell by his expression that his interest had been piqued. I clicked my fingers in his face.

"Hey, don't go getting any ideas."

He turned back to me, grinning again. "What? I didn't say anything."

"Your face said it all."

The look he gave me next had mischief written all over it. He rummaged in his pocket, coming up empty. "Oh, would you look at that, I'm all out of smokes. Think I'll just mosey on inside and buy a pack."

I tried to grab his arm, my voice low and threatening as I hissed, "Don't you dare," but he was already gone. I was about to hurry after him when another voice drew my attention.

"Lex," said Stu, stepping outside. He always called me Lex, and though it was nice to be given an affectionate nickname, it really just made me think of baldy old Lex Luther.

Drawing in a deep breath, I turned to face Stu. I could do this. Slowly bringing my gaze to his, I took in his appearance. Tall, built, with brown hair and hazel eyes, Stu's looks had never been a problem in our relationship. In fact, his looks, combined with his finesse in the bedroom, were the foundation on which our relationship was built. He might not have had much going on upstairs, but that dirty mouth of his always managed to make me forget my senses. The night he got arrested was the kick up the arse I needed to finally end things.

"Stuart," I said, giving him a nod. He smirked at my use of his full name and took a step toward me. Clenching one hand into a fist, I summoned my reserves of willpower. If the look he was giving me was anything to go by, he was about to lay the moves on thick and heavy, and I had no intention of succumbing to them.

"Missed ya," he said, now standing directly before me and looking down. His breath hit my cheeks, smelling of cigarettes and beer, which just said it all, given it was only eleven-thirty in the morning.

"Hmm, steal any cars lately?" I asked, my voice coming out clipped.

He laughed before his mouth formed a hard line. "That was all a big misunderstanding. I told you. My mate forgot he let me borrow his car."

I folded my arms and rolled my eyes. Did he think I was born yesterday? A moment of quiet passed, then a low, seductive murmur, "You look good."

I stepped backward to put some space between us, but he only advanced on me. My back hit the wall, and Stu crowded me in. Leaning down, his lips brushed my ear. "Fuck, but I've been dreaming about your pussy. Come back to me, Lex."

Okay, so I'd be lying if I said I didn't feel a little flushed right then. Sex with Stu *had* been spectacular, and life in my bedroom was decidedly dull since I'd handed him his marching orders. Still, giving in to him wouldn't be a good idea. Rekindling a relationship with a criminal was not something smart women did. And rekindling a relationship with a dumb criminal was definitely not something smart women did. I liked to think I was a smart woman. My vagina, on the other hand, was the equivalent of a dumb blonde. And that blonde wanted what she wanted.

"Piss off," I said, placing my hands on his chest and pushing him back. He didn't fight me, and instead chuckled, giving me a lascivious grin as I walked away.

He mimicked holding a phone to his ear. "I'm always available for booty calls, babe. Don't forget."

I flipped him off, which only solicited more chuckling, and stepped inside the supermarket. I searched through the aisles for Karla and finally found her idling by the breakfast cereals. There was a trolley in front of her containing a couple of items.

There was also a Lee Cross in front of her, and he looked determined. I caught the tail end of what he was saying.

"...fucking love this hair. You're gorgeous. Let me take you out."

"No, thank you," Karla replied stiffly before her eyes rose to mine and relief etched itself over her features.

"Hey, time to skedaddle," I said, and gave Lee a cheeky slap on the arse. His posture grew still, and I immediately wondered if that had been a good idea. Me and my trigger-happy arse-slapping hand. When he glanced at me, he wasn't wearing his cheeky grin anymore, and he was clearly pissed I was interrupting his attempt to woo my best friend...also, the arse slapping. Yeah, I already knew that despite his carefree, piss-taker attitude, beneath the surface lay a man not to be messed with. It was worrying that he'd set his sights on Karla. Nothing about that would lead anywhere good, and that was before you even factored in her profession.

He held up a finger to me, then turned back to the object of his affections. "One date. Come on. What's the worst that could happen?"

I resisted the urge to snort. Then Karla let out a small laugh. "I'm sorry, but no. Now, could you please move? I have groceries to shop for."

Lee stared at her for several seconds before leaning in and whispering something in her ear. I couldn't hear what he said from where I was standing, but I did see Karla swallow nervously. Giving her one final heated smile, he strode off with that confident swagger.

I let out a long breath. "Sorry about that."

She shrugged me off. "It's no problem. Was Stu out there?"

"Uh-huh." I let my eyes wander to the shelves as I scanned the items.

"How'd that go?"

"As aggravating as expected. What did Lee whisper to you?"

Karla looked away, embarrassed, before replying quietly, "Something a little too risqué for this time of the morning."

I finally decided on a box of cereal and picked it up before tossing it in the trolley. "Yep. Those Cross boys have some dirty mouths on them."

"Hmm," said Karla, and I didn't like the contemplative look on her face.

"Don't even think about it," I warned, wagging a finger at her. "Lee might be a hot little slice, but believe me, he's not worth it." I didn't mention that I was ninety-nine-percent positive he was involved in some pretty dodgy dealings. I didn't need to. Karla had been in her line of work long enough to recognise a criminal when she saw one. Don't get me wrong, Lee had a heart of gold. In fact, alongside Stu, he'd cared for his younger brothers from the time he was fourteen and his parents died. So yeah, he had a good head on his shoulders. Unfortunately, his circumstances in life had pushed him to channel his brains in the wrong direction.

Karla scoffed, but I could tell by the brief expression that crossed her face that she had been tempted, even if she'd never allow herself to admit it. "I'm not stupid, Lexie. I wouldn't touch that boy with a ten-foot bargepole. And I shudder to think what my dad would say if I did."

I gave her shoulder a reassuring squeeze. Karla's father was a superintendent and had raised her hard. It was where she got her tough side from. In any case, she was right when she said he'd disapprove. In fact, he'd see right through Lee the second he met him. Not that it was ever going to happen. Unless, of course he was arresting him for something.

The rest of the weekend passed, and before I knew it, I was waking up on Monday morning for work. I'd just slipped into a black pencil skirt and a purple blouse when my phone began ringing. Seeing it was Eleanor, I picked it up.

"Alexis, I'm glad I caught you before you left for the office. I won't be around today. Keith and I are seeing our estate agent about the house we're buying in France. You know Mr King's morning schedule well enough by now, don't you?"

"Yes," I said, nodding even though she couldn't see me. "I've got this. Don't worry about me." I had to use a little of my confidence-faking skills for that one. Sure, I knew King's routine, but that didn't mean I wasn't going to mess it up.

Eleanor let out a relieved breath. "Great. I'll see you tomorrow, then."

"See you tomorrow," I said, and hung up.

Rubbing my suddenly sweaty palms on my skirt, I began quickly throwing everything I needed into my bag. My hair looked a bit wild, so I twisted it into a bun and off I went. I managed to make it to the office a half-hour early, grabbed the credit card Eleanor used for office expenses, and then dashed out to the nearest newsagents. And okay, I might have gotten a little distracted chatting with the portly old fellow who was working the counter. It's a problem. When people start talking to me, I tend to get sucked in. This was why I took longer than planned to get the papers. I had ten of them tucked under my arm as I dashed into the elevator, only to be met with the icy blue gaze of Oliver King.

"Alexis, good morning," he said, nodding to me in greeting and grinning a little at my efforts to keep hold of all the papers. Then he gestured for me to hand him some. "Here, let me help."

I silently allowed him to relieve me of half the load, our fingers grazing as I explained, "Eleanor's not coming in today. Also, I have to confess, I haven't had a chance to read any of these."

King's lips twitched. "Well, given that you're new, I'll go easy on you. And don't worry, I've already been informed of Eleanor's absence."

"I'm sorry. I would have made a start earlier if I'd known, but I'm going to try my best not to screw up your day." Oh, God, if my hands were free, I would have face palmed at that. Way to show him I was a nervous wreck.

King's expression warmed. "I have every faith that you won't."

A few seconds of silence ticked by before the doors pinged open. As I walked alongside him, he commented, "You know, I hardly recognised you today without the leopard print."

I shot him an amused scowl, but strangely enough, his friendly teasing managed to ease some of my nerves. "Very funny, Mr. King."

It was nice to know that just because he was my boss, it didn't mean he was a slave driver. I was sure if I made a mistake today, he wouldn't berate me for it. And God, speak of a mistake and watch it appear. We walked into the office, and Gillian shot up from her seat.

"Good morning, Mr King," she greeted her boss brightly before her gaze came to me and her eyes flared meaningfully. King continued into his office. "Alexis," she whispered, "you forgot his breakfast." I swear, by the look in her eyes you'd think she was about to have a coronary at the horror of a breakfastless Oliver King.

"Crap, sorry! I'll take care of it right away."

"It's supposed to be waiting for him when he arrives."

"I know. It's my mistake. I'll go in now and apologise."

I left before she could stress me out further and slipped inside King's office. I held my hands up. "*Mea culpa* — I forgot your brekkie, but I'm remedying the matter right now. What ya got a hankering for?"

Brekkie, Alexis, really? For some reason my brain thought being funny about the mixup would make it less of a big deal.

King cocked a brow as he looked up at me from the newspaper he was scanning. "*Te absolvo*. Eggs Benedict and a double espresso. You speak Latin?"

I tried not to snicker. "Nah, I'm just clever like that. And that's one eggs Benedict and a double espresso coming right up. I'll be back quicker than John Travolta in a leather jacket."

King shot me a confused glance but just shook his head. He clearly didn't get my "Greased Lightning" joke, but whatever. I headed for the nearest café and got his breakfast. When I returned, he was in the middle of what sounded like a serious phone call, so I quietly set his food down on his desk. He gave my wrist a quick touch and mouthed a *thank you* before he was knee deep in his phone call again.

I returned to my desk and set to work, trying not to let my thoughts linger on the casual way he'd touched me. It was a touch of familiarity, and we weren't familiar. Well, not really. Perhaps the way I joked around made him think we were, but that was just my way. I was incapable of putting on airs and graces, and tended to act the same whether I was talking to my grandma or the Queen of England. Not that I've ever met the Queen, but you know what I mean.

Mid-morning came and went, and then there was a handsome dark-skinned guy in a suit arriving at the office to see King. His exotic looks, however, didn't match his public schoolboy accent. In fact, he sounded a lot like my boss.

"Ah, Mr Batage, it's good to see you again," said Gillian. "Is that a new suit?"

Mr Batage smiled at her and glanced down at what he was wearing. "Good to see you, too, Gill. And yes, it is new. Glad you noticed."

Gillian preened at him shortening her name to "Gill" and gave him a demure, "Well, it looks really good on you, and I love the way you're cutting your hair these days. Follow me — Mr King is just inside his office."

Mr Batage gave me a nod hello before following Gillian. I continued working until she returned and shut the door behind her. She made sure it was closed tight before sidling up to my desk and giving me the lowdown.

"That's Dilvan Batage. He's a good friend of Mr King's. They went to school together. Dilvan is a trader over at The Ring, but he comes from really old money. His family are wealthy tea exporters from Sri Lanka."

I glanced up at her. "Huh. What's The Ring?"

She looked at me like I was slow. "It's the London metal exchange. Busy place. Mr King took me along on a visit once. It's the only market that still trades solely in cash."

"Ah. Got ya. So he's some sort of hotshot, then?"

"Pretty much. He's really successful." I wasn't mistaken when I saw the dreamy look flash across her face.

"And easy on the eyes, too," I added, giving her a wink.

Gillian firmed her lips and straightened up. "That's neither here nor there."

"But you wouldn't mind his heres having a go on your theres, would you?"

Her pinched expression grew even more so, and I had to laugh. "I'm messing with you, Gill. Relax."

Without another word she returned to her workstation, and I thought I might have embarrassed her. Though I

54

found it hard to believe a woman who flirted as much she did could be embarrassed by a bit of friendly teasing, but hey, what did I know. I'd have to watch my mouth with Gillian in future so as not to cause offence.

I answered the phone then and scribbled down a message to pass along to King. The woman sounded adamant that I pass it on ASAP, so I rose and went to knock on his door.

"Come in," I heard him call before I turned the knob and stepped inside. King sat in his usual chair, while Dilvan perched on the edge of his desk. Both men were sharing what appeared to be a glass of whiskey. I swear, it was a scene straight out of *Mad Men*. I had to resist the urge to crack a joke about old broads and crazy dames.

"Ah, Dilvan, let me introduce you to Eleanor's replacement," said King as I walked into the room and passed him the note. "This is Alexis."

I turned and gave the man a polite smile.

"It's a pleasure to meet you, Alexis," said Dilvan.

"You, too."

Dilvan shot King a smirk. "I think your other assistant has a sweet spot for me."

King grinned. "Oh, really? Gillian?"

"That's the one."

When King's attention slid to me and I saw the playfulness in his eyes, I got a feeling I wasn't going to like what he was about to say.

"Alexis has a something of a theory about Gillian, isn't that right?"

"Oh?" Dilvan put in. Now both of their attentions were levelled on me, and I felt a bit hot under my blouse.

"I think you're getting me mixed up with someone else, Mr King," I said, quiet but firm, about to leave when he continued,

"No, I'm not. If I remember correctly, you said Gillian would marry a cup if — "

Before I knew it, I was taking a step back so that I could fit my hand over his mouth to shut him up. I'd left the door ajar, and there was a small chance Gillian would hear. I was so panicked for a moment that I hardly realised what I'd just done. My palm was fitted against King's sculpted lips, which, as it happened, felt really nice. He stared up at me, his bright eyes going unfathomably dark, before I snatched my hand away like I'd just been burned. Silence filled the room.

"Oh, my God, I'm so sorry, I shouldn't have…."

And then both he and Dilvan started laughing.

"You know, I do feel sorry for you, working with this beast," Dilvan told me.

"I just didn't want Gillian to hear," I whispered. "I didn't mean to…."

King waved my explanations away. "It's fine. Don't worry about it," he said.

I swallowed and nodded, turning and leaving even though I hadn't been dismissed. I needed to get out of there before I began stripping and giving him a lap dance. I swear, I did the stupidest things sometimes. I wouldn't be surprised if that somehow happened.

When lunchtime came, I wasn't sure if King's invitation for me to use his bathroom was still open. He was out of the office, though, and Gillian was dining out as usual, so I decided to chance it. I'd brought a packed lunch, because I needed to watch the pennies until I got my first month's pay.

56

Opening the door to the office and then to the bathroom, I furrowed my brow in confusion. The bathroom looked exactly how it normally did, only now there was a table and two chairs set up in the middle of the room, and on the table sat a chessboard. But it wasn't just any chessboard, it was King's. The one we'd played on at his apartment.

I didn't get the chance to ponder it further, because the next thing I knew someone was entering the room from behind me.

"Ah, you're here. Perfect. Fancy a game?" King asked, passing me by and pulling out a seat.

Five

"Well, are you going to just stand there all day, or are you going to come and play with me? I'm sure you're eager for a rematch," King went on as I stood by the door. I had to admit, I was flustered.

"Um, I...."

"Sit down, Alexis," he urged me, but it also sounded a little bit like a command. Who knew my boss had a bossy side?

I tried to concentrate on the chessboard situation, but I had to get the "my hand on his mouth" situation out of the way first.

"I'm sorry for earlier," I blurted. King only stared at me for a very long moment and arched a brow. "In your office, while your friend was visiting. I put my hand on your mouth, and it was so inappropriate I don't even know where to start." I glanced to the side and fidgeted with my hands.

"*Sit down*, Alexis," King repeated, this time with more force.

Unable to resist an order like that, I finally came forward and took the seat he was offering. His knuckles brushed my shoulder as he pushed my chair in, and I instinctively sucked in a breath at the contact. Not that he noticed. Walking around to the opposite side of the table, he unbuttoned his suit jacket and took a seat.

"What you did was fine. Dilvan is a friend. If it had happened in front of anyone else, it might have been a different matter. Maybe try to resist the urge to fondle me during work hours in future." His voice was lightly teasing, but there was also a stiffness that put me on alert.

He began to arrange the pieces to his liking on the board, and I didn't know how to feel. Was he actually okay with it, or was he just pretending? Nah, a man like King didn't pretend. He didn't need to.

"Well, I'll be more careful the next time. I wouldn't want to embarrass you."

He fingered his bishop and flicked his eyes to mine. "Embarrass me?"

"In front of your colleagues. I know this business can be all about appearances."

"You think so?"

I smoothed my skirt over my thighs and saw his eyes follow the movement. Huh.

"Oh, I know so." I paused hesitantly before asking, "Do you want honesty or the polite answer?"

"Honesty, always," said King without batting an eyelid.

I swallowed and gave it to him straight. "I've only worked here a week, and already I can tell the environment is all about appearing to be successful and acting like you're doing well, even when you might be failing miserably. And, let's face it, more people are losing than winning, especially in today's climate, but you wouldn't think it to look at them."

It was true. I might not have been working right in the middle of it all, but I'd been through the main offices often enough to be able to get the lay of the land. And the land around here was *highly* competitive. It was kind of a relief not to be a part of it. I had no clue why someone would actually choose this for a career. Well, okay, I did know. They chose it for the money. Though personally, I thought the amount of stress that came with the money wasn't worth it.

King seemed intrigued as he leaned forward and rested an elbow on his knee. "And am I one of the winners or one of the losers?"

"I've worked on your spreadsheets. I think we both know the answer to that question." King was winning hand over fist.

His mouth moved in something akin to satisfaction. "You have a very cynical view of my industry, Miss Clark."

My eyes grew wide. "Can you blame me? People have lost their homes, their jobs, because of bankers speculating with their money and handing out subprime loans like candy at a fair. But really, I just see it for what it is. If somebody's making money in this office, then it goes without saying that someone in another office is getting screwed over. There's cash everywhere, but seemingly never enough to go around. And definitely never enough to satisfy one person's desire for it."

I'll give him credit, King didn't show a single sign of annoyance at what I said. In fact, I'd go as far as to say he was actually enjoying the conversation. I was thankful my opinions hadn't offended him.

"If this is how you see things, then why come to work here?"

I let out a laugh and decided to make the first move in our game. I picked up a pawn. "Because I don't live in an ivory tower, Mr King. I live in a tower *block*. And I can't afford to be picky. The way I see it, the people who while away their days living by lofty ideals are the ones who have the money to do so. The rest of us are too busy trying to keep our heads above water to have time to play around with moral codes. So yeah, I don't believe the way the financial industry works is right or good, but if that industry is going to provide me with a way to pay my bills and keep a roof over my head, then I'm in no position to refuse."

"You're right," said King, eyeing the board and seemingly deliberating over his next move.

"Thank you," I said, feeling a small burst of pride that was quickly deflated.

"But you're also wrong."

I glanced up at him, surprised. "How am I wrong?"

"You said we all desire money, but I don't. My family is very wealthy, and I could live off that wealth quite comfortably for the rest of my life if I chose to, but I don't choose to. I want to excel, to do better than everyone else. Break records all on my own merit, no cheating, no shortcuts, no unfair advantages. *That's* what drives me. The money I make in excelling could very well be empty pieces of paper for all I care."

"A-ha, but don't you see, not caring about the money, only caring about winning, that's a luxury. You come from money, so you have the *luxury* of only caring about your accomplishments. If you had nothing to fall back on, if the threat of poverty was something to really be scared of, you'd care about the money then. The money would be all you'd care about, because it'd mean the difference between having food on your plate or going hungry."

Our game of chess felt long forgotten as King stared at me for what seemed like forever. He didn't say a word, but he didn't have to. He knew I was right. And speaking of hunger, I hadn't yet had the chance to touch my lunch, so I picked up my sandwich and began to unwrap it. I took a bite, chewed, and all the while King didn't say a word.

Finally, he spoke. "Have you ever considered joining a debate club? You'd be a formidable competitor."

I laughed. "Maybe I will."

King watched me eat for a moment (which made me unusually self-conscious) before opening up the small food container he'd brought with him. It looked like some sort of healthy Asian salad.

"Why did you bring your chessboard here? This is the same one we played at your apartment, right?" I asked as we both ate.

He cleared his throat. "It is. And to answer your question, I enjoyed playing with you. I thought we could make it a regular thing."

His answer caught me off guard, and yes, I was also a little bit flattered that he wanted to play chess with me on the regular. "And you put it in your bathroom because...?"

He gave me a hint of a smile. "You're oddly taken with my bathroom. I thought you'd be more amenable to playing if I put it in here."

I laughed loudly, because even though it was so weird, it was also so right. "Oh, my God, you know me too well. It's kinda scary." I waggled my brow at him.

"I wanted to make an effort for my very first Sapphic friend," he replied.

Christ, if ever there was a lie that would come back to haunt me, it was telling Oliver King that I batted for the other team. Still, it was a little bit funny he believed I was gay, and it was enjoyable to play along. I mean, even though I found him attractive, I had no intention of ever letting it go anywhere, so what was the harm in him believing I liked girls?

"If you'd really wanted to make the effort, you could have popped a few pictures of topless birds up on the wall. You know, so I'd have somewhere pleasant to rest my gaze."

King chuckled. "My apologies. I'll remember that for the next time I need to butter you up."

***

Mum: Dinner's on the table at 7. Don't be late.

I got the text right after lunch, and remembered I'd promised my parents I'd come around for dinner that evening. King and I hadn't managed to finish our game within the hour, so we'd left the board as it was with an agreement to pick up where we'd left off tomorrow.

Was he going to spend all his lunch hours playing chess with me in his bathroom?

The question gave me troubling butterflies in my belly, and I couldn't deny I was flattered by how much attention he was showing me. I had the feeling Oliver King didn't show attention to new people easily, so I knew there must be something about me that interested him. I was under no illusions that I was special, but I put it down to being different from the usual women who worked at Johnson Pearse. I didn't mince my words, I said inappropriate crap, I acted inappropriately, and seemingly King found all of this endearing for whatever reason.

All I knew was, he wasn't inviting Gillian to spend her lunch hours with him playing chess.

It was five past seven when I arrived at Mum and Dad's. They lived in Hackney, in the same little house I'd grown up in. It was far from a perfect place. The house was old and worn and in definite need of a lick of paint, but it was *home*, even more so when it was filled with the aroma of my mum's cooking. My mouth was practically watering at the scent of her special recipe moussaka.

"You're late!" Mum said, one hand on her hip, her usually plump lips drawn into a thin line. "We've all been waiting."

By "all" she meant her, my dad, and my younger brother Kain, who had just turned twenty-one and still lived at home. My older brothers, Leon and Matt, were married with children and had long since moved out.

"Sorry, sorry, today was my first day on my own, and it took me a little longer to finish up than usual," I said, raising my hands in the air. I loved my mum to pieces, but she had a fiery temper and got mad easily. Lateness was one of her many pet peeves, especially when she'd gone to the trouble of cooking.

I almost laughed as I took off my coat and saw she was holding a spatula. She pointed it at me like it could've been used as a lethal weapon. "The next time I will make fish fingers! Then you'll learn to be on time."

Now I did laugh. Mum had only moved to the U.K. when she was twenty-three, so she still had an accent, and "fish fingers" just sounded hilarious when coming from her. I stepped forward and gave her a hug, which seemed to placate her mood.

"I'm sorry, *mamá*, it won't happen again."

She sniffed. "Yes, well, see that it doesn't. Now come on, you look starved."

I followed her inside the kitchen, saying hello to Dad and Kain as I took a seat at the table. I filled them all in on the details of my new job, and I didn't fail to notice the look of pride in my dad's eyes when I spoke. I knew the fact that I'd gone back to school meant a lot to him. He'd always told me I had brains to burn, and that I was wasting my time working in a bar. I wasn't quite sure that I'd ever go much further in my career than working at Johnson Pearse, but at least it was something.

We were just done with dinner when my phone began to vibrate. Since texting at the table was another of my mum's pet peeves, I excused myself to the living room to check my message.

Oliver King: Are you busy?

Alexis: Just finished dinner. What do you need?

Oliver King: I'm at a meeting that's running late. I was due at my mother's an hour ago, but it looks like I'm not going to make it. Can you pick up some flowers and deliver them to her?

I frowned at his message. I didn't want to blow off my family, since I usually stayed and watched TV with them after dinner, but I was really curious to meet the elusive Elaine King. Okay, so I was morbidly curious. She hadn't been seen in the public eye for more than a decade, and there had to be a reason for it. Plus, she'd been the one to teach King how to play the piano so beautifully, and I was a little in awe of her for that. Finally, I replied.

Alexis: Of course. Send me the details.

Needless to say, Mum was none too pleased when I skipped out on her early. I left with a promise to visit again at the weekend, and that kept her happy. When I arrived at the florist, there was a huge bouquet of red and yellow lilies waiting to be collected. I picked them up, careful not to damage the petals, and went outside to thumb a cab.

Elaine King lived in a four-story period house in Bloomsbury, a very exclusive and expensive area of London. I stood outside for a moment, gathering my nerve. I'd never stepped foot in a house like this in my life, and it was slightly intimidating. Finally going for it, I pressed the doorbell, and a moment later a female voice came through the speaker.

"Hello, is that you, Oliver?"

"Mrs King, my name is Alexis. I'm your son's assistant. He had a meeting run late and asked me to deliver some flowers. I hope that's okay?"

"Flowers? Oh, yes, flowers. Okay, I'll be right there." There was something manic and airy about her voice that sounded kinda off. I was standing there for a good five minutes before I finally heard the door being unlocked. She opened it slowly, and I was met with an older pair of ice-blue eyes that were almost identical to King's.

She studied me for a moment, then craned her neck around the doorframe to ensure I was alone.

"Do you...do you have any identification?" she asked, a tremor in her voice. Jesus, was she okay? Resting the bouquet on my hip, I rummaged in my bag for my work I.D. before pulling it out and showing her. She took her time scanning the details, and then before I knew it, she'd reached out and grabbed my wrist, pulling me inside. Her hand was cold. It all happened so quickly that I barely had time to react. I was standing in the foyer, still holding the flowers and my I.D. when she began flicking locks and pushing over deadbolts.

Whoa. That door had *a lot* of locks on it.

When she finally turned to face me, I had a proper chance to take in her appearance. Her light blonde hair was long and raggedy, and she wore a cream silky robe over a pair of peach-coloured pyjamas, slippers on her feet. Her complexion was pale, and there was a nervousness in her expression that made me want to put her at ease. She was like a twenty-first-century Miss Havisham, locked away in her big old house. I could already see that the furnishings were dusty and uncared for, which meant she probably didn't have any household staff.

66

"Hi," I said, clearing my throat. "I'm sorry for intruding, but like I said, Mr King wanted you to have these."

She stared at me, seeming to flounder for a moment, and I got the feeling she didn't speak to new people very often. Then her eyes went to the flowers, and her face lit up in a smile.

"Oh, my, they're beautiful," she said, coming and taking them from me. Without another word, she carried them into the living room and placed them on the window ledge. I noticed that she needed to squeeze them in, because there were a bunch of other vases there already. Some of the flowers were fresh, and others looked like they'd died a long time ago. I felt a little shiver run down my spine. There was definitely something not right about this woman.

"Thank you so much for bringing these. Oliver knows I love my flowers. I remember when I was still performing, I'd come back to my dressing room, and it would be full to the brim with bouquets. Oh, the smell was just heavenly." She paused, and swallowed, her bloodshot blue eyes considering me shyly. "Would you like to…to stay for a cup of tea?"

I wasn't sure if I did, but there was no way I could say no to her. She seemed so lonely, and she had clearly sequestered herself away from the outside world. I wondered if King was the only person who ever got to visit her.

"Of course," I replied. "That'd be nice."

She smiled again and motioned for me to follow. A moment later, we were entering a large, unkempt kitchen. The sink was full of unwashed dishes, but thankfully she set a clean-looking mug down in front of me for the tea. As she busied herself making it, I felt my phone buzz in my pocket and pulled it out.

Oliver King: Did you deliver the flowers?

Alexis: Yes.

Oliver King: How did she seem?

Alexis: She seems okay. I'm still here. She invited me in for tea.

I knew saying she was okay was stretching it a bit, because there was nothing okay about this situation, but I didn't feel comfortable asking King about the state of his mother's mental health in a text message. There was a long stretch in between me sending the text and King replying. Elaine had made the tea and was pouring some into my cup with an unsettlingly shaky hand when I felt my phone buzz again.

Oliver King: I'm still in the meeting. I'll call you later. Be as sensitive as you can with her.

Well, it was obvious from his response that when King had asked me to deliver flowers, he hadn't expected his mum to invite me in.

Alexis: I will. Don't worry. Talk to you later.

Elaine sat down across from me, her hand still shaky as she lifted her cup to her mouth. She took a sip, then set it back down. I clasped my hands together in my lap. This was one of the oddest moments of my life, sitting in a kitchen having tea with a woman who was once a global superstar. I drank some tea.

"Goodness, you must think all this is terribly peculiar," said Elaine, gesturing around the room.

I didn't want her to feel bad, so I said, "Oh, give me peculiar over ordinary any day. It's far more interesting."

Something about my response made a tiny smile crop up on her lips. "I would have dressed if I'd known I'd be having company."

I waved her away. "Don't sweat it. Me and my roommate Karla practically live in our PJs when we're at home. In fact, it's the highlight of my day, getting home and slipping into a pair. And don't even get me started on bras. Taking those torture contraptions off after a day's work is pure heaven."

Surprising me, Elaine laughed, a light, tinkling sound. She settled into her seat, looking a little more at ease now. "How long have you been working for Oliver?"

"Not long. His other assistant, Eleanor, is retiring soon, so he hired me to replace her."

"I haven't met Eleanor," said Elaine. "But we spoke once or twice over the phone. She seemed very nice."

"She is. I'm going to miss her when she leaves."

So even Eleanor, the woman King trusted the most, hadn't met his mum? The fact that he'd trusted me to come here made me feel…I don't know, special.

Elaine shifted closer in her seat. "Alexis…what's he like, at the office, I mean?"

"Mr King?"

She nodded. I chose my words wisely when responding. "He's…extremely driven. People really respect him, and he's a good boss. He doesn't go crazy if I make a mistake or anything."

She seemed happy with that answer, and now I knew something else. Elaine King had never seen her son work, had never visited him at the office. She was a full-fledged hermit. We spoke for another few minutes, and then I got the feeling she wanted me to leave. Not because I'd done anything to make her feel uncomfortable, but just because being around someone new seemed to take a lot out of her. I said my goodbyes, and she walked me to the door. When I stepped outside, I immediately heard her re-doing the locks.

What on earth had happened to Elaine King?

I caught the tube home and was just settling into bed for the night when my phone began ringing. It was King.

"Hello?"

He exhaled a long breath. "Alexis, I…I'm sorry. I didn't realise she'd ask you in. She *never* asks anyone in. She comes to the door to collect deliveries, but she doesn't let people inside, except for me and her therapist. She won't even allow me to hire any household staff." Wow, he almost sounded upset. It was a little jarring, since he was always so suave and put together at the office.

"Look, King, it's none of my business. I know it must be difficult having a family member who…."

"Did you just call me King?" he said, cutting me off.

"Oh, yeah, sorry, I…."

"Don't apologise. I like it."

A silence elapsed, and then he said, "Alexis, I'd really appreciate it if you kept my mother's current condition to yourself. Every once in a while, journalists come sniffing about. It's a hard job keeping them away from her."

"I can imagine. But don't worry, you have nothing to fear from me. I won't tell anyone."

He seemed curious now. "I hope this doesn't sound like an odd request, but could you tell me what happened? The fact she let you into the house is a big deal."

"Of course," I answered, and then began to detail the encounter from beginning to end.

When I was finished, King said, "She must have seen something trustworthy in you. I'm not surprised. I felt the same way the first day you came to be interviewed."

What he said made me catch my breath. I just hoped he didn't hear it. "You did?"

"Yes, you have a warmth about you, Alexis. I sensed it even after you got prickly when I told you I liked your picture. Do you find that a lot of people you don't know very well open up to you?" he asked, and the accuracy of his question blew me away.

I did find that happening a lot. Whether I was sitting on the tube or having a quick coffee in a café, I'd find myself being drawn into conversations with strangers, where they'd tell me things about themselves you wouldn't normally say to someone you don't know. It had happened just this morning, when I'd gotten caught up chatting with the man at the newsagents, thus making me late with King's papers.

"Yes, actually, I do."

"You see. People must feel like they can tell you things without being judged."

Ha! That was a laugh. I was a judgey little bitch sometimes. Just ask Karla.

"Huh," was my only response.

"Well," said King, clearing his throat. "I'd better let you go. I'll see you in the morning."

"Yeah, see you," I said, and then we hung up.

Dropping my phone on my nightstand and making sure to set my alarm, I thought that today had been one for the books. I was exhausted, and as soon as I shut my eyes, I was out. However, in my dreams, King's words seemed to echo: *You have a warmth about you, Alexis.*

I found I kind of liked the sound of that.

Six

The following morning, I got another call from Eleanor informing me she wouldn't be in until after lunch, so I was responsible for the morning routine again. This time I felt more prepared. I had King's breakfast and his newspapers on his desk when he arrived. Once Gillian had talked him through the upcoming meetings for the day, he very subtly signalled for me to come into the office. It piqued my curiosity.

Closing the door behind me, I walked over to the window as King perused a paper. I had no idea what he wanted to talk about, and he didn't start speaking right away.

Perhaps he felt weird about the thing last night with his mum.

Glancing out and down onto the large open square beyond the office building, I spotted a new guy working the newsstand I'd been watching on the morning of my interview. A couple of customers came and went, but it was obvious that there was no longer any dealing going on.

King was still reading when I said, "Do you know there's a new guy working the newsstand outside?"

The corner of his mouth shaped into a grin before he swung around in his chair, holding a pen to his mouth as he considered me. "Does anything get past you?"

I gave him a toothy smile. "Very little."

He half-sighed, half-chuckled as he turned back to his desk. "I looked into the other guy after you mentioned him. Turns out you were right — he was dealing, so I got rid of him." He paused, letting out a derisive chuckle. "Apparently, he was well known by traders around here, went by the name of Bernie Black."

I was impressed that King had the kind of pull that he could get the guy removed just like that. I mean, he was obviously dealing for someone higher up, and this area would have been a highly profitable patch. Finally, I replied, "He actually told people his name? That's kind of dumb."

He stared at me sharply. "Think about it, Alexis."

I did. Then it hit me, and I laughed. "Ah, so Bernie as in coke, and Black as in hash."

"Now she gets it," said King with the tone of a patient schoolteacher.

I narrowed my gaze at him. "Do you know anybody in the office who bought from him? Because they're gonna be pissed when they find out he's gone."

Glacial eyes flicked up. "There's a few I suspect, but they'll just have to deal with it. It's a lifestyle a lot of people who come to work here fall into. If you're good at what you do, you can make an enormous amount of money in the blink of an eye. These people make that money, and all of a sudden they're buying expensive cars, luxury homes, and going out every night for extortionately priced meals. However, like you said yesterday, keeping up with the lifestyle and competing for all this money is also a big part of it. Competition equals stress, and when stressed, human beings seek a way to alleviate it. One of the main outlets for stress relief is drugs. Therefore, the City is a big market for dealers, especially since the people here have more than enough money to pay for what they want. It's a hard job keeping tabs on who's dealing and where, especially since I'm always so busy, so I have to thank you for the heads-up."

The warmth in his gaze made me flush. "It's no problem." What he'd said made me curious, so I went on, "What do you do to deal with the stress?"

He gave me a wan smile, and there was something in his expression that struck me as sad somehow. Rubbing at his chin, he answered, "Hmmm, when I'm stressed out...a nice glass of top-shelf whiskey usually does the trick."

"That makes sense," I said, and walked around his desk before taking a seat in front of him. "You know, I always thought it was poor people who did drugs, to escape the bleakness of their realities. Now I'm thinking maybe the practice is most common at the top *and* the bottom of the ladder. Perhaps the best place to be is somewhere in the middle."

"Not necessarily. I'm at the top. Do I look high to you?"

The deadpan way in which he said it made me laugh. I leaned forward and teased, "I'm not sure. Let me have a look at your pupils." Surprising me, King rose from his seat, walked around his desk, and came to kneel in front of me. Before I knew it, his face was mere inches from mine.

"Go ahead," he said, voice low.

Whoa, Oliver King's face right up close...I wasn't sure what to do with that. I guess he didn't realise the effect he had on this very non-gay lady, because he seemed entirely unselfconscious. His eyes were beautiful, his lashes long and golden, his skin smooth with a hint of stubble around his jaw, and his lips were just...I had no words. Sculpted and masculine was probably the only way I could think to describe them.

I realised I was staring at those lips a little too closely when my eyes flicked back to his. A moment ago he was smiling, but now that smile was transforming into a thoughtful frown.

I cleared my throat. "Your pupils look fine."

King exhaled a small breath, and I watched as his attention went from my eyes to my cheeks, nose, chin, and then finally to my lips. He looked like he was about to say something when suddenly Gillian's voice filled the room.

"Mr King, Jenson Gellar is on the phone. Shall I put him through?"

My heart beat wildly before I realised she wasn't actually there. She was talking through the intercom. I watched King swallow, smooth down his shirt, and then rise to a standing position. Walking to his desk, he hit the button to reply to Gillian.

"Keep him on hold. I'll pick up in a moment."

"No problem," she answered, and then the room was silent again. Whatever had passed between King and me, he seemed to be trying to push it from his mind.

Unable to stand the quiet, I asked, "So what did you want to see me about?"

I ran my hands over my skirt, noticing how King's eyes lingered on the movement for the barest second before he brought his gaze to mine. Another beat of silence passed, and my throat grew dry. Had he been…? I felt like maybe he had a thing for my thighs, because I'd caught him staring at them a number of times now. A moment later, he deftly set two newspapers down in front of me, each open on a different story. "Read both of these."

I cocked a brow. "Why?"

"Just read them, and then I'll tell you why."

"Aye, aye, captain."

He shook his head at my response and brought his attention to the phone. Picking up, he immediately began chatting a lot of numbers to the guy on the other end, while I tried to concentrate on the newspaper articles. Both were about different companies. One was a silicone manufacturer who had just announced an expansion to its production facilities. The other was a start-up for a new social media website. I read each of them to the end and was done before King was finished with his call. Glancing up, he noticed I was finished reading, and reached for a pad and pen. Still holding the phone to his ear, he scribbled something down, then passed it to me. It read: *Which of the two companies would you invest in?*

I pondered the question, unsure as to why he was asking me this. Did he need advice, or was it some kind of a test? Looking back at the articles, I tried to come up with an answer. Grabbing King's pen and paper, I began to write down a pros and cons list, and noticed his lips twitch when he saw what I was doing. All of a sudden, I began to wonder if I was some sort of amusement to him, or maybe a pet project. The thought disgruntled me, but I was determined not to let him see it. I'd told him at the end of my interview that I'd show him I had brains, and now I needed to prove it.

Five minutes later, he hung up the phone and turned to face me. Clasping his hands together, he asked. "Well, have you decided?"

I sat up primly. "Yes."

"And?"

"I'd choose the social media start-up."

"Elaborate."

Had it gotten hotter in here all of a sudden? My throat was feeling unusually dry. "Well, silicone is clearly a good investment, because let's face it, plastic surgery gets more and more popular year on year, and it doesn't look like it's going away any time soon. It's the safe choice if you don't factor in the possibility of a replacement being created that works better. However, the sky's the limit with the social media thing. It has the potential to go anywhere. And yeah, it's more of a gamble, but if it succeeds, the rewards could be huge."

King leaned forward, looking pleased. "So, let's say you're me and I'm my client. I come in and I want invest in either the social media start-up or the silicone manufacturer. You'd advise me to go for the social media?"

Narrowing my gaze, I nodded.

He smiled. "All right. That will be all."

"That's it?"

"I have a very busy day ahead of me, Alexis, but I hope to see you at lunch for our game of chess." His easy dismissal irritated me, and I felt like he was being sneaky.

"King, this was all hypothetical, right?"

The look he gave me when I called him "King" made my knees a little bit weak. He clearly liked it, and I wasn't sure if it was because I'd essentially given him an affectionate nickname, or if he just enjoyed being referred to as an all-powerful ruler.

"And if it wasn't?"

"I'm only an assistant. I know virtually nothing about investing. You shouldn't be using my advice in any kind of real life dealings."

Now I had his full attention, and he seemed annoyed with me. "Alexis, I have heard more intelligence from you in two weeks than I have from some of the people I work with in an entire year. Never underestimate the value of your decisions."

I swallowed. Blinked. Couldn't believe what I was hearing. Never in a million years had I expected him to say something like that. And then I felt tears prickling in my eyes. It was such a huge compliment, and I wasn't used to those. I needed to get out of there before I embarrassed myself. Not saying a word, I gave him a sober nod, turned, and walked out of the room. Despite what I'd proclaimed about having brains at the end of my interview, I suddenly realised that when it came down to it, I didn't really believe I could do very much with them. King's compliment showed me that I needed to seriously rewire the way I thought of myself.

For the next two hours, Gillian kept giving me furtive glances. She clearly wanted to know what King had talked to me about. I gave her nothing. Not only was the woman a flirt, she was also a gossip, and I didn't want her spreading rumours of me getting preferential treatment from my boss. Not that it had been particularly preferential, but I got the feeling he didn't often ask his assistants for business advice.

It was almost lunch when Gillian came to my desk and placed a small white envelope in front of me.

"This came for you," she said, looking curious.

I glanced at the envelope and saw it had been addressed to me in pretty cursive handwriting. Opening it up, I found it was a note from Elaine King telling me she'd very much enjoyed my company yesterday, and that she hoped she'd see me again sometime. Wow. I definitely hadn't been expecting this. I'd just finished reading it when I realised Gillian had been craning her neck and reading over my shoulder.

"You met Elaine?" she asked in a breathy, flabbergasted voice.

I shot her annoyed look before answering, "Yeah. Mr King had to cancel a visit and asked me to deliver some flowers to her house."

Gillian's eyes flared wide as she took a quick look at King's office door to make sure it was closed. Her voice grew hushed. "Nobody around here has ever met Elaine. Rumours say she went mad with paranoia after something happened with a stalker, and Mr King keeps her locked away to hide the secret."

For some strange reason, I felt the urge to cover for both King and his mum. "Well, she seemed normal enough when I met her."

"Oh," said Gillian, obviously disappointed. She was after a scandal, and I wasn't going to give her one. Finally accepting there was no story to tell, she went back to her desk and resumed working. I read Elaine's note once more, a warm feeling in my tummy to know that she'd liked me. It felt good to think I'd brightened up her day. Then I started to wonder about the stalker Gillian had mentioned. This tidbit definitely wasn't common knowledge, since I would have read about it in the media. Given the state of Elaine nowadays, it could just as easily be true as it could be a rumour.

When my lunch hour came, I waited until Gillian had left the office to head into King's bathroom. He wasn't around, so I tucked into my packed sandwich and browsed my personal emails while I waited. As I did this, a text came in from Bradley. He had news about the photo shoot he wanted me to do. In a nutshell, he'd shown the higher-ups at the fashion house some photos of me from my Facebook page. They'd liked my look and wanted me to model. It all felt so glamorous and exciting. I was just reading through the details for the shoot, which was to take place on Saturday, when the bathroom door opened and King stepped inside.

"Started without me?" he asked, taking off his suit jacket to reveal a perfectly fitted white shirt beneath. I really needed to stop noticing these things about him.

"Uh, yeah," I said, swallowing a bite as he neatly placed his jacket over the back of his chair. "I wasn't sure if you were going to make it."

He arched a brow and then began unbuttoning the cuffs of his shirt sleeves before rolling them up his arms. I didn't know why he was doing it, since it wasn't particularly hot in here. And really, I wished he wouldn't, because I couldn't take my eyes off his forearms. They were...yeah, quite pleasant to look at. He seemed to be hiding some sort of satisfaction when he nodded to my phone.

"Anything interesting?"

"What?" I glanced down, taken by surprise that he'd caught me staring. "Oh, right, yeah, actually. I was just texting my friend, Bradley. He's setting me up with some weekend work."

King's expression was wry. "We don't pay you enough here?"

I shook my head. "It's not that. It's more of a favour. He's a fashion photographer, you see, and the label he's working with at the moment need plus-sized models." I paused and gestured to myself. "Hence, my involvement."

He seemed both interested and amused as he leaned in. "You're going to model?"

"Eh, yes, no need to sound so cynical."

A small frown. "I wasn't being cynical. I think you'd make a great model," he said, and then his eyes seemed travel down my body, lingering on the flare of my hips emphasised by the pencil skirt I was wearing. "*Fuck*, you'd

80

make a perfect model." This last bit was said under his breath, and my skin began to tingle. Had he really just said that, or was I having a little mini daydream for a second? I needed to alleviate the tension his comment created, so I put on a haughty voice.

"Mr King, none of those F-words at the office, please."

He chuckled. "My apologies. I sometimes forget you work for me. You're so easy to get along with that you feel more like a friend."

"Aw, shucks, thanks." I grinned at him and took another bite of my sandwich. Well, that was kind of sweet. He seemed oddly sheepish about his admission, and picked up the lunch I'd ordered for him. It was now my job to order his meals from the local health food café each morning and schedule them to arrive by one. I swear, the man ate a diet straight out of *Men's Health* magazine, all eggs, lean meat, and fresh vegetables. And there was me thinking bankers subsisted on a strict regime of coffee, steak, and whiskey. Maybe that was the '80s *Wall Street* stereotype talking.

"So, you're working on a shoot this weekend?" King asked.

"Uh-huh."

"Can I come and watch?"

I gaped at him. "Are you serious?"

"Of course," he said, and pulled out his phone, fingers swiping over the screen.

"What are you doing?"

"Cancelling an afternoon tea party I was supposed to attend so that I can accompany you to your photo shoot."

"You're not coming."

He frowned and gave me this sad little puppy-dog pout that I swear made my ovaries wake up and say hello. The man was unfairly good-looking.

"Come on," I said, "you have to admit it is weird that you want to come to this."

Now he looked sceptical. "Will there be other women there who look like you?"

"I presume so...."

"You see? It's not weird at all. I enjoy looking at women, especially ones who are interested in cocks rather than vaginas."

I couldn't believe he'd just said that. I also couldn't resist the urge to give him a scare. Glancing over his shoulder, I said, "Oh, hi, Gillian. Were you looking for me?"

King's complexion instantly paled, and he went utterly still. I burst out laughing as he turned and found the doorway empty. "Oh, my God, the look on your face. That was priceless!"

"It was *cruel*." He scowled at me, but I could see the smile he was trying his best to hold back.

"It serves you right for talking about cocks and VJs at the office. I bet you don't say stuff like that to Eleanor."

"Eleanor is old enough to be my mother."

"And what am I? Chopped liver?"

"*You*," said King, voice low and gravelly, "are the perfect age to be hearing words like that."

On instinct, I licked my lips, and his eyes zeroed on it. Why oh why did he pay such close attention to the small details? It was too much, and the lesbian façade I'd been putting up was slowly beginning to crumble. If he kept giving me looks like that, he'd figure out sooner or later that I was lying, because my body language practically screamed my attraction.

He kept on staring at me, and I knew he was waiting for me to give in.

"Fine, you can come, but no manhandling the other models. I know what you Cambridge types are like. Frisky."

He laughed. "If by 'frisky' you mean uptight and socially awkward, then you know us very well indeed."

"Are you seriously using the words 'uptight' and 'socially awkward' to describe yourself? Because if you are, you're fooling no one."

King tsked. "I'm not talking about myself. I'm talking about the kind of people I went to school with. I was lucky to be born with natural charm." He flashed me a cocky grin.

"Self-professed charm is no charm at all."

"You find me charming."

"That's true. I find you about as charming as an '80s sex comedy."

King laughed loudly at my put-down, strangely seeming to enjoy it, and began eating his lunch while eyeing the chessboard.

"So, are we going to finish this game or what?"

We did.

And this time, I came out the winner. We were at a draw.

Oliver King: 1. Alexis Clark: 1.

Seven

The following morning I walked into the office, sensing an odd vibe in the air. It wasn't long before I discovered the reason. It was B-day at Johnson-Pearse.

And no, that wasn't B-day as in birthday. That was B-day as in Bonus Day. Apparently, investment banking, along with the vast majority of jobs in the financial sector, orbited around yearly bonuses. And those bonuses were announced at the start of each calendar year. I'd always read about this sort of thing in the newspapers, where left-wing journalists would criticize banks for giving out exorbitant bonuses to their employees while the rest of the country suffered one of the worst recessions in decades. I had to agree with the journalists; it was pretty fucked up. That still didn't stop it from happening, though, and now I was getting to witness it all first hand.

It soon became apparent that everybody wanted to achieve a larger bonus than the one they got the year before, which accounted for the nervous tension. Nobody wanted to get a small bonus, because that meant they were losing at the game of making more money than everybody else.

I learned all of this from Eleanor as we worked together to complete our morning tasks. She'd been very happy with the way I'd handled things during her absence, and was confident I was going to make an excellent replacement after she left. Her confidence in me gave me a boost.

The hours until lunch passed busily. The way things worked on B-day were as follows. Each employee was called into King's office, or the office of Daniel James, senior managing director. The bonuses were not announced

84

publicly. Instead, each employee was told his/her bonus in private. And the absolutely bizarre thing about it all was that every single one of those employees exited King's office looking confident and satisfied.

I knew some of them had to be bluffing, because not everyone got a larger bonus than last year. And here lay the competitive nature of the business. No matter what number those bankers got told when they entered King's office, they would never let their colleagues see their disappointment.

Like I said, it was all about appearances.

It was mid-morning, and another "pleased"-looking employee had just exited King's office when I went inside to bring him his coffee.

"Hey. How's everything going?" I asked, setting the cup down on his desk.

"Monotonous," he replied, running a hand through his short blond hair.

"Don't you enjoy telling people their bonuses? I mean, the ones who did well, at least?" I asked, curious.

King only shot me a look that said it all. So he didn't like B-day. Duly noted.

"Will you thank your mother for the note she sent yesterday?" I said just before I was about to leave.

King glanced up from the papers on his desk. "Note?"

"Yeah," I replied. "I got it yesterday. She wrote telling me she enjoyed my company when I'd stayed for tea."

A stressed look crossed over King's face. "Do you still have it?"

"Yes, it's in my drawer."

"Go get it," he clipped.

Frowning, I turned and went to retrieve the note. When I returned, I handed it to King, and he hurried to pull it from the envelope. His eyes scanned the words, and then a relieved breath escaped him.

"Yes, this is definitely her handwriting."

I let out a nervous laugh. "Who else's would it be?"

Shutters went down behind King's eyes and he stood, walking to me and handing me back the note. I took it and watched as he went to the drinks cabinet at the back of the office and pulled out a bottle of expensive whiskey. In less than a few seconds, he'd poured some into a glass and knocked it back. I recalled his words from yesterday.

When I'm stressed out, a nice glass of top-shelf whiskey usually does the trick.

Why had his mother sending me a note stressed him out? And why had he thought somebody else had sent it?

"King, is everything all right?" I asked, concerned.

He closed the drinks cabinet and turned back, his expression hard. Whoa. I'd never seen him look at me like that before.

"Everything is fine, Alexis. Now, I do believe you have work to attend to."

Brow furrowing, I gave him a quiet, "Yes, I do," then turned and left his office.

***

I didn't go to the bathroom for lunch that day, nor did I go the day after. Instead, I ate my sandwich on a bench outside, intermittently browsing my messages and throwing pieces of bread to the pigeons. I'd almost forgotten that King and I had anything even resembling a friendship until he sidled into the office on Friday morning looking like the cat that got the cream. And all of that smug delight was being firmly directed at me. He said his usual hellos to both Gillian and Eleanor, then came to stand in front of me, arms folded, a gigantic smile on his face.

86

"You're looking particularly lovely today, Miss Clark," he said with a flourish.

I glanced at him for a second, frowned, and then continued typing. What was his game? Eleanor got up from her seat and went to use the bathroom, and still he remained standing there like a complete and total oddball, as Gillian's voice talking on the phone filled the room. Finally, I gave in.

"Can I help you with something?"

"I could fucking kiss you right now," he beamed, and I sucked a breath.

Okay. Trying to play it nonchalant, I replied, "For what exactly?"

"That social media start-up we discussed the other day? Well, immediately after we spoke, I lined up one of my clients as an investor, and guess what?"

I stared at him. "What?"

"The site has gone viral overnight. Apparently, a couple of celebrities started using it, and now they're getting new sign-ups by the bucket load." He leaned forward and braced both his hands on the edge of my desk. "This client was an important one, and he currently thinks I shit daisies. *And* I have you to thank for it, Alexis. You're a flipping genius!"

I couldn't help my smile. He really was laying it on thick and heavy. "Shall I whip out my cock for you to suck now or later? Jeez, Ollie, tone it down a little."

He blinked at me, and then a second later he was laughing. It was good thing Eleanor wasn't around and that Gillian was too preoccupied with her phone call to hear what I'd said.

"Did you just call me Ollie?"

Supressing a smirk, I nodded, still typing. A beat of silence passed.

"Did you also just refer to me sucking your cock?"

"Well, you've already opened the button and pulled down the fly. You might as well finish the job," I quipped, and amusement lit his eyes.

He stared at me for so long that I began to get uncomfortable. His smile naturally faded, and now his expression grew serious. "I'm going to put a bonus in your first month's pay. Think of it as a consultant's fee."

Now I was frowning again. "You don't have to do that. Seriously, picking that start-up instead of the other business was just me thinking out loud. Hazarding a guess. I didn't do any research. I could have been completely bullshitting for all you knew."

King leaned closer. "Alexis, don't insult me. I know bullshit from real shit when I hear it. And what you gave me was the latter."

Now I was the one staring him down. I decided I wasn't going to protest further, because, hey, if he wanted to give me a bunch of money for my advice, I wasn't going to turn my nose up at it. Maybe I could use it to bring me and Karla away on a little weekend break or something.

"Fine," I said. "Give me the bonus."

"Not giving it to you was never an option," he answered before heading in the direction of his office. Once he reached the door, he turned back. "Oh, and don't think I've forgotten about Saturday. And I better see you at lunch today. No more standing me up."

Jesus, he said that right in front of Gillian. It was good thing she was still busy with her phone call. I could just imagine the gossip spreading like wildfire if she knew we were having all these intimate little lunches together.

Before I could shoot him a scowl for almost outing us, he'd disappeared inside his office.

I didn't stand him up for lunch. And this time King won the game. Damn, he was starting to get an advantage on me.

Oliver King: 2. Alexis Clark: 1.

* * *

Bradley: Don't wear any makeup. It'll be done at the shoot. Can't wait to see you. Smooches <3

Alexis: Is it okay if I bring a friend?

Bradley: Karla wants to come?

Alexis: No, she's working. Someone else.

Bradley: A *boy*?

Alexis: Maybe.

Bradley: Send me a pic and then I'll decide :-D

Alexis: Piss off.

Bradley: Fine. I'll just have to wait and wonder. If he looks anything like the last one, then I predict I'm in for a treat.

Alexis: He's not a boyfriend. Just a friend friend.

Bradley: Ooooh. I see. A gentleman's gentleman?

Alexis: Sorry to disappoint, but no. A lady's gentleman through and through.

Bradley: Sometimes I think you might hate me.

Alexis: Lol. See you later.

Bradley: Whatevs.

On Saturday morning, King insisted we take his car to the photo shoot. I told him I'd get the tube and meet him there, but he wouldn't take no for an answer. To be honest, I really didn't want him to collect me. I hated to admit it, but I was embarrassed by where I lived. Yeah, he was aware I wasn't exactly born with a silver spoon in my mouth, but the thought of King actually seeing the reality of my life made me break out into a cold sweat. I doubted he'd ever set foot in a building like mine in his life. It was going to be a rude awakening when he saw the graffiti-laden, grey block of despair in which I dwelled.

Giving in, I texted him my address, expecting him to call when he was outside. That wasn't what happened. Oh, no, Oliver King took it upon himself to ascend the many flights of stairs up to my flat and knock right on my door. Karla was at work, and I was just pulling on a top when I heard the knocking. Praying it was one of my neighbours coming to ask a favour, I padded my way to the door and peered through the peephole. And there in all his sexy glory was my boss. I let out a long sigh and thumped my head against the metal panel.

Well, he'd already seen the worst of it now. There was no point refusing to let him inside. I opened the door and stepped back, taking in his appearance. It had *quite* an effect on me. He wasn't wearing his usual fitted suit. No, today he wore a casual black jacket, a grey T-shirt beneath, designer jeans, and a pair of Caterpillar boots. I swear I had to consciously resist the urge to swoon. His hair was casually tousled with a bit of wax, and seeing him dressed like an everyday, normal bloke did a bit of a number on me. He looked just like someone I might chat with in a bar.

Catching my breath, I greeted him. "Hey, uh, you didn't have to come all the way up here, but come in."

Stepping past the threshold, King surveyed my small but tidy flat before bringing his attention to me. "Good morning, Alexis. I encountered a couple of young girls in the stairwell." He seemed a little flustered, and it made me smile.

"Oh, yeah, what did they say?"

His brow furrowed. "I'm not sure if it bears repeating."

I snorted. "Yeah, I can imagine. I just have to throw a few things in my bag, but make yourself comfortable. Be back in a tick," I said, and went inside my bedroom to shove my phone and wallet into my handbag. I was wearing a pair of black leggings, an old Madness T-shirt, and a long purple cardigan. Oh, and no makeup, as requested by Bradley. I hadn't bothered to dress fancy for two reasons. One: I'd be getting dolled up at the shoot. And two: I didn't want King "warming" to me any more than he already had. I mean, the man thought I was a lesbian, and he still wanted to hang out.

Perhaps it was my glowing personality that he enjoyed. Heh.

Returning to the living area, I found King sitting on the couch, perusing a picture of me and my family. The sight of all his masculine beauty in my very ordinary living room struck me like a whack to the chest. He was a fucking stunning-looking man, and I was pretty much doomed to lust after him for the foreseeable future.

"I'm all ready. Let's hit the road, Jack."

His eyes came to mine. "Is this your family?"

"Yep. Handsome bunch, aren't we?" I joked, and he chuckled softly, setting the frame back on the shelf. We left my flat and walked back down the stairs. The group of girls King had mentioned were gone, so he was saved from a second encounter of them leering at him. Girls around here could spot money a mile away, and King's every movement screamed privilege and wealth.

There were a couple of young kids and teenagers hanging about when we got outside, ogling King's car. It was a black Mercedes and came equipped with its very own driver. It was a good thing, too, because from the way the

91

local kids were eyeing it, I imagined it would have been stolen in a hot second if left unattended.

In a very gentlemanly move, King opened the door and gestured for me to get in. As I slid past him, he looked down at me, eyes intent on my face.

"You're not wearing any makeup," he said, his focus moving over my cheeks and down to my lips.

It didn't surprise me that he noticed the change, because I usually did wear makeup to the office.

"Yeah, they'll be doing it at the shoot."

He exhaled. "I quite like your face without it."

Well, okay then. I didn't know what to say to that, so I simply continued my way inside the Merc. King slid in after me, and then we were off. The journey was quiet as I fidgeted with my hands, a little self-conscious now that he'd seen where I lived. It was one thing to casually mention it in conversation, but it was another to have him actually go there in person. I could feel him watching me out of the corner of my eye, but I didn't look at him.

He must have sensed something was up with me when he asked, "What's wrong, Alexis?"

There was something about him saying my name in the small confines of the back seat that made the skin on the back of my neck tingle. I flicked my eyes to his for a second before looking back out the window. "Nothing."

"Don't give me that. You're not your usual chatty self. Out with it."

I sighed and crossed one leg over the other, causing King's attention to wander to my thighs for a moment. I was beginning to lose count of how many times he'd done that, and it made me swallow, hard. He was one of those real attentive types who picked up on body language. I could tell. I also wondered what he could read from me. Was I successful in hiding my attraction?

"I'm...." I began and then paused, feeling ridiculous. "This is stupid. I never make apologies for who I am or where I come from, but I just feel a bit embarrassed about my flat."

"Your flat is lovely, Alexis."

I pulled my lips through my teeth. "Thank you, but I mean the outside, not the inside. It's probably because I've been to your place and seen how fancy it is. I bet you've never even stepped foot in a building like mine before in your life."

He studied me, face drawn into a serious expression. I felt his shoulder brush mine when he said, "I haven't, but what does that matter? You don't always have to be stuck where you are. You can improve your life endlessly so long as you have the capability of doing it, and you, Alexis, have the capability. Don't ever let anyone else tell you otherwise. But back to the matter at hand. You're my friend — therefore, I don't care where you live."

I stared at him, dumbfounded and kind of flattered by all that stuff he said about my capabilities. I didn't want him to know I was flattered, though, so I ignored his compliment and blundered on. "And that's another thing. Isn't it a bit weird that I'm your friend and I also work for you? Do you normally make friends with your PAs? Isn't this, whatever we're doing, against the rules?"

"That's a lot of questions."

"I need a lot of answers."

He was close enough that I could feel his breath on my ear. "Okay, I'll endeavour to give you some. First, I wouldn't say it's weird that we're friends. It's more out of the ordinary."

93

"Same difference."

"Let me finish."

"Fine," I huffed.

"Second, no, I don't normally make friends with my PAs. In fact, I'd never planned to make friends with you. It just sort of happened. I like you. You make me laugh. And you're different from the other people I know. Having you around makes the day that little bit more interesting. I enjoy the spontaneity of never quite knowing what you're going to come out with next." He paused to laugh gently. "And third, no, it's not against the rules. I'm free to be friends with whomever I choose, employee or not." He went quiet then, and I turned to see why he'd stopped talking.

His eyes looked...heated.

Now he whispered, his breath kissing my ear, "If I were to fuck you, it would be frowned upon, but it still wouldn't be breaking the rules. I'm not your teacher or your college professor, Alexis."

Eight

Oh. My. *God.* I felt like I'd momentarily lost the ability to speak. What on earth was he playing at? I mean, his driver was sitting *right* in front of us. He didn't show any signs of having heard King, *but still.* I think I became a touch hysterical when I shakily wagged a finger at him. "You have all the wrong equipment for me, remember?"

Jesus, was that even my voice? I sounded way too high-pitched.

He was silent a moment, and when he replied his voice was low and quiet, "Oh, yes, how could I forget?"

Now he stared out the window, arms folded across his chest. This was turning out to be the most awkward, sexually frustrating car journey of my life. It was a relief when we finally reached the location of the photo shoot, a warehouse building in Shoreditch. King got out first and went around to the front of the car, leaning down and talking to his driver through the window. The man nodded and drove off after I'd gotten out, too.

King glanced at me and gestured that I should lead the way. I took a few steps over to the intercom and pressed the button to be let in. A female voice answered, and a second later we were being buzzed through. King was quiet as we went up the stairs to the studio. I was dying to know what he was thinking. What had brought all that on back in the car? I mean, he was often flirtatious, but never outright lewd, unless of course we were exchanging dirty jokes. But there was nothing humorous about what he'd said to me on the drive.

When we reached the first floor, we found the place a flurry of activity. There were makeup stations all along one side of the large open-plan room, and on the other side were racks upon racks of clothes. Some girls sat having their faces done by makeup artists, and others were standing about as stylists handed them clothes to wear. Music played from speakers set into the corners of the ceiling, and by the windows was a white, black, and red set where the photos were going to be taken.

It was all very chaotic and exciting.

King placed his hand to the small of my back, and I was just about to ask a passing girl where I could find Bradley when my friend suddenly appeared.

"There you are," he said, grabbing hold of my wrist. "I need you in makeup ASAP." Glancing over my shoulder, he saw King and gave him a quick perusal. He reached his other hand over to my boss for a shake. "Well, hello, I'm Bradley. And you are?"

I resisted the urge to snicker at the sweet, flirtatious lilt to his voice. Unlike the last time I'd seen him, when that girl had been rutting all over him on the dance floor, now Bradley was the one barking up the wrong tree.

"Oliver," said King, shaking Bradley's hand. "Thanks for letting Alexis bring me along."

"Oh, it's my pleasure. *Alexis* is one of my dearest friends." He was teasing now, because Bradley never called me by my full name; I had always been just Lexie to him. He took my bag and coat from me, then led me over to hair and makeup. A curvy, light-haired girl came and began talking me through the "look" they were going for, while Bradley asked King if he'd like any tea or coffee.

"A coffee would be great," said King, emitting his usual master of the universe confidence. He might have been a duck out of water in this situation, but it didn't show for a second.

"Coffee it is. Come with me while Alexis gets her face done."

They were already walking away when I suddenly realised Bradley didn't know about my lie. And he was chatty – too chatty. That meant he'd start grilling King on the nature of our relationship. And during that grilling it'd become pretty obvious that I didn't, in fact, bat for the other team. The makeup artist was smoothing on a base foundation when I began rummaging in my bag for my phone. My fingers glided fast over the screen as I typed out a message to Bradley.

Alexis: He thinks I'm a lesbian. Play along.

His response was almost instantaneous.

Bradley: And he thinks this why...?

Alexis: We're friends. If he thinks I'm gay, it eliminates the possibility of him coming on to me.

Bradley: And you don't want him to come on to you why...?

I snorted a laugh, the makeup artist getting cranky when I kept looking down at my phone. I told her I just had to send one more text and then she'd have my full attention.

Alexis: Because he's also my boss.

Bradley: No way! :O

Grinning, I finally put my phone away and let the girl do my makeup. She'd moved on to my eyes when King reappeared, holding a mug. He sipped on it, gaze grazing me, lingering on the curve of my chest. Those eyes of his were so...consuming. Then his attention wandered to another of the models who was passing by. I swear I'd never seen anyone with such perfectly proportioned junk in their trunk. King had noticed, too. The woman caught him looking at her and gave him a sassy little smile.

Bitch.

Okay, so I knew I had no right to be jealous. This was a predicament of my own devising. I'd had King's attention from the beginning, and it had been my decision to deflect that attention with a fib. Yes, I'd made my bed, but it seemed I no longer wanted to lie in it. I hated feeling like this, so I tried to shrug it off with a joke.

"I call dibs," I mouthed at him, allowing my eyes to flick to the model just before she disappeared behind a rack of clothes.

He took a step closer and leaned down to whisper in my ear. "I'll thank you for the lovely visual, but how do you know she's that way inclined?"

His words made me shiver. I turned my face to him, startled when I found our lips a mere inch apart, and tapped the side of my head. "Top-notch gaydar."

King chuckled and stood up straight again. "Whatever you say."

For the next few minutes we were both quiet as King took in his surroundings, i.e. the other models. The place was jam-packed with bootilicious females. When my makeup was done, I peered at myself in the mirror, liking the results. She'd outlined my upper eyelids with black liquid liner, and used a golden-brown eye shadow to create a smoky effect. It made my usually black eyes seem brighter, like a deep chocolate brown. My lips were a glossy peach colour, and my cheekbones had been highlighted with a shimmery blush.

A moment later a thin blond guy came and used a curling iron to style my hair into glossy waves. It took him less than five minutes, and right after he'd suffocated me with hair spray he was off, setting to work on the next model.

I turned my head from side to side, admiring my 'do, then looked up to see King standing behind me. His focus was completely on my face. I'd been so preoccupied studying my reflection that I hadn't noticed him watching me.

"You look...." he began, but then paused, shaking his head. "Never mind." He glanced down at his watch. "When do you think they'll start taking pictures?"

Before I could answer, Bradley sauntered over, carrying a clothes hanger. "Soon-ish. Here, Lexie, go put these on." I took the clothes and went behind one of the nearby privacy screens to get changed. King followed but remained standing on the other side of the screen.

"Have you ever modelled before?" he asked, curious.

"Nope. First time," I replied, and pulled off my T-shirt, trying to ignore the way my skin tingled to have him so close as I undressed.

"You're a photo shoot virgin," he continued, a smile in his voice.

"Ah, I gave you that one too easy," I said, grinning and slipping off my leggings and boots. I turned to pick up the outfit Bradley had given me. It consisted of a tight black sleeveless dress with a sweetheart neckline, sheer tights, and a pair of bright red four-inch heels. I had a bit of trouble fitting my boobs into the dress, since the fabric didn't have any give whatsoever. Standing in front of a full-length mirror, I tried some manoeuvring, letting out a quiet grunt. Ugh, I thought these clothes were supposed to be plus-sized. I felt as though I'd been sewn into the thing, like Sandy D and her slinky black pants.

"Need some help?" King asked, his voice a reminder that he was close by.

"Um," I said, "could you go get Bradley?"

Before I knew it, King had come behind the screen, and I heard him inhale a sharp breath when he saw me. Again, I tried to deflect the tension with humour. "Looks like I've been eating too many of the old onion bhajis. This dress is way too tight."

King stepped forward, and almost of its own accord his hand went to my nape before running down the length of my spine. My breathing hitched.

"No," he murmured. "It's perfect."

"King."

"Yes, Alexis?"

"That's enough touching."

His hand paused when it landed just above my bottom. He ignored my comment and asked, "What did you want Bradley for?"

I turned around, breaking the contact, and gestured to my chest region. "The girls can't breathe in this infernal contraption."

King laughed tenderly. "Well, they look fantastic."

I scowled at him. "You're not helping."

"I'm sorry," he said and took a step closer, his voice lowering. "What can I do to help?" His eyes were nowhere near my face. No, they were glued to my heaving bosom.

"You can stop ogling me, for a start."

"Sorry. Can't do that. Anyway, why do you care?" He tilted his head and arched a brow.

His question riled me. "Misogyny. That's why I care." Oh, God, I was officially grasping at straws. "All you men are interested in is boobs and bums."

King stepped forward again, and now he had me backed into a corner. "You forgot the third b-word."

"What?"

"Brains."

I snorted.

"Don't believe me?"

"Coming from the man who gave me an interview based on my looks." I glanced away, already sensing this was an argument I wasn't going to win.

"Ah, but I gave you the job based on your quick wit. And I've already told you how intelligent I think you are."

"Why are you trying to butter me up?" I asked suspiciously. His chest was dangerously close to brushing up against mine.

"That's not what I'm doing." A pause, followed by a thoughtful expression. "Can I ask a question?"

I hesitated a second. "Sure."

Now he closed the remaining distance between us. His breath hot and humid on my cheeks when he whispered, "Have you ever had a cock before?"

My heart stuttered as I swallowed, unable to meet his gaze. He continued talking. "You should try one, just to make sure. Who knows — you might even like it."

I still couldn't look at him, and a heavy silence fell between us. My head swam with visions of him prying my legs apart and ramming himself deep inside me. My knees grew weak at the thought. His voice sounded different when he finally said, "Alexis, are you...?"

"Lexie, you're up," Bradley called, interrupting whatever King had been about to say. Acting on instinct, I slid away from him and hurried to Bradley, needing an escape. I went and stood with the rest of the models who were awaiting direction. Giving my appearance one last look in a full-length mirror, I tried to summon some calm. Oh, King had been right — my boobs did look fantastic, even if they were being suffocated half to death. The cut of the dress and the push-up bra I was given worked wonders together.

I was being led over to the set to stand next to two redheads when I caught sight of King again. He was standing discreetly in the background, taking in the activity, but when his gaze caught on mine, it scorched. He was staring in the region of my cleavage like he'd just spotted the Holy Grail.

God, *boys*. So easily distracted by a pair of tits. Perhaps they also caused momentary insanity, and that was the reason for the way he spoke to me.

For the first half-hour of the shoot, Bradley focused on group shots. I enjoyed watching him work, because he got all serious and no-nonsense. He still kept his sense of humour, though, and I chuckled when he began trying to explain to a model the difference between fierce and smouldering.

"To smoulder, you combine a subtle pout with a slit gaze. To look fierce, you need to put your hands on your hips and stare at me like you want to fuck me and be the one on top."

I wasn't sure which was funnier, the look of shock on the model's face or the idea of Bradley letting a woman ride him. He caught me snickering and gave me a playful scowl before he was back behind the camera, snapping shots and shouting orders at people. Two outfit changes later, I caught sight of King again. I was kind of surprised he was still there, because even if there were attractive woman all about, this couldn't have been much fun for him.

And okay, maybe I'd been wishing he'd get bored and leave. It would mean I'd get to avoid the drive home and the possibility of him bringing up what he'd said earlier. He really was on a mission to push my limits today.

The outfit I currently wore was a lot more comfortable than the first. It was a plain white vest under a cream shirt with a pair of pale ripped jeans. Casual style. Bradley announced that we were taking a fifteen-minute break, which was a relief, because I was starving. I avoided searching for King and instead made my way over to catering. Picking up a plate, I loaded it with sandwiches and grabbed a bottle of water. Then I wandered to the far corner of the studio, sat down on a window ledge, and began to eat.

"Alexis." I heard King say my name right before he came and sat in front of me, close enough that I could smell his cologne.

"Oh, hi," I said, refusing to make eye contact. It was a good thing I had the window to stare out of.

I was just about to start in on my second sandwich when he caught my wrist. "Do I need to apologise for how I spoke earlier? If I do, just tell me, and I will. I don't want to jeopardise our friendship."

Now I finally looked at him, tilting my head as I considered his words. "Do you feel like you should apologise?"

He shifted closer, his knee knocking against mine. "I only said what I was thinking. I told you before that tact wasn't my strong suit."

I let out a breath. "It's fine. Just try not to be so…pushy in the future."

"As you wish," said King, holding his hand out for me to shake. He was so weird, but I shook with him anyway, trying to ignore how much I enjoyed the feel of his palm on mine. A silence elapsed, and I noticed he hadn't gotten anything to eat.

"Do you want to share some of these?" I asked, gesturing to my plate, on which I'd put way too many sandwiches. "I won't eat them all. My eyes are bigger than my belly."

King gave me a slow smile, then reached forward to pick one up. "Thank you. That's very generous of you to offer."

God, I loved how he spoke sometimes. It was like, if I closed my eyes, I could almost pretend he was Firth doing Darcy. We sat and chatted as we ate until I became aware of a third presence. Turning my head, I saw Bradley standing a few feet away, a camera held to his face as he snapped shots of King and me.

"What are you up to?" I called, and he stopped taking pictures, lowering the camera and walking towards us. King sat beside me, silently observing.

"You two look great together," Bradley gushed before shoving the camera at me. "Here, take a peek." I did as he said and flicked through the most recent shots. They showed me with King from various angles, chatting and laughing. We looked so...at ease with one another. And wow, King really did photograph well. He could pass for a model. And then Bradley almost echoed my thoughts when he looked to King.

"How do you feel about being in some of the shots? We'd pay you for your time, of course. Baha do a men's line, and there still some clothes left over from yesterday's shoot."

King eyed him, quiet for a long moment before he asked, "Would Alexis be in the pictures with me?"

"Of course!" Bradley exclaimed. "That's the main reason I want you to do it. You two look amazing in pictures." Now he took the camera from me and handed it

104

to King, who immediately scrolled through the shots. He didn't say anything for a minute, his expression thoughtful as he took them in. I had no idea what he was going to say when he finally handed the camera back to Bradley.

"I'll do it."

"What?!" I screeched.

"Wonderful!" Bradley exclaimed. He was already rushing off to find an outfit for King when I turned to face my boss. "You're going to model? Seriously? What if someone who knows you ends up seeing the pictures?"

He gave a tiny shrug and stared at me dead on. "What I do in my free time is my own business."

I narrowed my gaze at him, feeling like he was up to something, but I wasn't quite sure what. A minute later Bradley was back, holding nothing but a pair of pale blue jeans. They had tears at the knees and were almost an exact replica of mine, except they were the men's version.

"Here's your ensemble," he chirped, and handed the jeans to King.

I gaped and pointed. "That is not an ensemble. That's one item. Where's his shirt?"

Now Bradley waggled his brow. "He won't be wearing one."

To his credit, King didn't bat an eyelid. In fact, he chuckled while shaking his head.

"Oh, come on," I protested. "You can't be serious. This is a fashion shoot, not a…a sex shoot."

"Oooh," Bradley crooned precociously, "sign me up for one of those. And you forget, my darling Lexie, that sex sells." He pinched me on the nose, and I scowled.

Bradley shot me a confused glance then, obviously not entirely getting why I was disgruntled. It made me suddenly realise I was arguing about having to see Oliver

King topless. Yeah, I didn't understand it, either. Clamping my mouth shut, I let my friend give us both instructions.

Before I knew it, the rest of the models had been told to take an extended break and it was just me, King, Bradley, and a handful of other people left in the studio. King went behind one of the aforementioned privacy screens to change, Bradley telling him to take off his shoes and socks as well. Then he told me to do the same.

Good God.

What was I getting myself into? It wasn't long before a fancy lounge chair had been plopped smack bang in the middle of the set by the props guy. King emerged in jeans and nothing else, and I practically choked on my own tongue. My boss was ripped. Even his bare feet were beautiful. He had gorgeously wide shoulders, muscular pecs, defined abs, and a "V" to die for. Not to mention a light natural tan. He had an even better body than my ex, Stu, and I knew he had to be one of those annoyingly smug health freaks who got up at four in the morning just to exercise.

Yes, that was it. I needed to keep focusing on the vain smugness of someone who worked that hard on their body, rather than the fact that it made me want to crawl all over him. The problem was, he didn't look smug. King wore an expression that was all, *Here I am, take me or leave me,* which only functioned to make him even more irresistible.

Take him, some deep, feminine part of me pleaded.

I noticed Bradley looking at King in almost the exact same way I was. Biting on his lip, he muttered under his breath, "Oh, we are going to sell some serious amount of jeans after this."

I shot him a cynical look. There was a bit of manoeuvring with the set, and I went to stand next to my boss, silent and awaiting further instructions.

"Oliver," said Bradley, "go sit on the chair. Alexis, I want you on his lap. Act natural. Try to give me that vibe you both had earlier when you didn't realise I was taking pictures. I want you to seem like a real couple. Completely in love. Got it?"

Whoa, eh, okay. I was in love with the man's abs, if that helped. King strode over to the chair like he owned the room and sat down before his eyes found mine. Those eyes were commanding, their icy colour catching the light as it shone through the window. They were far too welcoming, those eyes, and I got the feeling he was going to enjoy this. He was going to enjoy it *a lot*. Mustering my trusty false confidence, I walked to the chair and tentatively lowered myself onto his lap. My hands instinctively went to his shoulders for balance, and his hand grazed my hip.

Our eyes met, and I sucked in a breath. I was up close and personal with Oliver King's face yet again, and I couldn't look away.

"Hi," I said, trying my best not to sound awkward.

He gave me a smile that lit up his eyes. "Hey."

"Are you regretting coming with me now?" I asked, voice quiet. Bradley had already started taking pictures.

King brought his mouth over my ear. "Never. It's the best idea I've had in ages."

I swallowed and looked down, my lashes shading my eyes. Unfortunately, looking down also meant looking at King's abs, and now I couldn't look away.

"That's perfect. I love it. You two are doing brilliantly," Bradley encouraged us. He was close, but he sounded far off. King had captured all of my attention.

"Oliver, bring your hands up to Lexie's shoulder blades. Lexie, can you move so that you're straddling him? I've gotten plenty of you side-saddle for now."

I sputtered a laugh. Side saddle? Really? Letting out a tiny sigh, I moved my legs so that I was straddling him and felt a small breath whoosh out. When my gaze went to his throat, I saw him swallow. Was he having just as much of a hard time with this as I was? I was painfully aware of my ever-hardening nipples and how easily King would see them through the thin bra and white vest I was wearing. Bradley had told me to lose the shirt, so I didn't have any coverage. Thankfully though, King's attention was locked on me, alternating between my eyes and my lips. A minute or two passed as Bradley continued to provide us with directions.

"Place your hand on her face, Oliver. I want lots of eye contact."

King didn't hesitate for a moment, his hand gently cupping my cheek. The heat of his palm sent a tingle shooting right between my legs. I tried looking anywhere other than his face until Bradley gave me hell.

"It doesn't work unless you're looking back at him, Lexie."

No other choice left, I lifted my gaze. My eyes met King's, and his deep stare held me captive. One of my knees was hurting a little as I held up my weight. I adjusted myself so that King was taking some of it, and that's when I felt him.

He was hard.

I gasped quietly, but King was the only one to hear. I didn't know what to say. I mean, how would a lesbian react to having a penis hardening against her? Maybe she wouldn't care. The problem was, I did care, and though I tried my best to ignore it, my traitorous body had other ideas. The spot between my thighs ached, and involuntarily my torso moved by the tiniest fraction. Delightfully exquisite pressure ensued. God, that felt good. And then I was wet. So wet.

King didn't fail to notice. His brow furrowed, his gaze searching, as I tried my best not to let him see the turmoil raging inside me. It felt like an eternity had passed, a million questions in his eyes that I didn't know how to answer. Then those eyes left me, and I felt a flicker of relief. It didn't last long, because when I saw where his attention had moved, my heart wanted to beat its way out of my chest. He was staring at my nipples, my nipples that were practically as hard as his cock.

He moved closer, his lips at my ear again, as I felt every muscle in his body go taut. His words were lethal. They held equal parts anger, triumph, and satisfaction when he whispered, "I fucking *knew it*."

Nine

Subtly, he moved his hips, his hard-on lightly pushing against me as he let out the tiniest masculine grunt. He felt heavenly, and for a moment I forgot that even though I hadn't breathed a word, my body had betrayed me.

The cat was very much out of the bag…or should I say, the fake lesbian was out of the closet.

"Oh, this is fabulous! Okay, both of you get up. I want some shots of you standing by the window. Oliver, you go behind Lexie. Put your arms around her and, I don't know, nuzzle her ear or something."

First of all, was he shitting me?

And second of all, I felt like I was having an out-of-body experience when I moved to get off King. Just before he let me go, he clutched my wrist, giving it a hard squeeze that said, *This isn't over.*

I walked to the window, sensing him follow directly behind. I felt like a small animal being preyed upon by an expert hunter. He'd caught me out, and I was under no illusions that he was going to make this easy for me.

But still, he was my boss. He shouldn't have been acting the way he was acting. Even though we weren't in the workplace right now, I needed to remind him of that. A moment later King's heat was on me again, this time as he wrapped his arms around me from behind. And oh, my God, in spite of everything, it felt so good to be held.

"You're attracted to me," he whispered with a touch of curiosity.

I huffed out a breath. "Can we talk about this later?"

"You're not gay, are you? You know I value honesty, so why would you lie?"

I felt the tip of his nose against the back of my ear, nuzzling me just like Bradley had asked him to do. My breathing stuttered; my heart hammered. Wow. His hand moved to my belly, fingers just barely slipping under the hem of my vest. I had tingles *everywhere*.

"I wasn't intentionally trying to be dishonest with you. It was supposed to be a joke, but then you thought I was serious, and it kind of got out of control. I didn't know how to take it back."

His hand moved a fraction further, his fingers digging hard into the soft part of my lower belly. "You take it back like this: *I lied, King. In fact, not only am I not a lesbian, but I also think you're hot.*"

"C-cocky much?" My words came out weird and choppy.

He didn't say anything, but I could tell he was grinning.

"Okay," said Bradley. "Turn around, Lexie. Put your arms around Oliver's neck and stare up at him. Make me believe you're infatuated."

Oh, jeez.

As I turned, my breasts brushed King's torso, and I heard his breathing deepen. How on earth did professional models do this every day? Perhaps I was just more sexed up than the average person, because every single touch got my mind racing to dirty, forbidden places.

I reached up, slid my arms around his neck, and hooked my fingers together. My chest was flush with his, but this way I couldn't quite tell if he still had an erection. Perhaps that was for the best.

"You really had me believing you for a while," he said quietly.

"Are you mad?" I asked, desperate to know.

"A little bit. I thought we were friends."

"We were. We *are*."

"Then why lie?"

"Because I wanted to keep it that way."

Understanding lit in King's eyes, his expression softening as his mouth firmed. "I see."

He went quiet then, and he didn't say anything more for the rest of the shoot. The other models were called back from their break, and I was still needed for a few more group pictures. I swear I was sick to death of smiling and pretending to be "having fun with the girls" by the end of it. When Bradley called a wrap, I went to change back into my own clothes. As it happened, I wasn't allowed to keep the ones I'd worn during the shoot.

Not like I was dying to squeeze myself back into that black number anyway.

Unable to spot King, I decided he must have gone home. I said goodbye to Bradley and the other girls, and was just leaving the building when I saw the Merc idling by the side of the road. I hitched my bag up on my shoulder, having every intention of continuing on to the tube, when the door swung open. King emerged, and before I knew it, his hand was on my elbow, steering me back towards the car.

"We need to talk," he said, voice firm.

"Oh, right, yeah okay," I mumbled, climbing inside, skin tingling where his hand cupped my elbow.

It was dark out already, and I was exhausted after spending the entire day in the studio. I think King must have seen me blinking my eyes to try to stay awake, because he murmured, "Come here." His voice had grown soft, tender. And as he held his arm out, I couldn't resist scooting over and resting my head on his shoulder. He stroked my arm as his driver started the engine and drove away from the studio.

"You're exhausted," said King, and my God, I'd never heard him sound like that before. I'd heard him strict. I'd heard him joking. I'd heard him business professional. But I'd never heard him bedroom-y. I really liked hearing him bedroom-y. It was almost like now that he knew I was into guys, some kind of wall had come down between us.

A long sigh escaped him before he said, "We're in something of a predicament, love."

I turned my face to look up at him. "We are?"

Reaching out, he stroked my cheek with the back of his hand. "Yes, my darling, because I very much want to fuck you."

I inhaled sharply at his admission, but he continued talking before I could say anything.

"In fact, I find myself thinking about it a lot. But I don't fuck my assistants. I've never wanted to. And the problem is, I value you far more as an employee and a friend than I ever will as a conquest."

I grew slightly rigid as I listened to him speak, but couldn't help sputtering a laugh. "A conquest?"

"Love and romance aren't things that enter my mind very often. They're too...time-consuming, and I have so little of that as it is. I enjoy the company of women in many different ways, but I don't have space in my life for a real partner. It would hold me back."

"Okay...."

"When you told me you were gay, I was admittedly disappointed. However, I was also relieved, because it meant nothing could happen between us. But now I find out that you're not, and I begin to want things that I shouldn't." He paused to give me a smouldering look. "Touching you today, being close to you, has been more arousing than anything else I can remember. It's a heady feeling to find someone you're highly attuned to, is it not?"

All I could do was swallow and nod.

"And so," he went on, "here lies our predicament. If I fuck you, I'm going to want to keep doing it, and I don't have time to keep doing it. Christ, even coming here today was a massive chunk of time I'd normally spend working." He stopped and ran his fingers through his hair. "I could lose the run of myself inside a woman like you, Alexis." He paused before muttering under his breath, almost absently, "And I fear if I made you my queen, I could no longer be a king."

I frowned at him, whispering, "There are lots of different ways to be a king, Oliver." It was one of the few times I'd ever called him by his given name, and it added a tenderness to the moment I knew he hadn't expected. The look he gave me told me that. But really, I felt a little sad for him. He was so focused on succeeding, on winning, that he would never have time for love. That was sad.

"That's true, but my life, it's, well, it's always been a certain way, and I'm afraid this may be the only way I know how to succeed."

I didn't know what to say, so I said nothing. Our journey progressed, and we were only a couple of minutes away from my flat when King began talking again.

"You have an addicting presence, one I don't want to give up, so I propose we try our best not to touch. I think that touching, for us, is where temptation lies."

I groaned and rolled away from him, covering my face with my hand. "What's tempting is when you talk like that."

114

Peering at him through my fingers, I saw him bite on his lip and cast me a considering glance. "Maybe just once...." He stopped himself, shaking away the thought. "No, that's a bad idea."

"Uh-huh," I agreed with him stiffly.

This was the best-paying job I'd ever had, and was ever likely to get. I couldn't go letting a fling with my boss mess it up for me. I mean, I'd spent half my life working for minimum wage in grotty pubs and bars. I knew a good thing when I had it, and I had no intention of letting it slip through my fingers. My dream was to one day own a home of my own, someplace nice, where there were low crime rates and no junkies hanging around every corner, waiting to jump you to pay for their next fix.

I knew all of this as fact. I knew it, and yet, there was no mistaking the disappointment in my gut to think we'd never explore the possibilities that lay between us.

"So, we have an understanding, then," said King. "No touching."

"Yep. Got ya." I nodded, a weird awkwardness settling in. The car stopped, and I saw that we were right in front of my building. I got out silently, while King insisted on walking me up to my flat. I told him he didn't have to, but he insisted. I don't think he liked the look of the gang of teenagers hanging around by the entrance.

I wanted to tell him he was doing more harm than good, because once the locals saw me with a man like King, they'd think I had something worth stealing. I didn't. Neither did Karla. That didn't mean it wouldn't be upsetting to come home and find our place broken into. My things held no monetary value, but they meant something to me.

When we reached my door, I slotted my key in the lock and turned back to King. He was staring at me with an intensity that caught me off guard, and my heart fluttered.

A moment passed.

I wetted my lips.

He saw.

I inhaled.

He clenched his jaw.

"I'll see you on Monday, then," he said with effort.

"Yes." I nodded. "Monday. Right."

His hand rose to my cheek in a soft, forlorn sort of caress. "Sleep well, Alexis."

At long last he turned and went, and I felt every foot of distance like a cord was snapping between us. Opening the door, I heard Karla utter a quiet "fuck" and found her holding a hand to her forehead.

"Give your nosy flat mate some warning before opening the door next time," she complained. She'd clearly been spying on us through the peephole and got clocked on the forehead in the process. I laughed, and she shot me a scowl.

"That man is beautiful, Lexie," she sighed, as though it was a bad thing. I definitely knew where she was coming from. Beautiful bosses who wanted to be your friend were a very *bad* thing.

"Tell me everything that happened today," she insisted, plopping down on the couch, looking cosy in her blue pyjamas. I smiled and went to join her.

"Okay, so first, I'm not sure if I want to murder Bradley or send him an early birthday gift."

Karla giggled. "Oh, my God, this is going to be good. I can already tell."

Had I mentioned how much I really, really loved this girl? Getting comfortable, I told her everything. And when I was done, she threw a blanket over me, because I'd already drifted off to sleep.

***

On Monday morning, King needed me to assist him with a small meeting in one of the conference rooms. It was with a client company whose shares he was supposed to value so that they could be sold on to investors. At least, that was the gist I got of it. I had a folder full of spreadsheets that Eleanor had prepared, so all I needed to do was hand them out, make tea and coffee, and take notes of what was discussed during the meeting.

Oh, and did I mention that King was being weird with me?

I couldn't tell if it was because of our conversation driving home from the shoot, or something else. To be honest, I thought it might be a bit of both. He seemed preoccupied, and it couldn't all have been because of me.

The clients hadn't arrived yet, and King had just finished having a chat with Daniel James, who had dropped into the conference room for a minute, when I lightly touched my hand to his elbow. I know we'd made that no touching rule, but I felt compelled to do it anyway.

"You okay, boss?" I asked softly.

His posture showed that he was definitely wound tight, and all the air seemed to rush right out of him. "Alexis," he said, and turned his body to face mine. His usually bright eyes seemed tired, and he looked like he hadn't gotten a wink of sleep. He spoke low, like he didn't want anyone else to hear. "My mother had a bad episode last night. She...I had to take her to the hospital."

Shocked by the admission, I gave his elbow a squeeze. "Oh, my God, is she all right?"

"She's stable now."

I wanted to ask him what had happened, but a moment later the clients arrived. King went to greet them, and I busied myself with the documents. It was a minute or two before I recognized one of them. Her name was Mila Rhodes, and I'd seen her before in a picture at King's apartment. She was his ex-girlfriend, the one he broke up with because she wanted more than he could give.

Well, this was interesting.

I wondered if they'd met through doing business together. King didn't seem at all affected by her presence. In fact, he still seemed preoccupied, probably over worry for his mum. He shook Mila's hand and said hello to her just like he did the three men she'd arrived with. After the pleasantries were over, we all sat and got down to business. I sat on one side of King, my work laptop open in front of me to type down notes. The entire thing would have been a complete snoozefest if it weren't for the underlying tension emanating from both Mila and her colleague, a middle-aged man named Vincent Jones.

I was good at reading people. Put it down to my years of bar work, watching how others interacted in social settings. And it was clear that something was going on between Mila and Vincent. I saw him touch her hand at one point during the meeting, but she'd very subtly pushed his fingers away, glancing surreptitiously at King, who was entirely oblivious to the exchange. Not me, though. I'd caught all of it, and surmised that Mila was having a relationship with Vincent that she didn't want King to be aware of. Perhaps she was holding out hope he'd change his mind about settling down and come back to her. She didn't want him to know about Vincent, that was for sure.

My seat was right next to King's, and my laptop was open as I took the minutes for the meeting. At one point King leaned over to glance at my screen, his shoulder brushing mine as he shook his head. He wanted to correct something I'd written, but instead of telling me to do it, he reached over and did it himself. Practically leaning over me, he deleted a section of my notes before correcting them. I had no idea what to do with my hands as he typed, and felt a hot blush mark my cheeks at his familiarity and closeness. His cologne smelled gorgeous.

Even though Vincent had been talking the whole time, his voice filling the room, Mila hadn't failed to notice. I saw her brows narrow in suspicion, and she cast me a considering look. And yes, just as before, King was entirely oblivious to it all, his mind focused completely on work.

The whole thing just made me feel awkward.

I didn't know how to deal with posh people drama. If something like this were to happen at home, for instance, if one woman was jealous of another, it'd be handbags at dawn, earrings out, and a hair-pulling session. But here, in this professional environment inhabited by the wealthy and privileged, it was all narrow-eyed looks, passive-aggressive comments, and repressed anger.

I was practically bursting with the need to simply shout, *There's nothing going on!* Because that's what I'd do in any other setting, but not here. Here my employment was at stake. Soon the meeting drew to a close, and I excused myself to go use the bathroom. I'd just left the stall and was washing my hands when the door swung open and Mila Rhodes strode in.

Oh, for fu….

"Hello, Alexis," she said, coming and setting her handbag by the sink. I nodded hello to her and turned off the tap as she pulled out a tube of lip gloss and began smearing it across her heart-shaped mouth. She was a petite little thing, at least a few inches shorter than me, and extremely pretty. She had one of those doll faces that always looked young, no matter the person's age.

I had just turned to leave when Mila asked blatantly, "Are you fucking him?"

Well. Maybe these posh types didn't beat around the bush after all.

I turned back around. "Excuse me?"

"Don't play coy. I've never seen him so comfortable with an assistant."

Any morsel of politeness I had in me swiftly fled as I gave her a sardonic look. "Ah, well, that means we *must* be banging, then."

"So you are sleeping together?"

"Oh, my God, that was sarcasm. But if you need me to spell it out for you, here it is: No, we're not sleeping together."

She snorted like she didn't believe me, but I saw a flicker of pain in her eyes that told a thousand words.

"You still love him, don't you?"

Her face hardened as she swallowed what appeared to be a lump in her throat. God, I was right. Sometimes I hated it when I was right. Gentling my voice, I took a step forward and placed a hand on her shoulder.

"Take it from someone who's been in many hopeless relationships. Move on. If he can't see what's good for him, then he's not worth it. Find someone who is." I paused, and Mila stared up at me, as though my kindness was the last thing she'd expected. "Vincent seems nice."

A long breath escaped her, and her entire body seemed to sag. "He is nice."

"You see? Mr King is a fool not to see what's right in front of him. Unfortunately, fools can never be taught. They have to learn on their own."

Absorbing my words, she nodded and sounded sincere when she said, "You're right. I'm sorry for how I spoke to you."

I smiled. "Ah, don't worry about it. Water off a duck's back."

She moved away and put her lip gloss back in her handbag. I was about to leave when she looked at me seriously through the mirror. "He pulls you in, you know. You start off thinking the ball is in your court, but it never is. Before you know it, you've fallen for him, and it's too late to go back to the way things were."

Absorbing her words, I couldn't quite tell if this was a warning or if she was just thinking out loud. Nevertheless, I gave her a sober nod. Leaving Mila in the ladies' bathroom, I made my way back to King's office, intent on having a serious word with him about his ex. However, as I reached his office door I paused, because a strange-looking woman was just leaving. She was probably in her fifties, had dyed red hair, and clothes that reminded me of a gypsy.

"Oh, hi," I said, stepping back to let her go by.

She only gave me an ambiguous smile before continuing on her way. "Odd" didn't begin to cover it. I'd never seen a woman who looked like her around here before. Shaking off the strangeness, I remained full of determination to confront King about Mila. That was until I walked into the room and saw him sitting on the sofa by the window, an open bottle of Macallan in front of him. He poured some into a glass, knocked it back in one go, and then repeated the process. Everything I'd planned on saying immediately fled my mind as concern took its place. I'd seen him drink at work before, but not like this. The bottle was more than half empty, and I knew it had been full when I'd seen it in the cabinet that morning.

Piano music was playing, something classical, but it was low enough that you wouldn't be able to hear it outside the office. I recognised it as the same piece he'd played when I'd visited his apartment. Memories of that night entered my mind, how absorbed he'd been, completely unaware of my presence, and how beautiful his music had sounded to my ears. Quietly, I sat on the other side of the couch and eyed him. He didn't look at me, just focused on the drink in his glass.

"Has something happened?" I asked tentatively.

King glanced at me, then shook his head.

"Then why are you drinking?"

He arched a brow. "Because I can."

There was something in his expression that made me think I shouldn't push the matter. Still, I couldn't help asking, "Who was that woman I just saw leaving?"

There was a long silence before he spoke. "Just a relative asking after Mum."

Clearly, he had no intention of telling me any more details and didn't seem in the mood to talk. I stood and turned to leave. Before I could do so, King grabbed my wrist.

"Don't go," he pleaded, those eyes holding me captive.

I sat back down. We exchanged a meaningful look before he spoke again. "I'm sorry. I'm a bit off today. I'm just worried about Mum."

Reaching out, I placed a hand on his. "That's understandable. Maybe you should take the day. Go be with her. Is she still at the hospital?"

King nodded, and then cast his eyes to mine; his seemed...desperate. "Would you do it? She enjoys your company." He stopped, ran a hand through his hair, mussing it up. "I'm just not in the right frame of mind to see her at the moment."

I stared at him, this man who at first had seemed so put together and in control. When I looked at him now, he appeared vulnerable. It showed just how much he cared for his mother. I guessed that maybe she was the only family he had. He had definitely never mentioned a father or any brothers or sisters.

I was so lost in studying him that I almost didn't notice when his hand went to my knee. I looked down, then back up to his eyes, which seemed to be begging me for comfort. God, how those eyes made me weak. They made me want to give him anything he might think to ask for.

"King," I said, a quiet warning.

He didn't breathe a word, just squeezed my knee and leaned in closer. His hand started to move up my thigh, slow and torturous. Every tiny hair on my body stood on end as I inhaled his fresh cologne mixed with the sharp tang of whiskey. It was an intoxicating mixture, and I had no words. No funny lines or sarcastic comments to defuse the situation.

I had nothing, and Oliver King was pushing a boundary I was helpless to defend.

"Oliver," I said then, swallowing thickly on his name.

He leaned closer, breathing me in, and before I knew it, his mouth was on my ear, his tongue flicking over the soft, sensitive skin. He sucked my earlobe into his mouth, and I felt myself grow wet and achy in an instant. I huffed out a breath, trembled, and fisted my hand in his shirt, meaning to push him away, but instead only succeeded in pulling him closer. He groaned and caught my chin in his hand, turning my face to his. His mouth was almost on mine when I quickly turned away, his lips colliding with my jaw. The waft of alcohol was the stark reminder I needed to be strong and put a stop to this.

King was drunk and upset about his mother, though I still wasn't sure exactly what had happened to her. He'd never be acting like this if it weren't for his current state. I needed to be the level-headed one right then. Plus, Eleanor and Gillian were right on the other side of the door. They could walk in at any moment.

Pushing away from him, I stood, still feeling his lips on my earlobe and my chin, the memory giving me unwanted butterflies in my stomach. God, he was beautiful. It would be oh, so easy to give in, but the momentary pleasure wasn't worth the long-term unemployment. And unemployed was exactly what I'd be if I were to let anything untoward happen with King. Maybe not right away, but I'd lose my job eventually. It was inevitable.

"You should go home and rest. You're not yourself today."

"Alexis, come here," he replied, completely ignoring what I'd said. He had sex in his eyes, and it was pretty much impossible not to melt at the way he was looking at me. There was something about having a strong, powerful man look at me with such need that just melted my bones. And it went to show how much self-control I actually had, because I didn't allow myself to give in.

I was already walking backward when I said, "I'm going back to work now."

I didn't allow him to get another word in as I turned and swiftly left his office.

Ten

Five minutes later I was sitting next to Eleanor, who was diligently typing away when King finally emerged. I felt safe in the fact that my coworkers were there. It meant he couldn't say anything about what had just happened between us. He stood in the doorway for a full minute, and I could practically feel him staring a hole in my skull before he spoke.

"Gillian, cancel my afternoon meetings. I have a family emergency I need to attend to."

"Of course," said Gillian, a mixture of concern and nosiness marking her features. "Is everything okay?"

"It will be," King replied stiffly before he strode right by her and out of the office. Once he was gone, I felt like I could breathe again. My brain was a scramble of thoughts as I tried to make sense of the morning. King had obviously been going through a tough time, and his behaviour was a moment of weakness. I was just glad I had the strength not to let it go any further than it did.

For the next few hours I plunged myself into work, keeping my head full of numbers and appointments so as not to think about my boss. Every time I found my mind wandering to the way it felt when he touched me, or how intoxicating it was to have his mouth on my skin, his lips sucking, I forced myself to concentrate on data. Data wasn't sexy. It was dull and flat and two-dimensional, and the perfect bucket of cold water for my wandering imagination.

I didn't see King for the rest of the day, nor did I see much of him for the following few days. I went out with Eleanor and Gillian for lunch and avoided our strange bathroom chess games. He never called me out on the fact that I was avoiding him, which was a relief. And after a while it became easier to simply concentrate on being good at my job, rather than cultivating a surreal friendship with my boss.

When it was finally Eleanor's last day, Gillian and I got together to organise for a cake to be delivered to the office. There wasn't a big going-away party, because Eleanor had stated firmly that she didn't want one, and you didn't eff with Eleanor's wishes. I thought the least we could do was get her a cake, especially since she'd been so helpful training me into the job.

It was just after five when a couple of the other admin workers came over to our area to share the cake. We'd ordered red velvet, since that was Eleanor's favourite. I stood chatting with my coworkers, a paper plate in hand, when suddenly I felt his presence. He'd been ignoring me somewhat, though I couldn't tell if it was because he was embarrassed by his drunken behaviour or angry at me for shutting him down.

In my peripheral vision I saw King come to stand behind me. He observed the gathering, which was comprised mostly of women, and I pretended I hadn't noticed him. Then I felt his hand lightly touch my elbow, followed by his breath on my ear.

"Alexis, can I have a word in private, please?"

I turned my head to him slightly and nodded, my posture stiff. "Sure."

He gestured for me to follow him into his office. Once I was inside, he shut the door. I still had my cake in hand, and found myself clutching the paper plate like a life raft, no clue what this was all about. Was I going to be given my marching orders? No, it couldn't be that.

King stood in front of his desk, leaning back against it and folding his arms as he eyed me. I wore a grey pencil skirt and a modest cream blouse, an ensemble I'd never be caught dead in outside the office. It was like a costume, something that made me feel like a different person, someone who belonged here in the City with the privileged and educated. King wore a navy suit with a slim red tie. He could have been a politician if he weren't so handsome.

I always wondered if men felt like they had the upper hand when they wore a suit. It certainly seemed that way to me.

"We can't go on like this," said King.

"Like what?" I asked, playing dumb.

"You know what. You're avoiding me, I'm avoiding you. There's an…awkwardness. I don't do awkward. I want to go back to the way things were." His huff of annoyance almost made me laugh. I swear, sometimes he was a terrible communicator, like a frustrated kid or something.

"Your behaviour the last time we spoke was worrying to me. I was trying to help."

"And I wanted you to help."

"Not in the right way, Oliver."

His eyes flared when I said his name, and I couldn't tell if it was because he liked it or because he didn't. Before I knew it, he stepped away from the desk and came towards me until there very little space left between us.

"I've missed you," he confessed.

My expression softened. "I've missed you, too."

He levelled his eyes on me, his attention wandering over my features. "Can we put it behind us?"

I thought about it for only a moment before answering, "It's already forgotten. Put her there, buddy." I held out my hand to him, and his lips twitched as we shook.

"So, is there enough cake left for one more?" he asked, smiling.

"Of course," I answered, and with that we went back out to join the others.

***

It was difficult getting used to not having Eleanor around at first, but I quickly got the hang of things. Soon enough Gillian and I were a team to be reckoned with, and although we didn't click quite so well as friends, we were perfect for each other when it came to work. Gillian was the best organiser, and I was the best bilateral thinker. In other words, I could see the bigger picture and was good at figuring out problems or working my way around time-sensitive emergencies. And when it came to this particular industry, there were a lot of those.

It was fast-paced and exciting, and no two days were ever the same. I also began to see how addictive King's job could be. He always said he only made decisions based on evidence and fact, but a lot of the time the whole thing felt like a bit of a gamble to me. There was a thrill to his position, not to mention a great deal of power, and I could certainly see why he'd chosen a banking career over playing piano like his mum.

We began having lunch together again, and often King would have a drink. I hadn't noticed it at the beginning, but it was now clear to me that he was pretty big into his liquor. Not in a way that seemed like he had a problem, but in a way that made me think it could easily turn into one. I supposed he needed something to deal with the stress of playing with millions of pounds on a daily basis.

It had been a long week, and I was looking forward to a relaxing weekend of doing nothing at all. I'd arrived home with Indian takeout, changed into my pyjamas, and settled in front of the TV. The forkful of chicken korma was literally halfway to my mouth when my phone began ringing. Sighing, I put it down and answered the call. King's name flashed across the screen. As soon as I hit "accept" and held it to my ear, he began to speak.

"Please tell me you have a valid passport."

His statement got me curious. "And if I do?"

"If you do, you can have another bonus. Gillian just called, almost in tears, might I add, to tell me she's lost hers and won't be able to get a replacement for at least three working days. She's being emotional, and I don't like that. You'd swear she ran over my cat or something."

"Oh," I said, brow crinkling. "You have a cat?"

"Turn of phrase."

"Right."

I was unsure if I should laugh or start to panic. I now understood what was going on. All week Gillian and I had been planning King's work trip to Rome. He was supposed to be meeting with some businessman who owned a chain of hotels, and who insisted on face-to-face business dealings. All of this was being done on behalf of a mysterious silent investor of King's, and Gillian was supposed to be going along on the trip. The idea of me going had never even come up. Until now, that was.

"I need you to come to Rome in Gillian's place, Alexis."

My voice was quiet when I responded, "Do you think that's wise?" We'd both been doing so well at keeping things platonic. Going on a trip and spending lots of one-on-one time together could potentially mess with that.

"At this point, I don't have another choice. There's too much work for me to handle alone. I need you."

It struck me that he wasn't *telling* me I had to go. He was leaving it open, giving me the option to say no. I couldn't say no, of course, but that didn't mean I didn't appreciate his sensitivity. We both knew that alone time outside the confines of the office was pretty shaky territory for us.

I let out a breath. "I'll come. The flights are for ten in the morning, right? Do you need me to contact the airline and change the name on Gillian's ticket?"

There was definite relief in his voice the next time he spoke. "Thank you. And yes, that would be hugely helpful."

"All right. I'll see you in the morning, then."

"See you in the morning, Alexis."

We hung up, and I just sat there for a minute, my appetite for Indian takeout momentarily lost, which was *so* not okay. Indian was my favourite, damn it! The idea of going to Rome was exciting, don't get me wrong, but the effort I'd have to expend keeping myself in check with King was scary. There was no denying we had a connection, and it was only amplified when we were alone together.

This trip was certainly going to be an interesting one.

***

I packed my swimsuit.

I wasn't sure why, because I was fairly certain it wasn't even going to be very warm in Rome at this time of year, but I packed it anyway. I hadn't been to the beach in who knew how long. Maybe I could fit in a trip while King was meeting with the "suits." That's what I'd started calling them, because they all looked the same to me, just a bunch of walking Hugo Boss advertisements.

King had his driver come collect me from outside my building that morning. His bags were in the car, which it was my job to have checked, and apparently he'd meet me in the VIP lounge before boarding. Well, I was sitting in that very same lounge, and there was still no sign of him. I was beginning to worry, since our flight was supposed to board in just twenty minutes.

In order to pass the time, I pulled out my phone and checked my emails. It was a pleasant surprise when I saw one from Bradley titled "**Some Pictures from the Shoot** ;-)." Opening it up eagerly, I quickly downloaded them and started to browse. There were a couple from early on in the day, showing me with the other models. Then I got to the ones of me and King, and I paused. They were…well, I wasn't quite sure how to describe them. All I knew was that they weren't what I needed to be seeing right then, especially since I was trying to keep my hands off the man.

The first showed me straddling him as he sat on the chair, leaning casually back and staring up at me with unmistakable heat in his eyes. Wow. Now I understood what Bradley had meant when he said we photographed well together. It was only a picture, and yet you could practically feel the need pouring out of both of us. Either we were really good actors, or we wanted each other…badly.

I swallowed and scrolled to the next one, where we stood by the studio window, King's arms around me and his lips at my ear. Seriously, this was more like porn to me than fashion. Without consciously realising it, I was squeezing my thighs together, my skin growing hot as I sat there, remembering. There were about ten pictures in total, and I flicked through them more times than bears mentioning. I was studying the one of me on King's lap again when someone suddenly spoke low in my ear.

"What *are* you looking at?"

Startled at hearing his voice, I jumped and turned around, clutching my phone tightly to my chest. King chuckled and gave me a suspiciously amused look as he held out his hand. "Let me see."

I snorted. It was pretty fucking elegant. "Noooo."

A moment later, I took in his appearance properly, noticing that he was still wearing the same suit from yesterday. He looked more tired than I'd ever seen him, and he smelled like a brewery. It was so disconcerting that I failed to notice him lunging for my phone and pulling it from my grip. I watched as his fingers zipped across the screen before he handed it back to me. Forcing myself to look down, I saw he'd forwarded the pictures to his own email.

"That was a dirty move," I complained.

He gave me a wry look. "I'm in those pictures, too. I have every right to see them."

Well, he had me there. Still, it didn't take away my embarrassment. Those photos were verging on soft-core porn, and he was *my boss*. It was so many levels of wrong, I couldn't even begin to count.

This was why I needed to say no to Bradley's propositions in future. Note to self: Don't give in to the mischievous pixie boy next time. My cheeks began to flush as King came and sat beside me, pulling out his phone. It was ridiculous, because I was never normally embarrassed about sex stuff, but with King everything was just opposite land. I never quite knew where we stood with one another. I was silent as he focused on his phone, and I didn't even have to look to know he was accessing his email and downloading the pictures he'd just forwarded.

God, I kind of hated him in that moment.

I tried to ignore him, but as the minutes ticked by, I lost the battle. Turning, I found his lips curved in what appeared to be a smug smile. The photos were displayed on the screen of his phone, and King kept scrolling back and forth, perusing them at his leisure as though taunting me to say something.

"Just delete them," I sighed.

He glanced at me, brow arched. "Why would I do that?"

"Because we look stupid," I huffed. We didn't look stupid. We looked insanely hot for each other, which was exactly the problem. King was about to speak when an air hostess's voice announced the flight was ready to board. I picked up my carry-on, noticing that King hadn't brought anything with him other than a slim black briefcase. All of his things were in his checked luggage.

He gestured for me to go ahead of him, and I self-consciously smoothed my hands down the back of my skirt, wondering if I had a visible panty line. I'd always had this sixth sense for when someone was looking at my arse, and right then it was telling me that was exactly what King was doing. Was he actively trying to make this trip more difficult?

He leaned close, his mouth at my neck as he said, "I think we look fascinating."

Fascinating. Right. What the hell was that supposed to mean? Once we were seated on the plane, King closed his eyes and let out a long breath. Despite his earlier playfulness, something was obviously up with him. I studied him a moment, then asked, "Care to share?"

One eye opened. He didn't say a word, so I continued, "You're wearing the same suit from yesterday, and you smell like you took a swim in a brewery. This isn't like you."

He sighed. "You've known me a couple of weeks, Alexis. You have no idea what is and isn't like me."

"Look, I'm not trying to be nosy. I'm just concerned, that's all. You've been drinking a lot, and coming from someone who used to work in a bar, I know a problem when I see one."

"There's no problem," said King.

I stared at him, disbelieving. If he wanted to fool himself into thinking he didn't have a problem, then fine, I wasn't going to push it. Getting up from my seat, I reached up to the overhead compartment and pulled out my carry-on. It had a brand new set of travel toiletries inside, including a mini-toothbrush.

"You can use these if you'd like to go freshen up," I said stiffly, holding the set out to him.

He looked up at me, not taking it. A long moment of silence passed, his light eyes turning stormy. Finally, and without saying a word, he took the toiletries and left to use the bathroom. About ten minutes later he returned, looking a little better than he had. Though if the smell of him earlier was anything to go by, he must have been suffering from one hell of a hangover. The flight progressed in silence, as I focused on reading a magazine I'd brought with me. When the air hostess stopped by to ask if we'd like anything to eat or drink, I practically held my breath. There was an array of alcoholic beverages available to order, and I just knew King was considering them. Instead, he shook his head, and the woman moved on to the next passengers. Well, that was a relief.

Before I knew it, we were landing in Rome. After we departed the plane, I went to collect our bags from the carousel, while King excused himself to the bathroom. By the pale look on his face, I thought he might be going to throw up. I knew I was right when he found me several minutes later, a little of the colour having returned to his cheeks. Perhaps he'd now learned his lesson not to overdo it in future.

A car was waiting for us outside, and drove us to a hotel a distance from the city near a place called Ostia. King had insisted on staying there because it was one of his favourites, and I could see why. It had an outdoor swimming pool and beautiful gardens, which got me excited. I had to remind myself I was there to work, not for a fancy holiday.

Rummaging for the folder of documents Gillian had sent me via email last night, I retrieved our booking and presented it to the receptionist, while King stood back, his phone held to his ear as he carried out a work conversation. I was vaguely aware of the receptionist informing me we had adjoining rooms as she handed me the key cards. King must have seen the WTF look on my face, because he lowered his phone for a second to explain, "It's easier this way. Gillian always books adjoining rooms so that we don't have to go traipsing halfway around hotels to find one another."

And then he was back on the phone. Well, that was...convenient. A bellboy came to take our bags, and before I knew it, I was alone in my room, flopping down on the bed and wondering what I'd gotten myself into. We didn't have to meet with the clients until dinner, and Italians ate late, so that gave me a couple of hours to rest up. I lay there for a while, tired, because no matter how short the journey, flights always seemed to drain me of energy.

In the end, I decided to treat myself and run a bath. I enjoyed a nice long soak and got out only when my fingers had started to turn to prunes. Wrapping a white fluffy towel around my body, I grabbed another and scrunched my hair dry. Usually, if I just towel-dried my hair and didn't brush it, it went really curly. Just as I was laying the black dress I planned to wear to the business dinner out on the bed, I heard a soft knock on the door that led to King's room.

Before I had the chance to react, the knob turned, and my boss stepped inside.

Eleven

Why hadn't I thought to lock the door? Jesus, though, he could have waited for me to call him in before opening it.

I stood there, frozen to the spot in my short towel and damp hair. King had clearly showered and changed into a new suit. In fact, he looked like a whole new man, no longer rumpled and hungover. The moment he saw me, he glanced away. Well, no, that's not *quite* what he did. His gaze made a quick perusal of my body, paying particular attention to the swell of my breasts. His jaw ticked, and *then* he glanced away. His close attention literally made me flush from my cheeks to the tips of my toes.

He cleared his throat. "I'm sorry. I thought you'd be dressed."

"Well, I'm not," I said, stating the obvious.

There was a strain in his voice as he echoed my statement. "No, you're not."

"Could you give me a half-hour? I just need to get ready."

King let out a breath. "We don't have the time. Mr Hirota's assistant just called to say they were moving the meeting to another venue. He's notorious for changing things around on a whim. Unfortunately, he's the one we're trying to win over, so we have to pander to it."

I looked back at him. He stared at me. We were locked in a moment, and neither one of us made a move to break it, even though I was standing there almost naked. King seemed unusually stressed, and it was curious because he was never stressed to meet with clients. Over the past couple of weeks I'd witnessed him secure a number of business deals, but there was something different about this one, like he was extra determined for it to be successful. It made me wonder why. Gillian had told me that Mr Hirota was the Japanese-American owner of a chain of hotels with a deep love for ancient Roman history, which was why he lived here. There was nothing particularly unusual about him, though, so I was lost as to why King was on edge.

"Okay, just give me two minutes, then," I said, finally breaking the silence and picking up my dress. King nodded, his eyes lingering on my bare thighs as I turned and went inside the bathroom.

Not helping, Oliver.

I wouldn't have time to put on makeup, so I guessed the *au naturel* look was going to have to do. I also wore ballet flats instead of heels. I had just enough time to give my appearance one last perusal in the mirror. I looked fine, definitely not business fancy, but fine nonetheless. I realised just how much taller King was than me when I stepped outside and stood before him without any heels on. He glanced down, eyes tender, and I wondered if he was noticing the same thing.

He shook his head as though to clear his thoughts, and I busied myself. Grabbing the contracts we needed for the meeting, I shoved them in my handbag and allowed King to lead me out the door. We took the elevator down to the lobby, King resting his hand on the small of my back for a moment. It reminded me of my first morning at the office, when he'd touched me in a similar way. It had confused me then. Now I knew it was intentional. I thought that maybe King was a man who enjoyed pushing the boundaries of his own willpower.

A car provided by Mr Hirota was waiting for us outside the hotel. King was busy working on his tablet during the drive, while I enjoyed the passing scenery. I got to see a few cool ruins and even the Coliseum before we entered a busy district full of bars and restaurants. Then we stopped in front of what was very clearly a strip club.

King glanced out the window, did an almost comical double take, then swore under his breath before letting his head fall back against the headrest. "You've got to be fucking kidding me."

A small moment of quiet elapsed, and I couldn't help it — I laughed. King turned to face me, his eyes narrowed, but I could tell from the set of his mouth that he was resisting a smile.

"This isn't funny, Alexis."

"Oh, come on," I said. "You have to admit, it's a little bit funny. I feel like I'm in some gangster film and we're about to meet with a scary mob boss."

I expected my joke to make him laugh. Unfortunately, it seemed to have the opposite effect. His expression grew serious and he turned away, clearing his throat. The driver emerged from the front of the car and came around to open my door. Kind of fancy behaviour for someone who was essentially dropping us off at a titty bar.

"Why, thank you, sir," I said to the driver in a humorous tone. It got a tiny smile out of King, which was something at least. I liked that I could still amuse him even when he was in a decidedly dour mood. As we approached the entrance, King slid his arm through mine. "You stick close to me tonight, Alexis."

"Why?" I asked, curious.

"Because," he answered low, "if Mr Hirota is willing to do business in a place like this, then I worry how he might behave with a woman who looks like you."

I chuckled and deadpanned, "Tell me about it. Wherever I go, I'm constantly terrorised by men getting spontaneous erections around me. It's such a chore being a sex bomb."

Again, King appeared to be fighting his urge to laugh. In the end, his serious side won out, and I gave in. "I'm joking. And don't worry — I'll stick to you like glue, Oliver."

He gave me a warm look, and then we were entering the darkness of the booby cave. Okay, I'll stop. Nudity just made me giddy like a five-year-old. A scantily clad woman greeted us and led us to a VIP section at the back of the club. All the while I was wondering if this was still going to be a business "dinner." I was far from stuck up, but the idea of eating food prepared in a strip club just didn't float my boat. Yeah, I was definitely going to wait until we got back to the hotel, and then I'd be making one hell of an order to room service. What with all the travelling, I'd hardly had the chance to eat all day.

It was kind of funny that I paid more attention to the topless dancing ladies up on the stage than King did. Call it morbid fascination. I knew King was slightly ticked off about the venue, but it probably wasn't the first time something like this had happened. I hate to stereotype, but businessmen liked to look at boobs. It was a known fact.

In the VIP section there were a few more dancing ladies and a large table where several men sat. I immediately recognised Mr Hirota as the Japanese guy in the white suit, black shirt, and white tie. A white suit! How oh how was I going to keep from commenting on that?

Mr Hirota immediately stood when he saw King, holding out his hand for a shake. King took it, and the two exchanged the usual pleasantries.

"This is my assistant, Alexis Clark," said King, distracting me from the glare of the white suit and ushering me forward.

"Alexis, it's a pleasure to meet you," said Mr Hirota while giving me a quick once-over.

"Likewise, Mr Hirota."

He grinned. "Please, call me Kei."

We sat, and the woman who'd greeted us at the door came and asked if we'd like any drinks. King requested a Scotch, and I just went with orange juice. Somehow, I got the feeling this wasn't a scenario I wanted to get drunk in. Knowing me, I'd end up doing something to embarrass myself. Even though it was a strip club, I was there in a professional capacity, so I needed to act like it.

"How was your flight, Oliver?" Mr Hirota asked.

"It was fine," King replied smoothly.

The woman returned with our drinks, and King picked his up, bringing it to his lips for a sip. I took in my surroundings, trying not to be weirded out by the tanned woman shaking her hips on a stage just shy of the table. She had golden tassels on her nipples and bright purple lipstick. Man, I couldn't wait to get home and tell Karla all about this.

"I understand your client wishes to remain anonymous," said Hirota.

"That's correct. He appreciates you agreeing to his terms."

"Yes, well, I haven't signed anything yet."

"Of course," said King, gaze now travelling around the room. He seemed disinterested as he scanned the half-naked women before returning his attention to Hirota. "Nice place. Is it yours?"

Hirota nodded. "A recent purchase. I've grown bored of the hospitality industry of late, which is why I'm interested in selling to your client. It will take a couple of years for me to offload the majority of my assets, though. This club is just the beginning. I'm hoping to make my foray into producing pornographic films once I learn the lay of the land."

I swear to God, I almost spat out my orange juice right then. King showed no outward signs of surprise or judgement, but then again, he rarely did. I, on the other hand, was practically bursting at the seams to make a joke.

You want to get into the porn industry. Is that why you're wearing a pimp suit?

"Well, I wish you the best of luck with all of your new ventures," King said, and turned to me. "Alexis, may I have the contracts?"

"Sure," I replied, and reached for my bag before pulling out a thick folder.

Hirota waved his hands in the air. "No contracts right now. Tonight is for pleasure. Tomorrow we'll discuss business." I put the folders back in my bag, and I could sense King's dissatisfaction. He didn't want to draw this out any more than he had to. Unfortunately, Hirota seemed determined to do just that.

"Are either of you hungry?" Hirota asked. "We have a spectacular menu here."

"That's all right. We both ate at the hotel," King lied, and I was glad he was just as against eating here as I was.

Hirota didn't seem bothered, and he began talking about his two sons, and how they were currently learning how to horse ride out on his countryside estate. Chatter filled the table, mostly from Hirota and his men. King seemed on edge, like he'd rather just finish the business they had with one another rather drag things out by being social. Usually he wined and dined his clients, but not this time. Right then I could sense his agitation, like he really wanted just wanted to get things over and done with. It was probably why he kept drinking, and that worried me.

About an hour went by, and most of the men were now paying attention to the woman who had just come on stage for a special performance. A slow, sexy number played through the speakers as she began her striptease. It was right about then that the humour I'd originally found in the situation began to dissipate. At that point I'd seen enough boobs to last me a lifetime.

"I'd much prefer to be looking at you on that stage, wearing nothing but that towel from earlier," King whispered, and my heart did a somersault. This was the first time he'd commented on the strippers, and it was more a comment about me than them. My chest fluttered and I tried to think of a funny response, but my brain let me down. I knew it was the alcohol that was prompting him to speak so freely.

"I'm tired," I said. "Would it be all right if I took a taxi back to the hotel?"

King's eyes flitted back and forth between mine as he studied me closely. It was a long moment before he finally nodded, pulling out his wallet and handing me some money for the trip. My immediate reaction was to tell him it was fine, that I could pay for my own taxi, but then I remembered this was work. He was supposed to be paying. It was so easy to forget the real nature of our relationship sometimes.

I stood and walked out of the club, while Hirota and his men were still fixated on the exotic dancer. It only took me a minute to flag down a taxi. The second I got back to my hotel room, I felt a huge flood of relief. There was something off about King and this trip, but I was completely in the dark as to what it might be. Changing into some boy shorts and a T-shirt, and relieving myself of my bra, I called for room service, then checked out what films were available on pay per view. I settled for a romantic comedy.

My food arrived soon after, a massive bowl of spaghetti carbonara and an equally massive glass of white wine. Now that I was off the clock, I could afford to indulge. About a half-hour into the film, while I lay in bed, sleepy from pasta and wine, a knock sounded from the door adjoining mine and King's rooms.

"Yeah?" I called.

"Can I come in?" King called back.

I hesitated. Why did he want to come in? I was trying to veg out and relax here, ferchristsakes!

"Uh, sure."

"Are you decent?"

I glanced down at my PJs. "Kinda."

"I'm coming in."

A second later he was in my room, wearing only his shirt and slacks, the suit jacket discarded. The first few buttons on his shirt were undone, and he looked like he'd been running his hands through his hair a few too many times, because it was attractively ruffled. He seemed...stressed, but he didn't seem drunk. He must have stopped drinking right after I left the club.

A moment passed as he took in the sight of me tucked up in bed, the empty plate and wine glass on the floor and the romantic comedy playing on the flat-screen TV.

"I'm sorry, am I interrupting?" he asked. His tired voice held a hint of humour.

145

I picked up the remote and pressed "pause" on the movie. King dropped down onto a seat, and I rose to a sitting position. I remembered I wasn't wearing a bra only when his eyes lingered a few too many seconds on my breasts. I said nothing, just raised an eyebrow at his obviousness. With the tiniest grin, he shook his head and looked away.

"Do you mind if I order up some food?" he asked then.

"Not at all, go ahead."

He stood and walked to the phone, dialling room service. "I haven't had the chance to eat yet," he said as he waited for them to pick up.

"Not in the mood for a side of gonorrhoea with your steak?" I asked, grinning.

King half-smiled, half-grimaced back at me before he began speaking down the line. He ordered a pizza, and I kind of liked the sound of that. What? I enjoyed eating, and I was in flippin' Italy, of all places. I was determined to take every chance to sample the cuisine that I could. King finished his call and returned to his seat.

"You look comfortable."

"I am."

A silence elapsed, King staring at me dead on, before I said, "Can I ask a question?"

His eyes pierced me. "Go ahead."

"What's up with this deal? Something about it has you agitated."

He sighed and ran a hand through his hair again before replying, "It's a little difficult to explain, but you're right, I am agitated. Let's just say I'll be happy when we have the contracts signed and are on a plane back to London."

"Huh."

A silence elapsed as I studied him, then asked gently, "How has your mum been?"

My question took him off guard, as he brought his eyes to mine. For a split second I saw the sadness in them, and it caused my heart to thump harder. "She's okay," he answered, then paused, shaking his head. "Well, no, that's not quite true. You saw how she's been living — there's nothing okay about it. But she's been unwell in her mind for a long time, and sometimes that's the worst type of illness. At least with a physical ailment you can find the cause and treat it. Mental illness is so much harder to get a handle on. Some days are better than others, but they're never what you'd consider normal."

"What's wrong with her?" I asked, my voice soft.

"Severe anxiety and paranoia, paired with a bad case of agoraphobia. She rarely likes to leave the house."

I wanted to ask what had caused all that, but I knew it was none of my business, so I simply took his hand in mine and squeezed. "That must be awful."

When he looked at me, his expression was pained, and for a second it felt like all the turmoil inside him was about to flood out. "It is awful. Do you ever wish, Alexis, that your heart was just that little bit smaller, so that you didn't have to care quite so much?"

His question knocked the air right out of me. When we'd started having this conversation, I never expected it would turn so deep. I squeezed his hand once more and whispered, "Never. The bigger our hearts, the more beautiful our souls."

Our eyes connected, his moving back and forth between mine as he absorbed my words, my meaning. I hadn't anticipated my answer; it just seemed to come out naturally. For a long moment we sat there in contemplative silence. I didn't want him to be down, though, and tried to cheer him up when I said, "So, how do you feel about romantic comedies?"

He blinked at me, bringing himself back to the present, and with no small amount of sarcasm, replied, "Oh, I adore them."

"Well, isn't that just fabulous, because you're going to join me in watching one," I said, ignoring his sassy attitude and patting the space beside me. King rose from his seat next to the bed and crawled on. I don't know, there was just something about the visual that gave me tingles. A bed was new territory for us, and it inevitably made my mind wander. I hit "play" on the movie and King settled in next to me, our elbows touching. I tried to ignore the clean smell of his shower gel and the familiar scent of his cologne, but it was hard.

Man, I could seriously go for a bottle of that stuff...you know, just to have at home and spritz on my pillows every time I wanted to torture myself.

"What kind of cologne do you wear?" I blurted, because I'm me and that's what I do. I blurt.

King's eyes came to mine slowly, and they seemed curious. "Do you like it?"

I sucked in a deep breath. "Uh-huh."

"It's Estee Lauder *Pleasures for Men*."

I let out a guffaw. "Ha! Why do they always insist on giving these things embarrassing names? It's almost like they don't want people to buy them."

King shifted in his place and sighed. "Cynical marketing ploy, I assume. By naming it 'Pleasures,' they imagine our brains will make the connection that if we buy the product, it'll somehow bring us exactly that: pleasure. I, for one, just like how it smells."

"Ah, but has it ever brought you *pleasure?*" I teased. "That's the question."

He shot me a lazy glance and tilted his head. "I'm still waiting to find out."

"Oh, you're a scoundrel," I declared, and slapped him lightly on the shoulder.

King just shook his head and returned his attention to the TV while muttering under his breath, "I wasn't joking."

I shot him a wide-eyed glance, but he was still staring at the screen. A silence filled the room. It would have been worse if it weren't for the movie playing in the background. I felt a blush creep up my neck and glanced down to see King flex his hand, repeatedly opening and closing his fist. He'd rolled up the sleeves of his shirt, so I could see his forearms, and as usual they were way too much of a distraction. I began to feel a funny sensation, both in my chest and between my legs. An *ache*. My imagination was working overtime, showing me just how easily it would be for him to roll on top of me right then and make me see stars.

I wondered what he was like during sex....

He said he wasn't one for love and romance, but I bet he put his all into a good old-fashioned fucking session. And really, if he put even half the effort into it as he put into his work, then he was probably more than I could handle.

And, funnily enough, I had a sudden craving for more than I could handle.

The tension had almost reached its boiling point when there was a knock at the door. It was room service, and King slid off the bed to go let them in. It was a good thing, too, because I seriously needed a moment. I feared the blush that had begun on my neck had spread all the way down my body by now.

"Do you want some?" King asked, picking the plate and his glass of wine up off the tray and carrying them to the bed.

"Sure," I answered. I never said no to pizza, and this one looked delicious.

King settled back in place and took a quick bite, then held the pizza to my mouth. Now, normally I'd say something cheeky in this circumstance, perhaps make a joke, but my sense of humour was no longer present. I was aroused, and King's eyes held a game. I wanted to play. Making eye contact with him, I bent forward and took a bite right from where he'd taken one. His nostrils flared, a new intensity in his eyes. He returned the pizza to his own mouth before bringing it back to mine again.

He was hovering over me, his fit, delectable body right there, and my hands itched to feel him. The movie was long forgotten as we continued our strange interaction. I had barely any clothes on, and since King was still in his shirt and slacks, I felt vulnerable and a little bit naked. His breathing grew heavy, and I saw his attention wander to the dip of my collarbone, fixating on it.

"We should…." he began, but then faltered.

"What?"

He looked down, his thick golden lashes shading his eyes. His voice was so quiet and gravelly when he continued, "I need to get this out of my system, Alexis."

"Get what…."

Before I could finish the sentence, he was taking the pizza crust from my hand, tossing it on the plate, and levelling his icy blues on me. "We can fuck." He paused, his accent over-emphasising the "K" and making my bones turn to jelly. "We can have sex once and still remain the same. I'm sure of it."

"Well, we *are* both very pragmatic," I agreed, my entire body coiled tight. I might not have believed a word I was saying, but right then I wanted him inside me, and my vagina was willing to let me lie to myself in order to make that happen. His hands were already on my hips, massaging.

"We are," he echoed, voice lowering to a whisper as he brought his mouth to my collarbone, to the spot he'd been staring at so intensely. A moan escaped me, and I tilted my head back to give him greater access. He licked at my skin, humming in approval as he trailed his nose across the rise of my bosom. He nuzzled lightly at my cleavage, then began planting kisses all the way up the centre of my neck. I undulated beneath him, and when he reached my jaw, he nibbled at my skin, soliciting another moan from me. His lips made a quick journey to my mouth. But once he was there, he pulled back to stare into my eyes, and it took my breath away for a fraction of a second. He looked at me like I was the sexiest thing he'd ever seen.

Leaning in again, King placed surprisingly tender kisses to either side of my mouth, and I kissed him back. These tender kisses continued for a while, each of us nibbling at one another, learning each other until the kisses began to deepen. He slid his tongue gently past my lips, teasing me, tasting me. I was melting into a puddle on the bed, gripping his shoulders, his hard pecs pressing into the softness of my breasts. It wasn't long before we were full-on snogging, grasping for each other, drinking one another in like we couldn't get enough.

My hands went to the buttons of his shirt, eager to get it off. He started to help, and as soon as he was bare, he

151

reached for the hem of my top, pulling it up over my head in one fell swoop. There was a moment where we both just stared, me taking in the perfect contours of his chest and abdomen, him studying the curves of my breasts, the flare of my hips and the hard peaks of my nipples.

I was so turned on, I felt empty. I needed him inside.

"*Fuck,*" he swore, all his breath escaping him.

He moved forward, lowering himself over me and bringing his mouth to my breast. The sound I made when his lips closed over my nipple would have been embarrassing if I wasn't so lost in arousal. His hand trailed over my thigh, squeezing before running up my hip and stomach until it came to my other breast. I arched my back off the bed, eager for his touch as he massaged and licked. He startled a yelp out of me when his teeth pressed down on my nipple in a teasing bite.

God, this.

Just this.

Sometimes you didn't realise how much you needed something until it was happening. I felt like I'd been unconsciously locking up my all desire for this man since the day we first met, and now it was pouring out of me like a waterfall.

"King," I moaned, and a grunt emanated from him as he moved his body, deftly pulling my thighs apart and settling himself between my legs. His fingertips dug desperately into my skin, marking me with his need. And I could feel him then, the thick length of him pressing into my core until I couldn't find enough air. My breaths grew laboured to match his, and my brain was completely out of the picture. I was nothing but feeling and sensation, and all I wanted was more.

Suddenly, his mouth left my nipple, and I wanted to whine in protest. But then he was at my ear, and I was hot, so hot I couldn't formulate words as he growled, "I want to fuck you so hard, Alexis, so hard you're still feeling me inside you tomorrow and tomorrow and tomorrow...."

Okay, did he just hit me with a side of Shakespeare in his dirty talk?

I died.

I died dead.

All right, I didn't die dead, but I did have a mini brain orgasm courtesy of the sexy-as-fuck Cambridge graduate who was currently trailing his tongue along the shell of my ear, sending goose bumps running all down my spine.

"Do you know how bad it's been for me, huh?" he growled. "Being around you at the office, you wearing those tight little skirts that made me want to bite my way up your perfect thighs and then sink my face between your legs until you screamed for it. And your fucking arse, Alexis — Jesus Christ, half the time I'm walking around with a semi just at the sight of it."

"Shut up," I gasped.

Don't shut up.

He was making his way down my body, licking and kissing the soft part of my stomach until he reached the hem of my sleep shorts. He paused, nuzzling my belly, face pressed to my skin as he let out a long exhalation.

"I adore your body," he breathed, almost like he was in pain. "I've been dying for this."

Whoa, it wasn't like I'd had a small amount of sex in my life, but this was definitely the most intensity I'd ever felt from a man. It was probably because I was reflecting that exact intensity back at him.

153

His fingers teased at the elastic, inching it down bit by bit until he was pulling the sleep shorts clean off and I was left in nothing but my black knickers.

King stared down at me, breathing heavily as I lay there watching him, enraptured.

"You are so fucking beautiful," he said, so quietly I almost didn't hear him. And then he pressed his face to my vagina, mouthing it through the fabric and miraculously finding my clit. He sucked it into his mouth, dampening the material and sending me to the edge of desperation. I needed my knickers gone. Now.

A second later they were; King pulled them off smoothly before returning his attention to my sex. I could practically feel myself pulsing with anticipation as his hot breath warmed my skin and his eyes devoured every inch of me.

"So pretty," he whispered, and then leaned forward to give me the lightest of licks. I shuddered, so turned on he could have kept doing only this and I'd have come within moments. He didn't keep doing it, though. Only a second passed before a wave of fierce need overcame him and his mouth was sucking hard, his tongue licking fast and his fingers trailing up my inner thighs. One hand found my entrance, a finger slowly dipping inside and a feral growl erupting from him as he did so. I fisted my hands in the sheets, pleasure filling my every pore as I felt him devour me. Own me.

Stu had been good at going downtown, but nothing like this. King possessed skill, yes, but it was the intensity with which he wanted me that made it so much better. It was royalty-level cunnilingus, and I momentarily wondered if any man who came after King would ever be good enough.

And honestly, I wasn't sure I wanted any other man after King. I was bewitched by him, enamoured. The concept should have sobered me, put a dampener on what we were doing, but it didn't. It only made me want him more. I wanted him to consume me; I wanted to consume him before life got in the way and ruined it for both of us.

This might be our only chance to forget about everything and just lose ourselves in the moment.

King levelled his eyes on me, his expression dark and sexual as he licked right up my slit, slow and hard - purposeful. My entire body shook, and the orgasm that had been quickly building hit me suddenly. Warm goose bumps spread across my skin, and my hands went instinctively to his hair and then his face, marvelling at him in wonder.

"You…I…we…." I mumbled incoherently, not even sure what I meant to say to him. There were no words to describe what he'd just done to me, what he'd just made me feel. I felt sated, but somehow even emptier. His mouth was all well and good, but it didn't satisfy the deep need I had for his cock. He climbed up the bed until his hands were braced on either side of my head.

He sucked in a deep breath, his eyes travelling back and forth between mine as he swiped his thump across my bottom lip. His voice was husky when he spoke. "The way you come is fucking devastating."

The way he spoke was fucking devastating. My eyes flicked down, taking in the sight of his erection standing to attention beneath his trousers.

I tugged on the belt and whispered, "Take these off."

One end of his lips rose in a smirk, and he leaned in to press a quick kiss to my lips. I could taste myself on him, something that had never particularly appealed to me before, but with King I wanted it. Some primal inner part of me wanted to leave my mark all over him.

"What's the magic word?" he asked playfully.

God, he was gorgeous all sex-mussed and turned on. His light eyes seemed even brighter.

"Please," I moaned with no inhibitions whatsoever.

"That's better," he purred, and sucked my earlobe into his mouth. "You need me inside you, love?" He was whispering now.

"Yes," I whimpered, nuzzling my face into his neck, loving how he smelled.

"What way do you want me?"

I didn't even need to think about it. I knew exactly how I wanted him because I'd fantasised about it many a time during quiet periods at the office. A wave of shyness came over me suddenly, and I hesitated to tell him.

"No, no, no," he chided me, still whispering. "There's no room for embarrassment here. You've thought about this. I know you have. Describe to me how you imagined it."

Oh, God.

Finally, I spoke. "We're in your bathroom, at the office. You corner me on the couch and flip me over onto my stomach."

King's eyes sparkled at my description and his hands went to my hips, one arm around my stomach. "Like this?" he asked, voice low, and then flipped me onto my belly.

"Yeah, just like that," I moaned as I felt him press his cock into my arse, his breath hot and heavy on the back of my neck.

"What next?" he urged.

"You're hard. You undo your belt buckle and pull down your fly, then you push my skirt up my hips and

156

shove my knickers to the side. You touch me, feel how wet I am." He moved as I spoke, hands completing the description I was giving him until his fly was open and his fingers were running over my folds, caressing them.

"You pull me up onto my knees."

He gripped my hips, lifting me to all fours.

"Then you pull yourself from your pants, and you run your erection over my arse before sliding it lightly over my vagina. You tease me with it, find my entrance, and push in just a little, torturing me until I'm begging for it."

I had to give it to him, King took direction *just perfectly*. His cock was free now, sliding inside me the tiniest bit before pulling back out. Sensation filled my entire body at the barest connection. His hand went to my neck, gripping it as he growled in my ear.

"I think this is your cue to beg, love."

"Please," I moaned.

"Not good enough."

"I need you, please, I'm begging."

"Almost there."

My voice grew strained and demanding. I didn't want to play anymore; I just wanted him inside. "Oliver, fuck me, please. I want to feel all of you," I cried out.

"That's better," he purred, his voice laced with deep male satisfaction as I heard him pull something from his pants pocket. There was the brief sound of foil tearing before he positioned his cock, then drove it inside me, hard and so deliciously deep. I felt myself pulsate around him, like my body was thanking him for finally giving it what it needed. We went still, and I felt his mouth move over my shoulder blade before his face sank into my hair.

"Jesus Christ," he groaned.

"Oliver, I need…."

"Hush, I know, darling, I know."

He rose up again, hands finding my arse and squeezing. He growled and gave one cheek a light slap before grabbing my hips and gripping them tight. My fingers dug into the pillows as I held myself up even though my body just wanted to go limp. Everything just felt too good, and my muscles had turned to jelly. King pushed back into me, in and out deliciously slow. Then his movements sped up, and I swear I lost the ability to think. I'd never felt anything so heavenly in my entire life. My little breaths and moans filled the room; I was unable to hold anything back. King delighted in my sounds, murmuring worshipfully how much he loved them, how much he loved my body, my pussy, how perfectly we fit.

I'd never forget his masculine grunts as he hammered into me, the thick, hard feel of him as he filled me up. I felt like I wanted to die when he suddenly pulled out, but before I knew it, he was flipping me over and pushing me onto my back.

"I want your eyes," he growled, lifting my thighs around his hips and driving back into me once more. He cupped my jaw in his hand, his thumb rubbing at my chin as he levelled me with his stare. He was beautiful in that moment, captivating. I wanted to look down, take in the sight of his gloriously chiselled body, but he wouldn't allow it. He held me in place, never allowing my eyes to leave his, and something clutched at my chest and throat. It was an emotion I wasn't quite sure I could identify: sharp and stingy but warm and lovely at the same time.

King's expression grew serious. "Do you feel that?" he asked on a laboured breath.

All I could do was nod, and in the next second we both seemed to understand that we were completely and totally screwed. No way was this going to be a one-time thing. Already I wanted to crawl beneath his skin and never leave.

"You're so beautiful, Alexis. You feel fucking beautiful on the inside, too."

"Oliver...."

"Yes, darling?"

"Will you come for me?" I asked, my words a desperate plea.

"Anything for you," he whispered, his movements slowing down but growing in intensity. He seemed to get even harder as his climax built, and just as I saw he was about to come apart, I pulled his lips to mine and kissed him desperately, swallowing all of his noises, letting them become a part of me. I felt him spill into me, groaning low and gravelly as he came hard, his body shaking a little with the effort. A soft layer of perspiration coated his skin as his delicious weight fell on top of me. His arms went around my body, pulling me to him tight and squeezing as he rested his face in the crook of my neck.

I stroked his hair, and he moved us into a more comfortable position so that his entire body surrounded mine. Feeling him plant light kisses to my neck, I let out a little purr of approval as his hand went between my legs.

"You think you could come again?" he asked in a sleepy voice.

"You're exhausted, Oliver. Go to sleep."

"But my hand is jealous of my mouth," he whined playfully. "It wants to feel you come, too."

My tender laugh soon transformed into a low moan as he started to stroke me. His fingers circled my clit, then dipped inside. I shifted and felt his cock begin to harden again next to my arse cheek, and already I could have gone another round. My body was sleepy, though, so I was content to simply lay there and let him work me up.

"I knew it would be like this for us," he purred. "Effortless." His other hand came around and palmed my breast, moulding it and then pinching the nipple. He began rubbing his thumb back and forth over the tight peak, the motion matching his fingers as they stroked my clit. In the next moment, I was coming with a stark cry. King murmured soothing words in my ear and I turned into his body, cuddling him tight and pressing kisses to his pectorals.

Soon after, we both closed our eyes, and then it wasn't long before sleep pulled us under.

Twelve

I woke to a warm mouth on my thigh.

Oliver King's head was between my legs as he kissed and licked. I stared down at him, and he gave me the most handsome of smiles.

"Morning, love," he said, voice scratchy from sleep.

"Morning," I murmured. "What ya doin' down there?"

He let out a low groan. "Teasing you, I'm afraid. I wish I could stay here all day, but unfortunately I have a breakfast meeting with Hirota in forty minutes. I need to shower."

"We could share one," I suggested, and he groaned again.

"Sharing one will last a whole lot longer than I have time to spare. I may lure you into taking a bath with me later, though."

"In that case, I looked forward to being lured," I replied, and King pressed one final kiss to my thigh before leaning up on his hands and bringing his mouth to mine. Our kiss grew hungrier than expected until we broke apart, breathless. King hummed and rubbed his thumb over my lower lip, eyes fixed on my mouth as he spoke.

"I'll need you later, but take the morning. There's a beach just a short walk from here," he suggested as he rose from the bed and began picking up his discarded clothes from last night.

My interest piqued. "There is? I haven't been to the beach in years."

King walked back and placed a final kiss to my temple. "Then go. Enjoy yourself. I'll see you later."

He disappeared through the adjoining doorway to his room, leaving me slightly flabbergasted. I'd half expected him to be distant this morning, withdrawn after he'd finally gotten what he wanted. Put it down to my experience with a whole bunch of real charmers in the past. But no, King had been warm and affectionate with me; it was almost like he'd completely forgotten the whole one-time agreement we'd made.

I glanced out the window to find it was an unseasonably sunny day, perfect for a trip to the beach. Hopping up from the bed, I went and took a quick shower, then packed my bag. I put my swimsuit on, red with a '50s vintage cut, and wore a light flower-print dress over the top with some sandals.

I definitely caught a few odd looks from the locals as I made the quick walk from the hotel to the coast, as they clearly didn't consider it beach weather. Having lived my entire life in cold, rainy London, though, it was positively tropical to me. As expected, there weren't many people around. I spread a towel out on the sand, slipped on my sunglasses, pulled my dress off over my head, and lay back to soak in the rays.

An hour or two passed in blissful peace as I listened to the waves crash against the shore. I never got to hear these sorts of sounds back home, only traffic and honking horns.

Sensing a presence, I opened my eyes and slid my sunglasses down my nose. King sat next to me on the sand, his chin resting in his palm and a thoughtful expression on his face as he stared out at the water. He looked a million miles away, and the fact was confirmed when I said his name but got no answer.

"Oliver," I repeated, and saw him blink.

He turned his head. "I thought you might be sleeping, didn't want to wake you."

"Wouldn't it be kind of dangerous to fall asleep on a public beach?" I asked, but he only shrugged and turned his attention back to the sea. I sat up, reached forward, and placed a hand softly on his arm.

"Hey, are you all right?"

Either he didn't hear my question, or he chose to ignore it. "I envy those with clear consciences," he murmured, as if to himself.

What he said made me frown. "Why wouldn't your conscience be clear?"

His eyes flicked to the side as he realised he'd voiced his sentiments out loud. A long breath escaped him. "Bad luck and circumstance."

"You're one of the luckiest people I know," I whispered. Yes, his mother was unwell, but aside from that he had a pretty spectacular life.

Turning, he levelled his eyes on me, and they seemed so much more beautiful with the sun glittering through them. "My luck is only on one side of the mirror," he murmured, and reached out to caress my cheek. "I haven't been able to stop thinking about you all morning." His words and his touch made me shiver.

"I've been thinking about you, too." What I said made him smile, but there was a sadness behind it. I wanted to find its source, snuff it out. He was having these episodes more and more lately, melancholy mixed with random philosophising.

"Mr Hirota is going to sign the contracts tonight. He's invited us to his villa for dinner. Did you bring a dress?"

"Of course. I always come prepared." I smiled and crawled over to kneel in front of him, placing my hands on each of his shoulders. Staring at him head on, I said, "A problem shared is a problem halved. Whatever's been troubling you, you can tell me about it. No judgement."

The moment dragged on forever as he breathed in and then out. I don't think I'd ever experienced such a long and meaningful stretch of eye contact with another human being before. Voices sounded from nearby, a family taking pictures. King's eyes went to them and then back to me.

"Stay here," he said, and stood up. I watched as he walked to the family and began speaking to the father, who had one of those vintage Polaroid cameras. Words were exchanged, and then the father handed the camera over to King. He walked back to me, and as I sat there on my towel, he lifted the camera to his face.

"Smile, Alexis," he said, and I had just enough time to plaster a grin on my face before he snapped the shot. The photo emerged from the front of the camera and King caught it, shaking it out.

"Hey, a little warning next time!"

"Come here," he said, voice low.

I went to him. He threw his arm around my shoulders and pulled me close, holding the camera up in front of us and taking another pic. This time I was the one to grab it from the slot. It had managed to capture us up close. I was staring into the lens, smiling, and King was in profile, staring back at me, a look of such affection in his gaze that it almost took my breath away.

"I'm keeping this one," I practically whispered as King watched me.

"Only if I can keep this one."

I shrugged, trying not to sound emotional. "Sure."

He went and returned the camera to its owner, and an odd atmosphere fell between us. I packed up my things, and we made the short walk back to the hotel. I knew exactly what accounted for the tension but was too afraid to voice how I felt.

I was falling in love with him, and if the way he looked at me in the picture was anything to go by, he was falling in love with me, too.

***

Since King had a bigger room, we went there to work for the rest of the day. I sat on his bed, my computer on my lap, while he sat at the desk. There were lots of small details to tie up before Hirota signed the contracts that evening, so both of us were buried in work for a couple of hours. I Skyped with Gillian so she could take care of everything that needed doing back at the London office. I'd just finished my call with her when King's phone began to ring. I saw him glance at the screen, and I swear his face instantly transformed. He was no longer relaxed and concentrated. He now seemed irritable and stressed.

Standing, he didn't glance at me once as he walked from the room and stepped out into the hallway. He only closed the door over halfway, so I could still eavesdrop on the conversation.

"Yes?" he answered, voice flat.

A pause.

"Of course. It's all moving forward as planned. The contracts will be signed tonight."

Another pause.

"Very well. Just remember our agreement. This is the last time."

I heard him let out a long, frustrated breath, and I could just imagine his jaw clenching. He didn't sound happy at all.

"Bruce, I mean it. This is the last time. You'll have your paperwork by the morning. Goodbye." A second later he stormed back into the room, and I practically yelped in surprise when he came right at me. He shoved my laptop away, then began undoing the buttons on my dress, revealing my bra underneath.

"All afternoon I've had to watch you sitting here, torturing me in this little dress cupping your perfect fucking tits," he growled, and brought his mouth to my cleavage, dragging his lips over the swells of my breasts. A whimper escaped me as my hands went to his hair. He wasn't the only one who'd been tortured. Having Oliver King close was always a test to my willpower.

"Oliver," I breathed as he pushed down the cup of my bra, then took my nipple into his mouth. His tongue circled, and I squirmed beneath him. "Oliver, who's Bruce?"

His entire form stilled, his mouth leaving me. "You shouldn't have been listening to that conversation, Alexis."

"I'm sorry. It's just that as soon as you got the call, you became really stressed out. It worried me."

"You don't need to worry," he said, and I could feel him withdrawing.

"But I do."

He was off the bed now, picking up his coat. "I'm going to take a walk. Finish what you're working on and be ready at seven. Hirota is sending a car for us."

And with that he was gone. I lay on the bed, equal parts turned on and confused. I didn't understand why he was being so closed off about this Bruce person. My gut sank, and I quickly fixed my dress back in place. Collecting my things, I returned to my own room, and this time I remembered to lock the adjoining doors.

The dress I wore for dinner was a deep purple colour, lace on top, velvet material on the bottom. My phone pinged with a text just as I was putting the finishing touches to my makeup.

Oliver King: I'm waiting in the lobby.

I tapped out a quick response.

Alexis: Be there in two minutes.

I saw him standing by a tall column when I arrived downstairs. His back was turned to me, and he wore a black suit that made his golden hair stand out. His broad shoulders and confident, masculine posture gave me a fizzy sensation in my tummy, and I immediately wished we weren't on awkward terms. Why did I have to be so nosy asking about this Bruce person? It wasn't like I had a right to know.

Anyhow, I'd put two and two together, and decided that Bruce either worked for King's silent investor or he was the silent investor. I knew that for whatever reason, King wasn't thrilled to be working on this deal. My guess was that he owed the investor a favour, and this was how he was repaying him.

"Hi," I said, and he turned at the sound of my voice.

"Alexis," said King, his eyes skimming my form before his hand went to my lower back to lead me from the lobby. He didn't say a word about my appearance, didn't give me any heated compliments, and my gut sank. We entered a sleek black limousine, where King immediately slid across the seat and went to open the mini bar. I sat and fiddled with my phone, while at the same time taking surreptitious glances at my boss. You could have cut the tension between us with a knife, and for once it wasn't sexual. Well, okay, it was sexual. It always was with us, but on this occasion the *tension* tension outweighed the sexual tension.

King studied the bottles, deciding on which drink he was going to have. His eyes flicked to mine as he held up a bottle of Scotch.

"Would you like a glass?"

I shook my head.

Something else I was starting to notice about him was that he was very specific in the way he made his drinks. He did it lovingly and with a certain finesse. I knew there were only three reasons why a person was that particular about their drinks preparation. One: They'd worked in a bar, and it was grilled into them for life. Two: They were collectors/hobbyists who collected vintage and expensive liquors. Three: They were alcoholics.

I hated to be so callous in my labelling, but it was true. I just hoped King fell into group number two, because I knew he didn't belong to group number one, and group number three was too painful to contemplate. I remembered our conversation about Bernie Black, the dealer who supplied drugs to those working high-powered jobs in the The City. I was reminded of what King had said, and not for the first time.

When I'm stressed out, a nice glass of top-shelf whiskey usually does the trick.

It took us just over thirty minutes to reach Hirota's place, which was a quintessentially Roman villa surrounded by acres of lush land and gardens. It was dark; however, the place was illuminated by lights placed all around the entrance and lawn. I noticed some horse stables off to the side, and there were a couple of fancy cars parked out front.

I'd been counting King's drinks on the drive, and he'd had no less than four large glasses of Scotch. The fact that he wasn't even acting tipsy indicated a high tolerance, which was also a worrying sign. It felt like the more time I spent around this man, the more clearly I was beginning to see him. The more I got the sense he had secrets he tried his best to keep hidden.

He slid across the seat until his thigh met mine, and I felt him lean down to smell my hair. His closeness caused me to tremble, and I knew he saw it.

"I'm sorry, Alexis," was all he said before the driver came around and opened the door for us. We both stepped out, and I saw King's eyes go to my hand a few times, as though he wanted to hold it. And I got the sense he wanted to do it for comfort rather than as a social show. The thought made my heart ache, because I always wanted to be able to comfort him if he needed it. In the end, he never touched me, and one of Hirota's household staff let us inside before leading us to a spacious dining room.

"Oliver, Alexis," said Hirota, standing. "So glad you both made it."

This time the businessman wore an even stranger outfit than before; he was decked out in British countryside chic. Something posh folks back home might wear to go on a hunt or clay pigeon shooting. We were introduced to his wife, a slim blonde who had the desperate look of a woman who took prescription meds just to get through the day. I felt bad thinking it, but it was the truth. He also had twin sons. Both were in the awkward chubby phase of puberty, and looked to be about fourteen or fifteen. The remaining parties at the table were the same men who'd been at the strip club the previous night. All employees of Hirota.

I sat next to King as the meal was served, our arms brushing every so often. King was left-handed, I was right-handed, which meant there was an awful lot of elbow knocking going on. My heart leapt as we were being served dessert and King's hand disappeared under the table to rest on my thigh.

His mouth was close to my ear when he said, "Stay with me tonight."

I wanted to say yes, but he had continued his drinking all through dinner, and my concern was outweighing my lust right then. So, even though his touch melted my insides, I pushed his hand away and answered, "I don't think that's wise."

I could feel him staring at me as I swallowed, trying to remain stoic when I really wanted to stand up and demand he tell me what was going on. I was so preoccupied that I was hardly able to take three bites of my dessert. Then the staff came and collected my plate before refilling the wine glasses of those still drinking.

"Laura," said Hirota to his wife. "Be a dear and take Alexis on a tour of the house. Mr King and I just have one or two matters to discuss before I sign the contracts."

Oh, for fuck's sake. The last thing I wanted right then was one-on-one time with Laura Hirota, but I didn't have another choice. Their sons had already left to go play video games in the lounge, and seemingly Hirota was a sexist ape who didn't think women had any place in business dealings.

"Of course," said Laura, eyes finding mine. "I'll show you my collection of china."

Laura's collection of china was truly riveting. I stood there as she oohed and aahed over the design details and boasted how expensive it all was, wishing I were anywhere else in the world. Oh, did I also mention that she expelled a shitload of venom about her selfish husband and her spoiled children along the way? It was like, oh, yeah, go right ahead and use me as an outlet for all your

170

dissatisfaction. She walked me through the various rooms, and then we did a quick sweep of the garden before returning to the house.

Laura yawned. "I think I'll go get some sleep now. It was lovely meeting you, Alexis." She didn't sound like she thought it was lovely at all; she sounded like it had been a burden. I made my way through a spacious lounge area, trying to find King, when I spotted him sitting in front of a grand piano that I was sure Hirota placed there purely for show.

King stared out the window, a glass of wine in his hand, as I closed the distance between us.

"Well, Laura Hirota hates her life," I deadpanned, and King shot me an arch look. "The contracts all signed and sealed?" I went on as I came to stand in front of him. He turned his head to face me and nodded.

"Everything's been finalised."

A silence elapsed. I leaned a little too hard against the piano, an off-key sound ringing out. I shot King an apologetic look and remembered again how beautifully he played. Our eyes locked for several moments, feelings passing back and forth but no words.

"Play something for me," I urged him.

His eyes went to the keys before returning to mine. "What would you like to hear?"

"Anything."

I stood back as he twisted around and ran his fingers across the ivories.

And then, just like that, he began to play.

Thirteen

The tune started out low and soft, but quickly sped up. It became faster, louder, until his fingers were dancing over the keys in a way that knocked the breath from my lungs. I'd expected him to play a little rendition of a modern song, something simple, romantic maybe. But this, this was on another stratosphere, and I knew from his skill that he played it often. Unlike the piano here at Hirota's, the one King had at his apartment was definitely not for show.

He was playing the exact same piece as he had at his apartment that night. Almost unconsciously, I lowered myself onto the bench beside him, both my eyes and my ears enraptured as he continued the melody. In that moment he was transformed; his entire body was at one with the instrument as he filled the room with perfect, heart-aching, sweet and soulful music.

I fell.

I'd already started falling, but the way he played finished the job. It was so beautiful in its realness that I couldn't help but be owned by him. Elaine King had obviously passed her talent down to her son, and it was almost a tragedy that this wasn't what he did all day, every day.

I wasn't sure how long he had been playing when the piece finally drew to a close. I sat there, staring at the piano in stunned silence, as he turned to face me.

"Why so quiet, darling?" he asked, taking my chin between his fingers.

"I don't know what to say."

"So say nothing." His mouth went to my jaw as he gave me a feather-light kiss.

"What was that song?"

King sat back and cleared his throat. "It's Rachmaninoff, Piano Concerto No. 2. It's the last piece my mother ever played to a live audience."

And just like that, it all made sense. The piece was clearly very special to him.

"I hope you don't take this the wrong way, but you're wasted as a banker. This is what you should be doing," I stated outright.

King laughed gently. "I think I told you before that Mum is the star. Pianists are ten a penny in this world, and that's usually how much they make for a living, too." His joke fell flat.

"I thought you didn't care about money."

"I don't. I care about prestige, and my mediocre piano skills will never bring me that."

"Mediocre? Are you serious?"

His low, affectionate laughter did something to the pit of my stomach. Well, it was the laughter combined with the music he'd just played. His fingers were trailing up my thigh, finding the hem of my skirt and dipping beneath when I spoke without thinking.

"Make love to me," I blurted.

King's gaze grew heated, and his mouth was at my ear again, whispering a single word, "Love?" The second it left his lips, his finger slid past my underwear and right inside me. My breath came out in a rush.

His voice grew dark. "One day I'm going to spread you out on my piano at home and fuck you until you forget your own name."

Jesus Christ. "Oliver."

"You're so *wet*."

The sound of approaching footsteps echoed around the room, and King instantly withdrew, leaving me feeling empty. A member of Hirota's household staff cleared her throat.

"Mr King, the car is waiting to take you both back to the hotel."

"Yes, very good. Thank you," King replied smoothly, and stood. I walked alongside him back to the same limo we'd arrived in. As soon as the door closed, King pressed the button for the privacy screen, and then he was climbing on top of me. He pushed me back so that I lay stretched out on the seat, his hard body over mine as his hand returned to where it had been before we were interrupted. I threw my head back and tried not to make a sound for fear of alerting the driver to what we were doing. King shot me a devilish grin. The bastard. He knew exactly what he was up to.

His fingers slid in and out of me fast, working me up into a heated frenzy. My hands were already fumbling for his pants, desperate to get them off. All day my mind had been fixating on last night, my body wanting more. Within seconds I had him free as I ran my hand down the hot, silky length of him. He felt beautiful, perfect, and right then I wanted all of that perfect beauty deep inside me.

His entire body shuddered as I fisted him, and his face fell to my neck as some realisation lit in his eyes.

"I didn't bring protection," he groaned.

Well, shit.

"Oh."

"The journey back to the hotel won't take long. We can wait," he said, but he didn't sound convinced. Our eyes connected, and I knew instantly that we were both thinking the same thing.

Should we risk it?

"I'm on the pill," I blurted. It was the truth. I'd been taking it for years and hadn't stopped even after Stu and I broke up.

His gaze held a warning. "Don't."

"I trust you."

He groaned again. "Fucking hell."

I wriggled beneath him, shoving my knickers aside and carefully guiding his cock closer. His resistance cracked and his hips jutted forward, closing the remaining distance between us as his hard, bare length pushed inside me. I moaned and closed my eyes, the feel of him with nothing between us a little more than I could handle. I was twenty-seven years old and this was the very first time I'd had unprotected sex with another person. I never imagined how amazing it could be, especially when you added my continually growing feelings to the equation.

"Alexis, darling," he murmured. "You feel…incredible."

I stroked a hand down his back and gazed up at him.

Barely a few minutes passed, but they felt as though they lasted an eternity. King made love to me slowly, his eyes never leaving mine. This certainly wasn't what either one of us had intended by having sex in a limo. I certainly hadn't thought it'd be so…emotional. I wanted to say something, anything, to warn him that I was beginning to grow attached, but I couldn't find the words. And then he was coming, his mouth capturing mine and his sounds reverberating through me.

And when it was over, we lay there in each other's arms, a startling awareness filling the small space and so many words being left unsaid.

***

In spite of our hunger for one another, we were exhausted. Arriving back at the hotel, we lay in my bed and just kissed for a while, King making me come with his hand before we both passed out cold.

The following morning we had an early flight back to London. A sense of dread filled my gut as I wondered if things would remain the same when we got home. It was unwarranted, because King was being warm and affectionate with me. He wasn't giving me any cause for concern, and yet I still felt it. I mean, we could hardly be a couple at work. Even if it wasn't against the rules, I didn't want people thinking I was some low-class hussy who slept with her boss.

Even though, let's face it, that's what I was, though I refused to accept the low-class bit. Damn me and my dumb blonde hussy of a vagina. She just couldn't keep her hands to herself.

Everything was a mad rush as we packed our things and made our way to the airport. I barely had a chance to catch my breath until we were seated on the flight. We'd just landed at Heathrow and were making our way to the baggage carousel when King's phone began ringing. I didn't pay much attention to the conversation until I heard the concerned tone in his voice.

"Mum? No, no, shit, stay where you are. I'll be there within the hour."

I placed a hand on King's elbow. "Is everything all right?"

He turned to me and looked down, his agitation clear as day. "No," he answered, almost absently. "No, it isn't. We have to go."

I nodded and grabbed our bags as we hurried to catch a taxi. King barely uttered a word, and I was half convinced he'd forgotten I was even there. It sounded like something had happened with his mum again. Perhaps she had to be taken back into the hospital, though I still didn't know what had happened the last time. King clutched his phone in his hand, his knuckles turning white. I wanted to do something to calm him, but I was at a loss. He was wound so tight I feared he might snap if I tried to touch him right then.

It took us longer than an hour to reach the house (London traffic), and King almost got into a fight with the taxi driver along the way. He was upset and stressed, and I knew his anger was only due to whatever had happened with his mum. I tipped the driver well when we got there, apologising for King's behaviour as my boss practically leapt from the car and hurried to the front door. He fumbled in his pocket before pulling out a set of keys, and then a second later he'd disappeared inside.

I brought our small suitcases into the entryway as King called out, "Mum, I'm here! Mum!"

"Oliver," came the sound of a weak, scratchy voice.

I followed King's calls until I found him in a small library room. His mum sat on the floor, her knees huddled to her chest and tears streaming down her cheeks. She looked like she'd just been through something horribly traumatic and wore only a silk robe, her long hair all tangled. Some of her chest was exposed, but King didn't even bat an eyelid; he simply pulled the robe tighter to cover her modesty. There was nothing weird or awkward about it. He did it with love and care, and it was in that moment, finally seeing them both together for the first time, that I realised this woman meant the world to him.

I got the feeling King had been caring for his mother for a really long time.

His hands went to her cheeks, wiping away the tears. "What happened?"

"He was here. He got inside. I don't know how, but he threatened me, Oliver. He said you were messing him around, and he wouldn't stand for it. He…he hit me."

King's entire body went still. "Where?"

Elaine slowly pulled up the sleeve of her robe to reveal an awful welt.

"He's the fucking devil," King fumed, and I'd never seen him so angry. "I'm going to kill him."

"No," Elaine cried. "That's what he wants. He wants to make you like him. Don't ever become like him."

"Mother, we can't go on like this. It's been…Christ, it's been too many years."

"Just call him," Elaine urged King frantically. "Explain everything. I'm sure it's all just a big misunderstanding."

King, kneeling in front of his mum, pulled back and slammed his hand down into the floor. "Don't you see, he'll never leave us alone. Not until one of us is dead or in prison."

"Please, Oliver, please, he said one last time, maybe he meant it. Maybe he'll go away after this."

King stared at his mother and ran a hand down his face. He looked exhausted, the kind of exhausted that only accumulates from years of worry and lost sleep. My heart was hammering in my chest, and I felt so out of place. I shouldn't have been listening to the exchange, but I couldn't take it back now. I'd heard everything, and what I'd heard had frightened me. I felt cold, colder than I'd ever been.

He'll never leave us alone. Not until one of us is dead or in prison.

A moment passed before King pulled his phone from his pocket and began scrolling through his contacts. Rising to his full height, he turned, and that's when he saw me. The startled look in his eyes told me he'd completely forgotten I was there. I'd never felt so uncomfortable in my entire life. King's gaze was hard, and it was only after a long few moments that it began to soften.

"Alexis...."

"I should go."

"No," he said quickly. "Don't go. I have an important phone call to make. Could you take Mum up to her room? It's on the second floor, the third door on the right. Then come find me and we'll talk."

I nodded, and he walked past me, lifting his phone to his ear. Elaine's reddened eyes found mine, and she seemed ashamed that I was seeing her like this. I hated that she felt that way, because she had absolutely nothing to be ashamed about. Going to her, I gently slid an arm around her waist and helped her up to a standing position. She was weak and I had to take most of her weight, but it was nothing. She was waifish, insubstantial, and it made her seem that much more vulnerable.

She didn't say anything as I led her to her room, but when I pulled her sheets back and helped her into bed, there was gratefulness in her gaze.

"Talk to him. Make him see sense," she urged me, and I wasn't sure what she was asking of me.

I gave her shoulder a reassuring squeeze before murmuring softly, "Get some sleep, Elaine. Oliver and I will be just downstairs if you need us."

Leaving her room and going back down, I found King in the library. The drinks cabinet was open, and half a bottle of Southern Comfort sat on the desk. His eyes rose to meet mine.

"Want one?"

Normally I'd decline, but the situation called for a drink, so I nodded and took the seat next to him. He poured, and I watched. Then he handed me the glass, and I knocked it back. The room was quiet for a long few minutes, and I wasn't sure why, but I felt the urge to hug him, to bridge the monumental gap that seemed to linger between us. I threw my arms around his shoulders, and he stiffened.

I didn't let go.

He resisted my embrace for so long that I was sure I'd have to give up eventually, but then he softened. It all happened at once. His body melted into mine as his arms went around my waist and pulled me close. He clutched me so tightly I felt the air rush from my lungs. It was in that moment that I knew I'd given him just what he needed.

He didn't need words or sex or platitudes. He just needed a hug. Human comfort.

His hands tangled in my hair, and mine laced around his neck. "I'm here to help. Whatever you need," I whispered, and his body sagged.

I didn't expect him to speak, didn't really expect anything at all other than for him to accept my hug, which was why hearing his voice startled me.

"Yesterday you asked me who Bruce was," he said, speaking into my neck. "He's my father."

I grew still, and King pulled away a little to meet my eyes. "He's also been blackmailing me almost my entire life."

My brow furrowed as I shook my head. "I don't understand."

King let out a long breath, picked up his glass, and knocked the entire contents back in one go. "My mother has been playing piano since she could walk. Her family were wealthy, and when they saw she had a natural talent, they invested a lot in her career. Once she hit her mid-teens, she began to get attention, and soon she was performing with orchestras, travelling around the world."

I stared at him, absorbing his words. King poured more liquid into his glass.

"She was playing at the Royal Albert Hall on a night when my father was in attendance. He saw her on stage and decided he wanted her. She was just seventeen, but Bruce Mitchell was a man who got what he wanted. He was a lot older and very rich, but he was also dangerous, which was probably what attracted Mum — the danger, the excitement. They were from different worlds, still are, and Bruce is not a good man. He's a criminal, a very powerful one. All of the most despicable things you can think of, my father has most likely had a hand in them."

"Oliver, I...."

"Hush. Just let me speak. I've never told anyone this before." He paused to meet my gaze, tilting his head. "I trust you, Alexis. That doesn't make me a fool, does it?"

I frowned. "Of course not. Anything you tell me will never leave this room."

He took a swig of his drink and breathed out. "Anyway, long story short, Mum had a brief affair with Bruce and fell pregnant with me. Her career really took off after that and she became very famous for a number of years, while Bruce sort of drifted into the background. Then, just after I turned eighteen, Mum started having trouble with a stalker. It was a scary time for both of us. We'd come home to find the house had been broken into,

181

the valuables left untouched but personal items of my mother's stolen. He'd write creepy, obsessive letters, and Mum had to set the police on the case. Months passed, and Mum started to go out in public less and less. She was frightened of running into her stalker, and a lot of what he'd written in his letters indicated he wasn't of sound mind. And then, one night during the summer before I was to start university, I came home and found my mother beaten up and restrained, a man readying himself to rape her. I lost the plot, went crazy, and beat the living daylights out of him. I couldn't stop." King's voice choked up, and I saw his eyes fill with emotion as he remembered. I was so absorbed in his story, so horrified by it, that I'd almost stopped breathing for a moment. I took his hand in mine, squeezed it tight.

"I...I thought I'd killed him. I couldn't find a pulse, so I panicked. I swear, Alexis, thinking you've killed a man is the most terrifying feeling in the world. It's like everything is over and your whole future is gone. I didn't know whether to call the police or start thinking about where I could bury the body, but then Mum spoke up. She told me to call Bruce. I'd only met my father a handful of times, barely knew anything about him, but I was in such a state that I simply did as she told me.

"A little while later he showed up at the house, finding Mum beaten and bruised, and me covered in another man's blood. I thought he was our saviour back then. He took care of everything. Got the man I'd beaten to a hospital, paid him to keep quiet, and made sure no one knew I'd almost killed him in my anger and fear. The experience would always stay with me, but at least it was over. And then, several months later, Bruce began making his presence known. He wanted to get to know his son, spend time with me. I was more than happy to oblige him at first. However, once I became familiar with my father and his way of life, I wanted absolutely nothing to do with him. Bruce, unfortunately, was unwilling to let me go. He told me he'd never taken Mum's stalker to a hospital that night, but instead had him killed and buried in a shallow grave. He told me that if I didn't start doing as he said, he'd see to it that the police found the body and I'd be done for murder."

I stared at him, flabbergasted and appalled. I clutched his hand so tight that I was probably cutting off his blood supply. "So...your dad, I mean, Bruce has been blackmailing you to do his bidding ever since?"

King leaned closer. "The things I've seen, Alexis, the things he's forced me to witness, don't even bear thinking about. I built my entire career cleanly, never cheating, never doing anything underhanded, for the sole purpose of never becoming like him. But now...." King sighed, his jaw working as his chest fell, "Now he's looking for new ways to clean his money, and he's decided to do it by having me invest for him. I told him just once, that I'd do this one deal with Hirota, and then I never wanted to see him again. But if coming here today and threatening Mum is anything to go by, he has no intention of leaving us alone." He glanced at me. "Remember when I told you Mum had to be taken into the hospital?"

I nodded.

"She'd overdosed on anxiety medication, because she was so worried about what Bruce would do to us if the deal didn't go through. I can't let her live like this anymore. My mother is the only family I have left in the world, and she's spent more than a decade as a ghost. She's too anxious and paranoid over Bruce's threats to even leave the house. I want to see her live again, see her go outside and be like any other ordinary woman on the street."

My heart pounded at his words, at the sincerity of them and the pain he had so obviously been harbouring for years. I wanted to fix this for him. I needed to. And I knew just the person to go to for help. I'd grown up in a lower-class neighbourhood, and having been best friends with Karla all my life, a policewoman raised by a superintendent, I knew my fair share about how criminals operated.

I sat up straight and levelled my eyes on King's.

"If Bruce is the man you say he is, then you have to fight fire with fire. Beat him at his own game. That's the only way you'll ever be rid of him. There's probably a wealth of information out there about things he's done he doesn't want anyone to find out about. You just have to know the right people to ask."

"Nobody talks about his business, not if they want to keep their lives, Alexis. Bruce is one of the most notorious and powerful crime lords in London. Only someone with a death wish would sell him out."

I moved closer, took his hands in mine, and met his eyes. "Do you trust me?"

He let out a breath. "You know I do."

"Then let me try something."

Fourteen

The following day at work was tense. King couldn't concentrate because he was worried about Bruce coming back for his mother, even though he was having security watch her house day and night. Apparently, after King had finalised the deal with Hirota, he hadn't had the chance to forward the documents to Bruce. Then we'd had to catch our flight, which delayed things further. Bruce had jumped the gun and thought King was giving him the runaround, hence the reason for him showing up at Elaine's and making threats.

We were dealing with a real prize.

Anyhow, we had a plan to set in motion. When I arrived home after work, I found Karla in the living room, watching TV and eating a bag of chocolate peanuts. She must have sensed my nervous energy because she sat up straight and eyed me curiously.

"What's up with you?"

"I'm having some people around tonight. I hope that's okay."

"Sure, go for it. Who's coming?"

"Um, King."

"And?"

"And Lee Cross."

Karla practically spat a peanut out of her mouth. "Oh, hell no. I'm not having that little shit knowing where I live."

"The little shit already knows, Karla. Stu's been around here lots of times, so if he wants to find out where you live, all he has to do is ask his brother."

"Yeah, but there's a big difference between him knowing and actually inviting him over. That's like

185

sticking a big 'come and get me' sign on my forehead," she sputtered.

"Oh, don't be so melodramatic. I'm sure he'll be able to resist you while he's here," I replied sarcastically, which only seemed to rile her further. It was a little bit funny, and I needed some comic relief right then.

"Hey! I wasn't saying it because I think I'm irresistible. I said it because I know how men like him operate. They want to shag a cop so they can brag about it to their mates. I'm just a trophy to him." She slumped back into her seat and folded her arms, muttering under her breath. "Nothing to do with my looks."

It had everything to do with her looks. She was gorgeous, she just didn't know it – probably because she had to wear that godawful shapeless black and white uniform every day.

"Anyway," I began, changing the subject, "I need to ask you something."

"Go ahead."

"What do you know about Bruce Mitchell?"

Karla's eyebrows shot right up into her forehead as she let out a low whistle. "That's some serious name to be throwing about."

"It is. So tell me what you know."

"I know he's a big-time criminal. Fingers in every pie imaginable, but mostly suspected of running a large drug ring in and around central London. He's been around so long he's practically his own institution." She paused, eyeing me suspiciously. "Why are you asking me about Bruce Mitchell, Lexie?"

And here was where I told her the lie I agreed upon with King. We wouldn't tell anyone Bruce was his father, nor about the past with his mum's stalker. What we would tell them was that Bruce had blackmailed King and threatened to frame him for crimes he didn't commit. Therefore, our plan was to ask Lee, who was shrewd as a fox and knew everything about everyone in this city, if he could get some dirt on Bruce. We'd then use that dirt to get Bruce to back off King and Elaine. Like I said, it was fighting fire with fire. Lee was a safe option because I knew him well enough to know he could be trusted, but he was also someone with his own level of power, so Bruce wouldn't try to retaliate against him as our middleman, so to speak.

After I'd finished speaking, Karla stared at me, gobsmacked.

"Are you seriously standing there telling me all this and expecting me not to report it? What planet are you living on?"

I reflected her indignation right back at her. "Are you seriously sitting there expecting me to let you report it? If I've learned anything from living with you, it's that the criminal justice system in this country is bullshit. Bruce has been getting away with murder for decades. What makes you think that's going to stop now? Don't you think hundreds of people have gone to the police about him over the years? And has any of it worked? No. We need to beat him at his own game."

Karla slumped back into the couch, giving up. "Sometimes I don't even know why I bother with this job."

I came forward and squeezed her shoulder. "You do it because you're a good person who wants to help those who need it. It's not your fault the system is corrupt."

She shook her head. "I just don't understand why you're trusting Lee."

"I'm trusting him because he's got an in. And yes, he might not technically live his life on the right side of the law, but he's a decent person. He's got a good heart, and when it comes down to it, he'd never intentionally hurt someone. He's not like Bruce."

Karla eyed me speculatively. "You seem very sure about him."

"I spent a lot of time around him when Stu and I were together. He might not make his money in a legit manner, but I've seen him use it to take care of his family. He even buys food for the kids next door whose junkie parents aren't fit to care for them," I told her. "So yeah, he's not perfect, but he's not a bad person, either."

Her expression softened for a brief moment before she gave me a sober nod and returned her attention to the TV. I could tell she still wasn't entirely happy with the situation, but she also wasn't going to continue protesting.

I'd just changed into a light T-shirt and some leggings when a knock sounded at the door. I called to Karla that I'd answer it, and then hurried to let King in. He'd changed out of the suit he'd been wearing earlier and now wore jeans, a T-shirt, and a khaki jacket. I swear, even with the current circumstances, the sight of him made my heart speed up.

"Hey," I greeted him quietly, giving him a tentative smile.

"Alexis," he said, and bent down to press a kiss on my lips. I could practically feel Karla's eyes bugging out of her head, because I knew she had to be watching us. I hadn't yet had the chance to fully explain my relationship with King to her, but I imagined she'd put two and two together. We hadn't had sex in almost two days, and despite everything that was going on, my body longed for his

188

touch. It felt like for the rest of my life, I was always just going to want more of him.

I stroked a hand down his arm before lacing my fingers with his. "How are you feeling?"

"Worried, stressed." He bent down to whisper the last part in my ear, "Horny."

A shiver trickled along the back of my neck as I tried to resist the urge to drag him into my bedroom. Instead, I led him over to the couch and introduced him to Karla.

"This is Karla, my roommate and BFF. I've already filled her in on the situation. Karla, this is Oliver, my eh, uh...."

"Your boss?" she finished for me, arching a brow.

I frowned at her. "Yeah, my boss."

Before the conversation could continue, there was another knock at the door. I went to answer it and was met by not just Lee, but his brother, too. Yeah, that's right, my ex had decided to tag along. Sometimes I wished I had a butler to answer my door and inform visitors on my behalf, *I'm sorry, but not today.*

Why the hell was he here? My first words voiced that very same sentiment as the two men stepped inside without even waiting to be invited.

"Uh, why is Stu here?" I asked, gesturing wildly.

Lee shot me a grin. "He's my muscle."

"As far as I can see, you've got enough muscle of your own," I shot back.

"Ah, yeah, but you know society's a bitch. Ya have to be a tall bastard for people to be afraid of ya these days. They don't realise us little guys are quicker on our toes." He paused, eyes darting across the room to give Karla a wink. "Plus, we have the advantage of a lower centre of gravity."

Lee wasn't exactly little, but I got where he was coming from. My ex was well over six feet, the big dumb oaf. I had to resist the urge to laugh when Stu gave his brother a vacant stare at his mention of "a lower centre of gravity."

"How's it going, Lex?" said Stu as his attention came to rest on me, his eyes doing a quick sweep of my body.

"It'll be going a lot better when you piss off out of here. None of this concerns you."

Lee held up a hand. "Now, now, don't go getting your knickers in a twist, Clarky. You called me asking for help. I was kind enough to answer, but if you want me to stick around, you'll have to deal with my brother being here, too." His voice was hard and broached no further argument. In the next second, King was beside me, introducing himself.

"We haven't yet had the pleasure," he said urbanely. "My name is Oliver."

Lee gave him a quick once-over before glancing at me, his lips twitching in amusement. "Bagged yourself a posh bastard, did ya?" He nudged his brother with his elbow. "She's moving up in the world."

"Don't be an arsehole," said Karla in an annoyed tone.

Lee seemed to enjoy her barb. "I'll never be an arsehole to you, Snap. In fact," he went on, his voice lowering, "I'll be so fucking pleasant, you'll never want me to leave."

Karla rolled her eyes, not bothering to retort. I noticed Stu was now eyeballing King, and I didn't like the angry slant to his mouth. Jesus, all of this would have gone so much more smoothly if Lee had just left his brother at home. Stu flicked his gaze between me and King.

"You together?"

My posture grew stiff. "And if we are?"

Stu snorted. "If you are, it's a fucking joke."

King, who was silently observing the exchange, spoke up, seeming unthreatened by Stu's presence. "I believe we have more important matters to discuss."

"Yeah, we do," said Stu. "Like how you're trying to take what's mine."

Oh, for Christ's sake. I cast Lee a pleading look while King stared emotionlessly at my ex. Deciding to be less of a prick, Lee nodded to the door. "Eh, Stu, go wait for me outside. Make sure no one tries to come into the flat."

Stu didn't look happy about his brother's order, but he did as he was told all the same. Between the two of them, it was clear who the alpha was. As soon as Stu left, I finally felt like I could breathe. I sent King an apologetic look as he leaned in and whispered, "An old flame of yours?"

"Unfortunately, yes."

"He wants you back."

"Well, he can go on wanting."

"I didn't like the way he looked at you," he went on, and the dark note in his voice made me shiver. I pressed a kiss to the underside of his jaw.

"It doesn't matter." I paused to eye him meaningfully. "He's my past." I left the second part unspoken. *You're my future.* If his satisfied expression was anything to go by, he caught my meaning. Turning, I found Lee had plopped himself down on the sofa beside Karla and was sitting a little too close. She shifted away, being none too subtle about putting distance between them.

"Oh, Snap," he chuckled. "It's so funny how you want me."

Karla bristled. "Don't call me Snap."

191

"You don't like it? It's short for Gingersnap. I thought you'd appreciate my creative efforts and shit."

"Well, I don't. Go focus your creativity elsewhere. In fact, pretend I don't exist."

He shot her a heated look, his eyes trailing slowly down her body.

"Sorry, can't do that," Lee whispered quietly. Karla took a deep breath, as though summoning the willpower not to slap him. I felt bad for subjecting her to Lee, but I needed her there for moral support.

Tugging King forward, I led him over to a chair and perched myself on the edge. His hand went to my thigh, and I savoured the warmth.

"So, what have you got for us?" I began, looking at Lee. "This needs to be good."

Lee scoffed. "Don't insult me with low expectations." Pausing, he eyed King. "Did you bring the money?"

Oh, yeah, did I fail to mention that Lee wanted 50K for this favour? It was pocket change to a man like King, but still, Lee had some balls asking for that amount. I'd expected it, though. He might have had a good heart, but he was a survivor, and surviving meant making money in any way he could.

King slid a briefcase across to him and Lee took a peek inside, letting out a low whistle when he saw the cash. One eyebrow went up. "Shit, should I have asked for more?"

It must have been Lee's tone that made King chuckle. Karla let out a long sigh and glared at me. "I can't believe you're making me be a witness to this. You seriously owe me one, Lexie."

Lee cocked his head to her. "I'll owe you one any day of the week, babe."

She scowled at him and he grinned in delight. I mouthed a silent "sorry" at her and thought maybe she should stop being so disgruntled with him, because it was obvious that he liked it. A moment of quiet passed before Lee clasped his hands together and started to speak.

"So, Mr King, it seems you're in luck. I've done some discreet asking around, and it appears Brucey's been getting sloppy in his old age. If you ask me, it's all the prostitutes. Syphilis fucks with the brain."

King grew stiff at Lee's words, and I reached over to lace my fingers with his. Silence followed. Lee chuckled. "What? Was that poor taste?" No response. He raised his brows. "*Okay*, I'll keep the jokes to myself in future. So, word has it that Bruce shot a copper a couple of months back."

Karla gasped. "What?"

Lee nodded. "True story. But don't worry, this cop was dirty. It won't happen to you, Snap. You're lily white. I can tell."

"Fuck off."

Lee flashed her a toothy smile. "Feisty. I like it. Anyways, shit went down. The cop was on Bruce's payroll but sold him out to the competition, a bloke named Tiny McGee. Ironic, since he's a fat fucker. I've managed to get my hands on the gun Bruce used to shoot the cop. He chucked it in the Thames, but one of his men, seeing an opportunity for blackmail down the line, as you do, fished it out and kept it for future use. This fella's agreed to sell the gun to me for 25K," he said, and glanced at Karla. "See, I'm not completely despicable. Half the money isn't even for me."

"Oh, yeah, you're a real saint," Karla deadpanned.

Lee brought his attention back to King. "So all you need to do is sit back, relax, and let me take care of the rest. Shooting a cop is bad business, and he's not going to want this to go public. I'll give Bruce a little call. Tell him how it's gonna play out, and see if he wants to be clever or stupid. I can't guarantee he'll be clever. Like I said, it's the syphilis." He paused, waiting for us to laugh. "What? Still not funny? Fine, I give up."

Lee stood as King addressed him. "When can I expect to hear from you?"

Glancing down at his watch, Lee answered, "Around this time tomorrow."

"Very good," said King, holding out his hand and shaking with Lee.

"It was a pleasure doing business with ya."

Lee stood to leave, but before he did, he bent over the couch, startling Karla by giving her a surprise peck on the cheek. It might have been a sweet gesture if it wasn't so brazen. She immediately recoiled, glaring daggers at him. He winked at her. "Little something for you to remember me by, Snap. Until next time."

"There won't be a next time," she called after him.

He flashed her one final grin. "We'll see."

When he opened the door, I saw Stu standing there impatiently. "I want to talk with Lex," he told his brother.

Lee put a hand on Stu's chest, pushing him back. "Nah, mate, you're good."

Stu grew irritable. "It'll only take a minute."

Lee held firm, eyeing his brother sharply. "If I say you're good, you're good. Now come on, she's not interested."

I knew Stu wanted to protest further, but he must have realised his brother wasn't going to budge on the matter. I wondered why. Perhaps Lee saw something in the way I interacted with King. He definitely had an intuitive nature; maybe he'd figured out there was no way I was going back to Stu, come hell or high water.

The door finally closed over, and King excused himself to use the bathroom.

"I'm sorry about Lee. He's such a flirt," I said to Karla.

"No worries. I can handle it." Her voice grew hushed as she leaned forward, eyes flicking to the bathroom door. "What the hell is going on with you and Mr Tall, Blond, and Perfect, though?"

I heaved out a sigh. "It's complicated."

"I can see that. Isn't it against company policy for you to be seeing one another?"

"No. He said it wasn't. We haven't really discussed things properly yet. I think we'll wait until this whole thing with Bruce blows over to start figuring stuff out."

I went quiet when I heard the toilet flush, and then King re-emerged.

"So, I should probably make a move. I need to check on Mum," he began.

Karla turned up the volume on the TV a little and focused on the screen, discreetly giving us some privacy. Bless her. I walked over to King and took his hands in mine. He raised them to his mouth and brushed his lips across my knuckles. I trembled, remembering our brief time together in Rome. It had only been two days, and yet it felt like a lifetime ago. But I knew now wasn't the time for sex. Everything was too tense.

God, life, why do you have to be such a cockblocker sometimes?

"Come spend the evening with me tomorrow after work," said King, his voice hushed. "I'm having someone watch Mum's house. You can bring an overnight bag. I'll cook dinner."

"That sounds perfect," I replied quietly, shivering when he rubbed the inside of my wrist with his thumb.

King bent in and pressed a chaste kiss to my mouth. Neither one of us dared to deepen it for fear of making things a little too raunchy. After all, we did have an audience of one, who was right at that moment doing her best to pretend to watch television.

"Until tomorrow, then," King murmured, and left.

As soon as the door shut, I leaned back against it and let out a frustrated groan. Eyes still on the screen, Karla let out a laugh and shook her head.

"Oh, Lexie, you are so fucked."

Fifteen

The following day I didn't see King until after lunch. He had meetings all through the morning and was away from the office. I missed him. This was probably why I went to him as soon as he got back, under the guise of having work for him to look over. Gillian had just left for a coffee break when I made my move.

"How's your day been?" I asked quietly as I closed the door and stepped inside, the printout of a spreadsheet from last week held to my chest.

King was typing an email when he heard me speak. He paused instantly and shot me a warm look, his eyes drinking me in, lingering on the flare of my hips.

"Come here."

I went to him. He caught my wrist and pulled me to his lap. I shifted in place, feeling him harden already. His hands moulded to my hips, squeezing them, as his mouth pressed against my neck.

"You fucking kill me with these little outfits."

"Oliver."

His hand moved up my body until it reached my neck. He cupped it, then rose, leading me backwards to the bathroom as his thumb applied the perfect amount of pressure to my nape. His speediness and lack of pretence surprised me. I'd expected him to at least protest a little about sex at the office. But no. A moment later he was lowering me face first onto the couch. I twisted in place as he began undoing his fly.

"Wait," I said, breathless, sitting up and reaching for him. "Let me try something." King remained still as I pulled him into me by his belt buckle and finished the job of undoing his trousers. I was aware of the heavy rise and fall of his chest, of his eyes glittering with heat, as I shoved them over his hips and pulled his cock free. I gripped him, licking my lips and looking up to meet his gaze. Without further hesitation, I brought my mouth to his head and licked softly. He felt hot and silky. I loved the feel of him. He let out an agonised groan, and I lowered my mouth onto him, taking him in fully this time. The deep, throaty sound he emitted made me instantly wet as I pressed my thighs together to dull the ache.

"Alexis," he murmured, his voice strained. "Da...arling."

I continued to work him with my mouth, my lips sliding wetly along his length, relishing the feeling of complete control. He might have been standing over me, but I held all the power. It was kind of exhilarating. I quickened my pace, and his words grew choppy.

"Take off your top," he said, face contorted with pleasure, eyes worshipful.

I continued sucking him off as my fingers trailed down my blouse, undoing the buttons one by one. Giving him a show. His breathing accelerated the more skin I revealed. Once I had the blouse off completely, I unclipped my bra, and the straps fell from my shoulders. King practically growled at the sight of my breasts and reached forward to cup them.

"Perfect," he whispered. "You're perfect."

Flickering my tongue and taking him in deep, I watched as King's eyelids fluttered closed while an agonised expression crossed his face. "Jesus Christ, you're good at this." His hips moved, matching my pace. Then he grew still as he came, warm liquid filling my mouth. I swallowed. His gaze turned fierce as he pulled me to my feet and spun me around, pressing my body flat into the wall. His hands were purposeful, authoritative, turning the tables from a moment ago. Now he was the one in control. A few quick movements, and my skirt was pushed up around my hips, my knickers pulled down, and his cock was inside me, hard and unforgiving. I was both flattered and impressed that he could get it up again so soon, and tried not to be too noisy while he pounded into me, making me forget my senses.

I felt owned, and I loved it. Loved him. God, it scared me, but I couldn't lie to myself. I felt so much for him, so, so much.

His hand around my stomach brought me back to my senses as he held me possessively.

Gillian was probably back from her coffee break by now. I could just imagine her sitting at her desk, typing away, totally oblivious to what was going on inside King's office. I swear it was almost like my mind summoned her when I heard a knock on the outer door. King didn't stop fucking me, his hand coming around to cover my mouth and muffle my whimpers. My heart rate picked up, panic setting in.

"Mr King?" Gillian called. Her voice was way too close.

King sounded completely normal, not at all breathless as he answered, "Yes, Gillian?"

Oh, my God, I could have killed him in that moment if I hadn't been so lost to him, my body grateful that he wasn't stopping while my brain screamed, *Cease this madness right now!*

Gillian sounded awkward, probably because she thought King was using the toilet. I wondered what she'd think if she knew what he was really doing.

"I have a couple of messages for you. I'll leave them on your desk."

"Thank you. I'll be out shortly."

How on earth did he manage to stay so calm? Sweat coated my brow, anxiety flooding my system. King's mouth went to my shoulder, playfully biting. I bit at his hand, which was still plastered to my mouth, and he let out a quiet, satisfied chuckle. The bastard was enjoying this. I heard Gillian's heels tapping on the floor as she made to leave. Relief flooded me for only a moment, until she stopped.

"Mr King, you haven't seen Alexis, have you? She's missing from her desk."

"I sent her out on an errand," King replied smoothly. "She won't be long."

After this she continued out of the room, closing the door with a click. Relieved air escaped me. King's hand left my mouth, trailing down my body and between my legs.

"I'm going to fucking kill you," I ground out.

He chuckled again. "No, you're not. I'll make you come, and then you'll like me too much to kill me."

"Not likely."

"Is that a challenge?"

I didn't reply. Couldn't. His cock was hitting all my sweet spots, and I no longer felt the urge to reprimand him. I kind of hated that he was right. He found my clit and started to rub, and I wasn't sure I could take it. The feel of him inside me and his skilled fingers working my clit was too much. I was going to come so soon. Too soon. I wanted to give him hell for playing with fire like that, fucking me while Gillian was right outside, but I couldn't summon the willpower. Everything felt too good.

"I can feel you squeezing me," he growled. "Do you like that?"

"Yes," I sighed.

"Will you come?"

"Yes," I repeated.

"You're beautiful," he breathed, and at the same moment I shattered under his hand. He groaned and continued to fuck me while I orgasmed, drawing out each and every wave until he was coming, too. I'd never felt so possessed, so owned, in my entire life. King filled me up, and it was only at that moment I realised we'd been so gone for each other that we didn't even remember protection. We hadn't used it before in the limo, either, so it wasn't a huge deal. Still, having unprotected sex with him felt closer than anything else. I wanted to tell him how I felt, but I was scared. I was usually a person who voiced what they were thinking, but not in this instance. My apprehension of the small chance that he might not return my feelings kept them locked inside, waiting for a rare moment of bravery.

King wrapped his arms around me from behind, his body melding to mine as he breathed into my skin.

"I…." he began, but faltered.

"Oliver?" I whispered.

"I can't stop thinking about you, love. Even with everything that's going on, I can't stop."

"I think of you, too. All the time."

His lips traced my ear. "What are we doing?"

"I think…." I paused, losing courage. *Come on, bravery, don't fail me now.* "Oliver," I started over and turned in his hold, bringing my arms up around his neck, my eyes searching his. "I think we might be falling for each other."

His throat moved as he swallowed, and his hand came up to cup my jaw. His eyes were so fierce right then, so full of words unspoken, that I found it difficult to breathe. Every tiny hair on my body stood on end, and his thumb stroked at my throat, sending shudders skittering through me. Then his mouth came to mine, his tongue sliding in deep, and I shut my eyes. He wasn't speaking, but he didn't need to. His kiss told me how he felt. Told me more than words could convey.

***

It took a bit of sneakiness to get me out of King's office without Gillian seeing. After we'd both cleaned ourselves up, King went out and asked if she could go to the kiosk outside and grab him a coffee. She hopped up immediately, thankfully providing me with the opportunity to escape.

That evening King changed our plans slightly, and I was a little disappointed. I wanted more one-on-one time with him, but his mum wasn't doing so well, so he decided we'd spend the evening at her house and he'd cook us dinner there.

I'd changed out of my work clothes, which were rumpled after our bathroom encounter. And yes, Gillian had been eyeing me suspiciously all evening. I think she knew something was up; she just didn't know what exactly it was. I sent King a message that read,

I think Detective Gillian might be on to us. No more office shenanigans. I mean it.

Right after I sent it, I heard him chuckle loudly from inside. He didn't reply, but his laughter said it all. I wanted to be annoyed, but I just couldn't seem to manage it. A smile shaped my lips. That man made me so happy inside it was almost frightening.

Anyway, I sat in King's mother's living room in a loose cotton dress and cosy knitted socks as the smell of roast beef wafted in from the kitchen. There was the tinkling of utensils and pots and pans as King cooked in the next room. Somebody had cleaned the place up a little, too. I knew it had to have been King, since Elaine wouldn't allow any workers into the house. It touched me to imagine him cleaning; I guess because it was so at odds with the boss I knew.

Elaine sat beside me in clean pyjamas, a photo album from King's childhood in her lap as she showed me his baby pictures. Unlike some people, who were awkward or ugly as children before growing into their looks, King had always been gorgeous. He was one of those little boys who you could look at and just know they were going to be a heartthrob when they got older. The only difference was that when he was little, his hair was snowy white. He looked almost Scandinavian. Then, as the years progressed, it got darker, became more golden than white.

About a half-hour went by, and I could tell Elaine was enjoying herself. She was remembering a simpler time before King's father began insinuating himself into their lives.

"Mum, would you like to eat at the table or in the living room?" King asked, standing in the doorway and watching us. There was something in his eyes that gave me pause; it was contentment, an affection for both of us. I liked how it made me feel all warm and fuzzy inside, like I was truly a part of his life now even if certain things were still up in the air.

Elaine glanced at me, a twinkle in her eye. It was so nice to see her relaxed and comfortable, such a contrast to the terrified, panic-stricken woman I'd encountered on our arrival back from Rome.

"Let's be uncivilised and have it in here," she suggested with a sheepish grin.

"Hear, hear," I agreed. "TV dinners are the best."

King shook his head, smiling, then went back into the kitchen. Five minutes later he returned, handing each of us a plate with roast beef, sautéed vegetables, mashed potato, and the most delectable gravy I'd ever tasted. He placed two glasses of wine on the coffee table for us, then went to sit on an armchair with his own plate. I noticed he was drinking wine, too. It was quite a large glass, but I chose not to comment on it. Obviously, the evening wasn't total domestic bliss for him. He still had his father on his mind.

We'd just finished eating when King's phone began ringing. Standing up, he stepped out of the room to answer it. I could hear him speaking, but his words were muffled. In the end, he returned to the living room, a sort of relief etched on his features…but there was also a hint of strain. His eyes came to mine, and his voice was light and airy when he spoke, disbelieving almost.

"That was Lee Cross. He said Bruce has agreed to back off. He's going to leave us alone."

Elaine gasped, her hand going to her mouth as her eyes grew wet with tears, though they were obviously happy ones. I stood and walked to King, giving him a tight hug and pressing a quick kiss to his lips. The moment I let go, he went to his mum, scooping her up into his arms and squeezing her tight. Their embrace lasted a long time. It was full of relief, years of worry and stress being let out all at once. I thought maybe I should give them a moment alone, but then King pulled back, his eyes on his mother.

"Come on, let's get you to bed. Maybe tonight you'll sleep soundly for once."

Elaine nodded and bid me goodnight before King led her from the room. I sat back down on the couch, picked up my wine, and knocked back the last of its contents. By the time King returned, I felt tired. I was relieved, yes, but there was also a knot of apprehension in my gut.

I knew this had all been my idea, but there was something about it that felt too easy. I didn't for a second think Lee was conning us. He might have been a criminal, but he was an honourable one. Yes, there was such a thing as honour amongst thieves. Besides, I'd seen enough dodgy characters during my years of bar work to recognise a good though slightly tarnished egg when I saw one. Still, something just didn't sit right with me, and I hated feeling like that. Like there were invisible loose ends we weren't quite grasping.

King returned to the living room and dropped down onto the couch beside me. He didn't say a word, but he didn't have to. I could sense his relief was short-lived, just like mine had been. He'd been putting on a brave face for his mum, trying to give her some semblance of peace, even if it might have been misleading.

He stretched his body out on the couch and pulled me to his chest so that my head was resting on his sternum. The silence continued as neither one of us spoke. I pressed my ear to his skin, listening to the steady beat of his heart. It was reassuring, amid the uncertainty, to have his strong body so alive next to mine. To know one beat would be followed by the next.

His hand started to stroke my hair, my bare arm, my shoulder blades. I closed my eyes, enjoying his touch.

"What you said today at the office, did you mean it?" King murmured, his voice almost hesitant.

His question gave me pause as I lifted his my head to meet his eyes. "What I said?"

"About us falling for each other," King whispered. "Do you believe it?"

"I don't need to believe it," I replied fervently before taking his hand and placing it over my chest. "I feel it."

King sucked in a breath, eyes flickering back and forth between mine. His voice was barely audible when he said, "I feel it, too, Alexis."

My heart stuttered, and a smile spread its way across my mouth. "Well, then, Oliver, that's all we need to know."

And then I kissed him.

***

Several weeks passed by. King began taking me on dates. The rest of the time we were both rushed off our feet, only stealing brief moments together. Some nights King came to stay at my place, and then others I went to his. I preferred going to his. It meant I didn't have to worry about scarring my best friend for life with our sex noises.

What was most surprising was the phone calls I'd started to get with job offers. Not for secretarial work, but for modelling. The shots from Bradley's shoot had been published in a popular fashion magazine, and I'd caught the attention of several agencies. I didn't want to give up working for King, but still, I thought it was a bit of good luck. I had a couple of shoots booked for the coming weeks, and, depending on how profitable it became, maybe I could quit my job as his assistant.

After all, I wanted to be his girlfriend far more than I wanted to be his assistant, and there was only so much sneaking around I could handle. Plus, Gillian was right on the cusp of discovering the truth. The other day she'd walked in on me standing by King's desk as he ran his hand up the outside of my thigh. He'd explained it away by saying he'd spotted a spider on my skirt.

And yes, it might have been the most obvious lie ever told. Amen.

It was a mildly sunny morning when I made my way to the newsagents to collect King's papers. I thought Arnold, the shopkeeper who I was now on first-name terms with, was acting a bit weird, but I didn't pay it too much attention. I picked up the papers and said my goodbyes before returning to the office. It was only when I reached the entrance to Johnson-Pearse that I noticed the swarms of journalists outside. They hadn't been there when I'd first arrived, but I'd gotten in earlier than usual. There must have been some sort of story going on. Perhaps the economy was taking another nosedive.

As I struggled my way past the crowd, I heard lots of chatter but couldn't make out enough details. In the end I tugged a youngish guy holding a camera aside and asked him what the deal was.

"Do you work here?" he asked excitedly.

"Yeah, but I'm only an assistant. What's with all the journos?"

His excitement seemed to deflate when he heard I wasn't anybody important. "One of the directors at the bank has been accused of illegal insider trading. It's all over the papers," he said, and nodded to the stack I held under my arm. My heart almost stopped beating, and I walked past him in a daze. As soon as I'd scanned my ID and made it by reception, I found a bench and set the papers down. There on the front page of the very first one was all I needed to know.

It showed a picture of King, which looked to be taken at some function a couple of months ago. He wore a suit and an aloof expression while the photo was being captured. The slant to his mouth made him seem cruel and uncaring, which I thought was probably the intention. The article read:

Oliver King, head managing director at Johnson-Pearse Bank, has been accused of insider trading after an investigation into the financial institution's public and private accounts. The claims were brought forward by an ex-employee of the bank, who wishes to remain anonymous. This individual is said to have left their job after discovering the unethical practices of the managing director. Mr King is the son of classical pianist Elaine King, who left the public eye over a decade ago after a long and successful career on the international stage....

And on the article went. I felt like I was going to throw up as I comprehended what was happening. I was on autopilot when I left the newspapers sitting there and hurried for the elevator. There were a number of other people inside, but I barely noticed them as I hit the button for my floor. Moments later, the door pinged open and I was out, almost running as I made my way to King's office. I saw Gillian first. She sat at her desk, her expression as pale as a ghost, and I knew she'd heard the news.

"Where is he?" I asked, breathless.

Her worried eyes came to mine before she nodded to the closed door of King's office. It was a rare moment that Gillian was lost for words, and this was one of them. Grasping the handle I turned the knob and stepped inside. King stood by the window, his hands buried in his hair as he stared out at the view. On his desk was an empty bottle of whiskey, his favourite tipple.

"Oliver," I whispered, and he turned, eyes bloodshot and face contorted in misery.

"Leave me," he said, his voice pained.

I took three steps. "No. We both know this story is bullshit. It's Bruce. I'm sure of it. He's orchestrated all of this, planted the evidence."

"Of course it's fucking Bruce!" King cried, startling me. "How naïve were we to think he'd back off? Men like Bruce don't back off — it's not how they're drawn. By backing off, he might as well be admitting he's a dead man. It's weakness, you see. I don't know why I ever allowed myself to believe otherwise."

All at once, the guilt hit me. Blackmailing Bruce had been my idea. Therefore, what was happening right now was my fault. Tears filled my eyes as the strength fled my body.

"I'm sorry," I whispered.

King's eyes came to mine, so blue, so beautiful, so sad. He shook his head, seeming to read my thoughts from my expression alone. "No, Alexis. Don't even think it. All of this was going to happen eventually. Bruce has always despised me for not being like him, for making it my life's mission to never be like him. He was always going to try to destroy me. It was only a matter of time."

"But King, I…."

In a few short strides he was in front of me, his fingers going to my lips to stop me from continuing. "I said no, my darling. No. You're one of the best things that's ever happened to me. Just by breathing, you make all this a million times more bearable. I've lost the respect of my peers, of everyone I know. I've lost." He paused, choking up, his posture projecting his misery. His hands fisted, his jaw clenched tight. "I've lost everything I worked years to build. The pride I held, the respect I commanded from others, it's all gone. I'm no longer the best at what I do, no longer surpassing anybody, because everybody thinks I got where I am by cheating."

"But you didn't cheat. You know it. I know it. Your mother knows it. We're the only ones who matter."

All the breath left him at once. "Oh, Alexis," he said, his voice the saddest I'd ever heard it. "You don't understand. If I don't have respect, I have nothing. I might even go to prison for this."

In that second, the whole world went still. My heart shattered into a thousand tiny pieces, and my legs almost buckled out from under me. I'd been so preoccupied with what Bruce had done to shame King that I hadn't even thought about the consequences. Insider trading was illegal, and breaking the law meant prison time. I stared at him, mouth open, despair filling me up, when there was a knock on the door.

We both turned our heads, expecting Gillian, but somebody else stepped inside. It was the strange woman I'd seen just once before. The one with the dyed red hair who looked like a gypsy.

"Oliver," she began, but he interrupted her.

"Get out! I don't want to see you!" King fumed, stepping by me to face the woman.

"But I can help," she insisted.

"You can't. You never have. All you've ever wanted from me was money. When I look at you, all I see is him, so leave. Leave before I have security come and physically remove you." The last part of what he said was dark, seething, and the woman's face grew frightened.

"Okay, I'm going. Just remember, I'm here if you ever need someone. I'm here, Oliver. All you have to do is come find me."

And with that, she went. I wiped the tears from my face. "Who was that?"

"Nobody."

"King."

"I said it was nobody," he shouted, and I stilled. Deathly quiet filled the room until his phone started to ring. I thought he was going to ignore it, but then he saw his mum's name on the screen. He picked it up and held it to his ear. The room was quiet and the volume was loud, so even though I was a foot away, I could hear the voice on the other end, and that voice didn't belong to King's mother. It was a deep, scratchy, seedy London accent, and my chest seized as I guessed who it belonged to.

King's entire form turned to stone as he listened.

"'Ello, son," said Bruce, layers of cruel satisfaction lacing his voice.

"What are you doing with my mother's phone?" King demanded, a tremor in his words.

"Thought you could fuck me over, you little shit. Me and your mum are just having some quality time now. You know, reminiscing. I was hoping you could come and join us."

A feminine cry rang out, and then an audible slap. Bruce's voice moved away from the phone. "Stop crying, or I'll give you something to cry about. You knew what he was doing, didn't you, you stupid bitch. The both of you tried to fuck me. Well, now you're gonna learn that no one fucks with me and gets away with it."

"If you harm her," King began, voice low and angry, but he couldn't seem to hide his emotion. His sheer panic

211

was evident, and I knew Bruce was enjoying it. "If you touch a single hair on her head, I will kill you. You think you've won, but you haven't. I have nothing left to lose now, Bruce. *Nothing*."

Cruel laughter sounded from the phone, and in a split second, King smashed it into the wall, the screen cracking to pieces. He grabbed his coat and fled the office. I ran after him, begging him to wait, but he wouldn't listen. I followed him to the back exit of the building where no journalists were waiting, and before I knew it, we were in a taxi headed for Elaine's house. I tried to hold King's hand, but he wouldn't let me touch him.

The air between us felt cold and I scrambled to try to think of something that would calm him down. Stop him from doing anything stupid. The journey was too short, and before I knew it, King was throwing money at the driver and running to his mum's. The front door, which I knew King had new locks put on after Bruce's last break-in, had definitely been meddled with. The door was closed, but the lock was bent out of shape. King pushed it open, and we both hurried inside. A tall, broad-shouldered man stood waiting in the hallway. He folded his arms over his chest and shot King a confident smirk.

He was obviously muscle for Bruce. He also appeared to think he could easily take King. That's why it surprised us both when King walked right up and elbowed him hard in the side of the face. I heard bone crack, and the man stumbled into a wall with a pained grunt. Then King brought his foot down on the guy's shin. The brute let out a strangled cry, but both of us were already gone, rushing to find Elaine.

The house was silent, which somehow felt more frightening than if she were crying out in terror like we'd

212

heard her on the phone. We entered the kitchen to find an older man standing by the sink, casually using a dishcloth to wipe the blood from his hands. He looked to be in his seventies, his hair almost completely gone. His face was lined with deep wrinkles, and there was a scar that ran just above his right eyebrow. He looked fit for his age, his build stocky, the only sign of weakness a little bit of pudge around his middle.

His eyes came to King, and his gaze narrowed. He wasn't laughing anymore. There was a coldness about him that chilled my bones.

"You're too late," was all he said. Dead voice. Dead eyes. Black heart. I knew all this within seconds of looking at him.

King was still, so still, and he wasn't looking at his father. It confused me at first, but then I followed his gaze to the floor. Time ceased to exist. There on the expensive stone tiles lay Elaine. She wore her favourite peach pyjamas – her favourite peach pyjamas, which were drenched in blood. She wasn't moving, wasn't breathing, but I refused to accept she was dead. She looked so…small.

No.

No.

No.

I didn't even realise I was shaking my head until King dove for his father, his hands going around the older man's throat. I couldn't hear over the sound of my heart thundering in my ears. Couldn't move. So I stood there, frozen in shock, as King started to beat his father to a pulp. Bruce lay in a couple of punches, but he was old, and his strength was no match for King's. I was about to scream when I saw him pull a gun, but King was quicker, knocking it from his father's hand and sending it sliding across the floor. He drove a final punch into Bruce's skull, and the man fell limply to the tiles. The heavy thud was an awful sound, and I thought I heard bone crack once more. A deep, all-encompassing shudder ran through my body. King's chest rose and fell rapidly as he stared down at his father's lifeless form.

I remained frozen, not understanding how this was happening.

"No, no, no, no, no," he began to mutter, running his palms down his face as he shook his head. "What have I done? What have I done?" King repeated his words over and over, his entire form shaking.

He went to his mother and dropped to his knees, pulling her into his embrace. "No, Mum, wake up. *Wake up.*"

Tears filled my eyes and ran down my face. This was all too much. Too much. This couldn't be happening. I didn't know what to do. What could I do? Should I call the police? Should I not call the police? I felt like calling Lee, but I wasn't sure I should be involving anyone else in this situation.

King's father had just killed his mother.

And King had killed his father.

It was a Greek tragedy come to life, and I felt like I'd suddenly stepped out of reality and into a dream. I'd woken up this morning to the sun shining. It had been just another ordinary day, but not anymore. I wanted to rewind the clock so I could erase it all. But that wasn't possible. King was crying now, holding his mother to his chest and just letting the tears flow. The sounds of his weeping filled the room. A cold sweat covered my skin, and my heart was thrumming a mile a minute. My hands were shaking. I took a few steps forward until I was beside him, and dropped to my knees. He didn't even register my presence until I put a hand on his shoulder.

He stopped crying.

Silence filled the room.

He turned his head.

He stared at me in horror and realisation that I'd been a witness to everything that had just happened. His face contorted, and so many emotions flickered past I could barely count them. Shame. Pain. Loss. Fear. More shame. So much fucking shame I could barely breathe with it. He reared away from my touch like it had burned him, his mother's body slipping from his arms as he stood, backing away.

"King," I said, a crack in my voice. "Oliver."

He began to shake his head, his eyes huge with fear as he took in the scene. And then he was gone. It took me a moment to get to my feet and run after him. I dashed from the kitchen, down the hall, and to the front entryway, where Bruce's muscle still lay crouched on the floor in pain. I ran outside, looked up and down the street, but he was nowhere to be seen.

I returned to the house, searching each room to make sure he wasn't still inside. The place was empty. I walked back down to the kitchen, my gut recoiling at the sight of Bruce and Elaine's bodies and all that blood. I'd never get it out of my mind, would never be able to wash my memories clean. I had to do something, had to act. I saw the phone on the wall and knew calling the police was the right action. King beating his father was self-defence. He wasn't in his right mind. Bruce Mitchell was a criminal. Bruce was the one with the gun, the one who killed Elaine. Any jury in the country would be able to see that.

I walked to the phone, picked it up, and started to dial nine-nine-nine. I was on the final nine when I heard a weak cough and looked to my left. My heart soared when I saw Elaine's eyes flutter open and her chest move up and down with her breathing.

She was alive!

There was so much blood I wasn't sure how it could be possible, but it was. I hit the final nine on the dialling pad.

"Nine-nine-nine emergency services, how may I help you?"

"I need an ambulance," I croaked out. "I need an ambulance right away."

Part Two
After

Sixteen

London, six years later.

My hands were shaking.

All I was doing was holding a piece of paper, and my bloody hands were shaking. I was standing by the open window, trying to get some air, but it wasn't working. I felt woozy. I had to sit down. I'd already read the letter three times. So I read it again.

Dear Alexis,

I hope you don't think my letter intrusive, but I found you through the agency you run and some of your past modelling work. My name is Lille Baker, and I'm an artist. I work in a travelling circus, the Circus Spektakulär. We perform all over, but right now we've stopped to do some shows in London.

I've wanted to send you this letter for weeks, but I held out. I had to wait until we were close enough for you to come. You're probably wondering why I didn't just email you. Or call. Letters are sort of a lost art form now, right? But what I have to tell you is of such great importance that I felt an email would be too impersonal. A call too abrupt.

I apologise. I'm going off topic. So yes, the circus.

It's run by a woman named Marina Mitchell. Perhaps you've heard of her? Anyway, Marina has a brother. His name is King, Oliver King. He stays with her most of the time; other times, he wanders on his own. I suppose you could say he doesn't really have a home. King carries around a picture of you, Alexis. It was taken six years ago on a beach in Rome. Do you remember? He treasures this picture, goes crazy if anyone tries to take it.

Why is the picture so important to him?

Did you love each other once?

218

Do you ever think of him, wonder about him?

I'm sorry. I ask a lot of questions sometimes. It's just that I worry for King. He's been on a destructive path for years, and I fear that if something drastic doesn't happen soon, he's going to kill himself. He drinks far too much, more and more each day, it seems. I try to help him, we all do, but there's no point trying to help a person who doesn't want it. Then I think, if you came, if he could see you, then maybe he would want to be helped. Maybe he'd have something to live for. I see glimpses in him, Alexis, glimpses of a fascinating mind, of a great man from whom circumstance has stolen everything.

Please come and see us. I think you're the only one who has a chance of saving him.

Yours sincerely,

Lille.

Tears filled my eyes again as my heart pounded. King. He was alive. For so long I'd lost hope. I hadn't seen him since that night at his mum's house, where he'd fled after he thought he killed his father. He hadn't killed him. The paramedics managed to revive Bruce, and just a few short weeks later, he was sent to prison for the attempted murder of Elaine. It was a hard time for all of us, especially since King had all but become a ghost. We searched high and low, spoke with everyone he'd ever known, but he'd vanished without a trace. I even quizzed Elaine about the gypsy woman, but she had no clue who I was talking about. She was the one missing link, and I knew deep in my heart that if I could just discover who she was, I would find him.

Now I held a letter in my hands that explained everything.

On the other side of it was an inner city location where the circus was currently camped for shows. It was no more than a car journey away, and my skin prickled to think he was so near. Was this real, or was someone playing a trick?

No, it had to be real. No one other than Bruce would think to do something so cruel, and he'd died in prison six months after he was put there, shanked by a young guy who didn't want him coming in and taking over. I thought it was a fitting death.

Bruce Mitchell.

Marina Mitchell.

King had a sister. How had I not known this? How had Elaine not known? A memory of the gypsy woman King once said was family flashed in my mind again. This Marina must have been his half-sister, born of Bruce and a different mother. That's why Elaine didn't know her. But why the hell would King be living with someone who had anything to do with that monster? It was all too much to take in, too confusing. I leaned back in my chair, trying to make sense of it.

After he'd disappeared, I'd gone through all the five stages of grief: denial, anger, bargaining, depression, and then finally acceptance. Now each of those stages were rushing back all at once, becoming a strange muddle of hope and anger, happiness and fear.

I'd finally settled into my life. How could a single letter flip everything on its axis?

Four years ago, I'd stopped modelling and started up my own agency. It did so well that I'd finally saved up enough money for a mortgage, and had purchased a small two-bedroom house in Waltham Forest. Elaine, who I'd grown close to over the years, sold her big house in Bloomsbury that held too many bad memories, and bought herself a small cottage in Waltham in order to be close to us.

Us.

The very thought made my tears increase. Life had been so hard since King disappeared. For a long time, I couldn't move on. My heart refused to believe he'd stay away of his own volition, but at the same time I understood the trauma he must have been suffering to think he'd killed a man with his own bare hands. Now I was being told he was out there, close enough for me to reach. To touch. To pull close.

And yet, here I was living in my little house with the love of my life. The one who'd come along after King and mended my broken heart.

I heard him pull on the doorknob and step into the room, probably wondering why I was upset, why I was crying. I wiped at my tears and tried to plaster on a brave face, not wanting to worry him.

"Mummy," he asked, "what's wrong?"

My boy was so beautiful, so like his father with his pale blond hair and blue eyes. I didn't even realise I was pregnant for a long time after King vanished. I'd put it all down to heart sickness. Yeah, I thought I was vomiting my guts up every morning because of how much I missed him. I soon came to realise that wasn't the case. Apparently, the pill isn't always one hundred percent effective.

But still, some small part of me was grateful. My love had disappeared, but he'd left something of himself behind. Nevertheless, I was depressed for much of my pregnancy. Karla and my parents were worried sick. Elaine, too. She wanted a grandchild so badly. And then, my Oliver came along, and I fell in love again.

My strength returned. I needed to live for the little one who needed me. So I put my all into my career, began modelling as much as I could. Elaine helped out with money until I was doing well enough to go it alone. I think the combination of Oliver's birth and Bruce's death changed something in her. She started going outside more, becoming independent. She even played piano every once in a while. She was often sad, as she grieved for her missing son, but she was no longer the shell of a woman she once was.

Even though I'd accepted the fact that he was gone, I grieved, too. Every day. For King.

I think it was the fact that we had so little time together that made it worse. I had all these possibilities to wonder about. What might our lives have been if certain events hadn't come to pass? It's different from losing your love at eighty after a lifetime together. The pain is so much sharper, more cutting. It guts you to the core, because you'd once held perfection in your hands, only to have it drift away like mist. You have to go on knowing you'll never feel how he made you feel ever again, knowing no one else will ever compare.

I had to go to him. And yet, I hesitated.

The words in Lille's letter frightened me. What would I find at the circus? What sort of man? Summoning some strength, I knew I still had to go. For him. For our son. For my heart.

I pulled Oliver up onto my lap and gave him a soft squeeze. "I was just thinking of a sad story, that's all."

"Why do you think about sad stories?" he asked, curious, fingers going to my damp face.

"Because sometimes my brain makes me," I answered, and his hands travelled to my forehead, giving it a poke.

"Brain, stop making Mummy sad." His words made me laugh. In just a couple of months he was going to turn six. The time was flying by so fast. Sometimes he'd ask about his dad, ask if he had one, because all the other boys at school did. I told him that his daddy was far, far away. I hated the sad tilt to Oliver's mouth afterwards and wished I could have come up with a better answer.

It felt unnatural to see him sad, because he was such a happy, gregarious child. He was never shy or insecure, always open to the world and the possibilities each day might bring. He made friends easily, too. The teacher of his Montessori class said he was always the one bringing the kids together, making suggestions for new games they might play.

I let him off my lap and went into the kitchen to prepare lunch. It was Saturday, my day off. Usually, either Elaine or my mum took Oliver when I was working, but I always had him on weekends. If I asked one of them to babysit tonight, they'd want to know why, and I didn't want to explain Lille Baker's letter yet, not to anyone. I especially didn't want to tell Elaine in case it wasn't real. Getting her hopes up would be too cruel.

After I'd made Oliver his food, I went and called Karla. We were still as close as ever, even though we no longer lived together. We didn't get to see each other as much as we used to, but we spoke on the phone almost every day. Having been my rock when Oliver was a baby, she loved my boy just as much as I did, and I knew she'd jump at the chance to have him for an evening. In fact, she'd be so happy she wouldn't think to ask questions.

Not asking questions was key.

I gave her a quick call, and she said she'd be over in a couple of hours. With that sorted, I tried to play with Oliver for a while, but my heart wasn't in it. I couldn't focus. Slotting a DVD into the player, I settled him in front of the TV so I could go shower. I was nervous. I'd gotten out and was wrapped in a towel when I began to shiver. My stomach twisted and turned. I hadn't been able to eat a bite since morning. My throat was clogged with nerves and hope, annihilating my appetite.

I stared into my closet with no clue what to wear. My fashion sense, if anything, had only become more distinct over the years. When you work in the industry, you tend to become a little obsessed with the latest trends. My hands were shaking again as I pulled out a pretty lace top and some skinny jeans. I paired them with some leather boots and allowed my hair to dry curly.

My heart thrummed.

I couldn't believe I was doing this. He was out there, alive and breathing. For a brief second, it took all my willpower not to rush out of the house right away and go find him.

Shakily swiping on some lip gloss, I gave my appearance one last glance before I heard Karla knocking on the front door. I hurried down to answer it and found I was wrong about her not asking questions.

"You look nice. Going anywhere exciting?"

I rummaged in my bag for my car keys. "Just meeting up with Bradley and his new boyfriend for some drinks. I should only be a couple of hours."

"Ah, right, well, have a good time." Her brows knitted together, which was usually a sign that she thought I was lying. I didn't know why she'd suspect anything, because my story seemed airtight. It was only as I slid into the driver's seat that I realised my mistake. If I was going for drinks with Bradley, then why the fuck would I be driving? I swear, this whole thing was turning my brain to jelly. My mind wouldn't stop racing, and I just wanted to get to the circus and see King with my own two eyes. Prove to myself this was real.

Hope flooded my veins, filling me with anticipation.

I could have him back. We could have him back for good.

It took forever to find a parking spot close enough to the circus, and in the end I had to leave my car a ten-minute walk away. It was seven-thirty, and the tent was all lit up for the night's show. People queued up outside to buy tickets, and I didn't know where to go. Should I buy a ticket? Should I ask around after this Lille person? I'd brought the letter in my purse, as though I'd need to show definitive proof before they'd let me see him.

Unsure of what else to do, I got in line and bought a ticket. I walked alongside a couple of young women as I went into the tent and took a seat close to the back. My skin prickled with awareness. My body hummed. King was here somewhere. It was almost like he'd shown up on my internal radar, sending everything into a fritz.

There were about another twenty minutes before the show would begin, and I was too antsy to just sit there. Standing, I made way down the aisle to an open doorway that led backstage. The place was a flurry of activity as I stepped through. A middle-aged woman wearing some kind of glitzy stage outfit passed me by.

"Excuse me," I said, and she turned to face me. "I'm looking for Lille Baker."

The woman smiled. "She should be out front at the face-painting booth."

A tall, dark-haired man who had seemingly overheard my question stopped, arching a curious brow. "You're looking for Lille?" he said. His voice was deep, his accent Irish.

I stared up at him, a little intimidated, if I was being honest. He had dark shoulder-length hair, and wore jeans, boots, and a wife-beater vest. His body was a fucking masterpiece of muscle and sinew, and it was a little much for me to take in all at once. I hadn't been with a man in a long, long time, and he was one of the hottest male specimens I'd ever seen. He must have been a part of the show. These types always were. Finally, I nodded.

"Who are you…." He paused for second, trailing off, as something like recognition lit up his eyes. He looked like he knew me, which made me feel weird. Running a hand over his stubbled jaw, he swore under his breath. "Fucking hell, Lille."

"You know Lille?" I questioned breathlessly, my heart rate picking up as I stepped closer.

"Yeah, I know her." He nodded to the back of the tent. "Come with me."

Instead of leading me out to the front, like the woman had instructed, he led me in the opposite direction. We exited the tent and he stopped, pulling out a smoke and lighting up. He side-eyed me, not saying a word.

"Um…." I began, feeling nervous. He might have been sex on a stick, but he was also scary and intimidating. These days I was used to hanging around my clients (who were all women) and my little boy. Men were an area I was completely out of practice with. Of course, I had my brothers, but I didn't see them very often.

"How did you know to come here?" he asked.

Anxious, I fumbled in my bag. "I got this letter."

Now he was swearing again. "For fuck's sake."

I frowned. "What?"

He seemed apologetic. "I'm sorry. My girlfriend likes to meddle. You shouldn't have come."

"You're Lille's boyfriend?"

He nodded. "Uh-huh."

My voice grew so quiet it was practically a whisper. "Do you...do you know King?"

His eyes went sad, like he felt sorry for me. Something thick and heavy lodged in my throat. Was I too late? Had his self-destructive path reached its end? The thought took the strength right out of me. I was about to ask him what had happened when another man exited the tent. He was tall, too, but with shorter hair and a smarter dress sense. He was also very handsome, and I wondered just how many drop-dead gorgeous men just so happened to be hanging around this circus.

"What's happening, bro?" he said. American. It was becoming hard to keep up with all the accents. Before the first man, whose name I still didn't know, could answer, the American's eyes wandered to me. He took me in quickly, shrewdly, and seemed to immediately recognise who I was. It didn't take him a few minutes like it had the first man. And his reaction to me was a whole lot different, too. A wide, almost giddy smile spread across his lips.

"Holy shit! It's you," he said with a gasp, and came to put his hands on my shoulders, squeezing them as he beamed down at me. "I can't believe you're here."

Okay, now I was confused. "Uh, me neither?"

"I'm Jay," he went on. "The grumpy one's Jack. He's my brother. Crappity crap, you're real, Alexis. You're a living, breathing woman. For a while there we thought you might be a ghost."

"Hold up a sec," Jack, the grumpy one, interrupted. "Don't fucking tell me you were in on this, too?"

Jay rolled his eyes and grinned. "Of course I was."

"And Matilda?" Jack asked.

"Nah, it was just me and your woman. We were kinda sneaky about it."

"This isn't a joke, Jay. This is serious. King isn't...."

"King will be fine," Jay intoned meaningfully, turning his head to his brother before looking back at me. "Once he sees his beautiful Alexis, he'll be doing fucking cartwheels."

"No, he won't."

"He will."

"He won't."

Seriously, I was going to get whiplash going back and forth between these two. I interrupted loudly, hands on hips. "Will one of you just bring me to him?" I stated, my voice on the shaky side.

Jay's face went serious. "Yeah, sorry, come with me."

"I'm going to find Lille," Jack muttered before stomping off. He sounded like he had a serious bone to pick with her, and I didn't fancy being Lille right then.

I tugged on Jay's shirt sleeve and he stopped walking to face me. "What's wrong, darlin?"

I bit on my lip, emotion filling my lungs and my eyes growing watery. "How is he?"

"Ah, shit, babe, don't cry," he said, and stepped forward, startling me when he pulled me into a hug. I'd been alone for so long, lonely, and this stranger hugging me just made things worse. His kindness was more than I could handle as I let him embrace me. It felt good to have a man close, to smell one, clean and warm. I couldn't have anticipated the emotional effect it would have on me.

He began rubbing the centre of my back soothingly, and I tried my best to blink away my tears. I stood back, shaking my head. "I'm sorry. It's just that I've been searching for him for years. This is all a little much right now."

Jay's brows drew together in empathy as he let out a gruff breath and placed his hands on his hips. He stared at the ground before meeting my gaze. "Look, I'm not gonna lie. He's in a bad way. Lille didn't exactly say it explicitly in her letter, but fuck, your man's got a serious drink problem. I'm gonna take you to him, you're gonna see him, but he sure as hell isn't gonna be the same as you knew him. You need to prepare yourself for that, Alexis, okay?"

I inhaled, and even though his words were a grave warning, there was something reassuring about them. "Okay."

Jay nodded, satisfied. "Good. Now, this isn't going to be easy, but I think that if he sees you, if he knows you still exist, then we can all work together to pull him back from the brink. You'll be the catalyst. You'll be the goal for him. I mean, if he knows he can have you back, then I think he'll even do all the hard work himself." A pause as he eyed me. "He *can* have you back, right?"

Without thinking, I nodded. Then I simply stared at him, absorbing everything he'd just said. A silence fell between us. Memories bombarded me, all the things that King had been through in his life.

Jay's voice was a soft whisper, his eyes flittering over me, studying me like I was a book and he was straining to see the words. "Jesus, Alexis, what the fuck happened to him?"

My face went sad. "So much and too fast. I have a feeling he still doesn't know that he didn't do what he thinks he did."

"What does he think he did?"

I wasn't sure what it was about this guy, but he had a way of pulling all the information right out of me. My voice was a whisper when I replied, "He thinks he killed someone."

Jay absorbed this quickly, his posture stoic. "But he didn't?"

"No, he didn't. He should have. If anyone deserved to kill that bastard, it was King, but he didn't."

"Christ."

"Jay."

"Yes?"

"Take me to him. Please."

"Okay, darlin', okay. Come on," he said, and threw his arm protectively around my shoulders. He led me farther from the circus tent and towards a cluster of mobile homes camped out nearby. In the centre of them was a large open-air gazebo with tables, chairs, and a few gas cookers. There were a couple of people milling about, but not many. My eyes scanned the space frantically, desperate for a glimpse of King. Jay stopped walking, and so did I.

That's when I saw him.

He was so changed, I wasn't even sure how I recognised him, but I did. My heart would know him anywhere, in any guise. He sat on a bench, his body slumped over the table, his fingers clasped around a bottle of liquor. His hair was long and dirty, his face heavily shrouded by a beard. He wore filthy, unkempt clothing, a grey jacket with a woollen jumper beneath, worn jeans and muddy boots.

I couldn't believe this was the same man who once sat in his office overlooking the Thames, a ruler of his own universe, the best at whatever he set his mind to. Now he was reduced to a homeless drunkard, completely

230

unrecognisable. I really didn't understand how the world worked sometimes.

At thirty-three, he'd been at the top.

Now thirty-nine, almost forty, he was at the bottom.

And yet, his very presence still made my heart pound, still made my lungs fill up with too much air. He was alive. He was breathing. And I didn't care what form he took, so long as I could have him back. My legs gave out, but Jay steadied me. I couldn't take my eyes off King, and he didn't even know I was there.

A small commotion sounded from nearby, and I turned to see a tall blonde woman come running up to us. She was followed closely by Jack and another woman, a short brunette. She stopped in front of us, hands going to her hips as she tried to catch her breath. Her beautiful grey eyes danced as she took me in.

"You're here," she breathed. "I can't believe you came."

I stared at her, taken aback, but I knew instantly that this had to be Lille. She confirmed my assumption when she threw her hand out and introduced herself. "I'm Lille, the one who wrote you the letter."

Slowly, I reached forward and shook her hand, feeling shy and out of place. "I'm Alexis."

She nodded, smiling, and replied loudly, "Yes, I know." She was clearly excited.

"Quiet the fuck down," a broody, scratchy voice demanded from nearby, and every hair on my body stood on end. His voice, so changed, yet so the same. I couldn't help closing my eyes, blinking away another tear. I'd turned my back to him when I shook hands with Lille, and now I heard hard boots crunching on the ground. I turned back around as he neared. His blue eyes, once so bright and sparkling, were now dull and reddened.

I sucked in a breath.

He stopped in his tracks.

Time slowed down, the world became as small as a grain of sand, as we stared at one another. It was a moment I'd never forget. The bottle he'd been clutching like a life raft fell from his grip. The harsh sound of glass shattering shot through me, making this all so real. King didn't even notice he'd dropped the bottle. He reached up, rubbing at his eyes to the point that it looked painful.

"Stop it, stop it, stop showing me. I don't want to see her anymore. No more."

He was hurting himself, and I couldn't watch. I stepped forward, my voice lighter than air. "Oliver," I whispered. I stood mere inches away, the smell of him hitting me. He stank of booze and dirt. My heart cracked in two. It was a physical pain to see him like this.

"No!" he screamed, hands flying out and pushing at me. I stumbled backwards but managed to find my feet before I fell. Grumpy Jack strode forward, his size formidable, and gripped King by the shoulders. "Calm down, friend, calm down." His words seemed to soothe something in King, whose body slumped forward. Jack's eyes wandered to his girlfriend, who stood frozen in place.

"I told you, I fucking told you, Lille."

"I'm sorry, I didn't think…."

"That's just it, you didn't think at all," Jack fumed, eyes now flashing accusingly at his brother. "Neither one of you did." There was something in the way he spoke that made me feel like this was personal to him, like he was truly angered that Jay and Lille had brought me here to King, who clearly wasn't in a fit state to see me. Again, my tears came. I felt like my heart, my very soul, was being torn in two. I didn't want him to be like this. I just wanted the old King back.

Now I wasn't sure if that was even possible. Then, all of a sudden, the anger hit me. How could he let himself become like this? How could he leave me for all these years and never once try to make contact? There had to be a reason, but I just wasn't seeing it. Perhaps it was the tears filling my eyes that caused my blindness.

Jack led King away, and I stared after my love, a lump in my throat and a brick in my stomach. Nothing about this was okay.

Nothing.

Seventeen

I cried all the way home, thankful it was dark and no other drivers could see me wailing like a crazy person in the front seat. After Jack had taken King away, I'd spoken with Lille and Jay for a while, and the brunette, Matilda, who turned out to be Jay's wife. They were all so kind and apologetic, pleading with me to come back in a day or so. They promised they'd do their best to clean King up, get him sober. I nodded vacantly, but all the while the image of him in his current state branded itself into my mind. I didn't know how to feel. Should I be angry? Sad? Happy to have him back even if he wasn't the same?

I thought it might be wise to give him space for a while, but I knew it was going to be impossible to stay away. I was already concocting plans, figuring out ways in which I might bring him back to his old self. Even though it had taken years, finding him had been the easy part. Healing him would be the greatest challenge I'd ever faced.

I decided not to tell anyone about our son yet, but I'd let King know that Elaine was alive as soon as I could. I thought that would ease his mind somewhat, give him hope. I also needed to tell him that he hadn't been the one to kill Bruce. He needed to know.

When I arrived home, I sat in the car for a few minutes, trying to compose myself. It was pointless, though, because Karla was going to know something was up the second she saw me.

The house was quiet when I stepped inside and dropped my keys on the end table. The TV was on low, and Karla sat on the couch, scrolling through the messages on her phone.

"Hey," I said quietly.

She turned to me and looked up, her eyes taking me in. "Hey, you're back."

"Yeah, how was he?"

"Well-behaved but chatty, as usual," she told me with a soft smile that quickly faded. "Lexie, is everything okay?"

I couldn't help it — I sniffled. She was up from her seat and taking me into her arms within seconds, holding me close. My words were tiny, barely audible, when I whispered, "I found him."

Karla sucked in a shocked breath and pulled back to look down at me. Several emotions crossed her face, mostly surprise. "King? You found King?"

I nodded.

"Where is he?"

"Not far, but Karla, he's changed, so changed. I'm not even sure if...." My voice broke and was replaced with sobs. Karla pulled me close again.

"Hey, hey, it's all right. You'll get through this, you have me. I'll do everything I can to help."

Her words soothed me a little, and even though I'd been there for her through some really tough times over the past few years, I felt embarrassed that I was crying. After a minute I pulled away and went to grab a tissue to dry my face.

"Can you take Oliver again tomorrow?"

Karla nodded. "Of course. Anything you need."

A few minutes later she left, and I climbed the stairs for bed, knowing I probably wouldn't sleep a wink. I ducked my head inside Oliver's room and found him sleeping soundly, his light breathing filling the space. I loved him just as much as I loved his father, but I'd only managed to keep one of them safe.

The thought almost broke me.

Closing the door over gently, I went to my own room and crawled into bed. I closed my eyes, but, as predicted, sleep never came. I finally drifted off after hours of racing thoughts, and was woken up the next morning by my son poking at me.

"I'm hungry," he complained. I'm not sure why, but there was just something about his cranky, entitled little face that made me laugh amid all the sadness. I sat up and pulled him to me, pressing a soft kiss to his head and cuddling him close. He giggled, and I lifted him up with me, tickling him under the arms and making him wriggle like crazy.

"Stop it!" he yelped in glee. His words instantly sobered me, and I set him down on the floor. They echoed what King had said last night, when he'd thought I was some spectre concocted by his mind just to torture him. Remembering, I led Oliver downstairs and began absentmindedly pulling out pots and pans to make breakfast. I let him help me put the bread in the toaster. He loved to help. Then he sat and watched as I cracked some eggs, stirred them up, and poured them into the pan to make an omelette.

"Are you sad again, Mummy?" he asked.

I wasn't sure if he was particularly tuned in to people's emotions, or if he was just good at reading me because we spent so much time together, but he always seemed to sense how I was feeling. I mustered a smile for him.

"No, I'm not sad, baby, just tired."

"After breakfast we can bring all our blankets downstairs and watch *The Lego Movie*," he suggested, like it was a sure fire way to cheer me up.

"I have to go somewhere today," I told him regretfully. "But your Aunt Karla is coming again to mind you. Maybe she'll want to watch it."

He scrunched up his nose. "But she always sings the song. I like Aunt Karla, but I don't like it when she sings the song."

His response surprised a laugh out of me, because it was true — Karla didn't have a note in her head.

"Okay, maybe I'll tell her not to sing during the movie. How does that sound?"

He looked appeased, replying fervently, "Yes, *please* tell her that."

After we ate I made quick work of bathing and dressing him, then did the same for myself. I put on some dark green skinnies, a yellow blouse, and ballet flats. I had an idea to get King to interact with me, but it was going to be a long shot. I planned to bring my chessboard to the circus and see if he'd play. We didn't have to talk at all, but if I could at least get him to play, it'd be a start.

Karla arrived and I was off, driving back into the city again. I'd exchanged numbers with both Jay and Lille the previous night, so I tapped out a text to them saying I was on my way. It was almost lunchtime, but I wasn't sure if the circus did daytime shows or just nighttime ones. Anyhow, I hoped it was quiet so I could find a decent parking space. A couple of minutes before I arrived, I received a text from Jay, telling me he'd meet me at the front of the tent.

I parked close by, got out, hitched my bag up on my shoulder (it was heavy because of the chessboard and all the pieces), and made my way to the entrance. When I got there I almost stumbled over my own feet, because standing beside Jay was the gypsy woman, Marina. King's half-sister. She'd hardly changed at all since I'd last seen her, and when she looked at me, her eyes held a mix of warmth and wariness.

"Hello, love," she said in greeting as she held her hand out. "I'm Marina. This is my circus."

"You're King's sister," I replied, not knowing what else to say.

She nodded, those wise old eyes of her eyes blinking slowly. A small capuchin monkey sat on her shoulder, which I would have found odd if she didn't own a circus. I could just imagine Oliver's excitement if he were here. Whenever I'd taken him to the London Zoo, he'd always gone apeshit for the monkeys – no pun intended.

"So Bruce Mitchell was your father?" I went on.

"That's right, though I'd say by blood only. That man was never much of a parent." Her voice was hard when she spoke of him, and I instantly knew she must have had just as much of an awful time with Bruce as King did. Perhaps that's how they bonded. Also, she used the past tense, so I presumed she knew he was dead, but did she know that King hadn't been the one to kill him?

"King didn't kill him, you know that, right?" I blurted.

Her eyes widened as she shook her head. "I didn't, but I do now. Young Jason here informed me." My attention wandered to Jay, and I remembered how I'd told him last night, how he had a knack for pulling information out of me. "Though honestly," Marina continued, "even if he had killed him, I wouldn't have blamed him. Bruce was a despicable human being."

For a second I was taken aback by the harshness of her words, the stark honesty in them. A silence fell between us, and I began to feel self-conscious as she studied me. What she said next almost knocked the wind out of my sails.

"You're a mother," she stated.

I sucked in a breath. "What?" How the hell could she know that?

She nodded to my hand, where there was a Disney-themed Band-Aid wrapped around my thumb. I'd cut it chopping vegetables the other day and hadn't had any other brand in the house. Embarrassed for some reason, I hid my hand behind my back. Marina gave me a soft smile.

"How many do you have?"

"Just one," I answered.

"What age?"

I didn't want to tell her, but I had no other choice. "Almost six."

She gasped, her face growing serious as she mentally added up the years. "King's?"

I nodded. She looked away, frowning. Beside her, Jay swore under his breath.

"You can't tell him," I pleaded. "Not yet. It's too early. I saw how he was last night. He's so vulnerable. If you put this on him, he'll freak."

"Alexis, nobody's gonna tell him," Jay reassured me. "It's your story to tell."

Something in his voice, in the way he spoke, calmed me. I shot him a grateful look. "Thank you."

"Come with us," said Marina, composing herself. "King spent the night in my camper. Jack washed him and gave him some clean clothes. He hasn't had a drop to drink since yesterday, so he's sober, but he's shaky, taciturn. He's not going to be in the best mood, love. It's the withdrawals — they make him sick because his system is used to having alcohol. Just know that if he's cruel or mean, it's not because of you or how he feels about you. It's because he's in physical pain." Her kindness surprised

239

me, because up until now I couldn't quite tell whether or not she was happy to have me there. Now I knew she was; she just worried how my presence was going to affect her brother. "Jack told him you were coming, so he knows. He hasn't said much, but I can see the change in him. I can tell he wants to see you."

Her words gave me hope. We came to one of the larger mobile homes, and that's when I saw him for the second time in so many years. There was a table and two deck chairs set up outside the van. King sat in one of the chairs, a half-finished cup of tea in front of him and what looked to be a bowl of porridge. I instantly noticed the changes from last night. His long golden hair had been washed, and hung over one shoulder. In a way, it was beautiful. He still had the beard, but it was clean. He wore clean clothes, too, a navy work shirt and dark jeans. I stood there, watching as he used a shaky hand to lift the spoon and bring some porridge to his mouth. It looked like he had difficulty swallowing, and it was a hard thing to witness.

His build was the same as before, but a little more filled out, less wiry and athletic. Don't get me wrong, he wasn't fat, just thicker around the neck and shoulders, as seemed to happen when men neared forty. His face had aged somewhat, but I thought that had more to do with the drinking than the years that had passed.

He must have sensed he had an audience, because he glanced up, and I swear air caught in my lungs the moment his eyes landed on me. He got up abruptly from the table, the deck chair falling to the ground behind him. My skin prickled with awareness when he started to move forward, my heart pounding fast the closer he came. His chest bumped mine softly, his eyes glittering in the sunlight just like they used to. I could hardly breathe as his hands rose to my face. His fingers started at my temples, then began to move slowly down to my cheeks. I swallowed harshly, my chest fluttering with butterflies to have him touching me. His fingers were callused, yet so tender, so gentle. I felt like I was holding still and allowing a wild animal to suss me out, realise I wasn't a threat.

His fingers came to my jaw, and I remained standing there, as still as a statue, my breathing intensifying the longer his inspection continued. His gaze was intent on me, so intense, and I found it difficult to meet his eyes. Finally, I lifted them and they locked with his. His fingers were at my throat now. It was a vulnerable spot, sensitive. His fingers dug in a little, and air whooshed right out of me. Uncomfortably, I became aware of my arousal. He smelled clean, like soap, and he was the only man I'd ever loved. My body was programmed to respond to his, no matter the circumstance. My nipples hardened, a long untended-to ache lingering between my thighs.

He was still touching me, his fingers exploring the rise and dip of my collarbone. I could feel that his hands were shaking and remembered what Marina had said about the withdrawals. I soaked him in, confused by how he felt so weak and yet so vital at the same time.

I saw his throat move as he swallowed before muttering a timid, "Hello."

It broke my heart.

"Hi," I whispered back.

I heard Marina speaking close by, but could hardly concentrate on what she said. "We'll give you both some privacy. Alexis, if you need anything just call Jay's phone, okay?"

"Okay," I replied softly, not taking my eyes off King. They left, and his body leaned closer until I could feel that he was hard inside his pants, just the barest touch against the lower part of my stomach. I must have made some small sound of surprise, because his eyelids began to flutter nervously and he looked away, pulling back. He seemed embarrassed and ashamed.

"I'm sorry, I...."

I put a hand on his shoulder. "Hey, it's okay."

"It's not," he grunted, and turned, stalking back to the deck chair and picking it up off the ground. He sat and grabbed the cup, downing the rest of its contents quickly. Letting my bag fall from my shoulder, I approached the table and took the empty seat. King watched my every move warily as I opened my bag and began to remove the chessboard. I didn't say anything, because everything seemed to have been going fine until we spoke. Sometimes words just overcomplicated things.

Memories flashed in his eyes when he saw what I had. I saw a kaleidoscope of images too, all of our private little games together. I opened up the board so that it lay flat on the table, then began to pull out the pieces. They were made of solid wood, so they were heavy, but they were quality. I'd bought the set just recently, having planned to start teaching Oliver how to play.

Oliver.

How on earth was I going to tell King he had a son? The prospect sent a sharp pang through my chest. He'd missed out on so much, and he didn't even know the half of it yet. *Slowly,* I reminded myself. I needed to take this one step at a time.

King's eyes didn't leave me, his gaze focused on my hands as I set up the game. Picking up a pawn, I opened the play. He watched me, and a silence followed. It seemed to go on forever, and I wasn't sure if he was going to join me.

Then, almost shyly, he leaned forward and made a move of his own. My heart leapt. It was such a tiny thing, and yet the fact that he was playing meant the world to me.

We sat in quiet for a long while. I kept taking surreptitious glances at him to make sure he was still engaged. Concentrating on the game seemed to be doing him good. His hands were still shaky, of course, but that couldn't be helped. I hated that he was in pain and there was nothing I could do to ease it. We were silent for so long that I startled when he spoke, staring at the board as though calculating his next move.

"How did you find me?" he asked, voice low.

"Lille," I answered simply, and his jaw seemed to tighten.

"That girl never stops. Bloody do-gooder."

"I'm glad of it. I searched for you for years."

He scratched at his beard and frowned, still not looking at me. "Why would you do that?" He seemed genuinely perplexed.

"Because I...." My words fell off, my throat clogging with emotion. I wanted to say it was because I loved him, but even when we were together, we'd never really told one another properly. We both knew; we just never said it. For some reason, I couldn't say it now, either. I felt like it might scare him off. "Because I care a great deal for you, Oliver."

He let out a long, pained breath. "You saw what I did."

I didn't speak, just waited.

"You saw what I did, and you still care for me. How is that possible?"

Disbelief coloured his every word. In an instant, I could see him that little bit clearer. He'd been so ashamed of what I'd seen him do that he thought he'd destroyed

243

himself in my eyes. He'd thought that any future we might have had together was destroyed, too. It had all happened years ago, and yet, I could see that he was still traumatised. It had simply morphed into something else, something ugly. Self-hate.

"King," I said, frustration building at how he wouldn't give me his eyes. "King, would you look at me?"

He lifted his head, and wow, every time he levelled me with his stare, I felt breathless. He was still so beautiful, even changed. "What happened that day, it didn't turn out how you think. You should have called me, made contact."

His chair legs scraped at the ground as he shifted in place, agitated. When he spoke, his words were stilted and gruff. "What do you mean, it didn't turn out how I think?"

I reached forward and took his hand in mine, but he pulled away sharply from my touch. "I mean that you never killed Bruce. He survived. He was sent to prison and was killed by another inmate. Your mother survived, too. She gained consciousness right after you fled."

The air all around us seemed to still as I comprehended the stupidity of just blurting all that out. King stood angrily, shaking his head in disbelief as he pushed up violently from the table, almost knocking over the board. "No," he said harshly. "*No.*"

Fuck. I was bombarding him with too much too quickly. What the hell was I thinking? King turned and stalked away, his gait slightly unsteady, like he might collapse at any moment. I wasn't sure if it was from the withdrawals or the shock of what I'd just told him. I ran after him and caught his arm. He reared back from my touch, so I threw my body in front of his. He stopped walking, barely an inch between us.

"I'm sorry," I said, breathless. "I shouldn't have told you all that. Not yet. You're not ready."

"I'm not an invalid," he hissed.

"I know that."

"Well, then, don't fucking treat me like one," he ground out, his voice choking up as his eyes grew watery with tears. He tried blinking them away, but it was no use. Agony marked his every feature.

"I'm sorry," I whispered.

His emotion didn't surprise me so much as it made me feel about two inches tall. How bloody tactless could I be? I watched his face, seeing all the realisations fall on him like a tonne of bricks. I knew exactly what he was thinking about. He was imagining all the time he'd lost because he thought he was a murderer. He'd hidden himself away, drinking himself half to death, thinking the only other option was prison. If only he'd reached out, gotten in touch. But no, he'd been too lost, too buried under a mountain of alcohol and guilt. I could see that I was losing him, and I couldn't let it happen. I couldn't let him get lost in regrets and what-ifs.

"Come back and play with me, please. We don't have to talk, just play," I said, desperate.

His face grew intense, and my skin prickled.

"No. You should go," he said irritably, moving away from me.

I stepped forward, closing the distance between us once more, and stared at him openly, not hiding any of the vulnerability I felt inside. "Please, King," I whispered.

A shudder went through him as I said his name, and we stood there, locked in a staring contest that felt like it might never end. After a long time, his distress seemed to die down as he realised I wasn't going to give up and leave.

Finally, he ground out, "Fine. Let's play, then."

Relief flooded me. I gestured for him to lead the way back. He turned. I followed him until we were at the table, sitting down to continue our game. It was mid-July, and the weather was warm. It was a bit too hot for a jacket, so I shrugged out of mine and hung it over the back of my chair. A couple of the buttons on my blouse had come undone, revealing the edge of my black lacy bra. I hurried to button it back up, feeling his attention on me. If anything, my boobs had gotten slightly bigger over the years, probably because I'd put on a few pounds after I had Oliver. King wore no expression, but his eyes practically scorched me, and I was already too hot from the sun. I was a little glad, though. At least this way he might be thinking of something other than how fucked up the past was.

We continued playing in silence, but I could feel his need now like a physical touch. I wasn't sure which one of us was more desperate for human comfort, him or me. Perhaps we were on an equal footing. However, I knew that, unlike me, King didn't want to acknowledge he felt it.

I was winning the game, which was out of the ordinary, because he always used to win more than I did. I glanced at him to see his brow was furrowed and his upper lip was sweaty. Without even thinking, I knew he was in pain. His head must have been thumping with alcohol withdrawals, not to mention the ugly truth of everything I'd just told him.

"Is this Marina's camper?" I asked, hesitantly gesturing to the van. He nodded. "Shall we go inside? It's getting too hot out here. I need some shade."

Without a word, King stood and opened the door to the camper van. He stepped back and let me go in first. By the décor, you could tell the place belonged to an older woman.

The couch was made of a flower print material, and there were doilies on the coffee table and old-fashioned ornaments everywhere. The moment King closed the door behind us, I regretted suggesting coming in here. It felt too small, too close. But I knew the sun was taking its toll on him, and he looked like he needed to lie down.

"Is it okay if I get a glass of water?" I asked.

King shrugged.

"Would you like one?"

Another shrug. If the way he was sweating was anything to go by, though, he must have been thirsty. I filled two glasses and walked over to where he was sitting on the couch before handing him one. He took it and downed a long gulp. There was nowhere else to sit, so I took the place beside him, a few inches between us.

"Alexis, do you...do you know how my mother is, where she is?" he asked, and he sounded so vulnerable right then it made my heart squeeze.

"Yes, of course," I hurried to answer. "She lives close to me now. I have a house in Waltham Forest. Your mum sold her place in Bloomsbury and bought a small cottage nearby. We grew close after what happened, became friends. You should see her these days, King. She goes out for walks all by herself, shops for her own groceries, she even...." I caught myself just in time. I'd been about to tell him, *She even takes care of Oliver when I'm working.* I needed to be better at censoring myself around him, at least for a while.

When I looked at him, he seemed conflicted, yet hopeful. The world suddenly wasn't as shrouded in black clouds as he'd thought. "So she's doing well, doing better?"

247

"She had a lot of help, Oliver. Me and my parents, we sort of took her in after…I mean, she still misses you every day, mourns for you, wonders where you are. We both do…we both did."

He went quiet, like he was dealing with some kind of inner turmoil. I cleared my throat and did my best to change the subject. "I started my own business a couple of years ago. It's a plus-size modelling agency. Only a small one, but it's doing well so far. I have a tiny two-room office space in Finsbury Park," I said, a little self-deprecatingly. "It was like, I saw how all these agencies worked and kept thinking to myself, *I can do this with my eyes closed.* And I always remembered you telling me I could do anything, go anywhere, that I had the ability. Your faith in me was where my confidence to go it alone came from."

I could see that my words meant a lot to him. "Thank you," he murmured. "Thank you for saying that."

"Thank you for showing me I could be more than just an East End barmaid," I said with a tiny smile, feeling more emotional all of a sudden. "If I hadn't met you, I'm not sure I ever would have gotten out of that shithole tower block."

"You would have." He stared at the glass in his hands, now empty.

"Want another?" I asked, gesturing to it.

He didn't answer, just handed it to me.

I went to the sink to refill it, then walked back to the couch. King had grown even paler, and he looked like he might want to get sick. He also seemed uncomfortable, like he didn't want me there to witness it. I set the glass down on the table and picked up my bag, making a show of looking at my watch.

"Well, I have a few errands to run while I'm in the city, but I'd like to come back later, if it's all right with you?" I said quietly.

It took him a second to respond as he swallowed thickly. "Yes, yes, it's all right."

"Good," I said, feeling awkward. "I'll see you later, then."

He didn't reply, only nodded. I hitched my bag up on my shoulder and made my way out of the camper. The sun beat down on me, making me feel a little woozy. I walked out of the circus and down a side street to where I'd parked my car. Once I was safely inside, I let my head fall back and exhaled. I hated this. I hated that I had to leave him there to suffer all alone, but I didn't want him to feel weak in front of me. I knew he'd be humiliated if I saw him being sick.

Once I'd calmed down, I picked up my phone and dialled the house. Karla answered after a couple of rings, and I spent a few minutes talking to her, asking how Oliver was doing. She was good at not prying into how my day had been, and that's what I needed right then. I needed to not talk about King, because if I did, I'd just end up having another crying jag.

We hung up, and I got out of the car. Taking a walk to a nearby café, I got something to eat, barely even noticing what I ordered since my mind was so elsewhere. I sat outside for a long time, nursing a lukewarm cup of coffee and wondering how on earth this was all going to pan out. I'd been gone about three hours when I finally made my way back to the circus. I went to Marina's camper first, but there was no one there, so I headed in the direction of the gazebo from last night. There were a whole bunch of people milling about, some eating meals, some chatting.

I spotted Jay, Jack, Matilda, and Lille at a table having dinner, and King was sitting by the end of it, drinking a beer. The sight of him with alcohol did a number on me, and my heart somersaulted in my chest. Why on earth were they letting him drink?

Eighteen

I took a few steps forward until I was standing by the table. It was Jack who spotted me first, and he must have seen where my eyes were trained, as he started to explain gruffly, "He can't go cold turkey. It'll kill him. The beer is light, good for weaning him off the hard stuff."

"Oh," I whispered, suddenly understanding.

"Yeah, remember what happened to that Amy Winehouse?" Matilda piped in. "Such a sad story."

There was an empty stool beside King, but I hovered, unsure if I was welcome. I locked eyes with Jay, and he shot me a look that said, *Stop being an idiot and sit.* So I walked around the table and sat. I could feel that King was aware of my presence, but he didn't say anything. Didn't look. I wondered what he was thinking, wondered if he was still coming to terms with everything I'd told him earlier. Tendrils of unspoken words hung between us. The others chatted a little, but an awkward atmosphere had descended upon the group, and I knew it was down to my arrival. That was why I did what I often did and tried to fill the silence with my own chatter, faking that I was comfortable when really I was the exact opposite.

"So, is there going to be a show tonight?" I asked, forcing a casual tone. "I'm sorry, I haven't even asked what you all do here yet."

"Don't be silly," said Lille, her voice gentle. "You've had so much else to think about." I caught her grimace slightly after she said it, like she thought she might have been a little clumsy with her words. I didn't mind. Not at all. I much preferred clumsy words to silence.

"Well," Jay began explaining, "Jack and I are both performers. I do illusions, and Jack's a fire-breather." He waggled his brows and flashed me a grin. "Real dangerous, like." Jack rolled his eyes at his brother and took a bite of his chicken. "Lille paints faces for the kiddos, and Matilda here designs the show costumes." He slung an arm around his wife's shoulder.

"Well, I'm only really starting out," Matilda added shyly. "I've designed stuff for Jay for a while, so some of the acts are letting me try my hand at creating some designs for them, too."

"Oh, that's cool. I work in the industry myself. Well, not in design, but I run a small modelling agency."

Matilda's eyes lit up with interest. "Yes, that's right. Lille told me."

We chatted for a while about fashion, but the whole time I never really felt at ease. I could sense King watching me intently. I didn't have the courage to look at him. His fingers were clasped tight around his beer bottle, and I wondered if he felt weird about me being there, trying to fit in with all these strangers who seemed to know him so much better than I did. Well, they knew the man he was now better than I did anyway.

My participation in the conversation died away as I became more and more aware of his attention and presence.

"Hey, Watson, did you get around to mending that shirt for tonight? I need it for the second part of my act," Jay asked his wife.

"Yep," Matilda replied. "It's all done. I left it in the closet for you."

"Good, I don't wanna go giving the ladies in the audience another eyeful," he said, and shot me a playful smile. "Last night I was doing a costume-change skit, and I had a wardrobe malfunction. Cheeky slip of the nip doesn't even cover it."

252

"You definitely gave Janet Jackson a run for her money," Matilda put in, chuckling.

I laughed and knew Jay had sensed my unease when he sent me a warm expression. That's why he'd made the joke. I was grateful to him. Lille laughed, too, while Jack smirked and seemed to be supressing another eye roll. I chanced a surreptitious glance at King to find he wasn't smiling at all. It made my skin prickle. Maybe he didn't want me there. The thought jolted me, and I suddenly wanted to flee. I picked my bag up off the floor and slung it over my shoulder.

"Well, it's getting late. I should probably be going. Maybe I could come visit again tomorrow?" The insecurity in my voice was palpable, and I hated how it sounded.

The second I made a move to stand, King's hand clamped on my wrist. It shocked me, since he'd barely registered my presence, and now he was touching me. The feel of his skin on mine sent a tremor through me, and I looked down at him, seeing a hint of desperation in his eyes. "Don't go yet," he said, voice low and pleading.

All of a sudden I realised what had really been going on. He wanted me there; he was just embarrassed and ashamed of how he was, of how I had to leave so quickly earlier so that I wouldn't witness him throwing up.

I lowered myself back onto the stool, and he let go of my wrist. "Okay, I can stay for another while," I said quietly.

My eyes remained on King as Lille announced, "We should all start getting ready for tonight's show. It was great seeing you again, Alexis."

I nodded to her, smiling, and everybody rose from the table to leave. A few moments later it was just King and me, sitting alone while the circus workers chattered and ate around us. My pores tingled as I felt King's close attention, his warmth right next to me. All it would take was for me to reach out a few centimetres, and I'd be touching him again. But I didn't do that because he was still wary, still feral in a way.

"Does my mother know you've found me?" he asked, a vulnerability in his voice.

My eyes softened as I whispered, "Not yet," then spoke a little louder as I cleared my throat. "Do you want me to tell her?"

Some kind of turmoil passed over his features, and he shook his head fervently. "No. I...I don't want her to see me. Not like this."

And there it was again, the shame. I hated it so much.

Out of instinct, I reached forward and tried to take his hand in mine, but he flinched away. *He's feral, Alexis, try to remember.* I had to keep reminding myself to treat him with care, like he was a wild animal not used to touch. It was hard, because I was so tactile these days, especially at home with Oliver. We were always cuddling or play fighting, or just generally goofing around.

"I have to tell her eventually," I said gently.

He just stared at me then, and it was too much. I had to look away.

"Am I so awful to you now?" he asked with chagrin.

Immediately, I brought my gaze back his. "Never. You've always been beautiful to me." I let my eyes wander over his features, older, kind of distinguished. His mane of golden hair and his full beard. No, he wasn't awful at all. In fact, he might have been more beautiful now that he was flawed, more human. He seemed to grimace in something close to discomfort, or maybe it was embarrassment. It was obvious he wasn't comfortable with people looking at him.

It was also clear that it had been a long time since anyone had used the word "beautiful" to describe him.

"Why did you never contact me?" I whispered. I thought I knew the answer already, but I wanted to hear him say it.

It took him a long time to speak, and when he did, the ferocity in his voice startled me. "After you saw what I'd done, the violence I was capable of, I thought you wouldn't want me. And I didn't want to know anything about my old life because it wasn't mine anymore. I'd destroyed it with my own two hands. All of that potential, gone in an instant. Mum was dead, and to you I was a killer. There was nothing left for me in that world." He held his hands up as though in pain.

"But what about Marina?" I went on. "Why had she never looked into Bruce or your mother?"

"Marina doesn't live like most people. This circus is her everything. The nomadic lifestyle is what makes her happy. She's never really embraced technology, doesn't use the Internet, doesn't even really read the papers. It's how she lives."

"I don't understand...."

King rubbed a hand over his mouth, like he didn't really want to talk, but was forcing himself for me. So that I wouldn't leave yet. I tried my hardest not to lose the run of my emotions. Every time I looked at him, I didn't know whether I wanted to cry and kiss every inch of him, or shake him in anger for mistreating himself so badly. It was a strange sensation to love somebody so completely yet fiercely hate their actions. His words broke me out of my thoughts.

"Marina was our father's first child, born when he was still a teenager. She bore the brunt of his cruelty because he was in her life more than he'd been in mine. And he was a brutish, violent parent. She wanted to get away from him, and she made it happen by disappearing. The circus was the perfect escape, the perfect way to vanish.

"It was only through the small contact she had with her mother, who was still married to Bruce, that she found out about me and how he'd been blackmailing me. So she got in touch. She wanted to help me because she'd never had a sibling, but also because she knew how awful Bruce's treatment could be. We became friends. She'd visit me whenever she was near London. I even helped her out with money when the circus wasn't doing so well. And then, when I thought I'd" — he stopped, his voice growing strained — "when I thought I'd killed Bruce, when I thought I'd lost everything, this was where I went. If Marina had managed to fashion a life of obscurity here, then maybe I could, too. I neglected to foresee that it didn't matter where I went. My own mind would become a prison."

I sat there, absorbing his words, for some reason feeling like this was the most he'd spoken to anybody in a really long time. I wanted to touch him, but again reminded myself that I shouldn't.

"What do you mean?" I asked, frowning.

He started to cough and it sounded terrible, heavy and wheezing. "The mind becomes a prison as it replays its images, and all you want to do is drown them out. Dull the repetition. Alcohol is such an easy way to do it, to quiet everything down. It becomes a basic need, like water or air. Suddenly, you can barely go an hour without having it in your system."

He rubbed at his eyes and then his temples, as though to soothe an ache. "I feel fucking awful when I don't have it. Right now it's like there are these purple ants on my skin, crawling all over me, and I can feel every single one of them as they *itch*."

I tried not to let my fear show as he expressed what he was feeling out loud. It was so easy to just accept that he was weaning himself off alcohol without thinking of how it felt. I wasn't the one inside his body, having to feel every second of the agony.

"Do you think you can quit completely?" I asked before amending my question. "I mean, do you want to?"

He looked at me then, his eyes full of pain and regret. "I really don't know."

I swallowed, trying not to let his answer hurt me. It would be ridiculous to think that just because I was there, just because I'd found him, that he'd suddenly make a miraculous recovery. That his addiction would simply be forgotten because the woman who loved him had come to find him. Yes, I was upset, angry, even, but I wasn't offended. It was unrealistic to think he could get better in the blink of an eye. I wasn't an angel or a magical princess. I was just a person, and he was just a person, and together we were scrambling in the dark to try to understand each other.

King began to fidget, peeling the label from his now empty beer bottle. I wasn't sure if it was a sign that he was antsy for more or if the conversation was making him irritable. I didn't have it in me to offer to buy him a drink. A subject change was all I could manage.

"Do you know that your apartment is still there? Your mother has been taking care of its upkeep. All of your things are still there, too, and your piano. Have you played…."

"No," King answered abruptly. "I don't play anymore."

257

I nodded, not pushing the matter, but simply told him, "You used to play so beautifully."

"All of those things…they might be there, but they don't feel like mine anymore. You should tell Mum to sell them, sell the penthouse, just, I don't know, get rid of it. I don't deserve any of it."

"Of course you do. You worked your arse off to pay for everything."

"There's no point if no one else believes it."

I didn't get what he was talking about at first, but then it hit me. "You mean Bruce's smear campaign? Oh, Oliver, all of that was exposed years ago. It came out during his trial. Your name has been completely cleared."

His mouth moved in an odd way as he comprehended what I was telling him. He looked distressed, and again I felt like an idiot for so unceremoniously laying the facts on him. I just didn't feel like there was any proper way to do it. No matter how careful or sensitive I was, the truth was going to be a difficult pill to swallow. King rose from his seat, standing in place for a second. I thought he was about to leave, distraught by the news that he'd been cleared of any misconduct. But then he started coughing again and sat down abruptly, his hand going to his chest like he was in serious pain. This time the wheezing sounded even worse, and my stomach tightened with worry.

"When was the last time you saw a doctor?" I asked, concerned. His look was all the answer I needed. He hadn't seen a doctor in years. I was suddenly desperate to take him to the hospital and have him looked over, afraid he might have some awful illness caused by his alcohol abuse. Once his coughing fit died down, I suggested quietly, "You should let me take you."

He shook his head. "I'll be fine."

His abrupt answer rose my hackles, and before I had the chance to censor myself, I told it to him straight. "You used to be the smartest man I knew. So don't give me that."

I expected him to get angry or to fight me, which was why I got a surprise when a pained smile shaped his lips. "You haven't changed a bit, have you?"

I returned his smile, the tiny expression practically lighting me up from the inside out. I wanted to keep that smile, box it up as proof that happiness was still possible for him. "Nah, if anything, I've only gotten better with age."

His intense eyes practically bored a hole in me. "I don't doubt it."

I shivered, and it was clear that he saw. "Cold?"

I shook my head. His eyes heated, and his chest rose and fell slowly as he took a deep breath. "What, then?"

"Just...." I sighed. "Memories."

He raised a questioning brow. I kept staring at him until he finally understood, and then something in his posture shifted. He was less of the sick, vulnerable man and more of the old, confident King I once knew. It was only a glimpse, yet it affected me right down to the tips of my toes. A shudder ran through me, and King shifted closer, gaze alight, his words barely a whisper. "Tell me."

"Do you remember the photo shoot?"

King smiled again, and my heart thudded. *More*, it urged, *I need more of those to place in the sacred box of smiles.* "The one where I figured out you were a dirty little liar? Why, yes, I believe I do."

He was teasing me now, and my stomach did a somersault of glee. I needed to keep this going, keep him from thinking about the pain he was in.

"Well, I was just thinking of you in those jeans and how you didn't even care that you were half-naked in a room full of people. You were so at ease with yourself."

He shrugged and glanced down at the table, then back at me. "Nudity never bothered me."

"I could tell. It was so fucking sexy. I was like, kill me now because there's no way I'm gonna be able to keep pretending I'm a lesbo with this perfect male specimen." I loved the sound of his soft answering chuckle and watched his reaction to my words carefully. I was delighted that they'd had the desired effect. They made him feel complimented, proud, to have once been worthy of female admiration. It meant he could feel that way again. I wanted him to see that there were things worth living for, and sometimes the small things were the best ones. Like when a woman notices you walking down the street, or when someone flirts with you and signals their attraction.

"I had started to become suspicious," King admitted. "The way you looked at me sometimes…."

"What?" I prompted, eager to know what he'd been about to say.

He levelled me with his eyes. "Sometimes you'd look at me like you wanted me."

I grew hot suddenly, and laughed to try to defuse the moment. "Well, your suspicions were spot on."

He turned to face me fully then, his head tilting to the side in curiosity as his gaze drifted down my body acutely. "How long has it been for you?"

His question both surprised and took me off guard. Oh, how he could read me so well, even after all these years. It made my pores tingle to think he'd been paying attention. Yes, I knew exactly what he was asking, but the honest

260

answer embarrassed me. In truth, it had been years since I'd last had sex.

King had been gone for months, disappeared without a trace. I'd just found out I was pregnant and was feeling terribly sorry for myself. Lee was still sniffing around Karla as they played their old *I hate you, but I want to fuck you* head games with each other. We were at a pub one night when the brothers had shown up. I wasn't drinking, of course, but I wasn't in my right mind, either. And when Stu came over and started laying on the moves, I succumbed to them. Admittedly, not my finest hour, but I was lonely and depressed and just wanted to feel the comfort of another human being. That was six years ago, and also the very last time I'd had sex.

I decided immediately that I wasn't going to tell King about that night with Stu, because it would be counterproductive and pointless. However, I also wasn't going to mislead him into believing I'd been with no one since him, either.

"Too many years," I answered finally.

His eyes lingered on my mouth before moving up to meet my gaze. "You're not with anyone now?"

I shook my head. He frowned and asked another question. "Why not?"

I pulled self-consciously at the hem of my blouse. I'd been wearing it all day, and it was starting to feel a bit clammy. "I've just been busy," I answered, then hastened to add, "With the agency, keeping everything running smoothly. You hardly get a moment to yourself when you run your own business." *And have a five-year-old to take care of,* my conscience put in.

King stared at me, and the silence lasted for a long time until I had to break it. "What about you?" I whispered, and now it was his turn to become self-conscious.

"I haven't, I mean…some of the women here, they try with me, but I'm always…I'm never really present enough, you know."

What he said caused my protective instincts to kick into high gear. "They never tried to be with you against your will, did they?"

King's eyes flared at my question, and he hurried to correct me. "God, no."

I let out a sigh of relief. "So you haven't?"

He shook his head, and my heart ached for him. He really had been imprisoned. So alone. It shocked me to realise that I might have preferred for him to have someone. Don't get me wrong, I hated the idea at the same time, because in my heart he belonged to me and no one else. But the fact that he hadn't had any companionship shone a stark light on his suffering. I would have wanted him to have a moment of relief amidst the turmoil, even if it did make me jealous as all hell.

We shared a moment of deep, intense eye contact, and then I heard music begin to play from inside the circus tent. It was a sound check, and light, tinkling piano drifted all around us. King's expression morphed at the very sound of it, and I knew he was remembering how much he used to love playing.

"I told you that Elaine started playing again, didn't I?" King stared at me. I cleared my throat. "Well, not for audiences or anything like that. Just at home. I think it's therapeutic for her. You should think about…."

"I'm not playing the piano again, so please stop pushing."

"I'm only trying to help you," I whispered.

"You are helping me. Just by being here, you're helping. Trust me."

I swallowed. "Okay." A pause. "Will you at least consider seeing a doctor? That cough doesn't sound too pretty, and if left unchecked, it could turn into something nasty." It already sounded like it had turned into something nasty, but I was just so desperate for him to go and get checked out that I'd latch on to any reason.

He stared at the floor. "I told you I didn't want to."

"Yeah, you did," I said, losing my gentle tone. "And do you know what else that tells me? It tells me that you don't care about yourself enough to worry that you might be badly sick, and that is the scariest fucking thing, Oliver. The scariest."

He let out a dark, miserable laugh. "Look at me, Alexis. Everything about me should tell you that."

Now I grew upset, my voice shaky with unshed tears. "But I want you to care."

I saw his self-hatred wriggle its way into his expression. It was awful to look at, so ugly. I wanted to kill it dead, but it had been corrupting him for years. You didn't kill corruption like that in a day. What he believed to be true had moulded him to hate himself.

"It's hard to care for something that's already falling apart," he said vehemently.

I stared at him, suddenly pissed off at the way he spoke. "That's a fucking cop-out, and you know it. Just because something's broken doesn't mean it can't be fixed. It's just takes guts, guts and a whole lot of effort. But clearly you don't want to even try." My words were a challenge, and I desperately needed him to stand up to them, counter them. I saw the flash of temper in his eyes and knew what I'd said had riled him.

He leaned forward, his expression sharp and his gaze narrowed. "There's broken, Alexis, and then there's irrevocably broken. Maybe I'm the latter. Maybe trying is futile."

The way he hissed his words made me stand quickly from the table, my stool scraping harshly at the plywood panels that had been set down to create a makeshift floor. "You're not irrevocably broken until you're dead, King. You can try — you just don't want to." My voice quivered as my anger was slowly overtaken by self-pity. "Perhaps you don't think I'm worth it." A single tear fell down my cheek, and King rose from his seat. The hardness in his expression had vanished, and in its place was remorse. He reached out to touch my cheek, and I stepped back.

"Alexis, I...."

"When you speak like that, when you hurt yourself with alcohol, you're being cruel to both of us. You know that, right? Don't think you're the only one suffering here. When I told you I care for you a great deal, I was telling the truth. Every bit of damage you do to your body, you might as well be punching me in the gut at the same time."

My words made him flinch. "That's not true."

"It is true! I know how I feel."

He grew incensed again and pulled at his hair. "Yes, but you don't know how I feel. You don't know how hard this is."

I shook my head at him. "Another fucking cop-out. The Oliver King I used to know never backed away from a challenge. He relished them. Challenges were what he lived for."

Before I could move, he was all up in my space, his face stormy. "But don't you see, I'm not the Oliver King you used to know. For fuck's sake, Alexis, I'm not him anymore."

He was fuming, but so was I. I was about to throw more words back at him when suddenly Jack was there, pulling King away from me.

"What the hell?" he said, looking between the two of us.

All of a sudden, the wind went out of my sails. What on earth was I doing, arguing with King like this? It wasn't going to help. He was sick, and I was putting my own feelings before his illness. In that moment, I felt horribly ashamed.

"I'm sorry," I whispered. "I should...I should probably go."

"Yeah," said Jack. "Maybe that's for the best."

Nineteen

I couldn't go back to the circus the next day. Mostly because I had to work, but also because I was upset and angry at myself for letting things get so out of hand the night before. I needed to have more control, needed to understand that King wasn't going to be completely logical when he was having withdrawals, and there was no sense arguing with an illogical person. It was just so hard not to get emotional. I was upset by how much he devalued himself just because he wasn't the same man he was before. I'd never judged people by their status in life or what job they had. I judged people by who they were as *people*.

Anyhow, I was thankful to have work to focus on to take my mind off things. Elaine had arrived at the house bright and early to watch Oliver, and I'd stood in the doorway, bag over my shoulder, car keys clutched in my hand, as I listened to them chatter. Grandmother and grandson. The strength almost fled me in that moment. I wasn't the only one King needed to be saved for, and it made me that much more determined to see him pull through this.

I'd concocted something of a plan, but it was going to take a bit of trickery. There were always lots of classical shows going on in London at any given time, but by some stroke of luck I'd managed to find a recital of Rachmaninoff's Piano Concerto No. 2 at the Royal Albert Hall. It was the same piece and the same location where he'd last seen his mother play. I thought the significance might bring him back to himself somehow. A step in the right direction. Anyway, the trickery would be needed in getting him there, because I knew if I suggested it outright he'd refuse to go, the same as he refused to see a doctor.

I'd purchased four tickets online, planning to ask Lille and Jack along, too. I could tell that Jack was closest to King; he seemed to have a calming effect on him. This meant that if my plan backfired and King freaked out, I'd have someone there who could calm him down.

Jay had told me that the circus was staying in London for the next three weeks, which gave me time to take things slow. I thought that was key, because forcing stuff to move too fast never worked. So, even though it killed me to do it, I decided to stay away from the circus for a day. I'd return on Tuesday evening after work, but this way I was giving King some space to get his head around everything. I was home from work and eating a bowl of spaghetti for dinner (Oliver's favourite) when I got a text from Jay.

Jay: Where you at? King's been asking.

The text made me want to hop up, throw on some shoes, and go to him immediately, but I had no sitter for Oliver, and it was too late to call Karla or Elaine. Therefore, it would have to wait until tomorrow.

Alexis: I can't make it tonight, but I'll visit tomorrow evening after work. About 6 or 7.

My attention was drawn away from my phone and across the table, as Oliver made a loud slurping noise sucking the spaghetti into his mouth.

"Today I asked Granny Elaine about the flowers," he said randomly. I would have called my son the master of random statements, but I knew that was just all kids. They said whatever they were thinking.

"The flowers?" I asked.

"The ones in her garden. She told me they're called tulips," he said, sounding out the new word.

"Oh, you went for a walk to Granny Elaine's house today?"

Oliver nodded, red spaghetti sauce all over his mouth. Elaine often took him out and about, especially when she was having a good day. If she was having a bad day, and feeling down about King, she usually stayed indoors. I took it as a sign that today had been a good day. I also took it as a sign that maybe I needed to tell her I'd found her son sometime soon.

"Yep. They're yellow with green…."

"Stalks?" I provided, smiling fondly.

"Yellow with green stalks. I asked her if the colours were the same to her as they were to me."

What he said made me smile. I swear my boy was already a little philosopher, thinking about perception in his own particular way. God, and now I was thinking about how I needed to tell King he had a son. Why did all the explaining have to fall on my shoulders, huh? The emotion hit me quite suddenly, but I reminded myself that although it might be a stressful experience at first, I was excited for King to find out about Oliver, to get to know him. I was certain he'd fascinate him just as much as he fascinated me.

"And what did Granny Elaine say?"

"She said the colours were the same for most people, but some people have colour blindness. That means they don't see the colours the same." He paused, his brow crinkling in concentration as he looked at me. "I have blue eyes and Granny has blue eyes. Is that why we see the same? You have brown eyes, Mummy. Does that mean you see different?"

"No, Oliver, that's not how it works."

He frowned, confused that his logic wasn't making sense, so I tried to explain it to him. "It doesn't matter what colour our eyes are — it's our brains that tell our eyes what colour we're looking at. So our eyes have three message receivers in them. One for red light, one for blue light, and one for green light. We see colour through the light. These receivers see the light and send a message to our brains, and then our brains interpret the message to tell us what colour it is." I tried to explain it to him simply, insofar as I could. "However, some people have a defect in one of their message receivers, which means they see the light wrong and send the wrong message to the brain. That makes them colour blind."

Oliver seemed worried now. "I don't want to have a defect in my receiver."

His statement caused me to let out a soft laugh. "You don't have a defect."

He rose up by levelling his hands on the table, totally distressed. "But how do you know?!"

Oh, my God, I honestly couldn't take how cute it was when he got stressed out about stuff, like it was a matter of life and death. "Well, actually, I don't. We'd have to test you."

I twisted some spaghetti around my fork, concentrating on my food again.

"What are you waiting for? I want you to test me now, Mummy."

I gave him my stern look. "I will, but first you have to finish eating your dinner." He wasn't happy with my answer, but he settled back in his seat nonetheless and finished his food. I had to go look up a colour blindness test online and do it with him afterwards. When he got the result that he wasn't colour blind, he literally jumped for joy, throwing his small arms around my neck and squeezing.

"Oh, Mummy, I'm so glad I'm not colour blind. I don't want a dog."

I laughed harder this time, realising what had caused him so much distress. He thought he'd have to get a Seeing Eye dog if he was colour blind. Seriously, sometimes he was too cute to handle.

"All those poor blind people. Not getting to see the colours," he went on, his words striking a chord in me. King used to see the colours, but he didn't anymore. The world was all in grey. I needed to teach him how to see them again.

"Yeah, baby," I whispered. "All those poor people."

***

The next day after I closed up the office, I drove straight to the circus. I lied and told Elaine I'd be home late because I had a business dinner. She accepted my explanation without question, which made me feel even worse for lying. It was a necessary evil, though. For now.

The same as the first night, I couldn't find a decent parking space because lots of people were arriving for the show. I spotted Lille out front, a queue of kids lined up at her booth, waiting to have their faces painted. I was just about to go over and say hello when I saw King. He was over by the entrance, pacing frantically, his eyes searching the faces of those who passed him by. The second he spotted me, he was on the move, determinedly threading his way through the crowds.

"Hi," I said awkwardly when he stopped a few feet away.

He ran a hand through his long hair. "You didn't come yesterday," he stated gruffly.

He sounded annoyed, and I don't know, there was something about it that satisfied me. I liked that he'd noticed my absence. Maybe it would help him realise he still wanted things, and that there was stuff worth getting better for. Or, more to the point, that there were *people* worth getting better for.

"I had to work," I answered.

He frowned hard. "Do you work all through the night?"

"No."

"Well, then, why didn't you come?"

I arched my eyebrow and restrained a laugh. Seriously, his entitled tone reminded me so much of our son right then it was too funny. I made sure to keep my expression neutral, though, not wanting to distress him further.

"Because I was exhausted, and I'm not sure about you, but some of us use the nighttime for a little thing called sleep." Being sassy with him was a risk, because it could have sent him off the deep end. It was a relief when it didn't, as he continued fingering his long hair and apologised.

"I'm sorry. I'm ten hours sober. It's making me tetchy. And I thought you might have stayed away because of how I spoke to you the other night."

I eyed him meaningfully. "We had a little fight, King. It was nothing, and certainly not enough to make me give up on you. But anyhow, I thought you weren't supposed to be going cold turkey?"

He let out a gruff breath. "I'm testing the waters, seeing how long I can go. I feel like shit, but I can handle it." His eyes came to rest on me, and their intensity made me a little breathless. "I'm glad you came. I need a distraction. And I've missed you."

I inhaled sharply at the stark honesty of his statement, and felt my heart give a hard pang of yearning. He was tugging at his hair now, but I wasn't sure he realised he was doing it. Stepping closer, I tentatively reached up and untangled his fingers from the long strands. It was a little dirty, and I wondered if he'd washed it since two nights ago when Jack helped him.

"You're going to end up pulling it out from the root," I said softly, and he let me lower his hand, watching me closely all the while. Feeling a strange need, I sank my hands into his hair and ran them right down to the ends. King didn't stop me from doing it, only continued stoically watching, and it gave me courage.

"You know, I really like your hair like this."

"You do?" he asked, perplexed.

"Yeah," I said, nodding. "It's gorgeous, but it's in need of a wash. What kind of sink does Marina have in her camper?"

King shrugged. "I don't know. Never really noticed."

"Well, do you think she'd mind if we used her bathroom for a half-hour to wash your hair?"

He narrowed his gaze. "You want to wash my hair?"

"Yes, Oliver, I do. Now, do you think she'd mind?"

Shaking his head and exhaling heavily, he answered, "No, she won't mind."

"Good. Come on, then," I said, and gestured for him to follow.

I led the way to the back of the circus where the mobile homes were stationed, feeling King's curious gaze on me as he walked a foot or two behind. I was wearing jeans again, and my spidey senses went on alert. I could practically feel him checking out my arse. He always used to do it before, and the thought gave me a rush of excitement. Any small sign of the old him was cause for optimism. When we reached Marina's camper, he shoved his hand in his pocket and pulled out a key to unlock the door. I let him lead the way inside as he walked to the bathroom.

"It's a bit small," he said, looking around.

I brushed off his comment and began rolling up my sleeves, sensing his apprehension. He was radiating want and...whatever the opposite of want was, like he was dying for me to wash his hair but at the same time dying for me not to. I understood. He wasn't used to people touching him these days, and if my gut feeling was right, he wasn't used to washing, either. He'd been living like a hobo, but I planned to gently guide him back into the land of soap and water. It was of the utmost importance.

I saw him pull a small packet from his jeans as I went to grab one of the chairs from Marina's kitchen table, and then he popped something in his mouth.

"What was that?" I asked, carrying the chair into the bathroom and setting it down in front of the sink.

"A mint. Jack said I should suck on them so that I have something to do with my mouth."

His words were said without any sexual undertones whatsoever, but still, they got my mind wandering to places it had no business wandering. I remembered him going down on me, the heavenly skill of his lips and tongue. He'd been really, *really* good at that. Blinking, I shook myself back to the present.

"Oh, right," I said, looking away and sticking the stopper in the sink before turning on the hot tap and letting it fill.

"He says it will keep me occupied, so that I don't think about having a drink."

"Huh. That's actually a good idea. Is it working?"

He lifted his shoulders. "A little."

"Come here," I said, gesturing to the chair. "Sit."

Warily, he stepped inside the tiny bathroom, and I realised he was right, it was small. It felt even smaller with the two of us inside and a warm, tingling heat began to creep its way to the surface of my skin. King sat down as instructed, then stared up at me, waiting for what I was going to do next. My black shirt had a sweetheart neckline; it was modest enough, but it showed a hint of cleavage, and I was distinctly aware of King's eyes resting there. Then he glanced up, saw I'd caught him, and looked away.

"You're allowed to look at me, you know," I said, picking up a bottle of shampoo.

He continued to stare at his lap, a frown causing his brows to furrow. What he said next made my heart hurt. "I wasn't sure if...you'd find it distasteful to have someone like me looking."

"Hey," I whispered fervently. He glanced up slowly. "I like it when you look."

He swallowed and his eyes grew dark, wanting. I swallowed, too, and set the shampoo down on the edge of the sink for when I needed it. I turned off the tap, then brought my hands to his shoulders. "Just lean back a little," I said quietly.

He did exactly as I asked, and my eyes fixed on the masculine line of his throat when he reclined. It was kind of sexy. I slipped a towel around his shoulders so as not to get his clothes wet. Then I filled a jug with warm water and lifted it above his head before pouring it over his hair. I repeated the process several times, King watching my every move like it was fascinating. Grabbing the shampoo, I poured some into my open palm, then sank my hands into his hair, massaging it in and creating a lather. King exhaled heavily as I dug my fingers into his scalp, massaging.

I saw his throat move, his blue eyes bright as he stared up at me. They dipped to my chest for a moment, and I let him look his fill. I wanted him to know I found nothing distasteful about his attention, that I wanted it, relished it. Leaning forward, I worked the lather through to the ends, which brought me closer to him, my breast brushing his cheek ever so slightly. He seemed to struggle for a moment, his hand clenching into a fist. I was struggling just as much, trying to concentrate on washing his hair rather than the fact that I wished he'd touch me. Run his hand up my thigh, maybe lean close and nuzzle his nose against my collarbone.

The room was way too silent, but I didn't want this to end. Being close to him, touching him, felt intimate, and I wanted to make it last as long as possible.

"Do you remember the first time you caught me having lunch in your office bathroom?" I asked in an effort to make conversation.

He gave me a warm smile, and I swear the heat of it thawed my lonely bones. "How could I forget?"

"I was so embarrassed when it happened, convinced you were going to fire me, but you didn't. You were so cool about it. You must have thought I was a complete nutter."

King shook his head. "It was endearing. You were like a breath of fresh air. I loved how impulsive you were. It made me want to be around you."

We locked eyes, and I knew I'd done all I could with the shampoo, so I began to rinse it out. I noticed a few lesions on his scalp, and a bit of redness, but they'd heal fine so long as he kept up a decent hygiene regime. It was his cough I was worried about.

"Have you given any more thought to seeing a doctor?" I asked gently, taking advantage of his momentary good mood.

"Would it make you happy if I did?" His eyes flickered back and forth between mine.

"Yes," I answered.

Determination formed in his gaze, and I knew my not coming to see him yesterday had given him a fright, made him realise he didn't want to lose me. "Then I'll go."

I opened my mouth, closed it. It was hard to find words for a second, and then I finally found the perfect ones. I hoped he heard my gratefulness. "Thank you."

I continued rinsing his hair then, and felt his hand come to rest on my hip. He left it there, and neither one of us commented on it. Warmth suffused my skin, radiating out from where he touched me. Once I'd wrung out all the excess water, I pulled the towel from his shoulders and wrapped it around his wet hair until it sat in a bundle atop his head. We shared a moment of eye contact as I laced my fingers through his and pulled him up to stand.

Leading him out into the living area, I brought him to the couch and sat him down while I went to rummage in my bag for a hairbrush. Then I came and lowered myself to sit beside him. I pulled the towel from his hair, let it fall around his shoulders, and scrunched it dry before I started brushing out the tangles. King sat there all the while, still as a statue, and allowed me to groom him. The act was so simplistic in its intimacy. He was turned away from me, and I'd just about finished when he suddenly moved, his eyes meeting mine.

I startled when I saw his tears and gasped when he suddenly grabbed me, pulling me into a desperate embrace. The speed at which he moved was shocking, but the tenderness of his actions stopped my heart. He rested his head on my stomach, and I couldn't find my voice. He was open to me in that moment, laid bare, and his vulnerability provoked tears of my own. His breathing was deep, the rise and fall of his chest heavy, as I brought my hands to his hair and started to stroke.

I felt his face move and realised he'd placed a kiss on my stomach over the fabric of my top. I swallowed deeply, unsure whether I should touch him back or allow him to take the lead. His hand came to the soft part of my belly and began to push up the hem of my top until it revealed skin. The old, faded lines of the stretch marks I'd gotten when I was pregnant with Oliver were a stark reminder of everything I still had to tell him. I couldn't stop him, though, didn't want to, and he didn't seem to draw the connection between the little silver lines and the fact I might be a mother. He simply marvelled at my skin, like it was a thing of wonder.

He started to stroke me, almost reverently, and every pore on my body drew tight. His hand was warm and big and manly, and I loved the feel of his callused fingers on my soft skin. I lay back, completely still, and allowed him to find his own way, go as far as he was comfortable. But he didn't try anything else, seemed content to simply run his hands over my bare stomach and concentrate on the movement of his fingers.

After a long time, his hands stopped and his eyes fell shut. I closed mine, too. I only realised we'd both fallen asleep when the buzzing of my phone startled me awake. King still slept, but I managed to reach inside my pocket to check my text without waking him.

It was a message from Elaine, asking when I'd be home. I had to go, but I didn't want to leave. I wanted to go back to sleep, lie here with King for hours, and just feel the peace of being with him. Unfortunately, life had other ideas. His breathing was loud and steady, with a little bit of a rattle. It reminded me that he'd agreed to see the doctor, and my heart felt suddenly lighter.

As quiet as a mouse I slipped out from under him and left the camper, and almost walked straight into Jack as I was leaving.

"Oh, my God, you gave me a fright," I whispered loudly, my hand going to my chest.

He seemed awkward. "Sorry. I get that a lot."

"You're one of those big men with silent feet, huh?" I went on.

Unexpectedly, Jack smiled. He was gorgeous when he smiled. Well, he was already gorgeous, but he frowned a lot. It made him seem closed off. The only time I'd really seen him smile was when he was with Lille or his brother.

"Yeah, you could say that," he agreed.

I glanced back toward the camper. "King's inside sleeping, but listen, he's told me he'll go see a doctor. I work during the day, so I won't be able to take him. Do you think you could do it? Maybe make an appointment for tomorrow."

He nodded. "Sure. I'll take care of it."

"Thank you. Oh, and there's another thing. Do you know that he used to play the piano?"

Jack shook his head. "No, but I did know that his mother played."

"That's right. Well, King used to play, too. Music meant a lot to him, and I've bought tickets for a concert I want to take him to see. I think it'll be good for him to hear a live orchestra again, therapeutic maybe, but I'm not sure I can handle taking him alone. So, do you think you and Lille could come along?"

Jack arched a brow. "Like a double date?"

He was teasing me now, and it made me grin. I didn't realise Jack had it in him to tease. I placed a hand on my hip. "Yeah, like a double date."

His lips twitched. "I think we can manage that. When's the concert?"

"Next Saturday. Will you have a show?"

"Yes, but I can fix to have the night off."

"Great. That's great. Thank you so much. This means a lot."

Jack's eyes wandered to the camper. "I'll do whatever I can to help you, Alexis. I'm sorry if I was rude before, but I've spent years watching that man suffer. It'd be nice to see his suffering come to an end."

His words made me slightly emotional, so all I could do was nod and turn to walk away.

The following day at the office, I couldn't help checking my phone every five minutes. I sent Lille a message, asking if she'd let me know how things went at the doctor's with King. It was almost the end of the day, and I still hadn't heard a peep. It caused me to worry. What made matters worse was when I called Elaine to tell her I'd be home late again, and she asked questions. She was starting to become suspicious, especially since I told her I'd be home by nine yesterday and didn't get back until after midnight. I hated lying to her.

In the end, Lille met me when I arrived at the circus. I'd worried myself sick, thinking something might be terribly wrong with King. She sat me down in her and Jack's camper to give me the details. It turned out that he did have quite a few ailments, but nothing that couldn't be dealt with. He had acute bronchitis, which accounted for the coughing. He also had a few patches of eczema. They'd done some tests on his liver but wouldn't get the results back for a couple of days. It was also looking likely that he had a stomach ulcer. The doctor had prescribed antibiotics for the bronchitis and the ulcer, some specialist creams for his skin and a drug called Disulfiram to help him stop drinking. As regards his liver, the fact that he was making an effort to quit was a big help.

Even though all this wasn't exactly news that he was healthy, I was incredibly relieved to hear that he didn't have anything incurable. I could see light at the end of the tunnel. When the door to the camper opened and Jack walked in with King following behind, I gasped. He'd shaved off his beard.

Standing, I walked over to him and instinctively brought my hand to his cheek.

"You shaved," I whispered.

His eyes, dull and bloodshot only a couple of days ago, had regained some of their colour. They look clearer, bluer. "I thought it was high time."

"I can see your face now," I smiled, noticing the lines that weren't there before. They gave him character. He also had a small scar on one of his cheeks. "How did this happen?"

"Honestly, love, I can't remember," he replied, and I shivered at his term of endearment. He always used to call me "love" when we had sex, and several goose bump–inducing memories swept through my mind all at once.

"Drink will do that to you," said Jack, giving King a firm pat on the shoulder. "It's the elixir of memory loss."

King shot his friend something of a smile while Lille widened her eyes at her boyfriend. "*Jack.*"

"We need to be able to joke about it. Takes away its power," Jack explained, and I thought he made a lot of sense.

I looked back to King. "Come for a walk with me?"

Without a word he moved to the side and gestured for me to lead the way. I said goodbye to Lille and Jack before exiting the camper. When we got outside, I gently slid my arm through King's so that we were linking. He glanced down at me, his eyes lingering on our linked arms.

"Where did you go last night?" he asked tensely. I was still trying to get used to the sight of him without the beard. Plus, his question made me strangely shy as I remembered his hands on me, his tender, worshipful touches. I looked at my toes as we walked.

"I had to get home and didn't want to wake you."

"You could have stayed," he said quietly, and I didn't know how to respond.

A silence ensued as we made our way past the front of the tent. A couple of the circus workers went by, and I noticed some of them doing double takes when they saw King. He'd cleaned up a lot in the last few days. I reached up and playfully tugged at a strand of his hair.

"I hope you don't plan on getting rid of this like you got rid of your beard," I said.

His eyes practically twinkled. "You like my hair long?"

"I already told you I do."

"Then maybe I'll keep it."

I shot him an amused scowl. "Only maybe?"

He laughed, low and deep, before shrugging. "If you like the hair, I'll keep the hair."

"Good," I said, satisfied. We chatted as we continued our walk. I asked him how he was feeling, and he told me he was still in pain but not as much as the day before. We entered a busy shopping district, buses and cars clogging the roads since it was rush hour. The streets were crowded with people, all scurrying by on their way home from work.

"Are you hungry?" I asked as I felt my stomach rumble. I'd been in such a hurry to leave the office today that I'd completely forgotten about dinner.

King looked away uncomfortably. "I don't have any money."

I didn't point out the fact that he did have money. He had a bank account full of it, not to mention a gigantic apartment that had been left unlived in for the last six years. He hadn't considered any of that his for a really long time. Perhaps he thought all his property had been seized by the authorities. After all, he never knew that his name had been cleared. Still, I had no intention of pushing the matter right then. I just wanted to eat with him and enjoy his company. I'd always loved the lunches we shared together in his office, the conversation.

"My treat," I said as I steered him in the direction of a small bistro.

He didn't protest, but I got the sense that he wasn't too thrilled about me paying. Neither one of us was dressed fancy. I wore a cream knit top, pale blue jeans, and ballet flats. King wore a work shirt and khaki combats. But the bistro was a casual affair, so it didn't matter. A waitress led us to a small nook at the back and handed us each a menu. I scanned down the list.

"The roast chicken looks good," I said, and was met with silence.

King was looking around the room, clearly uncomfortable. I didn't have to ask to know it had been a long time since he'd eaten in a restaurant. The waitress came back to take our drinks order. King seemed overwhelmed, so I hooked my foot around his ankle under the table for a second as a show of solidarity. It seemed to comfort him a little, but the waitress was still waiting for his order and he wasn't talking. In the end, I ordered two Cokes and told her she could put us down for two of the roast chicken dinners as well.

King seemed relieved after she left, glancing at me and muttering a quiet, "Thanks."

"She was being pushy, if you ask me," I joked to try to make him feel less uncomfortable. "So," I continued casually, "Lille and Jack invited us to go out with them next Saturday night."

His brows drew together. "Out where?"

"I'm not sure. Probably to dinner and a show or something. It could be fun," I said, trying to sound nonchalant. I didn't want him to know how desperately I needed him to say yes.

"Do you want me to go?"

I nudged him with my foot. "Of course I do."

"I'll go then, if I'm feeling well enough."

My heart soared. He'd said yes. We were going on a date. It was a little sad how deliriously happy that made me. "Lille told me you went to see a doctor today."

King nodded and stared down at the menu, where his fingers fiddled with the edge of the paper. "I'm taking some medicines, and I haven't had a drink since two days ago. I'm still not over the worst of it, but I don't want to go back. It feels like it's either win or lose at this stage."

What he said surprised me, since I hadn't even been certain he wanted to give up. "The other day you said you weren't sure you wanted to quit, but you seemed determined now."

His eyes flared meaningfully. "I'm trying."

"All you can do is try," I said, giving him a warm smile, remembering how he'd told me something similar years ago.

He smiled back, sending my hopeful little heart into overdrive. We sat side by side in our nook, the restaurant noises surrounding us. "Maybe in a week or so, do you think you'd like to see your mum?" I asked tentatively.

He cleared his throat, coughing a little. "Yes," he nodded. "I just need some more time to...get better."

"I can understand that," I said, glancing up at him. I'm not sure why, but there was something in his eyes then that held mine captive.

He leaned the tiniest fraction closer, and whispered so that no one else could hear, "I dreamt of you last night."

Twenty

"You did?" I replied, my voice more air than sound.

"I think it was something about having you close, your smell, your warmth. We were sleeping just the same, but we were skin to skin." His hand drifted across the table to mine, his fingers covering my fingers. I shivered, my throat growing tight with need. He stared at me so intently that I became self-conscious. It wasn't often that someone looked at you like they were seeing every piece that was on the surface, as well as every piece that lay beneath.

Almost instinctively, my head drifted towards his, mere centimetres between our mouths.

"Don't stop," I breathed.

"You were beneath me, all soft and languid. I ran my hands from here," he said, and touched a finger lightly to my temple before moving it down the side of my face, along my neck and chest until he reached the rise of my bosom. "To here."

I let out a huff of a breath. "Is that all?"

King's eyes sparkled as he slowly shook his head. His look, so carnal in its intensity, like he was vividly remembering the dream, got me wet. I let my head fall back against the seating, sighing heavily. "Life is so unfair."

The very corner of his mouth quirked upwards. "How so?"

I narrowed my eyes at him, irritable and well, horny. "Don't give me your demure little 'how so' — you know what exactly what I mean."

"Alexis...." he began, his tone apologetic, but he was cut short when the waitress arrived with our meals. I didn't know what to do – continue with the conversation or pretend it hadn't happened? In the end I dug into my food, happy for the distraction. At least this way one of my hungers was being satisfied. King picked up his utensils and began to eat, too. There was something soothing about the quiet that ensued. It was a salve to the ache inside me that yearned for him.

When we were both finished eating, I sat back a moment, hesitating. Finally deciding to hell with it, I laid my head on his shoulder. I heard him suck in a breath at my move, but I couldn't help it. I needed the contact. Tentatively, he lifted his arm around my shoulder and pulled me close. The waitress came and asked if we'd like some dessert. I ordered a cheesecake for us to share, mainly because I wanted to prolong our time together, but also because, well, I wanted cheesecake.

Once she delivered it, complete with two spoons, King and I ate from either end of the slice. We kept taking glances at one another. It became so ridiculous that we both burst out laughing in the end.

King set his fork down and reached forward to cup my cheek. My laughter died away, my smile fading, as his eyes drank me in. "You're so beautiful."

"I'm old and fat," I huffed self-deprecatingly. And look, I know I should have just accepted the compliment, but I was terrible with praise. Couldn't handle it when people said nice things. When I was younger I might have given him a sassy, *Aren't I, though?* But not now. Life had had its way with me. I wasn't so bright-eyed and sarcasm-tailed anymore.

King frowned. "You are not old or fat. In fact, you're somehow more beautiful now than you were before."

"Maybe I just wasn't very beautiful before," I joked.

"That's not true. You were stunning. I really shouldn't have employed you. Even when I agreed with Eleanor that

286

you'd be her replacement, somewhere in the back of my mind I knew I was fucked."

I laughed and shook my head. "Oh, come on."

"I'm being serious," he said, his voice lowering, his hand still at my cheek. "Sometimes we see someone and they just suit us. They're beautiful to us in every way. You're that person to me."

Well. How was I supposed to reply to that? He'd always had a way with words, always knew exactly the right thing to say to melt my bones. It seemed in all these years he hadn't lost that ability.

"You're that person to me, too," I finally managed to whisper in response.

King's chest rose and fell sharply, a turmoil in his eyes. I knew exactly how he was feeling, because I was feeling it just the same. We wanted each other, but it was too soon. He wasn't well, and I had to give him time to heal, to gain a level of stability. So I simply cuddled closer into him, and enjoyed what he could give me in that moment.

And it was enough.

***

The following day I had my assistant, Dara, cover for me for the afternoon so I could leave work early to go and see King. Our time together the previous evening had gone so well, and I was eager to spend more time with him. When I bumped into Matilda, she told me she'd seen him walking towards the gazebo, so I went in that direction. The place was crowded with people having lunch, a lot of hustle and bustle, and I couldn't spot King at first.

Almost every seat in the place was taken, and as I scanned the heads, looking for his recognisable long blond hair, I spotted him sitting alone in the far corner. I got the feeling that most of the circus workers tended to avoid him.

Making my way past the people, I saw that there was a meal in front of him. A dark-skinned man walked past, saw King, and pulled a small bottle of vodka from his coat. When he spoke, his accent sounded foreign.

"King, my friend, got a little something for you." He placed the bottle down on the table, patted him on the shoulder, and walked off. King's eyes went to the bottle, and I stood there, staring in disbelief at the man as he walked away. Did he not know that King was trying to give up drinking, or was he intentionally trying to sabotage him?

My skin began to prickle as worry coiled tight in my belly. King's hand moved toward the bottle then stilled, his palm resting flat on the table. His jaw firmed, and his hand formed a fist. I forced my feet to move until I was standing before him.

"What are you thinking right now?" I asked, keeping my voice level as his eyes rose to meet mine.

He was momentarily surprised to see me there, but then he winced when he realised I'd witnessed him about to pick up the vodka. He looked ashamed. "I'm thinking that I really want to grab that bottle and down the whole fucking thing."

"Why would that man give you alcohol?"

"His name is Pedro. We used to drink together a lot. I'm not sure he knows I've given up."

"Right now you don't look like a man who believes he's truly given up. You look like a man who's tempted."

King let out a long breath, his mouth firming into a hard line. "Of course I'm tempted. This isn't easy, Alexis."

My gaze softened, along with my tone. "I know it's not easy. I'm on your side, never forget that. But think about it this way — if you drink that bottle, you're back to square one. If you don't, you're taking another step towards getting better. You want to get better, don't you?"

His expression was fierce. "Of course. I don't want to go back to how things were, but fuck, Alexis, I...." He took another mournful look at the bottle, clenched his fist again, and then abruptly shoved it off the table until it smashed onto the floor. The shatter caused a few people to look up from their lunches, but nobody said anything. King ran a hand through his hair and stared up at me, his eyes pleading, "Distract me."

Taking a seat across from him, I dug into my handbag and pulled out my monthly planner. It was where I kept all my work appointments, because I preferred hard copy. From the inside of the leather cover, I pulled out the Polaroid I'd kept there for years. Often I'd take it out and just stare at it, remembering that day on the beach in Rome and how King had taken two pictures. I'd kept one, and he'd kept the other. I placed it down on the table and slid it across to him.

"Do you remember when you took this?" I asked gently.

King marvelled at the picture, picking it up carefully like he might damage it. "Yes," he whispered.

"I love how you looked at me."

His eyes flickered to mine. "I adored you."

"And I adored you," I replied with a sigh. "I still adore you."

His throat moved in a way that made me think he had difficulty swallowing, and his brows knit together. Quite like me, he wasn't used to accepting compliments these days. He placed the picture back down before rummaging in his pocket. My heart jolted when I saw he had the other Polaroid, the one of me in my swimsuit, smiling into the camera like I hadn't a care in the world. Lille had mentioned it in her letter, saying how King would go crazy if anyone tried to steal it from him. It must have been just as much of a comfort to him as mine had been to me.

"I kept mine, too," he said, a thread of sadness in his voice. "How funny that I've lost so many things over the years, have been so far gone that there are whole weeks I can't remember, and yet I've always managed to keep this picture safe."

A tiny silence elapsed before I replied thickly, "Maybe you didn't want to forget everything. Maybe there were some memories you wanted to keep."

His eyes found mine, intense and probing, "Yes, maybe so."

***

Almost two weeks passed, and I arranged for my parents to have Oliver for a couple of nights. I didn't like being away from him, but I needed the time with King. It was a critical period. He was making progress, and I felt like having me near was helping. That was only a tiny part of it though. After resisting the vodka, his own inner strength was beginning to shine through, his determination taking over. It was like when he was younger, and he'd work through the night in order to do the best job he could. That potent drive was returning, and he was using it in his quest to give up alcohol for good. Don't get me wrong, he had a few worrying moments where he really, *really* wanted a drink, but with my help and the help of his friends, he managed to stay strong.

And strong was what he needed to be, because he was sick a lot during those two weeks. In fact, it was a horrible time. I'd been doing a lot of reading up on alcoholism, but it felt like every case was different. Successful recovery all depended on the individual.

Marina let us have lots of time in her camper. I tried helping King with his medicines and such, but he didn't want me around for that. He even got a little cranky at one point, saying he was quite capable and didn't need a nurse. It might have rubbed me up the wrong way if it didn't make me so unbelievably happy. In fact, I was happier to have him do stuff himself than to rely on anyone else for help. Supporting himself meant he had a greater chance of succeeding.

Then the night of the concert came, and my stomach was doing somersaults the whole day leading up to it. I was scared that King would be pissed at me for tricking him, but I was determined to take the chance. The potential payoff was worth the risk.

Dressing up, I wore a dark blue body-con dress with black heels, and styled my hair into glossy curls. I wanted to look good for King. In fact, the anticipation of seeing him was almost too much. We hadn't really touched since our dinner together in the restaurant, but there was always that energy between us. It was a little addictive.

I decided to leave my car at home and instead splash out on a taxi. This way I wouldn't have to worry about finding a parking spot. I texted Lille as I sat in the back, having just given my makeup one last check in my vanity mirror. The driver gave me a sarcastic, "Yer gorgeous, lav." Total cockney geezer. He reminded me of my dad's friends. You know, the kind of blokes who can't help making these annoying little comments, like, *Smile, it might never happen.* It was a real special kind of wanker who came out with that one.

Alexis: Be there in 5 mins.

Her response was instant.

Lille: **Great. We're all waiting outside.**

My tummy started to roil with nervous tension as we pulled up outside the circus. I spotted Jack, Lille, and King immediately. All of them were dressed nice, but not as fancy as I was. I felt a bit embarrassed that I'd gone all out. Then they climbed into the cab, King sliding into the space next to me. He smelled clean, and his hair hung long over one shoulder. God, he was handsome. I clasped my hands together tightly.

"Hi."

"Hello, Alexis," he said, eyes dipping momentarily to my dress then back to my face. "You look beautiful."

In that moment, all the effort became worth it. The word "beautiful" on Oliver King's lips when directed at me was always worth it.

"Thanks."

The taxi started to move. I'd already told the driver our final destination; that way, King wouldn't know where we were going until we actually got there. He didn't ask questions, and seemed content to simply sit next to me, our thighs touching, arms brushing whenever the cab went around a corner.

The area outside the Royal Albert Hall was busy, so King didn't immediately recognise where we were. My heart was beating a mile a minute. And then, almost in slow motion, he glanced up and took in the location. I saw his throat move as he swallowed, and all the noise surrounding us seemed to quiet as I waited for his reaction. Jack and Lille were off to the side, hand in hand. Jack stood tall, watching King almost as closely as I was so that he could dive straight in if things took a turn for the worse.

King's gaze came to rest on me, his brows drawn together in consternation. "Why are we here?"

My throat went dry. "Because we're going to see a concert."

The second the answer was out, he spun around, checking to see if there were any posters on display. There was a big one right next to the entrance, and his entire body grew still.

He didn't turn back around as he spoke, emotion filling his voice. "I told you not to push this."

"I only push because I care." My words were uttered so quietly, I was surprised he heard them. Jack took a step forward, as though predicting King was going to fly off the deep end. He shot Jack a rather unfriendly glare.

"Leave it out, McCabe. I'm not an animal. I won't make a scene."

And then, without further ado, he walked towards the concert hall, determination in his gait. Jack, Lille and I all exchanged surprised glances before I hurried to catch up with him, fumbling for the tickets in my handbag.

I handed them to the attendant at the door, and he directed us to our section. We all bypassed the bar (obviously) and went straight into the hall. Our seats were on the ground floor, right in the middle. King hurried his pace and went ahead of us to take his seat. His posture was strung tight, his hands flexing into fists. I stood in the aisle and turned back to the others.

"Do you think he's all right?" I asked them with worry.

"I think he's trying to be," said Jack.

His answer caused me to emit a long exhalation, and then I made my way to our seats. Taking the one beside King, I sat. He stared directly ahead at the empty stage, and I tried to make conversation.

"This venue is beautiful, isn't it?"

Nothing.

"It's funny that I've never actually come here before. I should make it more of a regular thing."

Still nothing.

"Would you like anything to drink?" I asked, and then winced. "I mean, like water or orange juice or something."

"I'm fine," he finally said on a long exhalation.

"Oh, right, good." I paused, glancing around. Lille and Jack were being just as silent as King, which wasn't helping matters. I got the feeling neither one of them were the chatty kind, but it could just as easily have been the awkwardness causing them to flounder for something to say. All of a sudden, my dress felt too tight, and my throat clogged with nervous tension.

"Well, I think I'll go use the bathroom and maybe grab a programme before the concert starts."

King glanced at me for a brief moment, nodded, then turned his attention to the stage again. I stood, making my way past him because lots of people had already taken their seats on the other end of the row. I did my best not to brush off him as I went, and then I hurried to find the ladies'. Once I got there, I really wanted to splash some water on my face, but couldn't because it would ruin my makeup, so I settled for holding my wrists under the cold tap for a minute.

When I was done, I bought a programme and hovered, browsing the selection of CDs available. Then the final call for the start of the concert was announced over the speakers, so I made my way back inside. I had to go by King again to get to my seat, and my heel caught on the toe of his shoe, causing me to trip backwards. His hands went to my hips to steady me and I pulled myself back up, apologising profusely. Once I was safely seated, his hand squeezed my knee, the affectionate gesture surprising me. I was even more surprised when he leaned close to my ear and whispered calmly, "Relax, Alexis."

My skin heated everywhere his breath touched, and he moved his hand away. I wished he'd leave it there. A moment later the concert began, the orchestra musicians taking their places on the stage. The pianist was the last to walk out, a woman in her thirties wearing a long black dress. The audience clapped for her, and then the conductor was standing by his podium, signalling the start of the concerto. The lights in the hall were dimmed, which made the gigantic room feel small somehow.

The second the pianist started to play, I had chills. With each stroke of the keys, she moved her body with a fierce elegance. It reminded me of that night in Rome, when King had played the same piece and I'd been fascinated by his talent and skill. The orchestra joined in after a couple of notes, and I was swept away with the music. It was so...passionate and consuming. Several minutes passed before I even thought to glance at King. He stared straight ahead, his hands resting on his thighs, but his eyes were glassy, his jaw clenched firm. I couldn't tell if it was because he was angry or because he was trying to control his emotions.

Feeling brave, I reached out and slid my hand into his, our fingers intertwining. He didn't push me away. Instead, he clenched my fingers tight, almost to the point of pain. He hadn't heard music like this in a really long time, and I could tell it was having a profound effect on him. Hell, it was having a profound effect on me, and I knew nothing about classical music. There was just such beauty in the piece that it was hard not to let it capture your imagination.

Everything this man had been through flashed in my mind's eye. The fear of his mother's stalker. Thinking he'd killed him and then having his father come onto the scene, making it seem like he could fix everything, when really he was only going to make it worse. Bruce trying to force his way of life on King when he wanted no part in it. Making him bear witness to violence and crimes he could never wash from his memories. Blackmailing him for years. And then, the last straw when King finally snapped and almost killed his father. Running away and leaving behind everything he worked so hard to achieve because he thought he was a murderer.

The music continued, and before I knew it, the concerto had come to an end. When the audience rose in a standing ovation, King jumped up from his seat, hurriedly making his way out of the hall.

"Where's he going?" Lille asked, but I could only give her a blank stare. I had no clue, but I knew I needed to follow him. I pushed my way out, spotting him a couple of yards ahead of me. It was hard to keep up with his long strides, especially since I was wearing heels and had considerably shorter legs.

"King," I called out. "Where are you going?"

I didn't expect him to answer, but then he responded loudly over his shoulder, "I have to...I have to go somewhere."

I couldn't seem to catch up with him, so I pulled out the ballet flats I always kept in my handbag (I was practical like that) and quickly swapped them out with my heels. Finally catching up, I grabbed his elbow.

"King, will you wait a second?"

He didn't stop. "I just need to walk, okay? You don't have to come."

I steeled my resolve. There was no way I was leaving him alone right then. "I'm coming." Little did I know I'd come to regret that decision when we'd walked for over an hour, and my feet felt like they wanted to crawl away from my body and die. King didn't seem to be walking in any random direction, though; I sensed he had a destination in mind. It became apparent that was the case when I recognised his old apartment building in the distance.

"Your old place," I said, winded. Yeah, I definitely needed to work out more and, I don't know, eat more carrots or something. I was in worse shape than King, who was overcoming an addiction and some serious illnesses to boot. It was kind of ridiculous. *Damn you, cake!* I inwardly groaned.

We'd just reached the entrance to the lobby when King turned back to me, his eyes fierce as he took me in. "Are you all right?"

I waved away his concern sheepishly as I tried to catch my breath. "Yep, that walk was just a little more, uh, vigorous than I'm used to."

The fierceness quickly fled his expression as his lips shaped into something akin to amusement. He didn't comment on it, though, and his expression sobered soon after. He turned back around, walking toward the door and holding it open for me. We stepped inside, and the night doorman pulled out his earphones, eyeing us curiously.

"I've lost my keys," King announced with authority, and the doorman frowned.

"I'm sorry. I don't recognise you. What number is your apartment?"

"Twenty-two. The top floor. My name is Oliver King." The way he said it gave me a little shiver of awareness. This was the first time since I'd found him that he'd so confidently stated his name, like he had regained a sense of his identity. It felt monumental, made my heart thump hard.

The doorman's eyes widened. "Oh, you mean the penthouse? Do you have any identification?"

King's expression darkened in annoyance, and I suddenly remembered that I had keys. Elaine had asked if I'd drop by and check on things a few weeks ago, and had given me her spare set. I'd completely forgotten to drop by, of course, and the keys were still sitting safely in the inside pocket of my bag. I quickly began to dig for them before pulling them out triumphantly.

"Ah! Crisis averted. I found the keys," I declared, jingling them in the air. King shot me a perplexed look, and the young doorman appeared relieved to be able to avoid further disturbance. Whatever he'd been listening to on those headphones, he seemed eager to get back to it. I faked a confident tone.

"Come on, honey," I said, holding my hand out to King. "Let's get going. I'm exhausted."

He stepped forward and took my hand as I led him toward the lift. Once we were safely on board, King turned to face me. "Honey?"

I shrugged. "I was aiming for casual."

His lips twitched in amusement again. "You have the keys for my apartment?"

"Your mum gave them to me. She wanted me to stop by and check on things. Make sure the plants got watered."

"I never had any plants."

I made a weird sound in the back of my throat. "Oh, you know what I mean."

The doors to the lift pinged open, and there was a beat of silence where King just stared at me. I both loved and hated his stares in equal measure. I loved them because

298

they made me want him. And I hated them because they made me want him.

He made his way out of the lift, and I followed. When he reached the door, he stood and waited for me to open it. I did so quietly and he hurried inside, going straight to a drawer and pulling out a pad of paper and a pencil. I found it fascinating that he remembered exactly where he'd left things. Then he went to his piano, which sat by the large panelled window that looked out onto the river. I watched as he sat down and opened the lid, revealing the keys. He ran his fingers over them, feather light, as though saying hello to an old friend.

I watched him with rapt attention. His face rose, and I noticed he was staring at something. Following his gaze, I saw it was fixed on the drinks cabinet on the other side of the room. Elaine hadn't known about King's alcohol abuse, so obviously she'd never thought to clear out the cabinet. King was still staring at it when he spoke, his voice strained. "Can you empty all those bottles down the sink, please?"

"Sure," I said, slightly flustered, and hurried over. As quick as I could, I removed the bottles and carried them to the kitchen, where I promptly poured their contents down the sink. I was a mixture of nervous and triumphant, because the way in which King stared at the bottles was nerve-wracking, but the fact that he'd told me to empty them meant his strength had won out. Once it was all done, I turned back around and gave him a firm nod. King's body sagged in relief, and he shot me a stoic look in return before his attention was back on the piano.

I suddenly became aware of my sore feet, and I just knew I had a bunch of blisters from the long walk. Why the hell hadn't I suggested getting a taxi? Or even catching a tube? I'd been so anxious, so worried about how the concert had affected him, that my brain didn't seem to be working like usual.

Seeing that the door to the bathroom was slightly ajar, I left King to his own devices as I stepped inside and slipped off my shoes. Just as I thought, my feet were red and raw from the walk, the edge of the flats having dug into the backs of my ankles and the sides of my toes.

The place was spic and span, courtesy of Elaine's upkeep. In fact, there wasn't a hint of dust or mildew in sight. Perhaps she'd always known her son would come back here one day. I made my way over to the large corner tub and filled it with a couple inches of water, just enough to soak my feet in. I ran the tap for a while, waiting for the water to heat up, and heard King press down on a couple of keys, testing. The piano must not have been in tune, because I heard him fiddling around with it for a while.

With the tub filled, I sank my feet into the warm water and practically groaned in relief. King started to play something, a melody I didn't recognise, and I closed my eyes, savouring the sound.

He was playing.

I couldn't believe he was playing. The song was sweet, and somehow reminded me of springtime. I wanted to go inside and watch him, drink in the skilled movements of his body as he created something close to true perfection. But I didn't move, just listened, afraid if I went inside, I'd break the spell.

The music stopped, and I heard him muttering something absently to himself. Then it started up again, stopped, started once more. I got the sense that he was either trying to remember something old or compose something new. Whichever it was, I had no intentions of interrupting. I laid my head back against the tiles, enjoying the relief of the water at my feet and the sound of the music in my ears.

I wasn't sure how much time had passed when the door to the bathroom creaked and King stepped in. I opened my eyes, glanced up, and saw him studying me. His eyebrow quirked upward.

"What are you...."

"My feet were sore," I explained quickly.

"Oh," he said. "I forgot you might not be used to walking."

"And you are?"

Self-consciously, he scratched his head. "Sometimes, when the circus is on a break, I wander."

His answer intrigued me. "You wander? Where?"

"Anywhere. I never really care where I'm going, so long as it's somewhere different than before. Somehow, though, I always manage to find my way back."

Something painful hit me right in the chest, as I comprehended what he was saying. "And when you wander," I whispered, "where do you sleep?"

"On the streets."

"Oliver," I said, my voice wavering.

"You're upset," he stated.

"Of course I'm upset. You've been sleeping on the streets, and yet you've had this place here all along."

"I told you, I stopped thinking of it as mine."

"Well, you need to start again. Because this is your home."

His face grew strained. "Alexis, I haven't had a proper home, my own bed, in a really long time." He paused, looked around, and gestured with his hands. "All of this is going to take a lot of getting used to."

301

On one level, what he said irritated me. This place was his, for crying out loud. But on another level, I completely understood where he was coming from. The apartment was practically palatial, and everything in it was expensive and luxury. My own house was positively quaint compared to this penthouse.

My voice was quiet as I offered, "You can come and stay with me, if you like. My house is seriously tiny. It could be a way of phasing you in." I shot him a smile, for a moment forgetting that he couldn't come and stay with me until I told him about Oliver. I had to tell him about Oliver; I was just waiting for the right moment, which never seemed to arrive.

"I couldn't impose on you," he said, and walked to the rack to pull off a towel. He neared me, towel in hand, then knelt in front of the tub. I watched with rapt attention as he reached in and lifted out one foot and then the other, drying both with care. His thumb rubbed down the arch of my foot, applying just the right amount of pressure. I had to bite my lip not to groan, because it felt so good.

"You don't have to do that," I said, while at the same time not wanting him to stop. His eyes came to mine, and the towel fell away as he looked back down and started to examine my feet. Sucking in a harsh breath, he said, "You need to bandage these cuts."

"They'll be fine."

He shot me a look of reprimand, and I shut my mouth.

"I think I used to keep a first aid kit in here somewhere," he said, and looked in the cupboard over the sink. Sure enough, there was a white box inside. He pulled it out and began looking for antiseptic cream and Band-Aids.

"The song you were playing inside, it was lovely," I said as he worked.

"Yeah, I was watching the woman play tonight, and I realised something." He frowned, hands stilling on my foot.

"What was that?"

His gaze met mine. "That I was jealous."

I didn't know what to say, but then he continued talking. "I wanted what she had so badly, it was almost a physical type of pain. I've been away from real music for so long that I didn't realise how much I needed it. It used to be my favourite thing, something I did to decompress. But now it feels like I can't breathe if I don't get it back."

My lips grew dry, still not knowing what to say. "Well, I'm just glad you enjoyed the concert."

"I did. Thank you for taking me there. I know it took a lot of courage."

He held my foot in his hand, fingers deliciously warm on my skin. I stared, transfixed, as he began to feel his way up my shin. My lips grew drier. In fact, I was dying of thirst right then, and it wasn't for water. King's mouth hung open a little as he admired my bare legs, his eyes wandering as far as my thighs before they came to my face. We communicated silently, and seconds later he was pulling me to him, water splashing as he caught me. His hands gripped either side of my neck, and he lowered his mouth to mine.

The kiss was soft at first, maybe even a little hesitant, but then his tongue slid ever so slightly against my own, and I moaned deep in my throat. The sound caused King to let out a quiet grunt as his fingers dug into my skin and the kiss deepened. Every fibre of my being came alive as our tongues tangled, our lips biting, nibbling, seeking, and I felt the spot between my thighs grow wet and needful.

I might have come from the kiss alone, it was that intense. We kissed like our lives depended on it, like we were dying of thirst in the desert, and I would have been embarrassed by my obvious need if he hadn't matched it with his own. Long minutes passed, but his fingers never wandered from my neck and mine never left the front of his shirt, the material bunched in my fists. The fact that we were barely touching made it so much more feverish. It was only when I moaned a second time, much louder than before, and King gave a deep, masculine growl, that I knew I had to break the kiss. If we didn't end this, he was going to be inside me soon, and I knew I wouldn't have the willpower to stop him.

My chest was heaving as I broke away, seeing stars, all of them gold like his hair. We locked gazes, and it was at that very moment that I blurted out, "There's someone I need you to meet."

Twenty-One

King didn't want to stay in his apartment that night, and no matter how much I tried to convince him to give it a try, he was determined to return to the circus. He wanted what was familiar, and his old apartment was foreign to him now.

We shared a cab, and I made him promise to meet me the following day at two, because I wanted to go see the show and introduce him to a friend. What he didn't know was that the friend wasn't a friend, but our son. I'd decided that there wasn't ever going to be a perfect time to tell him, and that showing him would explain things far better than any words.

Elaine had come over for breakfast, and we were currently sitting at the table, drinking coffee and eating pancakes. You always knew I was overcompensating when I made pancakes. Oliver was in the living room, eating a bowl of Cheerios and watching television. He didn't want the pancakes for some reason and was determined to have cereal. Oh, the whims of a five-year-old.

"I have to tell you something," I said nervously, and Elaine glanced up from the magazine she'd been browsing. Her naturally pale eyebrows arched in concern as she sensed my apprehension.

"Yes, darling?" she said, giving me a warm, open smile. Did I mention how much I loved that she called me darling? She had this well-bred, upper-class fanciness about her. Sometimes I felt like maybe I could gain some of it by osmosis.

Okay, in for a penny, in for a pound. I didn't want to beat around the bush, and Elaine wasn't so vulnerable these days that she couldn't handle a bit of a shocker.

"I found Oliver."

She blinked at me in disbelief, her eyes darting to the doorway that led to the living room. "You mean, *my* Oliver?"

I nodded.

She got up from the table and began fanning herself with her hands as she paced back and forth. I watched tensely, worried that she might have a meltdown. Thankfully, that didn't happen. Her voice was breathy with emotion and excitement when she finally spoke. "How did you find him? I mean, where is he?"

I told her to sit down and that I'd explain everything. And I did. All about Lille's letter and how King had a half-sister who owned a circus, how he'd been living with her for years. How sick he'd become and how he was slowly trying to get better. She was wide-eyed and speechless by the time I'd finished recounting it all.

"Do you think he'll want to see me?" she asked timidly.

"I know he does. He just wants to get better first, make himself presentable."

She nodded, her eyes watery as she stared over my shoulder, and I knew her mind was elsewhere.

"I'm bringing Oliver to the circus today to introduce them. I can't hide the fact that we have a son any longer."

Elaine's face grew concerned. "Is he ready for that?"

"Yes," I said, "I think he is."

***

"Where are we going, Mummy?" Oliver asked from the back seat of the car. I'd dressed him in his Sunday best, a little navy blue shirt and grey corduroy pants. His hair was neatly brushed to the side, and as I glanced at him through my overhead mirror, I felt my chest constrict. He looked so fucking adorable. There was just something about little people dressed like big people that got me every time. But more than that, he looked so much like his dad.

"We're going to the circus," I answered before concentrating back on the road.

"The circus!" he screeched with sheer excitement. This was the reason I'd held back on telling him. I knew he'd get all hyper and would be impossible to control. He bounced up and down in his seat, a gigantic smile on his face. "Mummy, you sneak! You kept this under wraps." I burst out laughing at his turn of phrase.

"That I did." I grinned at him.

"Will there be elephants?"

"Yup."

"Oh, my God!" he exclaimed, putting his hands to his cheeks like he simply couldn't contain himself. He bounced with more vigour now, his giddiness amping itself up to eleven. Jesus, I loved him. I parked along the street leading up to the circus and felt my heart begin to thrum. My entire body was full to the brim with nervous tension, and I felt a bit like I was walking on air. Or about to vomit.

Glancing at the clock on the dash, I saw it was five to two. We'd be meeting King in five minutes. In five minutes' time, King was going to meet his son.

I took Oliver's hand and led him down the street. All the while, my skin was breaking out into a cold sweat. When we arrived at the circus, I went and bought two tickets, but as soon as I let go of Oliver's hand, he ran off ahead of me to the side of the tent, where there was a large cage containing two male lions.

"Liiiiiooooons!" he yelled giddily, waving his hands in the air. I hurried to catch up with him, swung my arm around his body, and lifted him into the air.

"Oh, no, you don't," I warned him. "You stick with me. You don't go running off like that again, do you hear?"

He pouted. "Yes, Mummy."

I let him down and then heard someone clear their throat from behind me. Jay and Jack stood a couple of feet away, both staring at Oliver with wide eyes. Oliver saw the two men and became uncharacteristically shy, grabbing my hand and hiding behind my leg.

"Is this...?" Jay began, and I nodded.

"Uh-huh."

"Does King know?" Jack asked.

I shook my head. "Not yet."

He ran a hand through his hair. "Well, shit."

Jay whacked him on the shoulder. "Hey! Language around the kid, bro."

Jack slid his hands in his pockets and shot me a sheepish look. "Sorry."

I blinked at him, hardly hearing what they were saying because I was still drowning in nerves. Oliver was staring up at them both like they were another species. Other than my dad, he wasn't around men very often, and especially not men who looked like this.

"Alexis," I heard a voice call from nearby, and had to close my eyes. What was I doing? This was way too soon. I silently wished I could teleport us right out of there, but I couldn't. I had no other choice but to face the music. Footsteps sounded as King approached, and I forced myself to open my eyes. He wore a T-shirt, jeans, and boots. It was startling to see him in short sleeves when usually he wore several layers even in the blistering heat.

"Hi," I said, hardly recognising my own voice. I glanced at Jay in panic, and he nodded his head in encouragement, as if to say, *You can do this.*

308

I could do this. I could.

King was still focused on me, a frown taking shape as he observed my nervous posture. Several beats of silence passed while my heart thumped loudly in my ears. It felt like the moment lasted an eternity, and then *boom*. King suddenly glanced down and saw Oliver. His glacial blue eyes returned to mine, a question in them.

"Your friend?" he asked, his voice a mixture of curiosity and apprehension.

I swallowed thickly and summoned my courage before blurting out, "This is my son."

"Hello," said Oliver, waving, entirely oblivious to the momentous occasion. His voice brought King's attention back to him, and I saw him take in his every feature, from his blue eyes to his blond hair, to the face that was almost a carbon copy of his own. They say that you resemble one parent more at different times in your life. Well, right then Oliver resembled his dad far more than his mother.

King's jaw moved and he swallowed thickly, his eyes not leaving Oliver as he asked, "How old is he?"

"Five," I answered, voice wavering even though I'd only uttered one syllable.

King ran both hands through his hair and looked away, a strain marking his form. I knew exactly what was happening; his mind was piecing together the information, doing the maths. When he looked back to me, his eyes were wet, and I felt the weight of everything he was feeling like a blow to the chest. Our gazes locked, the atmosphere heavy with unanswered questions. Finally, Oliver interrupted by tugging on my hand.

"Mummy, I want to go inside now."

"Hey, buddy," Jay said, stepping forward. "You wanna see something cool?"

Oliver nodded, and Jay pulled a deck of cards from his pocket, doing an impressive shuffle. Oliver let go of my hand and stepped forward, staring at the cards in fascination.

"Do it again!" he exclaimed with delight.

"I will, but first, do you want to come see the elephants before the show starts?"

Oliver nodded profusely, and I wordlessly let Jay take him, knowing King and I needed to talk. A moment later they were gone and we both stood there, people passing us by, wading through the ocean of questions that lay between us.

"I don't understand," he said, confounded.

I looked to the ground, shoving my hands in my pockets and muttering, "It's not that complicated."

King stepped forward hastily, his expression frantic and his voice airy. "He's mine, isn't he? Fucking hell, you only have to look at him to know he's mine." He turned away, staring at the people walking by, his mind clearly racing. Vaudeville fair music began to play through the speakers at the entrance to the circus, like a stark exclamation point at the end of his statement.

"He's yours," I breathed.

King rubbed at his jaw, where an attractive bit of stubble had started to grow. And then, just like that, he turned and walked away. Jesus. My shoes felt like they were stuck in a tub of cement as I stood there, not knowing what to do. When I finally regained my senses, I hurried after him. He'd rounded the tent and was making his way toward the camper vans when I got close enough to grab his elbow.

"Wait, don't be angry with me, please," I begged. He stopped walking and turned around, his features contorted in anguish. His eyes flickered between mine, his voice coming out strained and raspy.

"Christ, Alexis, I'm not angry at you. I'm angry at myself."

"Why? You had no clue I was pregnant. Hell, I didn't even figure it out until months after you'd disappeared."

He huffed out a breath, hands frantically running through his hair again. "Yes, but I've been hiding for years, burying my head in the sand, and all the while you were out there, alone with a child that was mine. It just...it makes me feel worthless."

I moved closer and lifted his hands from his hair, like I had to before when he was tugging it to the point where he was almost tearing it out. Sliding my fingers through his, I held both of his hands in mine and looked him in the eye. "You are not worthless, King. You're the strongest person I know right now. I mean, look at you, look at how far you've come since I found you. Don't you dare think for one second that I blame you for not being there. I had help. I had Karla and my parents, and your mum, too. The only thing I regret are the years you've missed, but I'm not going to dwell on them, and I won't let you, either. He's still young, King, and there are more years ahead of us than there are behind."

Tears streamed down his face as he stared at me. "He's so...perfect." He paused, brought his hands to my face to cup my cheeks. "He's like this perfect little human that we made together, and I don't even know him."

I reached up and placed my hands over his. "You'll get to know him. And I wouldn't go throwing around the word 'perfect' just yet," I joked. "When he's having a tantrum or coming into the house with dirt all over himself, he's far from perfect, believe me."

King let out a quiet, sad laugh and gripped me tighter. The quiet was punctuated by the pounding of my pulse, which I was sure he could feel. A long silence fell between us as we simply stood there, communicating without words. Finally, I spoke.

"Come on, let's go back so that you can meet him properly."

Indecision clouding his expression, he drew in a deep breath and wiped the tears from his eyes. There was something so heartachingly beautiful about the moment, and I wondered why I'd ever been scared to tell him. If anything, the discovery had brought more of the colour back into his eyes, and I was determined to replace every last bit.

We walked hand in hand to where the elephants were being kept, and found Jay with Oliver up on his shoulders so that he could reach out and pet one of their trunks.

"Hey!" I called, and he twisted around to see me.

"Mummy, I'm petting the elephant. Look!" he called back, and reached out again to touch it.

"I can see that, baby. Come here, there's someone I want you to meet." I could feel King's intense stare on me when I spoke to our son, and then I saw his attention go to Oliver as Jay let him down off his shoulders. He came running at me and I caught him, lifting him up into my arms. He was getting taller by the week, his long legs dangling down from my hold.

I turned him to face King and said, "This is my friend. His name is Oliver."

Oliver made a face. "But *my* name is Oliver."

"That's right. You're both named Oliver."

He let out a cute laugh. "That's crazy."

I laughed, too, and saw King smile. I could tell that he was still struggling with his emotions, but was making an effort to hold it together. "It's a pleasure to meet you, little man," he said, and reached out to take his hand and shake it. Oliver was quiet as he studied King, trying to suss him out. It was kind of adorable. I gave him a little nudge.

"What do you say back?"

"It's a pleasure to meet you, too."

King's smile grew larger, and I felt like my heart was about to burst. I'd visualised this moment for years, imagined it happening in so many different ways, but now that it was actually here, there was no comparison. It was like a little piece of me that was broken was finally being healed. And if the look on King's face was anything to go by, he was feeling exactly the same way.

"Oh, I know what we can do," Oliver announced suddenly. "I can be Oliver 1 and you can be Oliver 2."

"That sounds like a good idea," King chuckled, the tenderness in his voice as he interacted with our son causing a deep, feminine part of me to ache.

I really wanted to tell him he could call him Daddy, but it was too soon. Oliver was an open, accepting sort of kid, but still, I knew I had to ease him into the idea that King was his father. Letting him down from my arms, we headed inside the tent for the start of the show. I bought Oliver some candy floss, so he was quiet as a mouse as he concentrated on stuffing his face. King seemed at a bit of a loss for how to act, but I just squeezed his hand to let him know he was doing fine. When we found some seats and King sat down, Oliver made his way over and unceremoniously began to climb onto his lap.

"I'll sit here," he said without preamble. I laughed. King stared at him, a mixture of amused and perplexed.

This was typical Oliver behaviour, though; he befriended quickly. I shrugged and took the seat beside King as our son sat on his lap, happily eating away at his candy floss like he hadn't a care in the world.

I looked at King then and whispered, "You okay?"

He swallowed and blinked a few times before clearing his throat. "Yeah, I'm fine."

I smiled and shot a glance in Oliver's direction as he watched a few stage hands set up the props for the start of the show. "I think he's decided you're both going to be friends. Not sure you get a say in the matter. Sorry."

King laughed gently. "That's fine by me."

"Thank you for being so cool about this," I went on, voice soft.

"Honestly, I'm not sure I've fully comprehended what's happening yet."

His bemused tone made me chuckle, because I completely got where he was coming from. If I had been in King's shoes right then, I'd probably be freaking the hell out.

Oliver twisted in his lap and practically shoved the candy floss in King's face. "Want some?"

"Uh, sure," he said, and picked off a piece.

"Oh, yeah, don't bother to offer me any," I mock-complained, and then the candy floss was being shoved in my face. I picked off a larger piece.

"Don't eat it all," Oliver whined before looking to King. "She always eats it all."

King chuckled, his eyes alight and fascinated by every little thing that came out of Oliver's mouth. A second later, the lights were dimmed and the start of the show was being announced. It turned out that Marina was the ringmaster, and she walked out wearing a long red coat and a top hat.

Her capuchin monkey sat on her shoulder, and, just as I'd imagined when I first saw it, Oliver almost lost his shit.

"She has a monkey! Look, Mummy, she has a monkey!" He bounced on King's lap, who bent down to tell him,

"That's my sister Marina. Her monkey's name is Pierre."

Oliver looked up at him, a massive grin on his face and bits of pink candy floss stuck to his cheeks. "Can I meet him?"

King smiled at him, and again it made my heart go *whoosh*. "I'm sure I can arrange it."

"You're the best," Oliver declared, and without warning reached up and threw his little arms around King's neck for a hug. He seemed startled at first, but then his eyes came to mine and I saw the emotion in them. He squeezed him back, and somehow I knew in that moment that everything was going to be all right. I had to look away for a second and clear my throat to keep from getting all weepy.

The show began with Marina announcing the elephants.

"That's the one I got to pet," Oliver shouted, pointing to one of the large creatures.

He was mesmerised by the entire show, in particular Jay's part, which even had my jaw hanging open in slack-jawed amazement. After Jay came Jack, but Oliver didn't like this bit so much. In fact, all the fire frightened him, and he turned in King's lap, shoving his face into his chest because he didn't want to watch. King startled, hands in the air like he didn't know what to do. I gave him an encouraging look and gestured to his hands. Finally he got the hint and wrapped his arms around Oliver as though protecting him from what scared him.

Unlike my son, I wasn't scared by Jack's act at all. On the contrary, I was a smidge titillated, especially since the man wore jeans and no shirt. I caught King shooting me an arch look, so I shrugged and mouthed a *what?* at him. He only grinned and shook his head, but if I didn't know any better, I'd say he was jealous. The thought made me oddly giddy.

During the intermission, Oliver was a chatty cat, as per usual. And he was more than fascinated by King.

"Why have you got long hair?"

King gave me a devious smile before replying, "Your mum likes it like this."

Oliver turned to me, all inquisitive. "Why do you like his hair long, Mummy?"

I shot King an annoyed scowl, trying not to smile back, but my effort was useless. "Because it's pretty and blond just like yours."

By the look on his face, he didn't like the sound of that. "I'm a boy. I'm not pretty. I'm handsome."

His response made me laugh, and I was staring at King when I answered, "Sometimes boys can be pretty *and* handsome."

"Granny Elaine tells me I'm handsome all the time," Oliver preened.

A pained look crossed King's face at the mention of his mother, and I knew exactly what I had left to do. I had to get him to go see her. The show came to an end, and Oliver wouldn't hear a word about going home until he'd gotten to meet the monkey. King led us backstage, and Marina was more than happy to introduce Oliver to her furry companion. I even saw a bit of a shine in her eyes as she took in my boy. She kept looking between him and King, noting the similarities. I thought she might well up at one point, but she managed to hold it together.

"Do you want to come home with us for dinner?" I asked King quietly as Oliver giggled excitedly while Pierre stuck his monkey hands in my son's shirt and trouser pockets, searching for loot.

King breathed deeply, standing close enough for me to feel his breath hit my skin. "Yes, I'd like that, Alexis."

There was something intense in the way he said my name. It caused the tiny hairs on my arms to stand on end and my breathing to turn shallow. I started remembering our kiss from the night before, his tongue hot and wet in my mouth and his cock hard and ready in his pants. I blinked and looked away, trying to clear the images. I had no business thinking those sorts of thoughts right then.

A few minutes later, I finally managed to pull Oliver away from Pierre. Suddenly, all he could talk about was getting a pet monkey. We made our way to where I'd parked the car, and Oliver asked King to sit in the back with him so that they could talk. By the time we arrived at the house, he'd told him all about his friends at Montessori and how he was going to be starting at the big school in September.

Every once in a while my gaze would lock with King's through the overhead mirror, and every time it happened, my skin tingled. He was here, in our lives, talking to our son like it was the most normal thing in the world. Feeling dizzy with happiness, I got out of the car and went around to let Oliver out. King exited from the other side and stood in our small garden, surveying the house in front of him.

"This is a nice place," he said as I gestured for him to follow me inside.

"Thanks. It felt like it took me forever to save for the down payment. I'd put aside a bunch of money from my modelling work, but then when the agency took off, I could finally afford it." I stopped talking when I realised I was rambling

"You like living here?" he asked.

"I love it," I answered simply. "It's home."

Slipping my shoes off in the hallway, I padded barefoot into the kitchen and opened the fridge, pulling out the ingredients for dinner. I planned on making roast pork with potatoes and apple sauce. King took a stool by the counter and watched, while Oliver situated himself in the living room to play. He had this set of toy cars that he was currently obsessed with. All I'd hear was various renditions of *vroom vroooom* out of him for hours on end.

"It's a good look for you," King said randomly as I peeled potatoes.

"What is?"

"This place. I like how happy you seem here."

"Well, like I said, I kind of have you to thank for it. You always used to big me up, tell me I could do whatever I wanted once I set my mind to it. And owning a home of my own has always been a big dream for me."

His stare grew thoughtful. He didn't say anything in response, and I suddenly felt awkward. It was probably because of the way he was looking at me so intently. I fingered the collar of my shirt, bashful, and his eyes wandered to the movement. His breath escaped him all at once before he blurted, "Is it strange to feel like I love him already, and I've only just met him?"

My heart gave a single hard thump, and I knew instantly he was talking about Oliver. His words caused my

318

pulse to accelerate as I shook my head. "It's not strange at all. I loved him from the moment I saw him."

Now he frowned as he reached forward and clasped my hand. "I'm sorry I wasn't there for the birth. That's not something you should have had to go through without me."

I stared at him. "It is what it is. We can't change the past. You're here now, though. That's all that matters."

He squeezed my hand once before letting go, and I returned to preparing dinner. It was sort of disconcerting how he simply sat there and watched. Well, disconcerting and sexually frustrating, because the way he looked at me felt sensual. It always had. King had this intense way of studying people that was guaranteed to get any woman hot under the collar. Speaking of which, I was tugging on mine again, and he seemed to notice.

"You okay?"

"Yeah. It's just a bit warm in here with the oven on. I think I'll go upstairs and change into something lighter."

King nodded. "Is it okay if I use your bathroom?"

"Sure, come and I'll show you where it is."

He followed me up the stairs, and I indicated the bathroom door on the right. Then I slipped inside my room and opened a drawer, searching for one of my light cotton T-shirts. Finding it, I slipped off my top and pulled the T-shirt on over my head. I heard the toilet flush, and a few moments later, King stepped out of the bathroom, the floor creaking under his step. The house felt so silent then, save for the low volume of the TV playing downstairs. My skin prickled to have him there, so close to my bed. I heard him pause on the landing, not making his way back downstairs yet.

"King?" I called softly.

As though my voice was an invitation, he stepped inside my room. His eyes travelled around the small space, wandering momentarily to my bed, where a couple of my things lay unsorted. Mostly underwear. It added a new tension to the moment, and I stood frozen to the spot, unsure how to act. Sad though it was to admit, I'd never had a man in this room before, and his presence made the place feel smaller.

He frowned and turned away. "I'm sorry. I don't know why I came in here."

"You came in because I called you. Is everything all right?" I felt like I was always asking him this, but I couldn't seem to help it. I constantly wanted to make sure he was feeling okay and not overwhelmed at all. He finally lifted his eyes to mine, and my tension ratcheted up a notch, a heavy thickness settling in my throat. The weight of the atmosphere between us was almost unbearable.

"You named him after me," he whispered.

All I could do was nod, mouth falling open slightly, heart squeezing with so many different feelings all at once.

He breathed in and out, then took a step forward. I gripped the shirt I'd just taken off tightly in my hands and couldn't help admiring his form. His T-shirt fit nicely around his broad shoulders, his hair hanging slightly forward to shield his face. Even before, I'd rarely seen him in jeans, but they hugged his slim waist attractively, accentuated by a simple brown leather belt. He looked so earthy and, well, just plain manly. It was hard to imagine a time when he'd donned designer suits and had his hair styled in a top London barber's.

He continued moving toward me, and I started to back away. I wasn't sure why, but I enjoyed the feeling of being trapped. Before I knew it, my back hit the wall, and he was right there, eyes holding me captive. The shirt fell from my hands as I sucked in a sharp breath. His chest met mine, and then he leaned his entire weight on me until I was flat against the wall. His weight wasn't unpleasant — in fact, it felt nice. I savoured how our bodies aligned themselves together, and my breathing increased in speed.

"I like your bedroom," said King, voice low and seductive. I couldn't believe how confident he was being, how he so aggressively took the lead. Yet still, there was a tenderness, a certain level of hesitancy, as though he wasn't quite sure if I'd allow him to get close. Right then, he couldn't have gotten any closer.

"Thanks."

His head dipped forward, his chin at my temple and his nose and lips in my hair. He inhaled deeply, and a shudder ran through me. He felt it, leaning on me even harder then. I was so wound up I thought I might melt into the wall. The way his body felt was causing my heart to race and my head to fill with images. My bed was right there. How easy would it be for him to throw me down on it and take me?

In that moment, I wanted to be taken.

"I keep thinking about last night and kissing you," he murmured. I gasped sharply when he took my earlobe into his mouth and gently sucked. His tongue slid along the shell of my ear, and tingles radiated down my spine.

"*Oh, God.*"

He continued tonguing my ear, then shifted his body so I could feel his hardness pressing on my stomach. I wanted to moan, but bit down on my lip to keep it in. Oliver was just downstairs, and I didn't want him to hear.

"I want you so badly. I wanted you from the very moment you walked up to me that day in the circus." His words provoked the memory of him standing abruptly from his chair and walking towards me like I was the only thing he saw. How he'd touched me almost reverently, his fingers tracing my features like he didn't believe I was real.

I moved a little, squeezing my thighs together to dull the ache he'd created. He noticed, and his lips began to curve into a smile. "What's wrong, love?"

I stared at his throat. "Dinner. I need to go down and check on the food."

"The food is fine."

"It could burn."

"It won't. I want to touch you."

I lifted my gaze, meeting his fierce eyes, and whispered, "Then touch me."

The second the words left my mouth, his hands flew to the waistband of my trousers, undoing the fly and venturing inside. His fingers slid beneath the elastic of my underwear, and then he was feeling me, his touch warm and probing. We both trembled. He fingered my slit, then sank further, exploring my folds, and I felt my entire body spasm at the contact. I was soaking wet already, and when he found my opening and drove inside, I had to bury my face in his shoulder and bite down to keep from screaming. All at once he was filling up years of emptiness, and it was too much.

My body went limp, but his strength held me up. He moved his fingers slowly, fucking in and out as his eyes sparkled, soaking in my reaction. My nipples grew hard, rubbing almost painfully against the fabric of my bra. King continued to finger me, his thumb coming up to rub circles into my clit. I undulated beneath him, letting out a sigh that he captured with his mouth. There was no gentleness in his kiss. It was hard and demanding, his tongue moving in unison with mine, sending my every nerve ending into a tailspin. I was completely open to him as he explored.

"You feel incredible," he gasped, breaking our kiss for a split second before his lips were back on me. His thumb circled my clit one more time and I came in an instant, shivering and shaking against him. He let out a low groan as he kissed me, and it vibrated through me as the waves of my orgasm crashed over me like a tsunami. His kiss grew gentler, until he was nibbling at the edges of my lips, allowing me to enjoy the after effects. I was vaguely aware of my embarrassment, since I'd just been victim to the female equivalent of premature ejaculation. King didn't even seem to be aware of how quickly I'd come, though, so I didn't dwell on it. I met his kisses, exploring his jaw and then his neck. He groaned when I licked at his earlobe, just like he'd done to me.

My hand had just started to move along his stomach in the direction of his crotch when a voice called from downstairs.

"Something's beeping, Mummy!"

My hand paused its exploration as I dropped my head to his chest and sighed.

Twenty-Two

I became aware of several things at once. One, my son was downstairs – *our* son was downstairs. Two, I'd just let King finger-fuck me to within an inch of my life, and I wanted to take things further. Three, I didn't have time right then to take things further (sad face.) And four, I really did need to check on dinner.

I drew away from King, voice breathy. "I should go down."

"Yeah," he said, a little breathless himself.

I was aware of him going inside the bathroom to wash his hands instead of following after me. In the kitchen, I busied myself by turning off the oven and checking to make sure the roast was cooked through. I knew it was since the timer had gone off, which accounted for the beeping. Still, I checked it all the same, mostly to keep from thinking about what had just happened. It was weird, because I certainly hadn't forced his hand down my pants, but I had this ridiculous notion that I was taking advantage of him. I wasn't, of course. I'd never do that, but it was just how I felt. Probably because he was still in a state of recovery.

When King came downstairs a minute later, he went inside the living room to Oliver. I listened to them talk as I dished up the food, smiling at my son's never-ending questions and King's bemusement at the random small talk. I could tell he was completely besotted, though, and it made my heart soar.

After a couple of minutes, King came in and silently began setting the table. I cast him a look of thanks, and we worked together quietly for a couple of minutes. Once everything was ready, I called Oliver in, stuffing a napkin into his collar because he was a messy eater. All the while I was aware of King watching my every move, like how I cut Oliver's meat into small pieces, or how I reached over and dabbed some apple sauce from his mouth at one point.

Every once in a while I'd look up from my food and catch his eyes on me. His attention made me flush, because it was obvious that he was thinking about what had just happened between us in my room. When we were finished eating, King insisted on doing the dishes, so I brought Oliver upstairs for his bath. By the time I had him in his pyjamas and ready for bed, the kitchen was spic and span.

I'd just walked in when King was drying his hands with a tea towel. Stepping forward, I went up on my tiptoes and placed a soft kiss to his cheek.

"Thanks," I whispered. It was nice to have someone else do the dishes for a change.

"No problem."

"I was going to read Oliver a bedtime story. Do you want to come sit?"

A thoughtful look crossed his face before he cleared his throat and asked, "Would you mind if I did it? Read him the story, that is?"

I studied him, surprised by the request. "Of course not. I'll tell you what — I wanted to take a bath myself, so how about I do that and you read to him?"

King's answering smile took my breath away. "That sounds like a plan."

I tried not to be disgruntled when Oliver acted pleased as punch to discover King was going to read him his story. If it didn't make me so happy, I might have been jealous by how quickly they'd taken to each other. But then again, they were father and son. It was only natural for them to have a connection. The thought suddenly made me get a little weepy (happy tears, of course), so I quickly went to run my bath. Didn't want King seeing me acting like a hormonal mess.

His voice trickled in from down the hall as I settled into the warm water. It made me ache for his touch and to have him whisper naughty things in my ear. I had a sudden urge to touch myself, but I resisted. His voice just did strange things to me. I'd gotten out and dried myself off when I heard him close Oliver's bedroom door and quietly step out into the hall. Quickly slipping into a robe, I opened the door and found him standing there, staring at the floor in consternation. When he looked up, he took in my appearance slowly, and my tummy did a little flip-flop.

"Hey," I whispered. "Is he asleep?"

King seemed to be trying to muddle through a maze of his own feelings as he nodded and answered, "Yeah, he's sleeping."

He looked like he needed a hug, so I went to him and wrapped my arms around his neck, pulling him close. His arms went to my middle, his fingers innocently brushing against the curve of my bottom. We hugged for a long time, soaking up each other's warmth and breathing one another in. Then suddenly he was backing me into my bedroom, and I didn't stop him. We were already inside when he asked, "Is this okay?"

"Yeah, it's okay."

"I don't want to leave yet," he said, nose in my wet hair.

"I don't want you to leave yet, either." And it was true, not only because I savoured his presence, but also because my little urges in the bath hadn't yet dissipated. I swear, just hearing him speak could probably get me off. He looked down at me then, and he must have read something

326

in my face, because his eyes turned heated. His arms fell away from me as he seemed to consider something. Then, with a gravelly voice, he gestured to the bed and ordered me, "Lie down."

Whoa. That was unexpected. The authoritative tone he used got my blood up. Swallowing thickly, I took three steps backward until my legs hit the bed. I lowered myself onto the mattress until I was flat on my back, chest rising and falling heavily, and waited for what came next. King's eyes darkened as he sat on a chair and rubbed at his chin. I loved how his gaze traced me, eating up every detail.

"Undo your robe." Unlike his first order, this time I heard a slight tremor in his voice. Was he nervous?

I never took my eyes off him as my hands fell to the tie and followed his command. Slowly, I brushed either side apart until my nudity was bared to him. He hissed in a breath and sat forward, elbows on his knees. His eyes were levelled on my breasts and my nipples, which were hardened into tight peaks. Then they moved lower.

His voice was thick when he spoke. "Lift your knees up and open your legs." On the surface his words were crude, but it was the way he said them that held tenderness. Inside my chest, my heart was pounding with excitement. I loved this, loved how he was telling me what to do. Once I'd done as he'd asked, King let out an audible groan before muttering, "Jesus, you're wet."

He was right, I was. I was also aching, pulsing with a deep need for him to come and give me some relief. His next words, so tender and warm, made me moan.

"Touch yourself for me, love."

Instinctively, I allowed my hand to run down my chest, caressing my breasts and pinching my nipples. I could hear King's breathing fill the room, and when I looked at him, his hands were balled into fists. He must have been using all his willpower to keep from touching me, and I felt exhilarated. Slowly, I ran my hand down my stomach and between my thighs. My body shuddered when I brought my fingers to my sex and rubbed, my clit a tight bundle of need.

"Fuck," King swore, and I shuddered, rubbing my wetness up and down my folds before circling my clit gently. I met his eyes, silently communicating that this was for him. His nostrils flared, his gaze on fire, and he was leaning forward so much he was about to fall off the chair. I would have found it funny if I weren't so turned on.

"Put your fingers inside yourself," he said gruffly, and I moaned again. I tried not to be too loud, since Oliver was sleeping just down the hall, but it was hard. King's penis was a stiff length, outlined sharply against the crotch of his jeans. I stared at him, imagining it inside me, as my fingers slid in, filling me up. My hips rose off the bed as I moved them in and out. My eyes locked with King's, and I never looked away, never stopped fingering myself as he devoured me with his gaze. Then I pulled them out and caressed myself up and down before rubbing at my clit again. My skin was hot and feverish, and my stomach was tight with the need to come.

"Let go for me," King urged me, and I increased my speed, my little pants and moans loud in my ears. I was so wet it was almost embarrassing, because he hadn't so much as touched me yet. Feeling the pleasure rush forward all at once, I gave my clit one final, hard rub, and my vision went blurry for a second. I orgasmed with a sharp cry.

I was rubbing out the waves when suddenly King loomed over me, his intentions clear on his face. He wanted to make love. The tender look in his eyes made me feel truly cherished. He was pulling his T-shirt off over his head as I scrambled for my bedside dresser to grab a condom. I'd bought a packet only days ago, in the hopes that maybe something would happen between us. Never in a million years did I think it would be like this, mind-blowingly kinky and earth-shatteringly hot – yet so emotional.

His shirt was off first, and as he focused on his pants, I took in the contours of his body. He was thicker than he used to be, still muscled but not as defined, yet somehow it was sexier for its lack of contrivance. In fact, in that moment he was the most arousing thing I'd ever seen. I shivered as I watched him. There were a couple of scars on his arms and one on his chest. I knew he probably didn't remember where they'd come from, collected over the years he'd lost to his addiction. Life on the streets wasn't easy. It was hard and brutal, and I was certain he'd found himself in fights on more than one occasion.

Anyhow, it wasn't like my body hadn't changed. I had old stretch marks and had gained a few extra pounds. It wasn't a bad thing. It was just human. King's eyes practically glowed, and I knew I was just as sexy to him as he was to me. It wasn't so much about the shell but about the soul contained within.

When his pants were gone, I brought the condom to my mouth in an effort to seductively tear it open with my teeth. The foil wouldn't rip, though, and we both shared a laugh at my epic fail. King placed a hand on my cheek, and murmured, "Christ, I love you."

His words made me gasp and I stared at him in disbelief, the packet falling inelegantly from my mouth. I wasn't sure why I didn't believe him. I guess I'd just spent so long wishing to have him back that it was hard to believe it had become a reality. Anyhow, my disbelief didn't last long, because even if my brain was hesitant, my heart knew he meant what he'd said.

He chuckled and bent down to nip at my chin as he took the condom from where it had landed on my chest. Clearly, I couldn't be trusted with it.

"No need to look so shocked, darling," he told me gently. "I never stopped loving you, not even in my darkest hour."

"I'm not shocked," I said, choking up. "I'm just trying to…absorb. I never stopped loving you, either."

The smile he gave me in response made my chest ache. I watched as he tore open the condom with far more finesse than I could've mustered before rolling it down his hard length. I swallowed in anticipation as he brought his hands to my thighs and pulled them tightly around his hips. His erection brushed against me teasingly, and he bent to capture my lips with his. He kept his eyes open as he kissed me; it was both strange and captivating. I stared at him, fascinated by his every move. I loved the tension in his shoulders as he held himself up, and the strain of his biceps as he kept from entering me.

Then his hips began to move, slowly in and out, his cock nudging at my opening. I gripped his arms and moaned in frustration. He just barely slid inside before pulling out again and then finally drove himself in to the hilt with an almost feral growl. I cried out at the invasion, my body tight and out of practice. He felt amazing, so hot and slick. Not moving, he continued to kiss me, his tongue silky and wet, his eyelids fluttering closed from the pleasure. A shudder ran through him, but still he didn't move. I loved the feel of him so deep inside me, filling up every inch. On instinct, I clenched around him, and his mouth fell from mine as he let out a quiet grunt.

"Jesus."

"Oliver," I breathed, a quiet plea.

"Just... just give me a minute."

I lowered my mouth to his neck and sucked, causing him to shudder a second time. Then I ran my hands over his broad shoulders and down his spine until I reached his lower back. Pressing my fingers in gently, a silent urge for him to move, I looked up and found him staring down at me in fascination. His icy eyes danced in the lamp light, his mouth hanging open. I rose up a little and took his lower lip in my teeth, giving him a soft nip. He growled low in his throat, a sexy, playful sound.

"Make love to me," I whispered.

It was a sweet relief when he finally moved his hips, pulling out, then driving back into me hard. I let out a breathy sigh, fingers digging harder into the base of his spine.

"I fucking love your body," he whispered like a vow. "I'll never leave you again. Never."

His words fixed something in me, sealed up any lingering doubt. He was here to stay. And I'd never let him go.

And then he was driving into me fiercely, expelling years of hunger and loneliness. I knew the feeling. It was almost euphoric to finally have someone, to connect at the most base and human level. I ran my mouth over his jaw, tried to catch his lips in mine, but they evaded me as his body moved fast. His muscles were coiled tight, his breaths harsh. I wanted his kiss, dammit. Just as though he was attuned to my every need, he slowed his pace and gave me his mouth.

As we kissed, our lovemaking became slow and languid, but somehow more feverish. I felt every second, found myself shivering as I relished the push and pull and savoured every inch of him inside me. My pores beaded tight, my skin was hot and flushed, and a light layer of sweat coated my skin.

He lowered his face to my neck, still fucking me, and breathed in deep. There was an urgency to his movements, and I knew he was going to come soon.

"I love you," I whispered in his ear. "Always."

And then he grew still as he came, before falling hot and heavy onto my chest.

***

Something felt wonderful. I thought I might be dreaming, but there was this fluttering tightness in the pit of my stomach that set my heart thrumming, and I realised the feeling was all too real. I stirred a little in the bed, blinking open my eyes and looking down to find King's head between my legs, his tongue lapping at me hungrily. I inhaled shakily at the sight, and the first sound I made was a low moan.

"What are you doing?" I asked, my voice a whisper.

"Not teasing you," he said, his words recalling a memory of the first night we spent together in Rome, and how he'd woken me up by planting kisses along my thighs.

Before I could respond, his fingers were inside me, pumping fast as his tongue worked its magic on my clit. I had just enough energy to turn my head and check the time on my alarm clock. It was five-thirty in the morning, and therefore early enough that Oliver wouldn't be awake yet. I could enjoy this. I let out a sigh of relief that mixed in with my moans.

King had thrown my legs over his shoulders to give him greater access, and I swear to God I could have died from the heavenly sensation of his lips and tongue.

"Have I mentioned that I love you?" I sighed.

He chuckled into my skin, the sound vibrating pleasantly through my body. Then he hummed low in his throat, a sound of sheer pleasure like he was truly enjoying himself. I relished the feeling of lazy arousal, of just having to lie there playing me like a piano. The thought caused an image of him with his instrument to flash in my mind, and then I was even more turned on. God, this man.

Sinking my fingers into his hair, I pulled his face in closer, his stubble scratching maddeningly at my thighs. He chuckled again, and I huffed out a breath.

"Shut it."

He came up for air. "Tell the truth. This is why you wanted me to keep my hair long."

I ground my jaw and replied breathily, "I said shut it."

More chuckling, and then he was back at me, licking me until I was coming long and hard on his mouth. His hand stroked my stomach, trailing up my body and caressing my breasts, my nipples. I trembled from the after effects and grabbed his shoulders, pulling him up to me.

"Come here," I whispered, and wrapped my arms around his neck, holding him close. His breathing was deep and relaxed, and I loved how chilled out going down on me made him. My thighs were around his waist, his delicious body heavy on top of mine. I stroked his hair, enjoying the silky feel, and felt him drift off back to sleep.

I wasn't sure what time it was when I woke up, but I knew it had to be later than my usual hour. King and I had moved while we slept, and now he lay behind me, his big body encapsulating mine as we spooned. The duvet was pulled high, covering us completely, and it was a good thing, too…because I opened my eyes to find two curious blue ones staring back at me.

Oh, Jeez.

Oliver stood there in his PJs, an inquisitive look on his face as he held one of his teddy bears to his chest. He took in the sight of me and King in bed, but he didn't seem upset by it. He only seemed curious. I might have felt ashamed if the man in my bed wasn't his father and if I didn't plan on spending the rest of my life with him.

"Oliver 2 is asleep," he whispered, and pointed.

I gave him a tight smile, and honestly, I kind of felt like laughing. Hadn't I learned by now that there was no privacy when you lived in a house with a five-year-old? I really should have thought to lock the door. Then again, if he'd woken up and found my door locked, he either would've gotten scared and started crying, or thrown a hissy fit until I let him inside.

Well, it wasn't exactly perfect, but I guessed this was one way for him to find out that King and I were together.

"Why is he sleeping in your bed, Mummy?" Oliver asked, still wearing that curious expression. It was sort of adorable.

"Because he's my...special friend," I answered, immediately cringing at my choice of words. Seriously, I could've done better than pulling out the "special friend" card, but there just wasn't a right way to explain this situation to a child. "Will you do something for me, baby? Will you go downstairs and grab Mummy's handbag from the kitchen? The blue one?"

Oliver hopped to attention at my request, nodding and hurrying to complete the task. I sat up from the bed quickly and pulled on my robe before leaning over and shaking King's shoulder. He blinked his eyes open, saw me hovering over him, and smiled lazily. He slid his arm around my waist to pull me closer, his hand dipping inside my robe to palm my breast. I gently pushed him off.

"I'm sorry to wake you, but Oliver just came in and found us sleeping together," I said, not sure why I was still whispering. Everybody was awake now. King was too sleepy to interpret what I was saying at first, but when he realised, his eyebrows shot right up.

"Ah, hell," he said, rising to sit and running a hand over his face.

"Yeah, you need to put some clothes on. He'll be back in a second."

"Okay," he murmured, leaning close to press a kiss to my lips before going and pulling on his boxers, jeans, and T-shirt. I went about making the bed as he slid his belt through the hoops and fiddled with the buckle. There was something satisfied in his expression as he watched me, and I didn't like it. Okay, that was wrong. I liked it a lot, but I didn't *like* that I liked it. It said something to the tune of, *Yeah, I made you come several times last night, no need to thank me.* Real cocky, like. I had just enough time to narrow my eyes at him and suppress a smile before I heard little feet trundling back up the stairs.

"Here, Mummy, here's your bag," Oliver announced, holding up my handbag triumphantly.

I took it from him and placed a kiss on the top of his head. "Thank you, honey."

King stepped forward and ruffled Oliver's hair, the three of us standing together in a circle. I was momentarily hit with a pang of emotion to have them both so close. My two men. Our small family. King shot me a warm smile like he could read my exact thoughts.

"Come on, little man, let's go downstairs and make breakfast. Give your mum a morning off."

"Okay," said Oliver, bobbing his head. He seemed to enjoy how King called him "little man," like he was one of the grown-ups. He also seemed excited to have him there. It must have been because it was usually just the two of us, so having someone new around in the morning added an element of fun. I went and took a quick shower while the two of them chattered down in the kitchen. I had no idea what they were cooking, but they were making a hell of a lot of noise. When I heard King laugh, full and deep, it sent a pleasurable tremor right down my spine. It felt nice to have a man around, just doing normal man stuff, like making breakfast with our son and giving me orgasms.

Once out of the shower, I wrapped my hair in a towel and threw on a comfy navy dress with cream polka dots. Then, removing the towel, I twisted my damp hair into a knot and went downstairs to see what kind of havoc those two were wreaking on my kitchen.

Surprisingly, the place wasn't too messy, and the heavenly smell of French toast filled the room. King stood by the cooker, holding a spatula. He'd placed Oliver on a stool so he could sit and watch. I went and peeked in one of the cupboards, grinning happily when I found we had maple syrup. King hadn't even realised I'd come in, because he was too focused on cooking and talking to Oliver. The two of them were so cute together, the similarities in their looks particularly striking. It was like looking at two pictures of the same person, one as a boy and the other as a man. Somehow, even though he was smaller and not as strong, I felt like maybe the boy would be the one to save the man this time. Having my love was all well and good, but there was just something about King's eyes when he looked at our boy that brought the life back into them. It was in that moment that I truly believed he'd never drink again. I hadn't realised it, but I hadn't been certain before. Now, somehow I just knew.

Sitting by the counter, I placed my chin in my hands, watching them interact.

It made me happy.

King only saw me when he turned, holding the pan. His lips twitched with a smile as he plopped the food onto the plates.

"You look beautiful," he said.

"Shut up," I said.

"Oi! You're not allowed to say that," Oliver said.

I stuck my tongue out at him, and he giggled. King dished up the French toast, and I poured an unhealthy amount of maple syrup onto mine. Oliver made a face at me, because he didn't like maple syrup and preferred strawberry jam.

We were eating for a minute or two when I heard a key slot into the front door. My eyes widened and went straight to King, whose brow was furrowed curiously at the sound of someone entering my house, someone who had a key. It wasn't at all what he thought, though. I heard Elaine's light footsteps sound down the hall before she stepped inside the room. She often stopped by unexpectedly, but since she'd visited just yesterday, I didn't think she'd be back so soon. When I saw the bunch of flowers she was holding, I knew she'd come just to drop them off. Every once in a while she liked to bring me flowers. King turned in his place to see who'd come in, and his fork clattered loudly to his plate.

"Oliver," said Elaine, her voice laced heavily with emotion.

"Mum," he breathed, so quiet it was almost a whisper.

She looked to me, and I knew instantly that she hadn't intended to intrude. She lifted the flowers weakly, as though to prove her visit was innocent. And then her eyes filled with tears. Seconds later King was standing, taking long strides towards her and pulling her into his arms for a tight embrace. They hugged for a long time, the flowers getting squashed between them.

Oliver looked at me, his mouth open and his eyes big. He clearly sensed something important was happening, but he wasn't sure what. The long silence was broken when he whispered, "Why is Granny Elaine crying?"

I didn't know how to answer, but then I heard Elaine's soft chuckle as she pulled back from King and turned to face him. She stepped forward and ran her hand lightly over Oliver's hair. "Because this is my son," she answered gently. "And I haven't seen him for a very long time."

I watched Oliver as his little brain put two and two together. "You're his mummy," he said finally, and Elaine nodded. King had come to place a hand reassuringly on her shoulder.

"I belong to her the same as you belong to your mum," he explained.

"Oh," said Oliver. "I'd be sad, too, if I didn't see my mummy for a very long time."

His words made us all choke up, and I stood to go grab a plate for Elaine and some coffee. It gave me a chance to settle my emotions. She sat down at the table, talking to Oliver mostly. I got the sense that she really wanted some alone time with King, so once we'd finished eating, I made a suggestion.

"How about Oliver and I go out for a couple of hours? Give you both some time to catch up."

Elaine nodded like it was a good idea, but King looked a little more hesitant. I knew it wasn't because he didn't want to spend time with her, but more because he didn't want to talk about all the painful things they had to discuss.

"I don't want to go," my son complained grumpily. "I want to stay here with Oliver 2!"

In any other situation, his grumpiness would have annoyed me, but no. The fact that he'd grown so attached to King made my heart do wild flip-flops in my chest.

"Oliver 2?" Elaine asked, her lips tugging into a smile.

I sighed and smiled back at her. "He thinks it's crazy that they're both named Oliver. Don't ask. Do you mind if he stays? I have a few things I need to take care of anyway, and it'll be easier if I leave him here."

"Of course not, you know I always love having him."

And that was how I found myself grabbing my things and making my way to the front door. King followed me out, leaving Elaine and Oliver in the kitchen. Then he placed his hand to the small of my back, and my body gave a little shudder.

"Don't feel like you have to leave," he said quietly, his touch warm.

I turned and looked up at him. "You and your mum need to talk. I'll only be gone a couple of hours."

"Yes, but this is your house...."

I quieted him by placing a finger to his lips. "No buts. Seriously, you need to talk to her. Get it all out. If you put a DVD on for Oliver, he'll be quite happy to sit and watch it. He won't give you any trouble."

"It's not about that. You know I love him."

Without thinking, a soft sigh escaped me. "God, I love that you love him."

"Well," said King, leaning closer, voice low, "I love that you love that I love him. And I love you, too."

I shot him an amused scowl. "Don't try to sweet-talk me." My hand moved from his mouth to his jaw, my touch a caress as my expression sobered. "How are you feeling, though? Any headaches or nausea?"

His mouth firmed as he swallowed. "Honestly? Yeah, a bit of both. But I'm handling it."

"Yeah," I breathed, ready to burst, I was so proud of him. "You are."

His strength in dealing with all this as well as feeling like shit from quitting drinking continually amazed me. He backed me into the wall and bent to press a kiss to my jaw. "I'll miss you today."

"I'll miss you, too. Now, I'd better go. Otherwise, I might drag you back upstairs to bed."

His answering chuckle vibrated through my chest as I slipped out the door and headed for my car. It was only when I was halfway down the street from my house that I realised I had no clue where I was going.

Twenty-Three

"Oh, my God, don't even get me started," Lille harrumphed. "That flippin' monkey has stolen dozens of my hair ties, several tubes of lip gloss, packets of face paints, and any number of small coins since I started living with this circus. Somebody needs to call the cops on the little fecker. I swear, I don't know where he hides it all."

"Maybe he has a secret stash where he goes to admire all his pretty treasures," Matilda suggested with a grin.

Lille sighed. "He was walking around with green all over his tail the other day, and my green paint was suspiciously missing from the case."

"Well, this isn't good news for me. After meeting Pierre, Oliver is determined to get a monkey. I may have to dazzle him with a new toy just so he'll forget," I joked.

The girls laughed as we sat at the tiny kitchen table in Lille's camper van, sharing a bottle of wine and talking about Marina's monkey/thief, Pierre. When I'd tried to think of somewhere to go earlier, I found myself instinctively driving in the direction of the circus. I'd lied when I'd told King and Elaine that I had things to do, but it was a white lie. I could have gone to my parents' house, or even to Karla's, but for some reason I wanted to spend time with these women, talk to them about King because they were the ones who knew him best these days.

Somehow though, we'd managed to discuss everything other than the father of my child, and it was oddly relaxing. Sometimes it was a relief to just talk about random crap, like monkey hijinks. Matilda had a dress in front of her as she hand-stitched a detail into the neckline. Jack and Jay had been around, but mostly they were in the tent, rehearsing. I was interested by the dynamic between the two couples, and truthfully, dying to know how they'd all met. So, like the Nosy Noreen that I was, I asked.

An hour or so later, the bottle of wine had long since been emptied, and I'd lived through the stories of two pretty spectacular romances. It made me feel relieved to know I wasn't the only one whose heart had been twisted around, chewed up, and spat back out again. I thought that maybe the best loves had to suffer the greatest hardships. You had me and King, Jay and Matilda, Jack and Lille. Hell, there was even Karla and her husband, but that was a story for another day.

Matilda had just gone to use the bathroom when Lille bent forward and placed her hand over mine. At thirty-three, I was almost eleven years older than her, and yet, there was something about Lille that felt wise beyond her years. Her touch comforted me, and when she spoke, my heart felt too full.

"I'm so glad we found you, Alexis. Seeing King get better has been truly amazing to watch, and it's all down to you."

I stared at her for a long moment, then wrapped my fingers around hers to squeeze her hand. "I'm so glad you looked."

It was late evening when I finally said my goodbyes. I'd only had two glasses of wine, and that was hours ago, so I knew I'd be okay to drive home. When I got there, I found Elaine curled up on armchair in the living room, asleep and a blanket draped over her. King sat on the couch with Oliver, and a kid's movie played on the TV. Oliver was sitting comfortably in his lap as King absently stroked at his hair. If I wasn't so taken by the sight of them, I might have pulled out my phone to take a picture. It was just too bloody charming.

"Having fun?" I asked softly, careful not to wake Elaine.

King looked up at me, and I was struck by the calmness in his features, the sense of peace about him. He didn't answer, just shot me a lazy smile and nodded for me to come sit. I dropped my bag on the floor and shrugged out of my jacket before taking the place beside him. After a second of hesitation, I rested my head on his shoulder. He exhaled heavily, turning his face so he could nuzzle his nose into my temple.

"Did you and Elaine get enough time to talk?" I whispered.

"Yes," King whispered back and I could feel him smiling into my skin. "Thank you for giving us some time. We needed it."

"It's no problem. And Oliver wasn't too much trouble?" I asked, our son too engrossed in the film to hear his name.

King shook his head, still smiling. "No, love, he was good as gold."

Only a minute or two passed before Oliver bolted upright and announced, "I have to pee." He was up and out the door a second later, climbing the stairs to the bathroom. I let out a quiet laugh and glanced up to find King looking down at me warmly. Elaine stirred in her seat, Oliver's announcement having woken her.

"What time is it?" she asked, voice sleepy.

"Just after eight," I answered. She took in the sight of me and King sitting together, and smiled fondly.

"Well, I'd better be going," she said, running her hands down her dress and standing. King stood, too.

"Shall I walk you?"

She seemed taken aback by his offer, shy even. "Well, I'm just down the street, but I wouldn't mind some company."

King held his arm out to her, and she slid hers through it before he led her from the room.

"I'll be back in a couple of minutes," he called over his shoulder just as the front door opened and shut. I took the opportunity to go upstairs and get Oliver ready for bed. On a normal day he would have been asleep already, but this wasn't a normal day. Catching him just as he left the bathroom, I lifted him into my arms.

"All right, mister, bedtime."

"But I was watching a film," he complained.

"And you can finish watching it tomorrow," I said firmly as I carried him into his room. I needed to stop lifting him, because Jesus, he was getting heavy these days. I was going to end up doing my back in.

"Where's Oliver 2?" he asked as I went to get his pyjamas from the drawer.

I let out a breath and answered, "He's just walking Granny Elaine home. He'll be back in a few minutes."

"I like him."

His statement made me smile. "You do?"

He nodded and leaned forward, whispering, "If I ask him to be my best friend, do you think he'd say yes?"

I swear, I didn't know where he got his guilelessness from, because it certainly wasn't from me. I'd been a little terror at his age. There was something about the moment that made me feel like testing the waters.

"Baby, you know how Granny Elaine is Oliver 2's mummy?" He stared at me, nodding, and I continued, "And Granny Elaine is your grandmummy? Well, that means that Oliver 2 is your daddy."

He looked at me for a long time, his expression concentrated like he was trying to figure out the logic. "You said my daddy was far away."

"He was. That's why Granny Elaine hadn't seen him in a very long time, but now he's back."

Oliver was frowning then and I wasn't sure why, but his lips went all full, like he was going to cry. "Is he going to go away again?"

I pulled him into a hug. "No, honey, he's not going to go away again. I promise."

And just like that, the possible crying jag had vanished as he bounced in my arms. "He's my daddy. I can't wait to tell Timothy that I have a daddy now." Timothy was his friend from Montessori. And seriously, he needed to stop saying things that made me emotional. Trust my son to accept King was his father without a single hesitation. There was a knock on the door, and I went down to let him in.

"Hey," I said as I held it open and he stepped inside. "So, you and Elaine really had a good talk, then?" I'm not sure why I felt the need to reaffirm that everything was all right between them. I guess I just wanted to make sure he was okay and didn't feel like things were moving too fast, especially since I now had a another bomb to drop. Perhaps it could wait until morning.

He nodded and answered, "Yes Alexis, we're good. Stop worrying."

I told him I was just putting Oliver to bed, so he followed me up. The very second we entered the room, Oliver shouted out, "Hi, Daddy!"

Well, waiting until morning was out of the question then.

King stopped, frowned, looked to me, looked to Oliver, then looked back to me again. He wore an expression of disbelief, like maybe he'd been hearing things. I was sure I was wearing a terribly guilty expression.

Looking at the floor, I said, "Sorry, uh, I might have told him that you're his dad."

He let out a nervous laugh. "Okay. All right. Eh, that's…that's…."

"It had to happen sooner or later. Might as well bite the bullet."

"I'm not annoyed with you, Alexis."

"Oh, no, I didn't think you were. I just, maybe I should have talked with you first."

He stepped forward, placing his hand on my shoulder. "I'm fine. I'm more than fine. Relax."

His words worked to calm me. "Do you want to read to him again?"

"Sure."

I left them to it and went into my room, taking deep breaths. For a second there I was certain I'd fucked up. I lay down on the bed and tried to focus on reading the paperback I was currently working my way through. After about twenty minutes, I looked up to find King standing in my doorway. We locked gazes, and a pregnant silence fell between us.

"I should go," he said at the same time I blurted, "Stay the night."

Ugh, why was I being so awkward? King shot me a cocky grin, so I threw a pillow at him. "Don't give me that face."

He moved farther into the room and asked coyly, "What face?"

"That one." I pointed. "The face that says you think you're the shit. I hate that face."

He was at the foot of the bed when he countered, "You love this face."

"Okay, I'll adjust my statement. I love your face. I hate your expression."

He shook his head. "Nah, I'm pretty sure you love my expression, too."

He was leaning over me now, climbing onto the mattress and levelling his hands on either side of my head. I was about to say something clever, but it immediately fled my mind when he kissed me. His tongue swept into my mouth, and all I could do was moan.

"Thank you for telling him," he breathed as he broke away to kiss along my jaw, moving down to my neck. I strained beneath him, hands going to his shoulders. Everywhere his lips travelled, they left tingles in their wake.

"I thought you might be angry with me for a second."

"I wasn't angry. I was just taken aback. He called me Dad."

"Well, you are his dad."

He was lower now, his face levelled with my boobs as he nuzzled into my cleavage. "Yes, I am."

I closed my eyes, trying to concentrate on the trajectory of our conversation rather than the fact that his nose was brushing against my ever hardening nipple.

"I'm not gonna lie," I said breathily. "He got a little upset when I told him. Not because you're his dad, but because he thought you might go away again."

King paused to look at me, his face serious. "And what did you tell him?"

A beat of silence elapsed as I swallowed. "I – I told him you were here to stay."

His eyes held mine for a long moment before he nodded, "Good, because I am." And then he licked his way across the top of my breast, and my brain turned to mush.

***

The following morning, I woke up to my alarm clock bleeping loudly at six-thirty a.m. King was spooning me just like he had been the day before. His body was hard and warm, and I really didn't want to leave. Duty called, unfortunately, and I sat up in bed, which solicited a groan from him.

"Where are you going?" he asked groggily.

"I have work. Go back to sleep."

Despite my order, he sat up and ran a hand through his hair. The sheet fell to his waist, revealing his bare torso, and I had to use a good lot of willpower to look away. We'd made love well into the early hours of the morning, and I could still smell him on my skin. God, how I wanted to crawl back into bed and spend the entire day there, just the two of us.

"Could you drop me off at my apartment?" King asked, surprising me.

"Uh, sure." I didn't ask why he wanted to go there, but I took it as a good sign. I gathered my things for the shower and made my way into bathroom. I'd just turned it on and stepped under the spray when a large, warm body joined me.

Best. Shower. Ever.

Elaine arrived to take care of Oliver, and I drove us into the city, dropping King off at his old place first and then heading out to the office. It was a busy day, and though one half of me really wanted to go straight home and put my feet up, the other half wanted to go get King. I liked having him in my bed, in my home. In fact, if I had my way, he'd be moving in with me and spending every single night there. I knew not to push him, though, knew I had to take things one step at a time.

It was just after six when I parked outside his building and went in. He buzzed me up, and I took the lift to his place to find him sitting by his piano, sheet music everywhere and an electric sort of aura about him. The very sight caused an exhilarating tremor to go skittering down my spine. I took a peek at the pages, noticing a lot of them contained his own handwriting, musical notes scribbled down in pencil. Was he composing something?

He started to play a gorgeous melody, and I went into the kitchen to make a cup of tea.

"Do you mind?" I called.

"No," said King absently. "Go ahead."

I found a small box of peppermint that Elaine must have left there and turned on the kettle. When I returned to the living room, King was still sitting by the piano, practicing.

"So, you're playing again?" I asked tentatively as I lifted the cup to my mouth and took a sip.

King's eyes were alight when he turned his attention to me. I swear they almost glittered, and I could tell his mind was racing. The creative muse was upon him.

"Yes, the music, it's, well, it's pouring out. The focus is liberating. I've barely stopped all day."

What he said concerned me. "Have you eaten?"

He furrowed his brow as if trying to remember. "I think I ate some toast at lunchtime." Well, that was a lie if ever I heard one. Pulling my phone from my bag, I quickly dialled my favourite Chinese takeaway and put in an order. With that done, I stood in front of the piano and levelled him with a reprimanding look.

"You have to eat, King."

He reached forward to cup my cheek. "I will. Don't worry, darling. It's just that I get so absorbed when I play that I forget everything around me, and it feels like there's never enough hours. What Rachmaninoff once said was true: *Music is enough for a lifetime, but a lifetime is not enough for music.*"

"Yeah, well, what Selina Kyle once said is also true: *A girl's gotta eat*. I think that goes for boys, too," I told him with a wink.

He grinned. "I don't think Catwoman can trump Rachmaninoff, darling."

Oh, I could have smacked him right then for his superior little tone on "darling." Somehow though, it made me grin. Any signs of his old self always made me grin. They mixed in with his new self to create something I loved so much better. Anyway, I didn't bother to retort, because I was far too curious about the sheet music. "Have you been composing?"

His expression turned guarded, but he answered me anyway. "Yes."

"Will you play some of it for me?"

When his body stilled, I knew I'd made him uncomfortable. "I'm wary," he said and then paused, his eyes meeting mine. "Don't get me wrong — you're the one who inspires me, but I just don't want to fall into the trap of playing for praise. That's what I used to do before. I worked so hard so that people would respect and look up to me, praise me for a job well done and tell me how bloody fantastic I was. Then when I lost it all, I felt like I had nothing left to live for. I want this music to be something I

350

do because I love it, not for the sole purpose of being the best."

"That's understandable," I said, coming and taking a seat next to him. "I want you to do what makes you happy. And if you never play for me or for anyone, then that's fine. So long as it's what you love."

"Thank you," he whispered. "I'm sorry if I'm acting crazy. Sometimes the way my mind works baffles me."

I reached out and took his hand, sliding my fingers through his. "Don't be sorry. I like your mind. It suits my mind."

The smile he gave me lit up his entire face, and my heart beat faster at the sight of it.

I squeezed his hand as I continued meaningfully, "But just remember, your music doesn't have to mean praise for you. It can be the gift you give to other people."

He stared at me, thoughtful, before his attention wandered to the piano keys. I could tell he was thinking about what I'd said. A few moments passed as we sat there in silence, the weight of the years surrounding us and the love we held for one another making all the heartache worth it. I swallowed the last of my tea and bent to place my cup on the floor. My top rode up at the back, exposing skin, and I felt King's palm press down on the base of my spine. I went utterly still as he leaned down to murmur seductively in my ear.

"I think I remember telling you once that I was going to fuck you on this piano until you forgot your own name." He paused and lowered his voice to a whisper. "Shall we try that?"

I didn't need to speak, because my body had already told him the answer.

Yes, Oliver, let's try that.

Twenty-Four

Two months later.

King had a secret.

Well, I wasn't exactly sure if it was a secret, but he was definitely up to something. Every couple of nights he'd go missing, not telling anyone where he was going. If I wasn't such a good judge of character, I'd think maybe he was drinking again, or worse, having an affair. But no, he definitely wasn't drinking, nor was he having an affair. His love and desire for me was something that felt impenetrable. Solid. Constant.

In fact, he kept asking me to marry him, and it was becoming a bit of a bother. The first time he asked, he'd arranged for a romantic candlelit dinner in his penthouse. He was keeping it as a place to store his piano mostly (I know, weird.) But other than that, he'd basically moved in with me and Oliver. I loved having him here, loved his smell on my sheets and his voice in the mornings as he spoke to our son.

This was why I surprised even myself when he popped the question and I told him no, I wouldn't marry him.

At first he'd been upset, but when I explained to him that the answer was no for now, but yes for the future, he'd gotten a gleam in his eye, determined to wear me down. I just didn't want to rush into marriage. It felt superfluous to me. We loved each other. Neither one of us was going anywhere. A wedding was a pointless expense. Not to mention I wanted to be a bride about as much as I wanted to stick pins in my eyes.

No, if we were ever going to get married, it would have to be a small affair. Quick and painless. It also wasn't going to be something I dived right into. Unfortunately,

King was a singularly focused individual, which meant I was proposed to at least once a day. Sometimes two or three times. I'd find Post-It notes inside the tea caddy. Voice messages on my phone. Texts with picture attachments of "Marry Me?" written in sand or on foggy car windows. He'd even sent one of him topless, with the words scrawled in marker pen across his chest.

Kinda sexy? Yes. Bordering on ridiculous? Also, yes.

I was standing by the cooker, heating up some soup for Oliver, when King came up behind me, sliding his arms around my waist and resting his chin on my shoulder. I geared myself up for yet another proposal, but it never came. Instead, he told me, "I'm heading out for a couple of hours. Don't wait up for me."

I nodded quietly, he pressed a kiss to my cheek, and off he went. He'd started driving his old Merc, but he'd sold his other cars, which had been stored in the underground garage beneath his apartment, and donated the money to charity. In fact, he'd donated a huge sum of his wealth to foundations for homelessness and alcoholism, keeping just enough to live off. After years of living with nothing, I didn't think he felt comfortable with wealth anymore. I also didn't try to stop him. In fact, I supported the action. In my opinion, money only brought happiness up to a certain level. Any riches over and above that just made you as miserable as being poor. Okay, maybe not for everyone, because the Kardashians seemed pretty fucking happy with their lot. Perhaps I should adjust my statement. Vast riches for those with hearts and brains made you just as miserable as being poor.

Elaine was already spending the evening with us, so as soon as King left, I hurried to the living room, asking if she'd watch Oliver for me while I popped out for a bit. I was behind the wheel of my car and pulling out of the driveway just in time to see King's Merc turn the corner at the end of our street.

I followed a few cars behind him all the way into the city, biting my fingernails the entire time. Where the hell was he going? Finally, he parked down a side street in Camden, got out, and walked off. I hurried to park, too, then discreetly followed him. He didn't suspect a thing, never once looking back, and then he slipped inside the door to a hipster-looking bar.

Oh, shit.

A bar? He'd sneaked off to a bar? Maybe I wasn't such a good judge of character after all. This wasn't looking good. I stood on the street for at least ten minutes, freaking out and trying to convince myself that this wasn't what it seemed, while my brain was all, *Bitch, how can it not be what it seems?*

FYI, my brain was a skinny gay guy who worked in a hair salon and loved to gossip cynically about other people's love lives.

When I managed to calm myself down, I noticed that a long queue had formed outside the bar, but King had managed to walk right past it. Figuring I didn't have any other option, I got in line. It took forever for me to get inside, because the place was packed out and the bouncers were staggering the queue. The bar was dark and crowded, and I instantly hated it. That was, until I heard the music. It was beautiful, transforming the room from something annoying into something wonderful. It was a unique mix of classical and modern, and it was just one instrument. The piano.

I felt it all around me, right down to my toes, and instinctively I knew it was his, knew this was the music he'd spend days on end composing alone in his apartment.

I couldn't see the stage because it was surrounded by people, but my heart began to pound as my suspicions about King being back on the beer slowly faded into the background. Pushing my way past the bodies, I finally reached a spot where I could see. There on the tiny stage he sat, playing glorious music on a worn-out, beaten-up piano that looked like it had been in the bar for over twenty years. Nevertheless, his audience was captivated, and so was I.

The way his body moved as he played, the way his hands manipulated the keys so fluidly, set my every nerve ending alight. He'd kept his hair long, just like I'd asked him to, and it hung attractively over his face, making him appear elusive and mysterious. His eyes were closed, too, adding to his enigmatic vibe. He wore only a simple white T-shirt under an open grey shirt and jeans. Basically, he looked nothing like what you'd expect from a classical pianist, but then again, he wasn't exactly playing straight-up classical. It was an unusual sound, something new and different, which was probably why he'd attracted such a crowd. Somehow I knew that if King wasn't playing, this bar wouldn't be half as packed as it was right then. I could tell because the patrons were focused completely on him rather than chatting amongst themselves and socializing.

He must have been doing this for weeks, telling no one. The thought made me both happy and sad at the same time. But then I remembered our conversation weeks ago in his apartment, where he'd talked about playing for the love of it rather than the praise. I also remembered telling him that his playing didn't have to be either of those things, that it could simply be a gift to other people. In that moment, I knew he'd taken my words to heart, because every person in the bar was getting a gift right then.

A worker moved past me, collecting empty glasses, and I pulled her aside, nodding to the stage.

"Does he play here often?" I asked.

She glanced at King, then back to me. "Not often. He performs in different places around the city. A couple of weeks ago he showed up at a bar in Soho and asked the manager if he could play. The place was quiet, so the manager said yes. He's been gaining a following ever since, but he never announces a gig, just shows up randomly, and people spread the word."

"Oh," I said, absorbing her answer, skin tingling at the idea of King just randomly playing piano for people wherever and whenever it took his fancy.

"What's his name?" I asked just before she turned to leave.

"They call him Oliver," she answered.

"Just Oliver?"

"Yeah, just Oliver."

And then she was gone and I was looking back at King, everything about him holding me captive. The fact that he kept his eyes closed most of the time and never really looked at anyone in the audience meant he didn't see me there. Still, I made sure to stand behind a couple of other people just in case. For a second I thought of waiting around until the end, pouncing on him, and declaring I'd discovered his secret. But no, that wasn't what I wanted. I just wanted him to go on playing, to keep doing what made him and the people he managed to touch with his music happy. I'd never be the one who turned what he loved into something that required praise, something that had once destroyed him.

So, when he finished his final song of the night, I inhaled a deep breath, savoured the moment, and soaked in the reactions of those around me, the catharsis they felt from the emotions portrayed in his wordless song. Then I turned and left the bar.

***

A couple of days later, I found myself waking Oliver up on a Monday morning and getting him ready for his first day of school. I had his uniform all set out: a white shirt, grey tie, navy jumper with the school crest, and grey slacks. I swear he looked so handsome, tiny yet grown at the same time, and I felt like crying.

I bet all mothers cried on their kid's first day of school. It was programmed into our DNA. Oliver was full of questions and enthusiasm. He'd been gearing himself up for this for a year. Often we'd drive by the school and he'd see the kids, and I'd tell him that's where he'd be going soon. I marvelled at how he never acted frightened or apprehensive. No, his eyes lit up at the prospect of something new.

King was sitting in the kitchen, eating a slice of toast, when I came down with Oliver, all clad in his new uniform.

"Daddy! Look at me, don't I look handsome?" he said, and King turned to take him in. Unlike me, he didn't get-teary eyed. No, his lips twitched in amusement.

"You're looking very dapper indeed, little man," he said, shooting me a smile.

"What's dapper?" Oliver questioned.

"Your daddy's being fancy again. He always tries to be fancy," I teased. "And it means you look sharp. Sharp and handsome."

He seemed pleased with my answer, and King went about getting him some breakfast. Once it was time to go, all three of us left the house to walk him to school. It was only ten minutes away, and it was a sunny morning, so we decided to forgo the car. I held one of Oliver's hands and King held the other. All the while, our son strolled along between us, chatting away about how he was going to make friends with everyone and how he was going to play hopscotch in the yard during his break.

I glanced at King at one point to see him smiling down at Oliver, affection and love in eyes as he listened to his every word. Then, too soon almost, we were at the school, and the teacher was waiting outside as the children gathered.

"There's Timothy," Oliver shouted, spotting his friend. "I'm going over." Before he could run off, I pulled him back and knelt down, looking him in the eye and fixing his tie. There was something about how small it was that made me feel like welling up again. King noticed my ridiculously emotional expression and took over, bending down to give Oliver a hug.

"You be good today, son. Your mum and I will be back later to collect you."

And with that he was gone, running excitedly to his friend, his little blue rucksack on his back. All around me, parents said goodbye to their kids, and there was a lot of crying going on. I saw a girl bawling her eyes out at the prospect of being separated from her mum, and it kind of broke my heart. In a way, I wished Oliver had been more like her, more upset, because that way I'd feel like less of a wuss.

King and I stood side by side, watching Oliver as he got in line with the other kids. "I hope you don't think me a soppy fool after this, but when we go home, I might get back into bed and be weird for a while. And by that I mean I might get back into bed and have a good cry."

King slid his hand into mine, a quiet show of affection, as he cocked his head to me and smiled. "Don't you have to be at the office in an hour?"

"Stop effing with my plans, Mr King," I snipped, but there was humour in my voice.

"You know, you haven't referred to me as Mr King since you were my employee," he teased. "Want to take the morning off? Maybe go home and get into bed for a different reason? Do some role-playing perhaps?"

I shoved him in the shoulder and scowled. "Don't be a cad."

He bent and whispered in my ear, "Aw, but you love it so much." His voice gave me tingles, and I closed my eyes for a second to push the images of our sex life from my mind. This clearly wasn't the time.

"Nah, maybe we'll save it for later. I wanted to head into the city anyway, spend a couple of hours practicing."

What he said brought back memories of the other night, and how electric it had felt to see him play for an audience, how he finally seemed to be completely himself. No pain. No loneliness. No addiction. No evil father trying to fuck up his life. No frightened mother, too paranoid to leave the house. He was better, and that's all I'd ever wanted him to be.

Suddenly, I had a moment of clarity, a feeling that all was right with the world. And then I was feeling weepy again, but this time it was for a whole other reason. I couldn't hold back the tears, and my eyes grew watery as they ran down my cheeks. Of course, they were happy tears, but when King saw that I was crying, he sucked in a breath and pulled me to him. Still holding my hand in one of his, he reached up and wiped the wetness from my cheeks.

"Hey, he's going to be all right, you know. Look at him — he's so excited and happy. Half the kids here are throwing tantrums."

"It's not that, it's just…I love him so much, and I love you so much. It feels too good to be true, to have this much love inside me."

His body was flush with mine as he dropped my hand so that he could cup my face, his thumbs brushing back and forth over the rise of my cheeks. His eyes flickered between mine, so loving, so serious. "Oh, darling, we should get married."

I sniffled and let out an unexpected burst of laughter. He was never going to stop with this, but strangely, there was something different about it this time. He was just as sincere as he always was, but the change was in me, and I felt like my answer might be different now.

"Be honest, you only want to marry me for my money. Well, that and my world-class derriere," I joked, my voice a shaky tremble.

King smiled a glorious smile, his retort provoking memories from words he'd spoken to me years ago. "No, I want to marry you for your witty banter. Well, that and your world-class brain."

His response made me laugh once more as I took a final glance in Oliver's direction to see the teacher was now leading the kids inside the school. Once he was gone, I turned back to King. "You know what? I'm kind of in the mood to get hitched today. Must be something in the air."

I knew he hadn't expected my answer when his smile grew even wider on his gorgeously handsome face. He pulled my lips to his and kissed me deeply before pulling back and whispering, "Must be."

Epilogue

King

She walked into the room and I glanced up casually, my attention on my phone call. I looked away, then looked back. Fucking hell, she had a body on her, and I noticed something exotic in her dark features. Enjoying a brief yet detailed vision of sinking my fingers around her lush hips, I glanced down at her resume to check her name. Hmmm.

You have beautiful eyes, Alexis Clark.

Memories were a powerful thing. They could at once set you free or take you prisoner, hold your entire life captive.

I think that in the space between birth and death you can have one life, or you can have many. But in order to have many, you also need the strength to end the one that came before. And there lies the tricky part.

In the old life you might have been face down in the dirt, but that dirt held a seductive quality that kept you in its grasp.

There was once a time when I felt trapped in a dark tunnel, and the only light was a false one found at the end of a bottle. The only peace was the numbness that sang through my veins and blocked out the memories of the life I left behind. Edgar Allen Poe once said that he didn't indulge in stimulants for the pleasure they brought, but to escape from the memories that plagued him. In that sense, we were kindred.

When I was a young man, I was confident, ready to take on any challenge, free of fear.

When I was a grown man, I knew the world and I was winning, even though there were worries that tried to drag me down.

When I was an older man, I was broken; the things I thought I'd done had ruined the things I'd left behind.

Now I was an even older man, and I knew that my memories didn't have to own me, and nothing was ever lost forever, especially love. It was simply waiting to be reclaimed, and reclaiming required strength.

You see, I told you there was a tricky part.

And that part would never be truly surpassed. Much like a virus that can't be cured but simply maintained, I would always look at the dirt and see something alluring. It was the strength I drew from within that kept me from succumbing to the allure.

My strength was in my music. It was in my boy, who grew taller every day. And it was in Alexis, who even when I was nothing had looked at me like I was everything. Thinking of her, I felt a sudden need to see her and rose from my seat, my sister eyeing me suspiciously.

"Where do you think you're going?" Marina asked.

"To see Alexis. I'll only be a minute," I answered.

She tugged on my hand and pulled me back down with a surprising amount of strength for a sixty-year-old woman.

"You can't see her now. It's bad luck," she scolded me.

Jay, who was sitting on the other side of the room, made a noise like Marina had answered a question wrong on a quiz show. "Nope. Complete load of horse rap," he said, casually closing his book and leaning forward. "People made that shit up back in the day of arranged marriages. Picture it here: Dude walks in and sees his bride's a howler, then goes, 'Fuck this for a game of soldiers, I'm outta here.' Before you know it, the wedding's off." A silence fell, and my sister shot Jay a scowl. "Or you know, vice versa. Lotta butt-ugly dudes out there, too," he amended.

Marina pointed to him. "That's not why I'm scowling. I'm scowling because you're trying to bring bad luck to my brother's marriage by urging him to break an age-old tradition."

Jay threw his hands in the air. "Hey, I'm just laying out the facts. You'll find that a bunch of those old superstitions arose out of simple practicality. Marriages were little more than business transactions back then."

Marina scowled harder. "When my friend Rose broke a mirror, she was sick with a different ailment at least once a year for seven years. Then on the seventh year, poof, no more ailments. How do you explain that, Mr. Practical?"

"I explain it with one word: coincidence," Jay threw back.

I shook my head. Those two were always arguing over stuff like this. In fact, I thought they enjoyed it. Marina touched my hand. "Don't listen to him. The ceremony is in less than half an hour. You can wait."

Before I could reply, Jay spoke up again. "Oh, and more evidence to prove my point: veils. Why have a veil if not to hide an ugly face? You're already married by the time the priest tells you to lift it, and then it's like boom, here's what you just pledged your entire life to. Good luck with that."

Jack, who had been fixing his tie in the mirror, snickered a laugh. I think this must have been the first time I'd ever seen him in a suit. My best man. My best friend.

Marina continued scowling at Jay until he finally got the message to shut up. She'd become something of a substitute mother to the brothers, and though she often complained about it, I knew she loved being needed.

I squeezed her hand. "It's okay. I'll wait."

I didn't hear her enter the apartment. The music in my fingers was too loud and consuming for me to be aware of another presence. That was the best thing about it. Music could fill your head and allow you to escape the constant worries that consumed you.

A buzzing sound went off, and my playing ceased. I turned, saw her outfit, and tried to suppress a smile.

"Oh, go on, say it. You know you want to," she sighed.

God, this woman. Even when my deepest fears tried to drag me down, she always found some way to make me feel lighter.

I released the smile I'd withheld and replied, "What on earth are you wearing?"

The tent was full. I wasn't quite sure why, because I'd been nothing but a rude, careless drunk to these people for years, but it appeared the entire circus was there to attend our wedding. Every time they saw me now, they seemed taken aback by how much I'd changed.

Christ, every time I saw me now, I was taken aback by how much I'd changed.

I wore a fitted tux, designed by Jay's wife, Matilda. She'd also designed Alexis' dress, but I wasn't allowed to see it yet. I believed in my sister's superstitions about as much as Jay did, but still, I indulged her. Marina had kept me from going over the edge for a really long time.

Speaking of my half-sister, she was the one officiating the ceremony, and she wore her ringmaster's outfit, complete with top hat and tails. Jack stood by my side; I'd always found his presence soothing, even when I was so far gone I'd forget entire weeks. Just like Marina, he'd been a rock to me, and probably the only one brave enough to grip me by the balls (metaphorically speaking) and tell me the truth that the way I was living was going to kill me.

Of course, I didn't listen to him. It was only when Alexis came back into my life that I remembered I wasn't me. Drinking wasn't me. And that I was far stronger than I'd given myself credit for.

The music began to play, and I turned to see her walking down the aisle. Her dress was beautiful, her face radiant, and when she stopped to stand in front of me, I told her so.

She sat astride me, and I couldn't hide my arousal. She was well aware of it, too, but her reaction wasn't what I expected. Something forced my gaze down, away from her pretty lips and beautiful eyes, and I saw her nipples were hard. All in an instant, everything fell into place. She'd been lying; she must have been. And I was pissed. Pissed and aroused, and yes, smug as fuck. Mere seconds passed, and already I was imagining all the ways I was going to take her. I wanted to grip her thick, dark hair as I plunged myself into her soft, welcoming body.

She trembled when I leaned in close enough that our lips almost brushed and whispered, "I fucking knew it."

Oliver was our page boy. He also sat beside me throughout the reception, and I spent most of my time talking to him rather than mingling with the guests. I'd missed so much, and every moment felt like a new opportunity to reclaim something of those lost years.

"I think your wife might like to dance with you now," Alexis murmured in my ear, the husky quality to her voice sending a thrill down my spine. I'd spent weeks asking her to marry me, and she'd finally said yes. Now here we were, six months later. The circus had returned to London, and we were husband and wife in a wedding that had been nothing short of unique.

I took her hand in mine, and Mum came to take my empty seat beside Oliver. She looked happier than I'd seen her since I was a teenager. After all the time I'd spent thinking she was dead, it felt a little bit miraculous to have her before me, alive and so much healthier than she'd ever been.

Leading my wife to the dance floor, I slid my arms around her waist, pulled her close to my body, and swayed us both to the rhythm of the music. Her hair smelled of lilacs and her skin of the sun. Her light olive tan looked pretty against the white of her dress, and I fingered the hem at the back, hardly able to wait until tonight when I got her alone. She gave a little shiver and rested her head on my shoulder.

All around us, our family and friends enjoyed the party. Marina sat with Alexis' parents, chatting like they were old friends. Mum had Oliver on her lap now, and I knew that my boy was her world just the same way that he was mine.

Alexis' hand came to my neck, her fingers light and probing on my skin. "I can't wait for tonight," she whispered, echoing my own sentiments. "Maybe we could slip away for a little bit."

I groaned low in my throat, feeling her shift her body so that her breasts pushed harder against my chest.

"Not yet," I whispered back. "First, I have something for you."

Her body was a dream, her stomach soft and rounded, her breasts heavy and full in my hands. As I stared down at her, marvelling at the flare of her hips and her hair spread out like a dark halo around her head, I felt something strange and intangible take hold. My throat was tight, and the taste of her was still in my mouth. I already loved the taste of her.

"I think this is your cue to beg, love," I murmured.

She did. Christ, she begged so perfectly.

And when I finally sank myself inside her, the final piece of that strange and intangible thing fell into place. I was surely falling.

I sat on the stage in the middle of the tent, our wedding guests seated all around. Alexis was only feet away, and the gravity of what I was about to do caused a heaviness to settle in my gut. My hands hadn't trembled like this since I'd come off alcohol. I rubbed my palms together in an effort to still them. I couldn't play music if my hands were shaking.

The wedding band had taken a break, and I sat by the piano, the weight of two hundred pairs of eyes baring down on me. For months I had only played for strangers; now I was playing for everyone I knew in the world. There was a certain comfort in anonymity, but there was no comfort in putting yourself out there for the people who mattered most.

My courage won out, and my hands settled on the keys. My gaze rested on Alexis as I leaned forward and spoke into the microphone.

"Someone once told me that my music can be a gift I give to other people. So, my darling, here's my wedding gift to you."

I closed my eyes and played. The music looked like colours behind my eyelids, and I experienced a wonderful moment of synaesthesia. I saw the years flash through my mind, all the pain and loneliness expelled through the tips of my fingers. When I opened my eyes again, I saw Alexis before me, her gaze shiny with unshed tears. Quite like a present waiting under the tree, I knew hers had been opened. She saw me for all I was, and I saw her for all she was. The story in the music of all we'd been through wasn't pretty, and yet, in that moment I wouldn't wish to be anyone other than who I was right then. I was glad for my experiences, good and bad. I was glad for what they had made me.

And I was glad that I hadn't had one life, but that I'd had many.

She stood before me, a miracle made flesh, and God, so much more beautiful than I even remembered. Living without her for so many years had been like living in a world without the sun. I didn't feel worthy of touching her, and yet, my hands wandered anyway. They began at her temples before descending. Drinking her in with my eyes, I felt my way down until I reached her throat and a breath escaped her. She was from another life, the one I'd left behind, but having her there, my hands on her skin, made me feel like I was stepping out of this life and into a new one.

"Hello," I said quietly.
"Hi," she answered back.

End.

Look out for Karla and Lee's story, *Hearts of Blue*, coming in November 2015!

She upholds the law. He breaks it.

Two blue hearts, both alike in bravery

In not-so-fair London, where we lay our scene

From gun crime to petty theft

Where family is blood and survival makes hands unclean

In this place, we find two hearts who should be foes

And yet, amidst the turmoil their love still grows

Misadventure abounds and the divide will bring them strife

But with luck, death doesn't always mean an end to life

Hearts of Blue is a standalone contemporary romance that tells the story of star-crossed lovers Karla Sheehan and Lee Cross, a police constable and the thief who steals her heart.

Check out more books in L.H. Cosway's *HEARTS* series!

Praise for *Six of Hearts* (Jay & Matilda's story)

"This book was sexy. Man was it hot! Cosway writes sexual tension so that it practically sizzles off the page." - A. Meredith Walters, New York Times & USA Today Bestselling Author.

"There is a way that certain authors write that just grips me by the throat because I can see the world, I can smell the sounds, I can hear the voices, and I can feel their hearts." - Marie Hall, New York Times & USA Today Bestselling Author.

"I loved the twist at the end. I loved how sexy it was. (DAMN IT WAS SEXY!!)" - Penny Reid, Author of Neanderthal Seeks Human.

"Six of Hearts is a book that will absorb you with its electric and all-consuming atmosphere." - Lucia, Reading is my Breathing.

"There is so much "swoonage" in these pages that romance readers will want to hold this book close and not let go." - Katie, Babbling About Books.

Praise for *Hearts of Fire* (Jack & Lille's story)

"This story holds so much intensity and it's just blazing hot. It created an inferno of emotions inside me." - Patrycja, Smokin' Hot Book Blog.

"I think this is my very favorite LH Cosway romance to date.

Absolutely   gorgeous."   - Angela, Fiction   Vixen.

"Okay we just fell in love. Complete and utter beautiful book love. You know the kind of love where you just don't want a book to finish. You try and make it last; you want the world to pause as you read and you want the story to go on and on because you're not ready to let it go." - Jenny & Gitte, Totally Booked.

"Babies! I want to have babies with his book. Ladies, you will drool over Jack, want to run away to the circus and play with matches and hot wax. Definitely going in my top 10 favorite books of 2015." - Katie, Babbling About Books and More!

About the author

L.H. Cosway has a BA in English Literature and Greek and Roman Civilisation and an MA in Postcolonial Literature. She lives in Dublin city. Her inspiration to write comes from music. Her favourite things in life include writing stories, vintage clothing, dark cabaret music, food, musical comedy, and of course, books.

She thinks that imperfect people are the most interesting kind. They tell the best stories.

Find L.H. Cosway online!

www.facebook.com/lhcosway
www.twitter.com/lhcosway
www.lhcoswayauthor.com

Books by L.H. Cosway

Contemporary Romance
Painted Faces
Killer Queen
The Nature of Cruelty
Still Life with Strings
Six of Hearts
Hearts of Fire
The Hooker & the Hermit

Urban Fantasy
Tegan's Blood (The Ultimate Power Series #1)
Tegan's Return (The Ultimate Power Series #2)
Tegan's Magic (The Ultimate Power Series #3)
Tegan's Power (The Ultimate Power Series #4)

Thank you for reading *King of Hearts*. Please consider supporting an indie author and leaving a review <3

56221912R00227

Made in the USA
Charleston, SC
16 May 2016